Mary Jane Staples was born, bred and educated in Walworth, and is the author of many bestselling novels including the ever-popular cockney sagas featuring the Adams family.

THE LONGEST WINTER

WINTER

Mary Jane Staples

CORGI BOOKS

TRANSWORLD PUBLISHERS
61–63 Uxbridge Road, London W5 5SA
A Random House Group Company
www.rbooks.co.uk

**THE LONGEST WINTER
A CORGI BOOK: 9780552150910**

First published in Great Britain in 1978 by
Souvenir Press Ltd as *Appointment in Sarajevo*
under the name Robert Tyler Stevens
Corgi edition published 2009

Addresses for Random House Group Ltd companies outside the
UK can be found at: www.randomhouse.co.uk
The Random House Group Ltd Reg. No. 954009

The Random House Group Limited supports The Forest
Stewardship Council (FSC), the leading international forest
certification organization. All our titles that are printed on
Greenpeace approved FSC certified paper carry the FSC logo.
Our paper procurement policy can be found at
www.rbooks.co.uk/environment

Typeset in 11/12pt New Baskerville by
Kestrel Data, Exeter, Devon.
Printed in the UK by
CPI Cox & Wyman, Reading, RG1 8EX.

4 6 8 10 9 7 5 3

**To Dolly Sewell,
friend and counsellor**

He appeared, and I did not think of disaster then
Or of love
For he was only another man
And most men are ordinary
But on a day unlike all other days
He became a hero, his badge shining so sternly bright
That I, as much in fear as all unpretentious mortals,
Stood palely in his shadow
And when the trumpets brayed to call the heroes to war
He was more than a hero
And far above earthly men in his godlike infallibility
Showing neither the smallest weakness nor spark of love
But paying his tributes only to Mars
It is war
And though eagles soar to vanish and the hawk ascends
    invisible
He flies higher
I am destroyed, for once I was myself and now am
    nothing,
Living only to despise him
Yet I love him with such unrequited hunger
That even if every other joy were a banquet
I should still die famished
Is this what such men make of women,
Starvelings?

Sophie von Korvacs
Vienna
December 1917

BOOK ONE

THE LAST SUMMER

He was very old. As he slowly crossed an inner court of the Hofburg he looked as if he had lived for a thousand years. Perhaps he had burdened himself with all the years of his dynasty. But he still wore his uniform each day and still rose at dawn to go to his daily work. That was how it had been from the time he had ascended the throne.

But work, with its mountains of paper and its demands for orders and decisions, was not quite so easy to come to terms with now. It had kept him a prisoner for how long? Centuries? He would have preferred to have taken command of his empire from the saddle of a horse, not from a desk. But because he was what he was, the servant of his people, he had accepted his chains without complaint. Sometimes, however, he did wonder if his people had not made him more of a bureaucrat than an emperor.

It was not a change of heart which made the mountains more difficult to move these days. It was simply age. There were occasions when, having reached his desk, he would stand before it uncertain as to whether it was time to commence or time to go.

But there was one thing he was sure of. And that was that his life, his times, his triumphs and his tragedies were of the past. He had been Emperor for almost sixty-six years. It had been a long, long reign. The longest. That in itself was history. There could be only a little time left before he was laid side by side with Elizabeth.

Elizabeth. His Sisi, his empress. Assassinated years ago in Geneva. Everyone knew how much he had spoiled her. No one knew how much he had loved her.

Rudolph, his only son. Gone long ago in the tragic, wintry mists of Mayerling.

Maximilian, his brother. Barbarously executed in Mexico. An eternity ago.

Who was left to succeed? Who would come after him to ensure the continuance of an empire that was so self-divisive and yet so enduring?

He could not for the moment remember.

Ah, yes. His nephew, Franz Ferdinand. A strong-minded archduke who had obstinately contracted a morganatic marriage with some obscure lady-in-waiting. The archduke had his own ideas about what might be good for stabilizing the empire. Such as turning the Dual into the Triple Monarchy by making a kingdom of the South Slav peoples, this to act as a buffer between Austria and Hungary. Neither Austria nor Hungary would like that.

Nor would Serbia, which considered there was

an ethnic case for incorporating all the South Slavs within the framework of a Greater Serbia.

Ah well, it would be Franz Ferdinand's problem, and of his own making. But even under Franz Ferdinand the empire would survive. The man would at least be conscientious. And the dynasty, around which the empire revolved, was indestructible.

It was a beautiful day. Was it May? April? June?

It was May and it was a beautiful day indeed, the harbinger of a long hot summer.

He hesitated before a door, its meaning and his purpose escaping him for a second or so. Then, with the ghost of a smile, His Apostolic Majesty Franz Josef I walked from the sunlight into the shadow of the waiting mountain.

'You don't know,' said the Archduke Franz Ferdinand in a letter to his affectionate stepmother, Maria Theresia, 'how happy I am with my family.'

He was indeed happy, despite his critics, of whom there were many, some in high places. Various were their complaints. He was too taciturn and too sensitive. He was uncommunicative and gruff. His ideas concerning the well-being of the empire were too radical or too impractical. Nevertheless, Franz Ferdinand, well aware that the empire was showing signs of falling apart, persisted in his belief that entirely new policies were necessary, and he was preparing himself for the day when he would become Emperor. His policies would be strong but sympathetic. There were a dozen different nationalities to consider. He must win them all over.

Meanwhile, as Inspector General of the Imperial Army, he accepted an invitation from General Potiorek, Governor of Bosnia and Herzegovina, to attend manoeuvres in Bosnia at the end of June. General Potiorek had also asked the archduke to set aside a day when he could attend a reception in Sarajevo, the capital of Bosnia. Franz Ferdinand agreed.

News that the archduke would definitely grace Sarajevo with his august presence on 28 June reached the higher echelons of the anarchist organization, the Black Hand, in Belgrade. The information was passed on to Colonel Dragutin Dimitrijevic, Chief of the Serbian Army Intelligence and the shadowy figurehead of the Black Hand. The colonel, so industrious a plotter that he was known as Apis, the Bee, did not take long to decide what was required.

Simply, a select band of bomb-throwers willing to face subsequent martyrdom.

Among those who answered the call was Gavrilo Princip, a nineteen-year-old Bosnian student. Also interested was Boris Ferenac, a musician.

Chapter One

Vienna, 1914. The city of the Habsburgs, where the Hofburg, a maze-like complexity of administrative buildings, reached out to peer into streets, invade gardens and overlook parks. Through its ancient arch in the Michaeler Platz bowled the carriages of those privileged to attend its glittering social functions. If one did not have the entry through that arch, then in the eyes of Vienna one had so little standing socially that one was a nobody.

Vienna, which the waltz kings had made eternally gay and haunting, was in 1914 at the peak of its splendour, its colour, its culture. Its Ringstrasse captured imagination, its women were the most elegant in Europe, its officers the most dazzling and its emperor the most incorruptible. It was the city of the imperishable *Merry Widow*, of Lehar, Strauss and Mozart, of writers, poets, love and scandal. For the rich there was everything, for the people there were the dance halls and the Vienna Woods.

Baroness Teresa von Korvacs adored Vienna and thought the family residence could not have been better situated. It was on the nicer side of the Salesianergasse and within easy reach of elegant shops and fashionable restaurants. And not far away was the Hofburg, where the dear old emperor still kept his eye on everything, including the Hungarian Magyars, the most acquisitive people in the empire. They were always after more than they knew they were entitled to. Her husband Ernst said that was how they always got as much as they actually wanted. And Ernst should know. He had served the emperor in more than one of his ministries. He was in the Foreign Ministry now.

Their house, with its domed vestibule leading to a baroque-style staircase and a chandeliered ballroom the envy of the exalted, was fronted by a paved forecourt, high iron railings and a gilded, ornamental gate bearing their coat of arms. Nearly ninety years old, the house had the appearance of being graciously mellowed by time while remaining impervious to change.

The bright morning room overlooked the Salesianergasse. When she was in a busybody mood the baroness liked to observe who was driving by with whom. Open carriages and trotting horses gave the thoroughfare an air of dash and elegance. It was a pity motor cars had been allowed to intrude. The baroness did not think automobiles suited a city like Vienna. Berlin, yes, because that city was all boisterous bustle, the noisy upstart of Europe. Vienna was the established, cultured Queen.

Motor cars were only a fad, of course. They

would never last. Carl, their only son, wanted one simply because other young men did. Ernst had said he would see. Carl had smiled and said he would see that his father saw. The baroness hoped that whatever was seen would not be allowed.

The drawing room was her favourite. It was wallpapered in old gold on which clusters of roses danced. The printed chintzes were softly subtle, the deeply upholstered armchairs designed for comfort. Tall windows looked out on to gardens stretching as far as the boundary of the Modena Palace. Through the windows one could watch the four seasons come and go. In the spring the blossom hung fragrant in the sun or scattered sensitively before the wind. In summer the lawns were a green canvas for every other colour.

The gardens were lovely today. She mused on them from the quiet of the room, then turned her attention to new fashion plates. Heavens, ostrich feathers were in again. Ridiculous. And impossibly expensive, besides leaving the poor ostriches bald and bereft. Baroness von Korvacs, forty-four, was fair, aristocratic and still a handsome dresser. But she could do without ostrich feathers.

Life was very agreeable. Other mothers worried about their children. She did not. Well, very rarely. She was blessed with perfect offspring. Well, almost perfect. Carl at twenty-four was the most good-natured of young men. Anne, eighteen, was a delightful girl. A little impulsive, perhaps. And Sophie, just twenty, was so elegant and intelligent. But it was just a little disconcerting that she was not yet engaged. She could have been. A charming and infatuated French diplomat had enquired after her hand. The baroness received the enquiry cordially. Sophie did not. Neither did her father.

'I'm sorry, Mama, but really, he's too fat,' said Sophie.

'Darling, his figure is robust, that's all,' said her mother.

'He's not only too fat, he's too old,' said her father.

'He's mature,' said the baroness.

'Then let him marry Elizabeth Schaeffer,' said the baron, 'she's as mature as he is.'

'Elizabeth Schaeffer is all of forty,' protested the baroness.

'So is he,' said the baron.

'Perhaps you are right,' smiled the baroness.

'Thank you, Mama,' said Sophie in her winning way.

Sophie supposed she would fall in love one day. But she was less worried about it than her mother. She did not want to marry simply for the sake of it. Life was lovely, exciting, and there must be a man somewhere in this colourful world waiting for her. She was quite happy to wait for him. There was so much poetry to write until destiny brought them together.

The baroness looked up from her fashion plates as her daughters came in. As usual, Anne entered all animation and colour. As usual,

Sophie followed unhurriedly. Anne was as fair as her mother, her hair the colour of harvest gold, her eyes a warm green. Life for her was an exuberance. She adored shops, weddings, men, Strauss, Lehar and Austria. She was kind to everyone, even cab drivers, and considered the ageing, aloof emperor a monarch of benign fatherliness.

Sophie was vividly brunette, with richly dark chestnut hair, taking after her father. An inch taller than Anne, she carried herself with superb elegance, dressing her hair in Edwardian crown style and enhancing her height. Her face was classically oval, her brilliant brown eyes and beautifully white teeth giving her looks a striking quality, particularly when she was amused.

Anne dressed with apparently careless rapture and always looked delicious. Sophie rarely departed from long sweeping green or blue velvets in winter and the simplest of silk pastels in summer, and winter or summer she looked elegantly superior to fashion's frills and flounces. Sophie loved life. Anne found it breathless. Anne asked that men should be gallant, dashing, attentive and amusing. Sophie did not ask anything quite so specific of them, only that they shared her appreciation of the world and its wonders.

Neither sister lacked admirers. Anne was a flirtatious delight, Sophie with her smile was captivating. One young man who admired them both was Ludwig Lundt-Hausen, son of the police superintendent. Sophie assured him that if he preferred Anne she would not take the slightest offence. Ludwig earnestly assured her that if he came to prefer either of them he would press his suit vigorously. Meanwhile he hoped neither of them minded that he considered them equally charming. They did not mind a bit. Ludwig was rather a charmer himself.

The baroness regarded her daughters with a smile. Anne looked as if the sun had kissed her. Sophie looked exquisite. They had been out in the four-wheeler, jaunting gaily with a variety of other carriages along the Hauptallee in the Prater.

'Did you enjoy yourselves?' asked the baroness.

'It was lovely,' said Anne, to whom the most unimportant of outings was an excursion into the excitements of life. 'Just everyone was there.'

'Although riding out in a carriage isn't quite the last word in cultural bliss,' said Sophie, 'it can be very stimulating. Horses are so rhythmic, aren't they? I was inspired to begin the composition of an adorable poem. I shall finish it in my mind in a moment. Then I shall recite it.'

'Sometimes, Mama,' said Anne, 'do you have the feeling that even in the bosom of our family we're spared nothing?'

'Do you also have the feeling, Mama, that my sister is a philistine?' said Sophie, removing her little white tip-on hat.

There were questions from daughters that wise mothers passed by. The baroness in her wisdom said, 'Did you meet Ludwig?' She entertained hopes for Sophie there.

'Yes, I think we exchanged a word or two with Ludwig,' said Anne. 'Oh, and we saw Carl. He wishes you to excuse him lunch.' Her father came in then. She put her arm through his and he kissed her. He had spent this Saturday morning at his office in the Ballhausplatz. He was tall, thin and had a mass of iron-grey hair. He greeted his wife, who lifted her face for his kiss.

'How nice you are home in good time, Ernst,' she said. 'Anne, what was that about Carl?'

'Oh, you'll excuse him lunch, won't you?' said Anne. 'He and Ludwig are looking at motor cars. Ludwig is almost the expert, you know, now that he has one of his own.'

'You'll have to buy a motor car for us, Papa,' said Sophie, walking about in thoughtful pursuit of metre and rhyme, 'Carl insists we're incomplete without one.'

'We are not incomplete,' said the baroness, 'but we are certainly quieter.'

'Hm,' said the baron non-committally.

'With a motor car, you know,' said Sophie, 'we could drive all the way to Ilidze next month. It would be very adventurous.'

'Never,' said her mother, 'not while there are trains. I should shudder every metre of the way in a motor car. You will not even think about it, Ernst. I beg you will not.'

'Naturally,' said the baron, 'I'd not allow thoughts of the finest motor car to promote disharmony, my dear, nor would I make you ride to Ilidze in one.'

The family owned a house in Ilidze, a small attractive inland resort in Bosnia. The baron was fond of shooting and fishing, and both sports could be enjoyed to the full in the area around Ilidze. The family always spent a few weeks there in June.

'Mama,' said Anne, 'I hope it isn't disharmonious to tell you Ludwig is taking Sophie and me out in his new car this afternoon.'

'Oh,' said the baroness, torn between her dislike of automobiles and her hopes for Sophie.

'I promise you, Mama,' smiled Sophie, 'that if it's a truly shuddering experience I'll confess it so. Now, while there's still time before lunch, I wish you to hear my new poem. Papa, don't you dare sneak out.'

'I wouldn't dream of it,' smiled the baron. He listened, together with his wife and Anne, as Sophie recited.

> *'Oh, fragrant Prater's tree-lined courses*
> *Are daily thronged by trotting horses,*
> *Horses large and horses small*
> *Horses fat and horses tall.*
> *Some trot proudly, four wheels running,*
> *Some trot idly, using cunning,*
> *Saving wind and limb and grace*
> *For tomorrow's same old race.*
> *Whips flick whistling, hats are dancing,*
> *Single horses run on prancing*
> *Leaving those who came on later*
> *To the windfalls of the Prater.'*

'That is as far as I've got with it,' said Sophie, 'but it's my declared intention to have it trip merrily to a finish. Please express your feelings about its possibilities.'

'Ah,' said the baron.

'Ah,' said Anne.

'Ah?' said Sophie. 'Ah what? Isn't it just a little bit delicious?'

'It's delightful, darling,' said the baroness.

'Piquant,' said the baron, smiling. Both his daughters were an entertainment to him.

Chapter Two

At the Ecole Internationale in Vienna the pupils bent their heads over watercolours. James William Fraser bent his head over the essays he had set them the day before. Marie Corbière looked at him from under her lashes. His thick black hair, inclined to escape all too easily from the frictional prison imposed by the brush, hung over his forehead. She would bet a sou, even a franc, that he was asleep. It was warm in the classroom. She put out a hand to nudge her neighbour.

'Marie?' It was a cautionary murmur from her teacher.

He had not lifted his head, his hair was still in his eyes, but he was not asleep. Eleven-year-old Marie blushed. That Monsieur Fraser, he was a martinet by instinct. He could see even when he wasn't looking. However, he was a quite nice martinet on the whole, a change from Fräulein Coutts who was so fussy with one.

James was a temporary replacement for Fräulein Coutts who, in fright at a persistent cough, was spending some months in a Swiss sanatorium. The principal of the school was Maude Harrison, widow of a British diplomat who had been drowned when his yacht capsized in the Adriatic. Maude, an active and resourceful person, did not want to become a distressed gentlewoman. Using what money she had been left she bought a suitable house in Vienna and turned it into a school for the children of foreigners, particularly the children of diplomats.

She had met James in the middle of nowhere, in a wild valley at the foot of the Austrian Alps last September. She liked to tramp around the mountain valleys, and was inclined to laugh at friends who thought it inadvisable. In her fifties, Maude considered she was long past the stage where she might meet a fate worse than death.

James, an Anglo-Scot, shared sandwiches and fruit with her that day. And conversation. He was an automobile engineer and designer. So was his father, Sir William Fraser, who had been knighted for his services to industry. James had some of his father's talents and some of his own. He painted moderately in colour, expressively in black and white, he took honours at Edinburgh in French and scraped home with his German. His father thought German would be useful, for as engineers the Germans were as good as any nation and one ought to be able to talk with them.

James accepted the job his father wanted him to have in the Midland works. He told Maude he felt he owed the old boy the gesture of going into the family business. But after a couple of years he decided that although they had their fascination, internal combustion machines constituted the most antisocial device man had ever inflicted on his fellows. He spoke frankly to his father, confessing his growing aversion to the motor car and voicing his doubt about whether it would prove to be the blessing people expected.

'And to cap it all,' he finished, 'I can't stand the racket.'

'Good God, Jamie, what are you saying?' Sir William Fraser, a vigorous and leonine Scot, was warm-hearted but single-minded. He lived and breathed automobiles. 'That racket,' he pointed out, listening to the vibrations of a new engine in its test bed, 'is the most beautiful sound man in his puniness has ever created.'

'I must be honest, guv'nor,' said James, 'it's just a noise to me.' He was as tall as his father, but sparer and darker. He lived with a five o'clock shadow.

'With the greatest of respect to her,' said Sir William, 'that comes from your Sassenach mother. She puts her fingers in her ears if a teacup rattles.'

'Not quite,' said James, 'but God bless her for her sensitivity.'

'Praise the Lord,' said Sir William fervently. 'Jamie, are you going to be a disappointment to me?'

'Knowing you,' said James, 'I'm sure you'd rather I was a disappointment to you than to myself. The fact is, guv'nor, you're a modern and progressive person, and I'm afraid I'm an old-fashioned one.'

'Oh, aye,' said Sir William with mild sarcasm. 'Man, will you throw the Lord's gifts away? Your eye for design is almost as good as mine. You earn your salary. How can that be a disappointment to you? What is the principle of life? You put something into God's world, you take something out. That's more than a principle, that's as near to happiness as any man or woman can get.'

'I agree,' said James, 'but all the same I thought I'd take the Lord's other gifts around Europe for a while. My paints and my sketchbook and my eyes.'

'It doesn't make too much sense to me,' said Sir William, 'and I'm not sure whether it will to your mother, either. I think she'd prefer you to show up with an estimable young lady rather than with ideas about going off to paint the Eiffel Tower. It's a small point, no doubt, but what d'you expect to live on?'

'I've some money of my own, but if I do run short I thought I could benefit from a generous arrangement with you,' said James affably. 'I'm not proud and you've never been parsimonious.'

'D'you know what I was doing at your age?' said Sir William.

'Yes, building infernal machines,' said James, 'and bringing it all into the house.'

Sir William, in grey waistcoat, black trousers, stiff wing collar and grey tie, looked, as he always did when he was down to his shirtsleeves, as if he were ready for industrial battle on a high but practical plane.

'Jamie,' he said crisply, 'I don't believe in forcing any young man, especially my own son, to work at something that's gone sour on him. But I'll bargain. You take a year off and I'll no' argue. I'll give you that, a year. But if you don't come back after a year I'll sue you.'

'Sue me?'

'You're under contract,' said Sir William.

'Am I, by God.'

'You are, by God.'

'Damn me,' said James, mildly thunderstruck by the uncompromising nature of parental astuteness.

Maude liked the young man with the dark, almost gypsy look. The Alps soared above them, freezing the sky. Birds floated on still wings and the grandeur of space was beyond imagination. When she told him about her school and that she was starting the forthcoming winter term short of a teacher, James gave it only a second's thought before offering himself as a temporary replacement. Maude, happy about his French, the language of the school, and his Edinburgh University background, never dilly-dallied herself.

'I'll call your bluff,' she said, 'I'll accept you.'

'No bluff,' said James, 'I want to see Vienna, live it, not wander through it.'

He proved a find. He exercised a firm but benevolent masculine authority and the more impressionable girls sometimes brought him flowers and a blush. His salary was not very much. But he lived in a room at the top of the house and enjoyed free and very good board. He explored Vienna during his spare time and carried his sketchbook about.

'Marie?'

Marie Corbière pinked again. James smiled and beckoned her. She went to his desk. He had her essay in front of him. He had asked them to write three hundred words on a day in their life.

'M'sieu?'

'I like your essay, Marie. It's very natural. A day in your life is a day with your family, yes?'

'Yes, m'sieu.' His dark eyes made her shy.

'Tell me,' he said, 'why did you end with this line?' He turned the work towards her and pointed. She bent to look and blushed again.

The last line of her essay read, 'A good archduke is a dead one.'

It intrigued James. It had no connection with the essay proper, which was all about her family and her home. It had made its climactic arrival like a thunderclap at the end of a sunny day. He had felt astonishment. Its inclusion must have a meaning. To Marie at least. But Marie, having observed it and blushed, straightened up and blushed yet again. Perhaps she was aware of other girls watching her reactions to the enquiring smile of the darkly masculine Monsieur Fraser. At any rate, she said nothing.

'Marie?' said James questioningly.

'Yes, m'sieu?'

'It makes a rather irrelevant ending to a nice day, doesn't it?' he smiled.

Marie had rather liked the impressive sound of it herself. She felt Monsieur Fraser did not. He was smiling, yes, but grown-ups often smiled just before they pounced. And some of the older girls confessed that at times his smile quite made them shiver. Marie, who had reached the age of reason, but not the age of discovery, was unacquainted in her mind with the shiver delicious.

She was nervous, therefore, as she said, 'It's wrong, m'sieu?'

'I don't know. Is it?' James was aware of her nervousness. It was creating a mental blockage. 'Well, it's nothing to worry about, but if you can remember why you put it in you can come and tell me.'

'Yes, m'sieu,' she said and gratefully escaped.

He was on the steps when the pupils streamed out at midday. It was Saturday, when there were only morning lessons. Several maidservants and governesses were waiting to collect their respective charges. A girl was at the gate, a girl in the grey cape and black skirt of a nursemaid, a young man with her. Marie emerged on to the steps and smiled shyly at James.

'Au 'voir, Marie,' he said.

'M'sieu,' she dimpled, and then, 'Oh, there's Rosa.'

'Rosa?'

'She looks after my small brother and

sometimes comes to meet me. And that is Boris.'
She dimpled again. 'He is walking out with
Rosa.' She skipped away to join the grey-caped
nursemaid and the young man, who wore the
wide-brimmed black hat and floppy bow tie of
the bohemian or musician. The three went off
hand in hand.

James buttonholed Maude a few minutes later
and showed her the last line of Marie's essay.
Maude read it, then cast a quick eye over the
essay itself. She returned to the last line.

'How very odd,' she said.

'I think it was an American politician who was
quoted as saying that the only good Red Indians
were dead ones. Could Marie have seen that in
some book, do you think, and used it in this way?
But if so, why? It makes no sense when you try to
relate it to the rest of the essay. And she's French.
Archdukes mean nothing to her.'

'They mean something here,' said Maude.

'None of her family would have made such a
remark?'

'Never,' said Maude. 'Her father holds an
important secretarial position on the staff of the
French Embassy. Neither he nor his wife would
commit such a blunder, even within the privacy
of their own household. A diplomat is as much
one by instinct as by training. James, whatever
Marie's reasons for using such a phrase, we
mustn't make a song and dance about it.'

'I'm intrigued,' said James, 'but it's tightly
under my hat, Maude, and will stay there.'

After lunch he borrowed Maude's deep blue

two-wheeler and drove out of the city with his sketchbook. The afternoon was fine, the sky a delicate blue, the Danube a gunmetal glitter. Compact villages nestled in the hills like red-roofed clusters of colour. Several miles out of Vienna he turned off the road to take a winding lane that offered a gentle descent to the bank of the river.

'Ludwig,' said Sophie, 'I think you'd better stop.'

'Oh, no,' protested Anne, 'drive on, Ludwig, this is whizzing adventure.'

The young baronesses were perched in breeze-blown, sun-caught elevation on the high rear seat of Ludwig's spanking new Bugatti as it ate up the road taking them back to Vienna. Their afternoon of motoring had been exhilarating and carefree up to now, both sisters impressed by the power Ludwig had at his command. But now, for some reason, steam was escaping, issuing in hissing little puffs from under the nobly wrought radiator cap. Sophie, always more sensitive to an atmosphere of approaching crisis than Anne, who would never worry about a leaning wall until it fell down, was sure the spasmodic puffs represented vaporous birds of ill omen. She had a presentiment. Ludwig, apparently, did not. Ludwig, in fact, was whistling cheerfully. But then Ludwig, a pleasant and easy-going young man, had the same tendency as Anne to let life happen and worry not.

'I'm sure something is wrong,' said Sophie.

'What can be wrong with a little steam?' said Anne. 'Train engines are always doing it.'

'Dearest ignoramus,' said Sophie, 'this isn't a train engine. I'm as much for progress as anyone, but I do feel there's no need for us to roar up every hill as if we were charging into battle. I'm sure we're overdoing it and that's why it's steaming.' She waited for a moment for Ludwig to make a reassuring comment. He did so.

'Nothing to worry about, dear girl,' he said, 'and we've not far to go.'

'Yes, dear man,' said Sophie, 'but I'd still prefer it if we stopped and you investigated the machinery.'

The Bugatti was new. Ludwig had been its proud owner for only two days. He had a manual he could investigate, he had only a vague idea of what was entailed in an investigation of the machinery. Better, with only a few miles to go, to let well alone.

'I'll look at it when we get back,' he said. The wind tugged at his words and tossed them away.

'Ludwig?' said Sophie as clearly as she could through her gauzy motoring veil.

'Don't worry, dear girl,' said Ludwig.

'Whizz on, Ludwig,' said Anne. She was in stimulated rapture and Ludwig in careless bliss. He sat capped, coated and goggled and upright, dedicated to the marvel of motion. His gloved hands gripped the wheel firmly, his attitude towards the emissions of steam one of cheerful resolution. He refused to be intimidated. Powerful and beautiful though the Bugatti was, it had been built by man to be controlled by man, not to get the better of him. Of course, when they reached Vienna he might perhaps look at the manual. It was not worth stopping now. The road was their guide and companion, the vista delightful and the Danube a broad shining flow through the valley on their right.

The steam hissed more menacingly as they began to climb another gradient.

'Ludwig, why is it doing that?' asked Sophie.

'Doing what?' called Ludwig.

'Steaming,' said Sophie, the ends of her veil fluttering.

'Ah, that's it, why?' said Ludwig cheerfully.

'Yes, why?'

'It's the proud spirit of internal combustion,' said Ludwig, and the sound of that was a pleasure to his ear. He climbed on maximum revolutions.

'That sounds like something to do with anarchy,' said Sophie.

Anne laughed, enjoying the thrill of it as Ludwig took them roaring up the hill. He reached the top with a smile of triumph. The low gear whined and he changed up. He gave the surging engine more throttle and the shining monster of black steel and brilliant brass careered towards a bend.

'Oh, glorious,' exclaimed the exhilarated Anne.

'I do hope so,' said Sophie.

'Control, dear girls, that's the secret,' said Ludwig.

34

And he was in perfect control until they rounded the bend and saw a two-wheel carriage beginning to emerge on to the road from a leafy turning on the right.

'Ludwig!' Anne put her hands over her veil, hid her eyes and prayed. Admirably but disastrously Ludwig swung the wheel and roared across the road, missing the carriage horse by a whisker and running into a half-submerged boulder in the long grass of the verge. There was a sickening crunch of fender and wheel buffeting stone, a shriek from Anne, a cry from Sophie, and both of them were thrown forward in a heap. Ludwig's chest hit the steering wheel, robbing him of breath, and the engine died of outrage and shock.

Escaping steam hissed. Ludwig hung his mouth open to suck in air. Anne, on her knees, felt sweet relief at only being shaken and not dead. Sophie, wondering why she was on the floor of the car instead of the seat, had a vague feeling that her support of progress had taken a grievous knock and her presentiment of disaster had been justified. While Ludwig sucked in air the shocked baronesses edged shakily back on to the seat and set their hats straight. The driver of the two-wheeler, having pulled safely on to the verge and soothed his horse, climbed down. Sophie and Anne, a little pale, saw him approach. He was as dark and ferocious as the devil himself, his cursory survey of the immobilized Bugatti anything but sympathetic. His black trousers were tucked into old calf-length boots, his leather belt fastened by a battered brass buckle and his dark green shirt marked by smears of old, dried paint. He was hatless, his black hair unruly and his expression a scowl. Sophie could not conceive him to be other than an unprincipled desperado quite capable of massacring them. Ludwig was helpless, leaning over the wheel, a hand to his chest as he hoarsely tried to recover his wind. Sophie groped for the only weapon to hand, her parasol.

The man, however, did not attack them. He bowed with what Sophie construed as sarcastic deliberation.

'I trust you are not too gravely injured,' he said in English.

Ah, thought Sophie, an abominable Englishman. She took a firm grip of her parasol. She said with proud aloofness, '*Würden Sie das bitte noch einmal sagen?*' Would you say that again, please?

'Ah,' said James almost evilly. His temper was a simmering furnace. '*Sprechen Sie Englisch?*'

'We prefer German,' said Sophie.

'Very well,' said James. He posed his question concerning their well-being in German. Grammatically it was execrable, but it was a necessary courtesy.

'I really don't know whether we are injured or not,' said Sophie, 'we are still too shocked to search for broken bones at the moment.'

'I see,' said James. He turned his attention on the car again and in a mixture of French, German and English damned it for a machine infernal and destructive. Anne blushed and Sophie broke into indignation.

'How dare you, sir!' she said in English.

'How dare I, how dare I? I'll have you know,' said James severely, 'that never have I seen a more baleful attempt to send four people and a horse to perdition.'

'Oh, goodness, you are cross,' said Anne.

'I disagree with you, sir,' said Sophie defiantly, 'it was simply the consequence of unavoidable circumstances, and I thought we did very well considering.'

'Well? Well?' James regarded the veiled young ladies darkly and launched into heavy sarcasm. 'You failed miserably, let me tell you. You had every advantage of weight, impetus, fire and fury, yet you killed nobody, not even yourselves. If you could move this miserable mountain of iron, perhaps you'd like to reverse far enough back and try again?'

'Oh!' Sophie's indignation was reborn on a speechless note. Anne, however, grateful that no fatality had occurred, refused to take James seriously.

'There's no need to be as cross as that,' she said from behind her pink veil, 'you'll feel sorry later on when you realize you concerned yourself more with our faults than our health. Fortunately, my sister and I are only shaken, but I think you might look at poor Ludwig.' Ludwig managed to wheeze that he was in fine fettle. 'There,' went on Anne sweetly, 'we are all quite well, but thank you for asking.'

'Oh, let us count our blessings, by all means,' said James. He walked around the car, inspecting it. Sophie quivered. The man was outrageous. She raised her folded parasol and bravely pointed it at him.

'Stand back, sir,' she said.

Ludwig sat up, breathing hard. James muttered. His acquired suspicion that automobiles were not a benefactory invention was not a total condemnation. But he was intolerant of people who drove them badly. The escaping steam told him the new engine was overheated. The driver had been carelessly exceeding the recommended revolutions.

'Look at this thing,' he said, 'an offence to civilization, an affront to peace and quiet. Is mechanical obscenity all we can offer future generations?'

Anne stifled a giggle. He was an uncompromising brute but he did know a great many German words in keeping with his temper, however deplorable his grammar and funny his accent.

'I'm not responsible for its invention,' she said very reasonably.

'I wish my conscience was as clear as that,' said James, knowing that while he may not have invented anything he had worked in the industry. He took a look at Ludwig. Ludwig was recovered enough to take his man's measure.

'Ah, the driver, I presume?' said James, sarcastic again.

Sophie saw dark little devil glints in his eyes.

He might not be a brigand but he could very well be first cousin to one. Ludwig, suspecting that the damage to his beautiful machine was calamitous, knew he would have to get down and endure the ordeal of finding out. He composed himself for it. He pushed back his goggles, his pleasant countenance a little sorrowful.

'I am the driver and the owner, sir,' he said, 'and I must say this is all very unfortunate. And most distressing to the ladies.'

'We are quite recovered, thank you, Ludwig,' said Sophie.

James regarded the ladies. Anne lifted her veil and smiled sweetly, roguishly. Sophie remained gauzily camouflaged. James softened under Anne's smile.

'I had no idea anyone would spring their two-wheeler on to the road,' said Ludwig. 'I hope you'll allow that was a little unexpected, sir.'

James was inclined to meet that reasonable argument halfway.

'I suppose I must take my share of the blame,' he conceded.

'There, now we all feel better,' smiled Anne.

'For the moment,' said Sophie, 'I wish to remain a little aloof.'

'And the car, I'm afraid,' said James, 'is going to remain wounded.'

'Is it bad?' sighed Ludwig.

'You'd better see,' said James.

'Courage,' murmured Ludwig to himself. He alighted. They all alighted. With James they inspected the damage. Ludwig shuddered. The fender was a mess, crushed back against the rim of the wheel, which was sadly buckled.

'What can be done?' asked Sophie.

'I should leave it, if I were you,' said James, 'and perhaps in the night it will go away and disappear. Quite the best thing, you know.'

He has the coolest cheek, the ruffian, thought Sophie. She tossed up her chin and pointedly said to Ludwig, 'What do you think can be done, Ludwig?'

'I shall consult the manual,' said Ludwig.

'If you'll pardon me for saying so,' said James, 'you might as well consult a railway timetable.'

'One must attempt something,' said Ludwig.

'Such as changing the wheel?' said James.

'The very thing,' said Ludwig, bearing no animosity.

'If we can ease that fender back,' said James. He resigned himself and added, 'Would you like some help?'

'What a good fellow you are,' said Ludwig.

'It is only fair, of course,' said Sophie. She lifted her veil back over her white hat. James looked into very fine but very cool brown eyes.

'Of course,' he said.

Ludwig took off his motoring coat, tightened his gloves, bent low, grasped the fender and pulled. It creaked but scarcely moved. He reddened with further effort. James went down on one knee and applied his own muscles. Together he and Ludwig wrenched at the fender. It cracked along the line of worst damage and hung clear of the wheel. Ludwig found the manual and began to leaf through it. James extracted jack and tools from the long box on the running board and set about practical matters. Ludwig recited instructions for jacking the car. James paid no attention. He did what was necessary briskly and efficiently. He loosened the wheel nuts, jacked the car, took off the damaged wheel and fitted the spare. His paint-soiled shirt became car-soiled, his hands turned black. Anne watched in admiration, Sophie with her coolness evaporating. She thought of something. The steam, which was still wispily escaping. She asked James if he could help with that too.

James, sweating, looked up. The young baronesses were colourful and picturesque in the summer light.

'No, I'm sorry,' he said, 'that's either a fault in the cooling system or a fault in the driver. A new car must be nursed like a baby. It must purr and hum, which it won't do if it's driven like a fire engine. When it's growling and roaring the permitted revolutions are being exceeded.'

'Oh, you are very knowledgeable,' said Anne.

'My relationship with these monsters is a love-hate one,' said James. 'I've crawled over them, into them, under them, and all for love. Realizing, however, that they're only going to make the world a noisier place, I'm currently engaged in a hate crusade against them. Would either of you care to join?'

'Although I'm fascinated,' said Sophie, 'I really don't think I could take it seriously enough.'

41

'In forty years time you'll regret that,' said James.

'I think you are joking, aren't you?' smiled Anne, her green eyes swimming with the high tide of life and adventure.

James was impressed by both of them. Neither had swooned nor had hysterics. They were both remarkably self-possessed and, it had to be said, engagingly attractive. She of the pink hat, with its cloudy halo of upturned veil perched enchantingly on hair the colour of golden corn, was gloriously young. She of the fine brown eyes, not quite so cool now, was undeniably striking.

'In my present mood,' he said, 'I'm far from joking.'

'I am not so cheerful myself,' said Ludwig.

James jacked down. He put the tools away, wiped his hands on a cloth from the box and said, 'If you'll switch on, I'll turn her. If your axle is damaged you'll have to leave her. If it isn't you may be able to roll her into Vienna.'

'Let us see,' said Ludwig. He climbed in, switched on and James cranked. The engine fired. Ludwig reversed the Bugatti off the verge and straightened up on the road. Then he moved slowly forward. James detected the slightest of wheel wobbles.

'You'd better follow me into Vienna,' he said, 'and if you get there drive straight to your engineers and leave it with them. If you wish, I'll take the ladies up with me.'

'It may be safer,' agreed Ludwig. 'I'm Lundt-Hausen, the ladies are the Baronesses von

Korvacs. Do you care to exchange cards, Herr – ?'

'Fraser,' said James, 'James Fraser. I carry no cards, I'm afraid.' He was not surprised the young ladies were titled. They had the look, the air. He was aware that his old, well-worn clothes must make him seem more of a tramp than a gentleman. That, however, had not made the baronesses turn their noses up at him. Which, considering his initial reactions of anger and disgust, represented a triumph for their well-bred social qualities.

'Unfortunate, the accident,' said Ludwig, 'but you're a helpful chap, Herr Fraser. You – ah – you are visiting Vienna?'

James smiled and said, 'You can find me at the Ecole Internationale. I teach there.'

'You're a teacher?' Sophie was agreeably surprised. He looked anything but academic. 'I wish sometimes I might be as useful as that. To teach is to make a real contribution to life.'

'Do you think so?' James seemed amused. 'You should tell that to the pupils. I feel they consider teachers, teaching and learning all rather boring.'

'Herr Fraser,' said Anne, 'you have really been very kind and I shall be pleased to ride back to Vienna with you.'

'In that case,' said Sophie, 'I shall naturally accompany my sister.'

'Of course,' said James.

'Of course,' said Ludwig.

'Dear me,' said Anne.

They drove to Vienna, Anne and Sophie up with James, Ludwig following with his front offside wheel running very slightly out of true. Anne was natural, friendly. Sophie was curious. She asked James about the school and how he came to be teaching there. He explained that he had left England to travel around Europe for a year, doing a little sketching and painting, and had met Maude Harrison, the principal of the school, in the Tyrol. Sophie and Anne thought his decision to take on the temporary post highly commendable.

'Oh, I'm doing very well out of it,' said James, 'I'm enjoying Vienna.'

When they reached the city, Ludwig left them to drive to the automobile engineers, while Anne gave James instructions on how to reach their house in the Salesianergasse. He handled the two-wheeler skilfully in the traffic. As they turned in through the open gates of the forecourt Sophie saw a motor car standing before the house. Around it were her parents, her brother Carl and a sleek gentleman. Two interested servants hovered in the background.

'Herr Fraser,' said Sophie, 'please will you tell no one we had an accident? It will put my parents against progress for ever.'

'Baroness,' said James, 'allow me to put you both down and to go on my way. I too am against some progress.' He brought the two-wheeler to a halt on one side of the forecourt. The people around the car looked up.

'Anne,' said Sophie, 'can we allow him to make us look ungrateful?'

'Certainly not,' said Anne, 'the least he can let us do is offer him some refreshment. I'm sure he will not really say anything to Mama.'

James regarded with interest the great, square-fronted house. Carl arrived, a slim tall young man with dark hair and blue eyes. He gave a hand to his sisters as they alighted and looked up at James in some curiosity.

'I thought you two girls were out with Ludwig,' he said, 'but never mind, come and look at the motor car and help me persuade Father we must have it. If you back down I'll skin you.'

Anne called up to James.

'Herr Fraser, please get down. I wish to introduce you to my family and to have you take some refreshment.'

'You must excuse me,' said James, 'but I'm really not presentable.'

'Ridiculous,' murmured Sophie, getting a little of her own back. It made James smile.

'Carl,' said Anne, 'this is Herr James Fraser. He has been indispensable to us this afternoon and knows absolutely everything about motor cars.'

'Then he's just the fellow,' said Carl. 'Will you come and tell us what you think of this one, old chap?'

'I warn you,' said James, climbing down, 'I'm much more likely to be frank than helpful.'

'I can't deny that,' said Sophie, 'Herr Fraser can be very frank. His opinion is that motor cars are monsters.'

'Good Lord,' said Carl disbelievingly, then laughed and added, 'you'll get on famously with my mother, then.'

The baron and his wife were far too civilized to show the astonishment they felt at the layer of paint, oil and grime anointing James's garments. Anne took their minds off the worst of it by emphasizing the sterling qualities of his character. She declared him to be the most invaluable of men in the way he had stopped on the road to change a wheel for Ludwig. This might have induced the baroness to ask why a wheel change was necessary, but with so much interest focused on the motor car the salesman had brought for inspection, the moment passed without comment from her.

The model was a Benz of dark green. Ludwig's Bugatti was new enough, but the Benz was pristine bright and immaculately beautiful. Carl was more than keen for the family to acquire it. At twenty-four he might have made his own decision, but he would rather hear the family express united favour. Also, if the family acquired it his father would pay for it and bear the running costs, which would suit Carl admirably. A fellow had so many other expenses to meet.

Anne was enthusiastic. Sophie was impressed, and although Ludwig's mishap was still a little black spot in her mind, she hoped, for Carl's sake, that Herr Fraser would not begin to abuse this gleaming machine of power if his opinion were asked. His expression was just a little threatening, she thought.

Anne's enthusiasm made the suave salesman feel the day could be a winning one.

'Papa,' she said, 'you simply must let Carl have it. It would set him up as the most popular dasher in Vienna, and he'll attract all the most eligible girls, which would please Mama no end.'

'However dashing Carl would look,' said the baroness, 'I should hope no young lady would consider that more important than so many other things.'

'Oh, you'd be surprised at what sweeps some of us off our feet these days,' said Sophie. 'But I must agree, Mama, it would do very well for Carl. Don't you think so, Herr Fraser?'

She knew he did not really want to be drawn in, but a little spark of feminine capriciousness, even of curiosity as to his reaction, compelled the question from her.

'Ah, well,' said James and coughed politely and got out of it in that way.

But Sophie, her eyes meeting his in sweet challenge, was too intrigued to yield. She wondered if he really would metaphorically strip the proud Benz of its beauty and leave it looking monstrous. She said to her parents, 'Herr Fraser is simply the most impressive man I've ever heard on motor cars, and I'm sure he could tell you Carl could not do better than have this one.'

Carl put an arm around his sister and squeezed her.

'What is your opinion, then, Herr Fraser?' asked the baron politely. He knew nothing of automobiles himself.

'That it's better for a family to make the decision between them,' said James, 'and for outsiders to stay very much on the outside.'

'Oh, you are funking it,' murmured Sophie.

'For myself,' said the baroness, hoping that if she remained on the scene long enough the thing would go away, 'I don't really need to know how marvellous it is, I'm convinced it would always be more of a noise than a miracle.'

'I'm not going to contradict that,' said James.

On his left side Anne whispered, 'But you must, think of Carl.'

Carl, aware of murmurs and counter-murmurs, was inclined to let things take their course. Obviously, his sisters found something rather intriguing about the disreputable-looking stranger. He knew them well enough, however, to be sure that they had not brought home a man who would blow the house up, even if he looked as if he might. The point was, the gathering was wholly about motor cars, and more especially about this Benz. Carl was willing to bet that the gleaming splendour of the model, together with the fact that his sisters were on his side, would win his parents over. They only needed a little push.

'Excellency,' said the salesman to the baron, 'I venture to suggest that if you and your family would care to let me take you for a short excursion, I could demonstrate and explain all the virtues of the model in the most practical way.'

'But you'd be biased in its favour,' said Sophie, smiling to let him know she did not hold that against him, 'and you'd never be as illuminating as Herr Fraser. He is a marvel of candour and expertise.'

'Are you?' Carl asked James.

'I've been close to design and development,' said James modestly. He was not sure whether he should involve himself. An enthusiast like Carl would only want to have his enthusiasm justified. But he was very aware of Anne, her eyes warm with appeal on behalf of Carl, and of Sophie with that mischievous challenge in her smile. They could not have thought much of his bad temper. He did not usually give way to it like that, but he had been violently shocked – as much for them as for himself – by the closeness of the mishap to real disaster. However, it was not a man's temper people like these considered important, it was his background. They thought him an impecunious, wandering artist temporarily turned teacher, no doubt. He had made various friends in Vienna. He had not entered any aristocratic circles. Nor had he met any young women as striking as these young baronesses. This was a time to sacrifice one's anonymity. 'My father,' he said, 'is Sir William Fraser of Edinburgh. I expect,' he added casually, 'that you may have heard of him.'

Carl had. His blue eyes lit up and saw James in a new light.

'Sir William Fraser? Of course I've heard of him. Who hasn't?'

'Me,' said Anne winsomely.

'I,' said Sophie, but with a smile for James.

'Darlings, much as I love you,' said Carl, 'you're not expected to be anything else but ignorant of him. You live in a different world. Sir William Fraser is one of the most respected and inventive designers in the world. My dear man, if I may?' He reached across the Benz and shook James vigorously by the hand. 'I congratulate you on your auspicious parentage—'

'I'm really quite proud of ours,' said Sophie.

'Thank you, darling,' said her mother.

'That's not to say we aren't impressed by yours,' said Anne to James.

'I'm more than impressed,' said Carl. 'What luck that my sisters found you. Usually they find only the most ghastly people.'

'That's not true,' said Anne.

'I take it, old chap,' said Carl, 'that you know more than a thing or two about roadsters like these?' He put his hand on the Benz.

'Herr Fraser,' said Sophie before James could answer, 'are you a teacher or not?'

'I am, temporarily,' said James, 'at the Ecole Internationale.'

'A teacher?' said the baroness. It was becoming confusing. And more confusing than anything were Herr Fraser's clothes. They looked as if he had borrowed them from a ruffian.

'Yes,' said James. 'The principal is Maude Harrison, I met her in the Tyrol. She was short of a teacher, so I offered to help out for a while.'

'Maude Harrison?' said the baron. 'I know Frau Harrison, I knew her husband. Very unfortunate. But a remarkably resourceful woman, she runs a most useful establishment. Excellent is the word, I believe.'

'Papa,' smiled Anne, 'now that we know what an exceptionally versatile gentleman Herr Fraser is, I'm sure we can be guided by his opinion on the Benz.'

She too knew that her father only needed a little push, and he was a man who knew when a push came from the right quarter. The salesman only knew he had to be patient as he stood first on one foot, then the other. This would go on for hours, they would all talk their heads off and then suddenly someone would toss a categorical yes or no into the melting pot and that would be it.

'Do please give us your opinion, Herr Fraser,' said the baroness, hoping he would be sensitive enough to take hers into account.

'Let me see,' said James and decided he might as well show off a little. He began to talk in highly technical terms of the Benz and its motive power. The baron excused himself for a moment. He went into the house and telephoned Maude Harrison. She was touched to hear from him, he had been kind and helpful during her late husband's tour of duty in Vienna. She told him now all he felt he wanted to know. He returned to the forecourt. James, with the salesman gawping, was expounding in his own mixture of French, English and German on transmission, intake valves, pistons, cylinders, carburation and manifolds. When he emphasized that the ideal manifold should, among other properties, have a low resistance in order to maintain high volumetric efficiency, the salesman quivered and the family looked numbed. Except Carl. Keenly he followed as much of it as he could, although he was left behind on some points. Nobody else understood a word. Only Sophie had the courage to catch James's eye and to beg for mercy with an expressively rueful look. James, answering her silent appeal, said, 'That, I feel, is as much as I need say about the technical merits of a motor car such as this.'

The baron, no wiser than before, decided to shift the responsibility of comment on to his wife.

'Well, my dear,' he said, 'now what do you think?'

The baroness was not completely unequal to it.

'Quite frankly, Ernst,' she said, 'I think if any motor car were only half as complicated as Herr Fraser describes, then we should all be mad to even sit in one, let alone ride in it.'

'No, no,' said Carl, who had enjoyed every moment of dialogue and discussion, 'that isn't quite the way to look at it, my sweet. Our friend James, in describing the essential desirabilities of a sound engine, was relating these to the virtues of the Benz engine.'

Our friend James? Oh, thought Sophie, has that devilish-looking brigand suddenly become a family friend? She laughed to herself, she glanced at James. He was looking very innocent.

Anne said, 'I must say, Mama, it all sounded terribly impressive.'

'And nothing like anything he said about Ludwig's Bugatti,' observed Sophie. With her veil tipped back over the brim of her hat, her chestnut hair swept upwards, her creamy skin accepted the warm touch of the afternoon sun. Anne's complexion was fair, the light liquidly reflected in her eyes. Amusement glimmered in Sophie's eyes, her glance another challenge to James.

'Yes,' he said, 'but you must remember that when I came up against—'

'Don't you dare,' whispered Sophie.

'Herr Fraser,' said the baron, 'we should like to be guided by you, since you're the son of the redoubtable Sir William. Will you help us to conclude this matter? Would you tell us whether the Benz is a perfectly safe and reliable automobile?'

'Safe?' said James. Anne sensed a compulsive urge for candour quivering on his tongue. 'Will you please excuse me for a moment?' he said and went and sat on the step of the two-wheeler.

'Intriguing chap,' said Carl.

'Oh, indeed,' said Sophie. She looked at Anne. Together they walked across the forecourt to confront James.

'Herr Fraser,' said Sophie, 'I don't feel we are quite strangers to each other now. Therefore, may I presume on our short but illuminating acquaintanceship to beg that for the moment you abandon your crusade?'

'We should both like to presume, for Carl's sake,' smiled Anne.

'I'm composing myself,' said James.

'We are all quite in love with the Benz,' said Sophie.

'Except Mama,' said Anne. 'It's for her that my father asked the question.'

'And he only asked if the car would be safe,' said Sophie.

'Having composed myself,' said James, rising, 'let me say that if I were offered the best car there is I'd lock it away to keep it very safe and very quiet. But as far as your brother is concerned, the Benz is a masterpiece of engineering perfection and as reliable as you could wish. If it's driven with due respect. If I were Carl and not myself, I'd have it, drive it and take great care of it.'

'Then if you'd care to tell my father that,' smiled Sophie, 'you'll be Carl's friend for life.'

'Very well,' said James.

'Oh, you are really most agreeable,' said Anne warmly.

James delivered his opinion. That settled the matter. The salesman looked sleekly happy and the baroness looked resigned. The baron began to discuss details of the purchase.

'I must be on my way,' said James.

'Indeed you must not,' said Anne, 'we should not dream of letting you go without giving you the promised refreshment. Should we, Mama?'

'Of course not,' said the baroness, conceding defeat with a gracious smile.

James plucked at his shirt to indicate his sartorial unsuitability.

'Goodness,' said Anne, 'we aren't as stuffy as that.'

'You'll find,' said Sophie, 'that we are all very nice and ordinary. At least, I am.'

'Come inside,' said Carl, delighted by the outcome, and he linked arms with James and took him into the house.

'When I first saw him,' murmured Sophie to Anne as they followed on, 'I thought he was going to murder us all.'

'It's all that poetry you write,' said Anne, 'it makes you imaginative.'

Chapter Three

Occasionally James went out with Kirsti, Maude's housemaid. Maude was not sure she approved, Kirsti being a scatterbrained servant and a notoriously fickle coquette. And she did not think James's parents would approve at all. They would not consider a flighty servant girl a suitable social companion for their son. But James liked Kirsti. She was an engaging minx with an aptitude for goodnight kisses that came like a soft, warm bombardment. They were her way of thanking a man for taking her out, but any man who asked for more received what she called a punch in the pinny.

Kirsti was not looking for a husband, only for fun. She and James enjoyed each other's company, and she showed him how the ordinary people of Vienna made as much of its gaiety as the upper classes. The ordinary people, in fact, enjoyed a more combustible engagement with revelry.

Wednesday was a half-day at the school. Kirsti had free time. James took her out. They crossed the Schwarzenbergplatz and entered the wide boulevard of the Ringstrasse. James immersed himself in the atmosphere of old Vienna, bounded by the Ring and the magnificent lines of trees. It was a cloudy day, the light softening the ancient buildings, and the tall spire of St Stephen's Cathedral looked almost delicate in its Gothic tracery. Carriages in stately unhurriedness impeded the progress of impatient automobiles, much to James's delight. People were strolling the leafy thoroughfares, leisure an art, not a time-killer. Bicycle bells rang, cabbies whistled as they ran their fiacres at a lazy trot, while here and there a two-wheeler in the hands of youth bowled by in rakish exuberance.

Kirsti tripped along, James ambled. She wanted to look at the shops in the Graben. She had looked at them a thousand times before. Then she would want raisin coffee and cakes, and later they would go to one of the dance halls that abounded in Vienna. Kirsti had a store of nervous energy and a capacity to dance all night. James, fortunately, had the stamina to absorb whatever punishment her vivacious quest for fun put upon a man.

Vienna was a city as much for the young as the old, and Kirsti was nineteen and very young. She was appalled by the interest James showed in monuments and museums. People would think he was one of the old. Who on earth except fusty old professors could waste time wandering around marble and masonry?

'Oh, come on,' she said.

'I'm coming on,' said James. It was always

'come on' with Kirsti. Each new pursuit was only a forerunner to the next. He pulled her back as she stepped blithely off the pavement. The driver of the approaching cab hollered 'Lunatic!' Kirsti put her nose up. They reached the Graben. She feasted on shop windows while James looked at people. The women, he thought, were more interesting than those of Paris. They were taller, their colouring diverse. But then Vienna had always been the confluence into which Germans, Slavs and Magyars had poured during centuries, the fair had mingled with the dark and produced all shades. In Paris it was nearly all Gallic darkness.

After an hour of window-worship Kirsti manhandled him to a coffee house. There she drank raisin-flavoured coffee and ate her way through a huge slice of layer cake.

'You'll get fat,' he said.

'Some like them fat,' said Kirsti creamily.

'Some like who fat?'

'Oh, go on.' She giggled, then waved to a young man drinking coffee at another table. He blew her a kiss. 'That's Frederic,' she said.

'Notorious or otherwise?'

'He hires out cabs,' said Kirsti, licking a finger, 'he says he'll be rich one day. One day. But what good will it do him? He'll only put it in the bank and call on Fridays to count it. Do you know, when he kisses a girl I think he's still counting schillings.'

'A very good way,' said James, 'of mixing pleasure with business.'

'It's not flattering,' she said, all buttoned up in pillar-box red, 'being kissed by a man who's thinking of money.'

'Well, we can't all afford to forget about it,' said James, lankily draped in a suit of light grey, 'and aren't there the loveliest young things who don't think about anything else?'

'They're thinking about your money,' said Kirsti, 'which is not at all the same as thinking about their own. Come on, it's time to go and meet Rosa and Boris.'

'Rosa and Boris? They sound familiar,' said James.

'But of course,' said Kirsti, rising and brushing herself down, 'Rosa works for the Corbière family. Marie Corbière, she attends the school. Boris is Rosa's young man. He is very earnest.'

'Is he, by God,' said James, remembering the young man in the bohemian hat.

They met up in a dance hall popular with the young people. The atmosphere was informal, and the orchestra played the music of Lehar, Lanner, the Strausses and others for whom there were no substitutes as far as the Viennese were concerned.

They shared a table and James ordered champagne, which delighted Kirsti and broke the ice with Rosa and Boris. Rosa was from Galicia, her plump curves accentuated by a small waist. Boris Ferenac was a Bosnian, a dark Slav who smiled as if amusement was a secretive business. A violinist, he thought little of those in this orchestra. It was one thing to tuck a violin

59

under your chin, he said, it was another thing altogether to clasp it to your soul. Only Slavs could do that.

He smiled as he made the observation. Secretively.

Rosa gossiped with Kirsti. Both in service, they were addicted to topical titbits concerning their employers and the employers of others. Rosa said her own employers were returning to France soon and had asked her to go with them.

'But, of course, I'm not sure if Boris would like that,' she said and looked at Ferenac. He smiled again but said nothing. 'You'd not care for me to go, would you?'

'We both have our destinies,' he said, 'and who can say whether they will intertwine or diverge?'

Pretentious ass, thought James. He danced with Kirsti. Ferenac remained at the table with Rosa. He could not, he said, dance to an orchestra as inferior as this. Everyone else managed it and the dance floor was a whirl of couples all evening. James took Rosa round a couple of times. He found her dull.

Towards the end of the evening the orchestra played 'Tales from the Vienna Woods'. It sent the patrons into raptures. And when it finished with the Emperor Waltz ecstatic revellers rose to their feet to sing and to drink the health of Franz Josef and the Habsburgs.

Ferenac, his meaningless smile now beginning to irritate James, lifted his glass, looked at Rosa and said, 'Health!'

'Health,' said Rosa.

'The dear old emperor,' cried Kirsti.

'And the good archdukes,' smiled Ferenac, looking into his glass.

The good? Strange, thought James, and wondered if Ferenac's smile was so meaningless, after all. The good? What was it Marie had written?

A good archduke is a dead one.

In between goodnight kisses which, probably because of the champagne, she turned into a more prolonged bombardment than usual, Kirsti said, 'It was very nice tonight. Did you like Rosa? She asked me why you weren't married.'

'If she asks again,' said James, 'you can tell her that it's only now that I've begun to think seriously about it.'

Kirsti reacted with a perceptible withdrawal of warm bosom from manly chest.

'You don't mean me, do you?' she said.

'You're a delicious young thing,' said James, 'but no.'

'Thank goodness,' said Kirsti, re-engaging, 'I thought it wasn't going to be fun any more.'

He looked at Marie's essay again the next morning. It was a bright piece about her home and family on a particular day, what she did, what they did, and what was said. Rosa was mentioned. And Boris.

'In the afternoon I walked home from school with Rosa and Boris. Rosa comes to meet me sometimes

*and then she meets Boris too. Rosa held my hand and
Boris held Rosa's hand. Sometimes they whispered
and sometimes he made her laugh and push him. My
brother Louis ran out to meet us and fell over and
hurt his hand. He is too big to cry now so he just
got up and asked me to come and look at his new toy
soldiers.'*

That was all there was about Rosa and Boris.
The paragraph was in the middle of the essay.

That last line still made no sense.

But it worried him a little and he began to
wonder about Boris Ferenac.

'Is the son of the redoubtable Sir William with us
again?' asked Sophie.

'James? He's with Carl, in the stables,' said
Anne. 'It's all to do with the Benz and nothing
to do with us. He doesn't seem to realize how
eligible we both are. Myself, I'm very eligible.'

'I know, darling.' Sophie smiled. 'And you're
keeping scores of suitors on tenterhooks.'

'I'm really only keeping them attentive. One is
only young once. And I shan't marry until I fall
madly in love.'

'There's Ludwig,' said Sophie, 'I'm sure he's
excessively keen on you.'

'Sophie, he's quite excessively attached to
you.'

'He's a dear boy,' said Sophie, 'and much the
age for you, darling.'

'Of course, James is very adult,' said Anne, re-
garding the bright sweep of the gardens.

'Oh, how did James creep in?' smiled Sophie.

'Well, he is very provoking,' said Anne, 'always coming to see Carl and having so little to do with us.'

'Oh, the devious fellow,' said Sophie.

'Devious?'

'Certainly. A young lady ignored is a young lady susceptible. He is out to catch you, my sweet.'

'Or you?' said Anne and laughed.

The baroness entered the drawing room.

'Ludwig and Helene are here,' she said. 'Ludwig has gone to the stables and Helene is waiting for you to receive her, Anne.'

'Yes, we're all to go driving in the Benz,' said Anne.

'That is news to me,' said Sophie.

'Well, it's all arranged,' said Anne, 'and you must come or we shall be odd.'

'I shall save you from that terrible fate,' said Sophie.

The carriages were out of the stables. In their place stood the gleaming Benz. The bonnet was up. Immersed in the mechanical functionalism were Carl and Ludwig. Sitting on a pair of steps, overlooking the amateurs, was James in his light grey suit with a striped shirt and grey tie. The stables smelt of horses, straw and linseed oil. From their stall on the far side the horses chewed hay and blinked suspiciously at the monster threatening their purpose in life.

'No,' said James, 'use the plug spanner, Carl.'

'Ah, you've caught me there,' said Carl.

That was how it was. Carl was learning the mechanics under James's supervision. Carl did not want to merely drive the Benz, he wanted to understand it, to comprehend the fundamentals, to know what to look for if anything went wrong and what to do to put the fault right. He had telephoned James two days after taking delivery, complaining about a stiffness in the gears. James thought he should have contacted the dealers but did not say so. He came round. He came again, several times. Now it was an involvement and a friendship, something that took up his time out of school hours. It also included teaching Carl how to drive. Carl wished to be a fully orientated owner-driver. It would help him to be father and mother to the Benz. His interest in it was such that he was as happy tinkering with it as driving it. James indulged one eccentricity of his own. If Carl ran the engine in the stables James went outside to escape the noise.

'I must say,' said Carl once, 'that considering you don't really care for autos it's damned decent of you to bother about the Benz.'

James bothered for a reason that had little to do with the Benz. He sat on the steps now, watching the bent heads of Carl and Ludwig. Ludwig realized he could learn a few things himself.

'Well, really.' It was Anne's voice. She stood at the wide entrance to the stables, the sun behind her. With her was Ludwig's sister, Helene, a fair but not entirely brilliant young lady. Sophie thought her a little giggly, the baroness thought her a little flighty. She was rather keen on Carl, but Carl, while as cheerfully disposed towards her as all girls, hardly thought about her at all.

'Carl, you're utterly fiendish,' said Anne.

'Oh?' said Carl from the mechanical deeps.

'Oh? Oh? Come out from there,' called Anne, 'you promised to take us all out. We've been waiting ages already. James, is that you up on high?'

'Ladies,' said James and bowed from his perch. Anne was good to look at. In her favourite blue she was as colourful as summer itself. Helene Lundt-Hausen looked a little insipid beside her. Helene was white-skinned, pretty. Anne was warm, lovely.

'James,' said Anne, 'as you're the king of all you survey, kindly command your subjects to rise up and sally forth, for there are beautiful maidens impatiently awaiting them.'

'That's almost a proclamation,' said James.

'Beautiful maidens?' Carl lifted his head. 'Where are they? Do you see any, Ludwig?'

'Isn't he hideously hopeless to have as a brother?' said Anne to Helene.

'Well, he is rather naughty sometimes,' said Helene. 'You are, aren't you, Carl? Are you going to be awfully sweet now and take us driving?'

James winced. Helene's conversation never reached celestial heights. At the best it was as coy as her archly pouting bosom.

'Just give us five more minutes,' said Carl.

'No,' said Anne, 'it's either now or never. James, order them.'

'Gentlemen,' said James, comfortably on the fence, 'I order you.'

'We're filthy,' said Ludwig. He and Carl were both in rolled-up shirtsleeves and their hands were black.

'Oh, you beasts,' said Anne, 'now you're going to spend hours scrubbing yourselves. Carl, Sophie said if you don't bring the Benz round to the house in two minutes she's coming to smash it to pieces with a hammer.'

'Dear Sophie,' said Carl. He and Ludwig began to wash their hands under a cold, running tap, using a large bar of yellow soap.

'James, don't just sit there, please,' said Anne, 'you can bring the Benz round. You are accompanying us, you know, we don't want to be odd. So please come down, or *you'll* get smashed to pieces with a hammer.'

'Whatever you say,' said James, climbing down.

They were all ready in the end. Carl offered to drive. So did Ludwig.

'James, I think,' said Sophie.

'Yes, he is the master engineer,' said Anne.

'Thank you,' said James, 'but I'm really a horse-and-cart man.'

'James, we command you,' said Sophie.

So James took the wheel. Anne sat up in front with him and Carl, Sophie and Helene on the high rear seat with Ludwig. They sailed smoothly through the gates and into the Salesianergasse.

'James, the other way!' screamed Anne as he turned left.

'What other way? I haven't been told,' said James as he adjusted the course of the car. The day was full of changing shades of light, clouds

66

scudding across the blue sky and under the sun, Vienna looking alternately soft and bright. The traffic was a mixture of trotting carriages, scurrying fiacres and portly automobiles. It was Saturday afternoon and the city was preparing for a gay evening.

'Oh, do let's go to Demel's,' cried Helene.

'I've been there,' said James.

'To Demel's, James, please,' said Anne, 'I should like a big fat cream pastry.'

'I can't believe that,' said James. He slowed to a stop to allow two ladies to cross the road. They smiled their thanks. He lifted his grey, black-banded hat to them.

'You're very considerate,' said Anne.

'Ludwig,' said Sophie, 'is your Bugatti better, is it recovering?'

'In a day or two,' said Ludwig, 'it will be out and about again.'

'Yes,' said Helene, giggling, 'and then you can ask James to teach you how to drive it.'

'That,' said Carl, who knew all about the mishap, 'is a blow beneath the belt.'

James turned right, making for the Kohl-market. He took off his hat and Anne placed it on her lap for him. His thick hair blew in the wind. Helene began to hum a song. Ludwig, looking at Anne's back, thought what a nice neck she had. James passed ambling vehicles. He drove smoothly, economically, and Carl watched his manipulation of gears with interest.

'This is quite lovely,' said Anne, enjoying the changing patterns of traffic and pavements.

'I seriously prefer a horse and cart,' said James.

'You're a reactionary,' said Ludwig.

Helene said, 'Is that the same as—'

'No,' said Sophie, leaving Helene puzzled as to how Sophie knew she was going to say revolutionary. 'James,' Sophie went on, 'horses and carts are for vegetables. We shouldn't want you to become just another cabbage.'

'I don't think James will ever be as green as that,' said Carl.

The Benz purred. Carl felt proud. The thoroughfares were busy, the traffic containing a fair proportion of automobiles. The Benz outshone its rivals. James, however, was more aware of the fumes, fuss and bullying look of the motor traffic. He said something inaudible.

'I didn't catch that, James,' said Sophie, wondering a little why she had consented to career around Vienna when it was just the afternoon for composing poetry in the garden.

'It's absolute sacrilege,' said James in English. He frequently broke into English when the most suitable German words eluded him, but all the von Korvacs understood the language and so did Ludwig. 'Look at it, my lovely Vienna strewn with smoking monstrosities.'

'James, you are sweet,' said Anne.

'Except that he's in the wrong position to criticize,' said Ludwig.

'Oh, not really,' said Sophie, 'our Benz may be a monstrosity but it doesn't smoke. James would never allow it.'

James looked critically at the belching exhaust of a vehicle in front of the Benz.

'Criminal,' he said.

'Now, James, don't get cross,' said Anne. She found James amusing, stimulating. She was sure he was tempted to butt the offender. He might have done when it stopped abruptly and without warning. He managed, however, to swerve adroitly round it. He pulled up alongside.

'Cannibal!' he called.

'*Mein Herr?*' said the startled driver.

'That's not a rocking horse you've brought on to the streets,' said James severely, 'it's a man-eating machine of fire, capable of cooking and consuming every citizen in Vienna. I shall report you to the emperor.'

'God in heaven,' said the bewildered recipient of this crisp homily.

James went on his way. Sophie was laughing, Helene giggling.

'James, the poor man,' said Anne, 'you were rather hard on him.'

'Not at all,' said Sophie, 'that poor man was an idiot. Well done, James.'

At Demel's in the Kohlmarkt, the uniformed doorman advanced as James drew up. The passengers alighted. Anne and Helene entered the celebrated establishment in a froth of blue and pink, Sophie in willowy white simplicity that commanded attention. Carl followed on. James bent over the car, looking for his hat. Ludwig found it for him, handed it to him. A dark young man in a wide-brimmed black hat passed by.

He saw James, then Ludwig. He looked hard at Ludwig for a moment, then passed on.

Demel's, the most fashionable pastry and coffee shop in Vienna, was crowded. The coffee aromas were fragrant and ecstatic. Austrian army officers in sky-blue jackets slashed with gold sat with ladies of such radiant grace that even the pyramids of whipped cream had a muted richness. One lady, observing the dark, thin and slightly Messianic look of James as he brought up the rear of his handsome party, caught his eye over the shoulder of her escort. Her rouged lips parted in an inviting smile. She winked. James reciprocated.

'I think I've made a hit,' he said, seating himself with the others at a round marble-topped table.

'With whom?' asked Sophie and he pointed the lady out. 'That,' smiled Sophie, 'is Fany Giesel, the celebrated musical-comedy actress.'

'I'm flattered,' said James.

'She's also very short-sighted,' said Sophie.

'That's a blow,' said James.

The little lights of laughter danced in her eyes. She was creamy. In her white hat with little touches of pink, and her white silk dress, she was also symptomatic of the elegance and charm he was coming to associate with the women of Vienna. She and Anne set each other off, Sophie a rich brunette, Anne's fairness warm and lovely.

'We'll all have strudel, shall we?' said Anne.

'Do they serve griddle cakes?' asked James.

'What are those?' asked Helene, pink-mouthed.

'I've a vague idea that they're a Scottish breakfast,' said Carl.

'Invented by Vikings,' said James.

'Oh? For their friends or enemies?' said Sophie, at which Carl laughed his head off and thereby caught the eye of several young ladies, one or two of whom sighed wistfully over his good looks. He looked very dashing in his striped blazer and white ducks.

'Carl,' said Sophie, 'I think we should educate James. Order strudel for him, the one with curds and raisins.'

'An education,' said James, 'should not be as punishing as that.'

'There, Sophie,' said Anne, 'you have met your match.'

They all ate the strudel in question, the paper-thin pastry baked around sweet curds with cream and raisins. James said it would make them all fat. They drank hot black coffee with it. Helene wanted to know what they might all do together that evening.

'We shall whirl around Vienna with James,' said Anne.

'Oh, dear,' said Sophie, given to less rowdy pastimes.

James could have said he had whirled around Vienna several times with Kirsti. Instead he said, 'Is it possible? On top of so much strudel?'

'Oh, it's just the thing for a visitor,' said Sophie,

71

'and although I've grown out of it I'll whirl around very agreeably for your sake.'

'Oh, yes, let's have fun,' said Helene.

'We can only get arrested,' said Carl.

'Let's be people,' said Anne.

So they drove later on to the Prater and joined the people in the amusement park. They rode on the Big Wheel and from the top looked down over the panorama of Vienna as the summer evening turned into illuminated night. Ludwig shot the head off a clay pipe at a booth and won a rag doll. He did not know whether to present it to Anne or to Sophie. James took it from him and gave it to a young girl, relieving the amiable Ludwig of the worry of making a decision.

They returned to the city at play. The boulevard lamps, curtained by leafy trees, spread diffused light over the charivari of Vienna's night life. They patronized taverns in which musicians, writers, painters, students and young would-be politicians argued away day and night. Anne suggested that as they were not dressed for formal dining they should have bread and sausage in one of the taverns. So they did.

'Sometimes,' said Sophie whimsically, 'it's good to be people.'

'I'm just hungry,' said Carl.

'I'm starving,' said Ludwig.

'I'm eating like a horse,' said Anne.

'The noblest of creatures,' said James.

'For that you must have some of my sausage,' said Anne and popped a piece into his mouth.

'We'll all get fat,' said James.

'Don't keep saying that,' said Helene.

'I suppose we're lucky to have the chance to get fat,' said Sophie. 'I've just finished reading a book from Papa's library about brigands. They become brigands, most of them, because they are born in wretched conditions with not enough to eat.'

'They're natural-born scoundrels,' said Carl.

'Oh, perhaps they have a trait,' conceded Sophie, 'since it is a fact that in many Balkan countries brigandry is a family tradition as well as an occupation. Although they're constantly harassed by the authorities, brigands are basically as free as the air. They conform to no conventions, only to their own customs. One magnificent adventurer called Dragovich ruled like a king in the Albanian mountains. He amassed a fortune from being a most provident scoundrel and divided it all among his followers, keeping for himself only the women he had captured.'

'Oh, the dreadful beast,' said Helene.

'But generous with his fortune,' said Anne.

'Even if he was greedy with his women,' said Carl.

'Dragovich,' said Sophie, warming imaginatively to her subject, 'was seven feet tall, had a huge black moustache and a Russian cannon. He lived until he was eighty-six, had nine wives and forty children. James,' she said, lights in her eyes, 'do you know any man who enjoyed a life of more glorious abandonment than that?'

'I'd call it worrying multiplication,' said James.

'James,' said Anne, 'do you think Sophie should be sent to Albania to look for a provident scoundrel of her own?'

'I don't think she'd go,' said James. 'Sophie, after all, has a higher intelligence than some of my pupils . . .'

'Thank you, dear James,' said Sophie.

'. . . even some of my pupils know that an old goat seen on a distant mountain always appears to be a far more majestic creature than the one eating up your garden. Distance lends illusion.'

They laughed and talked on.

Three nights later they all went to the Dianabad, the incomparable home of Strauss music. They listened to the orchestra, watched the dancers and drank Moselle wine. Anne in jewelled white was, thought Sophie affectionately, lovely enough to float with angels. Sophie in shimmering jade green was, thought Anne admiringly, dressed to bewitch all men. Helene, in frilled, off-shoulder cerise, flaunted her pink-framed bosom with the archest of poses. She will catch Carl's eye with such décolletée, thought Anne, but it won't make him fall in love with her. Carl is very easy-going but I'm sure he will look for more than low décolletée in a woman. Is Sophie falling for James, I wonder? No, I hardly think so. She would be much more intense in her behaviour if she were. She has hidden fires, I think. It would be better for her to fall in love pleasantly, not head over heels. How nice Ludwig is, always ready to fall in with what others want to do. It's rather delicious that he simply cannot make up his mind whether Sophie is more of a challenge than I am. I'm not sure that the possibilities and prospects aren't vastly intriguing, and how enjoyable it is with the six of us to consider the infinite variations. I should be in a hopeless quandary if either Ludwig or James proposed, I should simply not know what to do or say. I think that means I'm not in love, only having fun.

Sophie, her hands clasping her wine glass as delicately as if it had been summer's first rose, mused on the lights reflected in the pale translucence of the wine. It has really been rather satisfying, she thought, showing James my Vienna. Especially as other people always seem to enjoy Vienna more than the Viennese. We take it for granted, we're seldom fully aware of the jewel the emperors have laid at our feet. One day I shall complete a volume of poems on Vienna and have it published, and everyone will say here is an exquisite appreciation of everything we see and pass by daily without giving thanks. James is an artist, I wonder if he'd like to look at some of my poetry? No, I can't ask him to, he must ask me. It's a great mistake to press one's poetry into the hands of one's friends. It's a self-inflicted defeat from the start. Either they're flattered that you want their opinion and so only give you the highest praise, or they know you want your highest praise and do nothing about it, knowing they're going to force you in the end to ask what has become of my poems you've had for a year? Oh, my poor Sophie, I quite forgot all about them, do forgive me. But you can't forgive them, your artistic soul is too wounded. So no, I shan't ask James to look at any of my poems. He'd probably paraphrase his criticisms in motor-car terms and tell me my metre has a flat tyre and my stanzas are out of gear. What *is* out of gear?

He's getting on very well with Anne, I think. I wonder if they would suit each other? Anne is so happy with life's blessings and James, I fancy, has just enough of the devil in him to keep her interested, happy but not disturbed. Ludwig would make a very cheerful husband, probably, if she chose him. Myself, I'm sure I'd want more from a husband than simple cheerfulness. I'd like him to be intellectual, conversational and extremely fond of my poetry. I should wish to like him very much but not be off my head about him, as I think that is too unsettling for a wife. What is Anne saying to James now?

Anne was asking James if he had been to Oxford or Cambridge. James, held by her blue-green eyes, came out of an agreeably mesmerized state to say, 'At Edinburgh University no one's ever heard of Oxford or Cambridge. Would you care to dance, fairest of Vienna's blossoms?'

'How can I say no to that?' said Anne.

They glided away, melting into the whirling kaleidoscope of movement and colour, prompting Ludwig to offer his arm to Sophie.

'Thank you, Ludwig,' she smiled, 'how timely. Anne and James have launched themselves into perpetual motion, and we must fly after them.'

They flew. Into the gyrational gaiety of the waltz.

'What did Sophie mean by that?' asked Helene of Carl.

Carl, putting out his slim, gold-tipped cigarette, said, 'Nothing painful, dear girl. May I have the pleasure?'

'Oh, that would be nice,' said Helene and was on her feet in an eager gush of frothy pink. She adored Carl. But then she adored most of the young men she knew. She had no brains at all but was of such a generous disposition that her mental vacuity was always forgivable. She was due to be adored herself by a senior army officer who considered brains in a woman entirely undesirable and who accordingly decided Helene would make an eminently suitable wife. And she did. But at the moment, in this summer of 1914, she was flirtatiously and archly happy in company with Carl and the others.

Anne was warmly vivacious to dance with and James, whirling around with her, was frankly captivated by the atmosphere she and all his new friends created. True, they were without serious responsibilities, they did not have to work, to toil, to labour, they only had to live, and they lived fully, gaily and extravagantly. The von Korvacs were among the leading families of Vienna, and around Sophie and Anne moved the most eligible men. They were not always at home when he and Carl were tinkering with the Benz in the evenings, they were out at summer balls.

He had no false ideas about his own eligibility. He was a friend of the family and it stopped at that. He had nothing to offer an aristocratic Austrian woman which he would not have to work for. His father would not make him more than a reasonable allowance if he got married, but would pay him well if he went back into the business. But however well that was, he could not see it keeping Anne or Sophie in the luxury they were used to. He was not even sure he would go back into the automobile industry. He had turned his back on it to be as irresponsible as his aristocratic friends for a year, and the longer he was away from it the less it appealed to him as a career. If he did go back he would set his creative sights on the development of noiseless engines and on the social desirability of turning the motor car into a vehicle with as much grace and elegance as a carriage. I'm so damned old-fashioned, he thought, that I'm almost an anachronism. Or a freak.

'What are you thinking about?' asked Anne, spinning with him, her eyes full of the joys of waltzing.

'Horses and carts.'

'You are funny. Horses and carts indeed. You mean a carriage and pair, that's the gracious phrase.'

The chandeliers of bright, glittering light revolved, the swirling dresses foamed with colour and Sophie went spinning by in the arms of Ludwig. A little later, when they had all recovered their breath, James said to her, 'Sophie, will you engage again? Will you join the hoi polloi with me?'

'Join it?' Sophie's smile was sparkling. 'James, I *am* the hoi polloi, don't you know that?'

He found her an elegance of poetic motion, her dark shining hair regally dressed, her gown shimmeringly clasping her slender body.

'James, you're very accomplished.'

'I manage to keep up? Good,' said James.

'Quite truthfully, you know,' said Sophie, 'I haven't been to this dance hall since I was a girl.'

'That must have been quite three months ago,' said James.

'Ah,' she said, head back, eyes brilliant, 'you're much more gallant than when you nearly ran us down in your two-wheeler. What a beast you were then. Your language was dreadful.'

'So was your driving, you came round that blind bend like a racing chariot—'

'That was Ludwig. I was an innocent passenger.'

'You were nearly an innocent victim,' said James. She was laughing at him, it was in her eyes, her smile. 'What an air you have, Sophie.'

'What kind of an air?'

'Oh, full of the dash of the hoi polloi.'

Sophie laughed. It was true she had not been to the Dianabad for two or three years, and she was surprising herself in her enjoyment of it tonight. She observed James with interest. Ludwig always looked clean-cut and freshly shaved. James had a thinner face and a slight hint of blue shadow.

Ludwig was an entirely likeable young man. James was definitely a trifle devilish, with little glints in his eyes. A tiny suspicion darted into her mind, a suspicion that she might be more susceptible than she thought. She was perfectly happy with life, perfectly content to wait for an intellectual and sophisticated suitor to arrive on her doorstep, and she did not think James quite fell into this category. He was very adult, of course, and slightly whimsical, but the picture she carried in her mind of a prospective husband, while not sharply clear, was based on a learned, professorial figure, a university lecturer, perhaps, a man of dry, academic wit. She looked at James again as they came off the floor. He had rather a good profile but was as darkly visaged as a Corsican freebooter. She had thought him a brigand when she first saw him.

'James,' she said lightly as he escorted her through the retiring dancers, 'do you have any scoundrelly ancestors?'

'On my father's side I think we had some clansmen hanged,' said James, 'and on my mother's side we had two or three Regency highwaymen who just escaped the gallows.'

'I expect you've inherited a sense of adventure, then,' said Sophie. 'I am not so fortunate. My family on both sides has been terribly dull and respectable.'

'You'll get over it,' said James.

They danced the evening away, all of them. The Dianabad, where 'The Blue Danube' had first been played, gathered them into its melodious and infectious embrace and poured them finally into the clear, cooling atmosphere of the summer night.

Carl drove the Benz home. Sophie sat between him and James. Before he was dropped off at the school James said to her, 'Sophie, if someone told you that a good archduke is a dead one, what would you think?'

'I'd think I was listening to an anarchist,' said Sophie, 'or to someone who really meant it's a bad archduke who's better dead. Why do you ask?'

'Oh, just curiosity.'

Chapter Four

Night after night the Benz carried the six of them into the brightly lit playground of Vienna. They dined, they danced. James spent precious capital. No one ever asked about money, who would pay or who could not.

They went to see *The Merry Widow*. Anne said they must take James to that. It was traditional. She had seen it often but would always see it again. Sophie had seen it twice and said she really preferred Rossini. James had not seen it at all but said he quite liked Gilbert and Sullivan.

'Who,' said Sophie in demurest tones, 'are Gilbert and Sullivan?'

'I think they move furniture,' said Carl.

'You're all infidels,' said James.

And they went another night to Grinzing, the garden village on the outskirts of Vienna, where people from all stratas of society met on equal terms. The air was warm and sweet, Grinzing itself so picturesque that James wished he had brought his sketchbook. The place was famous for its arboured wine gardens, wherein the music of zithers and harmonicas encouraged the wining and dining patrons into singing as well. The clear evening turned into fairyland night.

'Hans Andersen slept here, I presume,' said James.

'Did he? I've never heard,' said Ludwig.

'If he didn't,' said James, 'he missed a large slice of magic.'

'I don't think the magic is just Grinzing tonight,' said Sophie.

'No, indeed,' said Anne.

Helene and Carl were singing. Ludwig was looking at Anne. Sophie was looking at James. The wine was putting dreaminess into her eyes.

'It's Grinzing, the night and my friends,' said James.

'Ah,' said Sophie to Anne, 'he did not take too long to catch on.'

'It must be obvious, even to James, that we are rather special,' said Anne. 'I am almost matchless.'

'I am matchless without qualification,' said Sophie.

'You're both nicely mellow,' said James.

'He's not terribly trustworthy with his compliments, is he?' said Anne. 'James,' she said, 'will you come to Ilidze with us? We are going in a week or so and you would love it there.'

'I am asked myself,' said Ludwig, 'but can't get there until the beginning of July. You must go and keep them in order, James. They run about wildly in Bosnia.'

'I appreciate the invitation very much,' said James, 'but there's the school. The term doesn't close until late July. I'm committed until then, do you see?'

Sophie, who had been thinking about asking her parents to invite James, felt a little twinge of disappointment. She also felt slightly disgusted with herself for not having had the sense to realize his teaching post meant he would not be free to join them, anyway.

Anne said, 'Oh, but you must come, James, you must talk to Frau Harrison.'

'Anne, he can't do that,' said Sophie.

'Can't you, James?' said Anne.

'Not really,' said James, and Sophie thought that while the rest of them sailed blithely through the summer days he alone had been making a worthwhile contribution to life in his teaching of children. Compared with James, she thought, I'm not much more than a butterfly. Perhaps that is what he thinks I am. Perhaps that is what he thinks Anne is. Perhaps that is why he doesn't take either of us seriously. 'All the same,' she heard him saying, 'it's nice to know I was invited.'

Colonel Dimitrijevic Apis had satisfied himself that the death of Franz Ferdinand was now of major political importance. For there was a growing belief that the archduke, when he became Emperor, meant to make generous concessions to Bosnia. That would not suit Serbia at all. Greater Serbia would only come about when Bosnia in disaffection threw off the Austrian yoke to unite with Serbia. The major reforms

Franz Ferdinand had in mind would eliminate the causes of disaffection and turn Bosnia into a co-operative province of the Austrian empire. That made the archduke a serious and unacceptable threat to Serbian ambitions. Many Bosnians might be ready to assassinate a tyrant. Not so many would consider murdering a man whose reforms would be benevolent. Franz Ferdinand must go before he grew a halo, while there were still Bosnians who believed he had horns. Bosnians must do it. Not Serbians. Serbia must not be directly implicated.

Sarajevo would present the perfect opportunity and the right timing.

Colonel Dimitrijevic's principal assistant in the Black Hand was a kindly officer and gentleman, Major Voja Tankosic. Major Tankosic was good to his family, contributed to charities and went regularly to church. He also held incorruptible political beliefs. Therein lay his Mr Hyde. For the sake of his beliefs he would unhesitatingly shed his everyday cloak and reveal the man willing to plot murder.

It was Major Tankosic whom Colonel Dimitrijevic placed in charge of the arrangements for the Sarajevo operation. This meant that Tankosic was responsible for the recruitment and briefing of a suitable number of dedicated assassins. He had seen to this. He reported to his chief early in June.

Dimitrijevic never concerned himself directly with anything but objectives. Everything bearing on the achievement of an objective he left in the hands of others, and kept his own clean. Nothing that was relevant to preparations and arrangements could be traced back to Dimitrijevic. From Major Tankosic he wanted to hear only that everything was proceeding satisfactorily. Tankosic was naturally inclined to say more than a bald yes. He had done a lot of work. He wanted his chief to know that. He began to talk about his band of recruited assassins.

'How many are there?' asked Dimitrijevic brusquely.

'Twelve. Not all will go. Only the best of them. I anticipate seven or eight. All these will be in Sarajevo on the day, positioned at different points along the route the archduke will take to and from the City Hall.'

'It will be enough if only one of them is in the right position as long as he is in the right frame of mind at the right time,' said Dimitrijevic.

'One will be.'

'One must be.'

'With seven or eight to rely on we could not duplicate our chances of success much more,' said Tankosic. He went on to say that he was particularly impressed with three of the men. Nedjelko Cabrinovic, Trifko Grabez and Gavrilo Princip. They were the very stuff of fearless bomb-throwers. 'And there's one man coming from Vienna with a fine, fierce reputation. Boris Ferenac. Success is assured, Colonel.'

Dimitrijevic, icy in his distaste at having unwanted and paltry details thrust on him, said, 'I've heard of assured success before.

Events usually prove it to be the father of certain failure.'

'Failure is written in many men,' said Tankosic solemnly, 'and is allowed for in some of ours. But if as many as six fail, Cabrinovic will not. Nor will the eighth man, Boris Ferenac, providing he can slip the police and reach Sarajevo. You'll excuse me now? My wife and I have to go to a meeting in aid of church missionaries in Africa. A dreadful place for missionaries, Africa.'

Sophie had been shopping with her mother. They had bought themselves new hats. Her mother's was a colourful extravagance of lemon silk and pink and red blossoms. Sophie's was a little round boater-style creation in pale green that perched to tilt. She glimpsed Anne in the gardens, sitting at the ornamental white table. She put the hat on and glided out. She stopped. James was there, sitting in a farther chair, a sketch block on his knees. Anne was posing for him. Sophie felt a small pang. It discomfited her because it hurt a little. They had not seen her. She took off the hat and walked up to them. It was rather unkind of James. Well, unfair, then. He was flaunting his art in a way she could not with hers. Would you like me to sketch you? was a much more acceptable question than Would you like to see some of my poems? One was flattered quite genuinely if one was asked to pose, but one was likely to make oblique comments if asked to read someone's poetry. Oh, what is the matter with me, I'm being stupid.

'Sophie?' Anne turned. Her hair was shiningly brushed and drawn over her ears and black-ribboned at the neck. She looked incomparably fair and priceless. 'James is sketching a little portrait of me.'

'How nice,' said Sophie. 'Please, would anyone like to read some of my poetry?'

James looked up. He was in a white silk shirt and grey trousers, which was casual to the point of bohemianism in the well-dressed environment of the von Korvacs. The white shirt emphasized his darkness.

'I'd like to, Sophie,' he said.

'Oh, I wasn't serious,' said Sophie. 'What has happened to your school?'

'Half-day,' said James, 'and I was serious about your poetry even if you weren't. Let me see some, won't you? I'd like to take it away with me and read it at leisure.'

'It will be very punishing on your leisure,' said Sophie, and went behind him to look over his shoulder. He was using a soft black pencil and his sketch of Anne had reached the stage of distinctive likeness. Already it was a light but exquisite little portrait, thought Sophie, he was catching Anne's warm, alive look with only the black lead of a pencil. Perhaps it was a light, gifted labour of love. He and Anne got on so well with each other. Impulsively, generously, Sophie said, 'Oh, James, that is going to be so good.'

'Is it? May I see?' said Anne in pleasure.

'Well,' said James. He sounded as conserva-

88

tively reluctant as any artist preferring to keep the sitter away from the work until it was finished and he himself satisfied. But he pushed the sketch block across the table to Anne and she looked at what he had done so far.

'James, that is me?' she said.

'It's supposed to be when it's finished.'

'It's lovely,' she said, 'and I'd be happy with it as it is.'

'It isn't finished,' he said and took the block back.

'You will sketch Sophie too, won't you?' she said.

'I don't think so,' said James.

Sophie felt shocked and really hurt. Even if he was in love with Anne he did not have to be as unkindly discriminating as that.

'Oh, James doesn't sketch hideous women,' she said.

James smiled and shook his head.

'I'm sorry, Sophie, I meant I already have a sketch of you. I had one of Anne too but wasn't happy with it. So I thought I'd get her to sit still for a while and give myself a better chance. Would you care to see the one of you?'

'As you are caring to see some of my poems, yes, I would, please,' said Sophie, the hurt melting away.

He leafed back a few pages and showed her the sketch of herself. It made her feel warm with pleasure. Perhaps it flattered her, she wasn't sure, but if it was what he really thought she looked like then his artist's impression of her was very

very acceptable. She had not seen pencil used so giftedly.

'Sophie, let me see,' said Anne. She got up and sank to the lawn with Sophie. They sat with their heads together. They leafed through sketches. They were mostly outdoor impressions of bits and pieces of Vienna. The entrance to St Stephen's, the face, the arm and the whip of a cabbie, the corner of a house, a girl looking into a shop window, a standing carriage horse with its nose in its bag of oats and the upper half of a proud Vienna matron in an enormous hat. Part of a bridge with its glimpses of the river attracted Sophie, and she thought that even in crayon the water reflected bright light.

'James, they're so good,' she said. There were others, they were all enchanting little peeks at Vienna. How well they would illustrate the volume of poems she had in mind.

'They're better than good,' said Anne, 'they're lovely.'

'Oh, sketches,' said James. 'A very limited branch of art, but suitable for a limited talent. I'd like to paint but I only achieve pretty-pretty pictures. I did some of the river the day I ran into you. Watercolours.'

'Where are they?' asked Sophie, her new hat out of sight on the grass behind her.

'I drowned them in the Danube.'

'Modesty should not be suicidal,' said Sophie.

'Don't you sometimes tear up a poem?' smiled James.

'With some poems I commit murder,' said

Sophie. She leafed back to her portrait. She hesitated, then said, 'James, will you let me have this? I mean, please may I have it?'

'Of course. Take it,' he said. She carefully extracted the leaf and returned the thick pad to him.

'Thank you,' she said as he went to work again on Anne's sketch.

'A pleasure,' he said, 'and a compliment. But I shall charge you for it.'

'Oh,' she said. Then, 'Naturally, you must, but what?'

'I'll tell you one day,' said James.

'James, now you can't refuse to sell me the one you're doing of me when it's finished,' said Anne.

'It's yours, but I'm not selling it to you,' said James, 'there's no charge.' Which left Anne shaking her head and Sophie disconcerted.

'James, I'm not complaining,' she said, 'but why—'

'We won't go into it now,' said James.

Which left her puzzled. She and Anne watched him putting the finishing touches to the sketch. He was absorbed, so Sophie put her new hat on again. Anne looked at it and loved it.

'Oh, Sophie, that's delicious,' she said.

James sketched on.

'It might be delicious,' said Sophie, 'but it's not commanding universal attention.'

'It commands mine,' said Anne, 'it's turning me green with envy. You're impressed too, aren't you, James?'

'Not with this,' said James, viewing his work critically, 'I think it's coming out wrong again.'

'Since he seems to be taking more notice of you than of me at the moment,' said Sophie to her sister, 'will you please tell him that if he doesn't look at my new hat I shall get up and bite him?'

He looked. The little green boater perched lightly, tilting piquantly on her dark hair. It made him think of joyous spring kissed by gay summer.

'Is that a hat, Sophie?'

'Beast,' said Sophie.

'Words can't describe it,' said James.

'Hate you,' said Sophie.

'It's not even a creation,' said James, 'it's a little miracle. What words are there? Divine? Exquisite? I think I'll go for stunning.' He returned to his sketch, musing on it.

'Do you think he means it?' said Sophie to Anne.

Anne, laughing, said, 'Do you have reason to believe he doesn't?'

'Well, I don't think he's given to weighty and ponderous judgements,' said Sophie, 'he's more inclined to be frivolous, especially about ladies' hats. The only thing he's very serious about is automobiles. Now if I were wearing not a hat but a brass motor lamp, I could rely on him passing the most earnest and sincere of comments.'

Carl arrived. In a grey jersey and old dark grey trousers he looked slightly out of touch with the clean, civilized impeccability of the gardens. He came with grease and oil about him.

'James, old chap—'

'Go away, you disgusting creature,' said Anne. 'We are being quietly cultural. You may ask Ludwig to join us if you like, but you must please go away.'

'Ludwig is in a more disgusting condition than I am,' said Carl. 'James, there's a knocking.'

'Impossible,' said James, 'unless you've left something undone.'

'Will you be a good fellow and come and inspect?'

'In a few moments,' said James.

'I'm obliged,' said Carl. 'Sophie, my word,' he said as he went on his way, 'that's a new hat and it's a beauty.'

'Am I a sensation?' said Sophie, colourfully arranged on the lawn. 'If one's brother actually notices, that is a sensation, isn't it?'

'More than a brass motor lamp,' said James. 'There, that's the best I can do, Anne.' He gave her the portrait. It delighted her. However self-critical he was, she could find no fault with the sketch.

'James, thank you,' she said. 'Oh, you are so clever and extremely nice. Why aren't you married when you could be such an agreeable husband?'

'I can't afford it,' said James, putting his things into an old satchel.

That produced a moment of uncomprehending silence. What did he mean? He was the son of Sir William Fraser, who was surely rich. Neither Anne nor Sophie knew any young man who would have answered that particular question in the way James had.

'You aren't serious,' said Sophie.

'I'm very serious,' said James.

'But, James,' said Anne, 'you—'

'I could, of course, go to work again for my father,' said James, 'that would pay reasonably well but it wouldn't be a fortune. Well, I'll go and look at the knocking Benz.'

When he had gone Anne said, 'I don't understand, his father is rich, isn't he?'

'I don't know,' said Sophie. She added a little quietly, 'In any case, perhaps James isn't the sort of man who'd let his father keep him.'

'But what are families for except to provide for sons and daughters?' said Anne.

'It isn't like that in every family, my child,' said Sophie. She took off her hat and looked at it. It had been very expensive. It seemed at this moment to be a silly extravagance.

At breakfast two days later Maude Harrison looked up from a letter she was reading. It was from Fräulein Coutts, she informed James. Fräulein Coutts was quite recovered and wished to return.

'I'm delighted for her,' said James.

'So am I,' said Maude, 'but it's a little hard on you, James.'

'Not at all. The agreement has always been that I'm a temporary substitute, nothing else.'

'You've been a perfect love,' said Maude, 'and a great help, and I'm very grateful. But I did promise Fräulein Coutts, and of course the post is so necessary to her.'

'Say no more,' said James. He thought of something. 'As a matter of fact, it could suit me very well for her to return as soon as you like. Next Monday would be fine. I've a trip in the offing if I could get away on Saturday.'

'A trip?'

'To Bosnia. A place called Ilidze. My friends in high places invited me. I told them I couldn't manage it. If Fräulein Coutts comes back on Monday, I can.'

Maude smiled.

'Oh, the von Korvacs,' she said. 'I don't think they consider they inhabit high places. They're too charming for that. Who is the one you favour, James, Anne or Sophie?'

'Maude, I stand impecuniously on the side-lines.'

'You stand in a state of nonsense, then,' said Maude in her forthright way. 'You're intelligent, ingenious and you have a very bright future. Do you imagine you have to own a gold mine to be eligible?'

'Yes,' said James.

'Well, you'll find out by the time you've finished a holiday in Ilidze with them. The daughters of Baron von Korvacs are both modern girls. So I should not have too many old-fashioned ideas if I were you.'

At the end of classes that day James supervised

the seemly departure of the pupils. He saw Rosa at the gate, Boris Ferenac with her. Boris lifted his black hat. James nodded. Marie came out.

'Rosa has come for you, Marie,' he said, 'and Boris. I went dancing with Kirsti and met them a little while ago.'

'How nice, m'sieu,' said Marie.

'Yes, very nice. Do you like Boris?'

'He is very funny,' she dimpled, 'it was he who said—' She stopped and blushed.

'Oh, about good archdukes,' said James casually.

'Yes, I heard him say it to Rosa. It wasn't wrong, m'sieu, was it?'

'Wrong? No. It was amusing, wasn't it?' James was smiling airily. 'As you say, Marie, he's very funny.'

Marie looked pleased and relieved. He did not watch her as she went to join Rosa and Boris at the gate, but he had a feeling that Boris was watching him.

'What was he saying to you?' Ferenac asked Marie as they strolled away.

'Oh, nothing,' said Marie.

'He was talking about me, I suppose,' said Ferenac, 'we have met, you know.'

'Yes, he said so,' confessed Marie. Rosa took her hand and Ferenac put his arm around her shoulders, chatting to her as they went on their way. Marie, responsive, chatted back.

Later, outside the Corbière home, he spoke to Rosa.

'That Herr Fraser, he's not what he seems.'

'He's only a teacher,' said Rosa.

'I'm not so sure,' said Ferenac, 'I saw him once with the son of Count Lundt-Hausen, the police superintendent. And now he's asking Marie questions about me and she's told him what I said to you.'

'Well, you should not have said it,' remarked Rosa, 'then she wouldn't have heard.'

Boris Ferenac chewed his lip.

'By the way, I have to go to Salzburg tomorrow,' he said, 'I'm engaged to play in an orchestra there for three weeks.'

'Oh, I shall miss you,' said Rosa.

'I need the money,' said Ferenac, and seemed to be full of brooding images of darkness as he added, 'But I tell you, unless they pay me more than they've promised I shall only take my violin, I shall not take my soul.'

James was modestly diffident when he told Carl that if the invitation to Ilidze still held he was now free to accept. Carl, who had joined with Anne in trying to get him to go with them, clapped him on the shoulder and said, 'James, you're more than welcome. The family will go by train, you and I will drive the Benz. That will be an adventure, won't it, driving from Vienna to Ilidze? And you'll be company for the girls there. I'm not sure they aren't both getting rather fond of you, old chap. Kindly don't get things too complicated. It's my opinion that women are more difficult to handle than a motor car.'

'You're speaking from experience or instinct?' asked James.

'From instinct. I tread a light path myself, you know. It's safer.'

James smiled a little ruefully. He was not too smitten with the safer courses of life. He preferred, to a reasonable extent, the hazards of winding ways. But some hazards, however well overcome, produced consequences not so easy to deal with.

The June weather was glorious. The sun bathed Europe in warm, golden light, and travellers who journeyed in less comfortable fashion than others blessed the kindness of the weather. Those who had a conspiratorial appointment to keep in Sarajevo were thankful for the clement conditions for, on the instructions of Major Tankosic, they travelled cautiously, in short stages and by whatever 'underground' means were available.

The three main conspirators, Cabrinovic, Grabez and Princip, had left Belgrade in late May in order to arrive in Bosnia well before the Austrians strengthened all border posts and crossings, which they intended to do just prior to Franz Ferdinand's visit. The young assassins, all nineteen years old, went their separate ways after a day or two, travelling independently. Before they parted company, however, Cabrinovic, an extrovert, wrote exultant postcards to friends, and on one of them he quoted brave lines written by Kara George, nineteenth-century Serbian hero.

Noble waters of the Drina
Frontier between Bosnia and Serbia
Soon will come the time
When I shall cross you
To enter faithful Bosnia.

Gavrilo Princip, an introvert, was disgusted by such indiscretion and was more than glad to detach himself from the incautious idiot. In any event, they all succeeded in entering Bosnia by their different routes and under the hot sun journeyed on to Sarajevo, where seven in all would rendezvous. Agents of the terrorist Black Hand helped them on their way at various points.

Boris Ferenac slipped quietly out of Vienna. It was time to commence his own part. If there was glory to come out of the assassination of the archduke, Ferenac intended that glory to be his.

The archduke had decided he would take his wife with him. They could stay in Ilidze, which was a pleasant place and conveniently close to the manoeuvres. And to Sarajevo, which he was to visit on the 28th.

Chapter Five

Ilidze, six miles west of Sarajevo, meant a healthy change for the baron. On the south side of the resort he had a comfortable stone-built house set in spruce parkland. Hunting and fishing were within easy reach. The forests of Bosnia were abundant, many of them untamed and impenetrably virginal. Sportsmen could find chamois and deer as well as wild boar and even the elusive, predatory wolves. The River Ivan was full of fish.

The baron was an amiable shot rather than a good one. He cared little for amassing a tally. It was the tramping, stalking, open-air adventurousness of the sport, not the results, he enjoyed. Carl shared his father's enthusiasms and intended to spend the best part of most days with him on the river or in the game regions. The baroness relaxed and enjoyed long, peaceful hours in which the pressures of Vienna's demanding social life were forgotten. She entertained in Ilidze, but as informally as possible.

Friends called to leave their cards and their

invitations. The latter embraced a host of light-hearted events, including parties and receptions. The atmosphere of Ilidze was one of charm. It was a pretty town, sunny and well-kept, with cultivated parks and a wealth of pines, laurels and flower gardens, and the inevitable quota of oriental architecture, symbolic of past Turkish occupation, added Byzantine curves to its picturesque appearance.

Anne and Sophie were not disposed to have James go off hunting. They thought the sport an activity of dubious graces. Not only was it unfair to the poor creatures on the receiving end, but it deprived deserving young ladies of the stimulation of male company. Anne was adamantly opposed to her brother's suggestion that James should take it up.

'Why don't you and Sophie take it up too?' said Carl. 'It's a fine, invigorating activity.'

'I think I can manage without it, Carl dear,' said Sophie, 'and I'm simply not the type to stalk inoffensive rabbits—'

'Rabbits?' said Carl hoarsely.

'Or whatever it is you like to shoot. I should be so hopeless at it and such a dunce with a gun that I'd be much more likely to shoot you. Or Papa. How would Mama take it if I came back and told her I'd bagged you? Or Papa?'

'Ah, hrmph,' said the baron.

'What's your fancy, James old fellow?' asked Carl looking every tweedy inch the intrepid hunter in check jacket and pepper-and-salt knicker-bockers. A feathered felt hat was on his head.

'In the best interests of everybody,' said James, 'I'll just laze around.'

'James, that isn't the idea at all,' said Anne. 'Carl and Papa have their guns, we shall retain the Benz. You can drive Sophie and me on outings. There's always somewhere to go, and there are some delicious shops.'

Until Ludwig arrived in early July, James was the only permanent escort available, and Anne was lightly possessive with him. He raised no objection to driving her and Sophie around, and did so. Sophie did not know whether her vivacious sister was flirting with him or seriously involving herself with him. Sophie herself was not quite sure what she wanted from him, except that the image of a would-be husband of distinguished looks and subtle wit was becoming even vaguer in her mind. And she was sometimes aware of a little quickening of her nerves when James was close by. She could not really tell what he thought of either Anne or herself, he was always pleasant to both of them.

There was a ball at the Hotel Bosna one evening. Sophie was detained in the ornate reception hall by a Captain Fabrovic, a Bosnian aristocrat known to her family and who had lightly pursued her on previous visits to Ilidze. She thought him an extrovert dandy. He wore so much gold braid on his gaudy uniform that he seemed festooned with it. In the crowded hall she was divorced from Anne, James and Carl as the delighted captain cornered her, swept her hand to his lips, expressed himself bowled over by her presence and dazzled by her beauty. Sophie said she did not think she was quite as beautiful as he was himself, at which he laughed, brought her hand to his lips again and said, 'Ah, if there were only two of you, one to enchant Vienna and the other to delight Ilidze.'

'Two of me would be one too many for every-body,' said Sophie. 'As it is, one of me is problem enough.'

'To whom?'

'To me,' said Sophie. She could hear the music from the ballroom. She wanted to be rescued, she wanted to dance. She looked around, seeking James. There was a galaxy of ballgowns, uniforms and tails orbiting around the hall and the ballroom but she could not see James. It was a little while before she was able to detach herself from her flamboyant admirer, but James was still not visible. Nor were Anne and Carl. To enter the ballroom alone was to make her a little cross. That sense of pique, so foreign to her, had her biting her lip. She lifted her chin and began her entrance, her white silk gown shimmering.

'Sophie?' James was suddenly there, offering her his arm.

'Oh, thank you,' said Sophie in a rush of gratitude, and her entrance was buoyant and floating then.

'You have an admirer,' said James.

'Oh, I have a hundred,' she said, 'but they come and they go. My poetry frightens them off.'

'Well, I haven't been frightened off,' said James, escorting her to an arranged pattern of silver and gold chairs, 'but then I still haven't seen any of your poems.'

'Are you an admirer, then?' asked Sophie, her warm blood quickening to the sound of the music.

'Just one of the hundred,' said James. 'May I mark your card?'

Anne was dancing with Carl. Sophie engaged with James. He took her into the exhilaration of the dance. She melted into it. She felt warmly, sweetly alive. James was adept, easy to follow, sure in his guiding, but quite without the cloying familiarities of gallants like Captain Fabrovic. James, she thought, was really a pleasantly masculine man, with an even, engaging manner. He did not have up and down moods. He would suit someone like Anne very well indeed. Anne, she thought, had begun to look at him as if she realized this.

'Sophie, aren't you enjoying this?' James's voice came to her out of the clouds and the music.

'Oh, yes, excessively.' A little pink tinted her. 'I was thinking, you see. I'm inclined to think very deeply when I'm dancing, I go off on sailing clouds and get swept through the skies. I take wing, but only when my partner is very accomplished. You are quite the most accomplished.'

'Ride your clouds again, then,' smiled James.

She watched him dance the polka later with Anne. They flew as they captured the infectious rhythm of the Bohemian-inspired steps, Anne's face alight with the joy of living, James in laughter.

'Come on, Sophie,' said Carl, 'you're hiding from me.' He was always willing to dance with his sisters. He was extremely attached to both of them. Sophie he talked to, Anne he teased.

'Look at Anne and James,' said Sophie.

Carl picked them out from the lines of adventurous dancers.

'My word, that's a dash they're cutting,' he said.

'Carl,' said Sophie, smiling very brightly, 'do you think that Anne is—'

'Falling for James? I don't know. If she hasn't confided in you, it can't be on. Except that she's in love with everybody, isn't she? Come on, let's polka, we can cut a dash as fresh as theirs.'

Sophie granted a waltz to Captain Fabrovic later. He told her he would not be denied. He was as flamboyant a dancer as a gallant. She found him overpowering. She realized she liked cool-bodied men, modest men. There were some, she supposed. James was very cool. In every way. Pleasantly cool, but cool. Pressingly ardent at the end of the dance, holding her hand to his colourful chest, Captain Fabrovic implored her to view the night from the adjacent conservatory.

'Naturally, I would love to,' said Sophie, 'but all those potted plants, I find them quite eerie at night. They close in on one. I am, in fact, allergic to potted-plant jungles when the sun goes down.'

'My heavenly baroness, my allergic Sophie,' he said, 'there's a door that leads to nothing but pure night air, then. Allow me to breathe it with you.'

'Will you please give me back my hand?' said Sophie. She was not embarrassed, although people were looking and smiling at Captain Fabrovic's extravagant possession of her gloved hand. She held her ground.

'Into the night, shall we?' he said, his white teeth brilliant beneath his neat black moustache.

'Captain Fabrovic—'

'Sophie, may I claim you? You'll forgive me, Herr Captain?' It was James, and Sophie experienced a little sensation of simple pleasure at his second timely arrival of the evening. It occurred to her that it meant he was keeping an eye on her. Did it also mean that perhaps he was a little jealous? He did not look so. He was smiling. Captain Fabrovic released her.

'Thank you, James,' she said as he took her away, 'I don't mind him too much, and one doesn't like to kick one's admirers, even if there are a hundred of them, but he suffers from the effects of his exotic way of life and is inclined to treat one as a bloom to be worn in his buttonhole. He is quite beautiful, you see, and when he's in company with a lady he regards her as an adornment of his beauty. Where are you taking me?'

'To the buffet,' said James, 'for champagne and smoked salmon. You were saying?'

'I was saying how glad I was to be rescued.'

At the buffet Anne, who usually enjoyed the colour which officers' uniforms brought to a

ballroom, declared on this occasion that the
brightly plumaged Captain Fabrovic was the
first headless peacock she had ever seen. Carl
roared with laughter. Sophie shook her finger
at Anne. And Anne, in her turquoise gown, her
enjoyment of life rich and uninhibited, was like
summer coming to harvest in blue and gold.

*I saw a man upon a horse, one summer
    afternoon,*
*He whistled as he rode his nag, a melancholy
    tune,*
*He went along clip-clop clip-clop, I envied him
    his seat,*
*A gentle joggle up and down, and slowly
    swinging feet.*
*Down the winding lane he rode, the sun so warm
    and fine,*
*And up above one heard a lark, and from the
    church a chime.*
*I wondered why on such a day, with beauty all
    around,*
*He did not whistle in a way to make a gayer
    sound,*
For in this age of melody one may pluck with ease
*Many sweet refrains of joy, and many songs that
    please.*
*I spoke to him, he smiled at me, his face a cheerful
    brown,*
*For though he whistled mournfully he did not
    wear a frown.*
*'What a lovely day,' I said, to make a friendly
    start,*

*'So it is indeed,' he said, 'and one to cheer my
    heart.'*
*So then I said if that was so, how strange it was to
    hear*
*A tune that spoke of mournfulness, instead of joy
    and cheer.*
*At which he laughed and smote his thigh, and said
    in kind reply*
*That if it were a sorry tune he really knew not
    why,*
Only that he liked to hum or whistle on his way,
*It helped his horse and he himself to pass the time
    of day.*
*'But why not whistle other songs, songs to make
    one glad,*
Why whistle only this, Mein Herr, *so woeful and
    so sad?'*
*He laughed again, quite full of mirth, then
    chuckled deep and low,*
*'Because, my friend, quite truthfully, it's the only
    song I know.'*

James smiled. He read the poem again. It
tripped silently off his tongue. Sophie had given
him several of her compositions to read, after
all, handing them to him with a little dissertation in praise of the light fantasia of life, which
may have sounded irrelevant but was designed,
James felt, to take his mind off any suggestion
that he needed to regard her work seriously.

'James, what is so amusing?' Baroness von
Korvacs, venturing into the garden to write
some letters, found him laughing. She liked the

Anglo-Scot, she liked his agreeable way of letting life happen and his lack of fuss.

'Baroness, this is far more than amusing,' he said from his relaxed position on the grass. He held up a sheet of notepaper. 'This is Sophie,' he smiled, 'this is a man on a horse.'

The baroness, seeing a folder on the grass beside him, said, 'You mean it's one of Sophie's poems.'

'Have you seen it?' he asked and passed it to her. She read it. She smiled.

'What do you think of it?' she said.

'Tripping?' suggested James.

'Tripping?' enquired the baroness, youthful in white silk.

'The metre. In any event, it's a poem, isn't it? A summer poem.'

'And what do you think of the others?'

'They're all poems,' said James.

'But good or very good? Sophie,' said the baroness, 'rarely shows her poetry to anybody, she's quite sensitive about it. Since she considers you an artist of talent she'll want you to consider her at least a good poet.'

'Listen,' said James and read from another sheet.

> *I stood on the bridge and watched the river*
> *Which passed by*
> *As life does*
> *For life is never still. Is it?*
> *It is only a transient moment*
> *That turns tomorrow into yesterday*

> *Each second comes and is gone*
> *As soon as it arrives*
> *Even a year is a time that has gone*
> *And tomorrow is another year*
> *Full of many things unknown*
> *That a day later are forgotten.'*

'Yes,' said the baroness as if in agreement with the thoughts Sophie had written down. 'I always felt poetry had to rhyme but apparently it's stylish today to write in split prose.'

'I think it's poetry,' said James, 'but I'm no expert. I only know what I like the sound of and I like the sound of these.'

'James?' Anne was calling. She came floating over the garden in a summer dress of apple green and a matching hat. She carried a closed parasol. Sophie, in cool loose-sleeved cream silk, followed on with her habitual unhurried elegance. The wide brim of her hat shaded her face. 'James, what are you doing?' said Anne. 'Aren't you ready?'

'Ready? Oh, calamitous moment,' said James guiltily.

'Well,' said Sophie, arriving with a whisper of silk, 'I suppose there had to come the time when ladies surrendered to gentlemen the prerogative of not being ready. To be quite honest, I'm not sure that this prerogative is one it would be wise to surrender. Anne, we must consider this an exception, not a precedent. James, kindly rise up. Or are we not going to Kontic?'

It was his own idea to drive to a spot where the views were grandly and ruggedly Bosnian, where the hills were imposingly wild and the mountains like naked stone giants. Sophie knew of the right place, a little hillside village, with a tavern where they might have a simple lunch. Anne thought a picnic would be rather nice but Sophie said although picnics could leave nostalgic memories of the al fresco, they were more likely in Bosnia to leave one with memories of the flies. Bosnian flies spent the whole summer lying in wait for picnics.

James, once immersed in Sophie's poetry, had lost count of the time. He got up, restoring sheets to Sophie's folder. She made no comment as he put the folder on the table and asked her mother to keep an eye on it for him. He wished, he said, to read them again.

Sophie said then, 'Are they so incomprehensible?'

'For me,' said James, 'poetry in German has to be read very carefully, I need to think up an English translation that does it justice. I haven't done too badly but I'd like another go at them.'

'They are hopeless in English?' said Sophie.

'I should think,' said James, 'that they're poetry in any language. I'll get my stuff.'

'Hurry, James,' said Anne, 'I am longing to be whizzing off.'

'No whizzing, darling,' said the baroness.

James disappeared for a moment.

'Mama,' said Sophie, 'did he say if he liked them?'

'Liked them?' The baroness regarded her elder daughter fondly. 'He was captivated.'

'Captivated? Are you sure?'

'He was so amused by the one about the whistling man on the horse.'

'Amused?' Sophie did not seem too delighted. 'But, Mama, that poem was a moment of summer delicacy, a wistful look at the incomprehensibility of man.'

'Yes, darling, delicious,' said the baroness.

'Did he really think it was funny?' asked Sophie.

'I have never seen a man so full of appreciation.'

'He laughed,' said Sophie.

'Well, in a way – '

'I shall speak to him,' said Sophie.

'Oh, poor James,' murmured Anne.

But Sophie was laughing herself.

They departed a few minutes later, taking the road to Jajce. They promised to be back before tea.

In Sarajevo the palely passionate Gavrilo Princip was discussing a brave new world with the other conspirators. They had all arrived safely and sat under the noses of passing policemen as inconspicuously as the good citizens of Sarajevo. They did not look like the kind of young men who would prime bombs and load revolvers to do away with a majestic archduke.

Meanwhile Boris Ferenac, his violin put into safe keeping, was travelling by quiet ways to meet and confer with others who belonged to the cloak-and-dagger fraternity.

Chapter Six

The road to Jajce was winding and pitted, crumbling in parts, but the solid Benz did not fuss. They turned off for the village of Kontic after an hour's drive, and the road became little better than a loose-surfaced cart track. It got worse as they approached the village, so they left the car and walked the last hundred yards. There was a valley on their right, beyond which hard brown hills rose starkly, only to be dwarfed by distant mountains soaring to ravage the sky. On the hills gigantic boulders were cupped so precariously by hard ridges that it seemed a touch would topple them. In the valley a river wound its way over a rocky course, the banks and the waters strewn with fallen stone. At the foot of the hills trees had forced their way into the light and bushes had sprung from cracks. The sun poured down to give life to colours invisible at grey dawn.

The walk was uphill and the village itself climbed steeply. The stone and timber cottages looked warm but quiet, their overhanging roofs shading the upper windows. Doors stood open and interiors, defying the outside heat, seemed dim and cool. Somewhere a kid goat bleated for its mother. Two women, scarves around their heads, black hats over the scarves, emerged from a path leading up from the river. They were carrying baskets of wet washing. They cast quick, shy glances as James and the young baronesses entered the village. Anne and Sophie, parasols up, looked in their bright elegance as if they had just come from a garden party. James was bareheaded, the sun deepening his dark tan. His white cotton shirt was tucked in comfortable knickerbockers, his jacket and sketchbook under his arm.

The little tavern, with its whitewashed front and faded awning, stood at the lower end of the village. Outside were a few round, marble-topped tables, their wrought-iron pedestals pitted with rust marks. There were no customers.

'So quiet, so lovely,' said Anne, 'now we can have coffee.'

They stopped. Sophie regarded the village, its hilly, rutted street, and then the harshness of the sunlit view on their right.

'Is this God's own end of the world? I always think so,' she said.

'I always think that in this part of Bosnia there must be brigands,' said Anne.

'Oh, Dragovich and his kind grow corn and keep goats now,' said Sophie.

James wished he had a bold, imaginative talent with oils. It was colour, rasping and brazen, which these vistas demanded. The village, built on the hillside above the river, was a dream vantage point for any artist. Here, by the tavern, one might sit and commit the primitive grandeur to memory, while sketching outlines.

As he stood in absorbed contemplation of light and shade, Anne and Sophie delicately inspected the chairs around one of the tables. James put his sketchbook on the table, took out his handkerchief and dusted the chairs.

'James, that is so nice of you,' said Sophie, 'and although there's a certain masculine superiority about some men which I fail to understand, considering the invaluable contribution women make to the continuation of life, I do enjoy the little courtesies which most men accord us. I confess—'

'Won't you sit down?' said James gravely.

'Thank you, James,' she smiled. She and Anne seated themselves. James joined them. The baronesses awaited the next move in sun-mellowed graciousness. The village seemed even quieter, as if the advent of strangers had made all life retreat behind curtains. No one came out of the café to serve the arrivals. James got up to see who was dead and who was only sleeping, and the proprietor emerged. He was white-aproned, bushily moustached and fatly amiable.

James asked for coffee in German. Croatian or Serbian was beyond him, but German was the second language in this Austrian province of Bosnia. The proprietor smiled, showing gleaming white teeth, and polished the tabletop with the hem of his apron. He beamed at the summery baronesses.

'Beautiful,' he said in German.

'Yes, quite the loveliest day,' smiled Anne.

He chuckled and waddled back into the tavern.

'I don't think he meant the day,' said James.

'Well, everything is beautiful,' said Anne, 'or at least impressive.'

'Striking,' said James.

'What is?' asked Sophie, willing to simply sit for the moment and wonder about the world in summer, and why her nerves were becoming so sensitively on edge at times.

'Both of you,' said James.

'James, this is very sudden,' said Anne and laughed. Sophie thought how the summer always made her sister look radiant.

'Oh, after this last month or so,' said James, 'I count myself an old friend of the family. Or at least of the Benz.'

'You are our very good friend,' said Sophie, 'and I should hope you will always be.'

If Anne was the kind the sun made radiant, Sophie in summer looked exquisitely impervious to its heat. Except that now, as James smiled at her, a faint flush invaded her coolness. Anne saw the flush. She smiled. She got up and wandered across the dusty street to stand on the dry grassy verge that dipped a little way beyond her to merge with the bracken-strewn slope leading down to the river. She stood there in the sun, the skirt of her dress fluttering.

At the table James said, 'Another thing. Your poetry, Sophie. Loved it, I assure you. Well, as much as I could in German. You're far better with words than I am with paints.'

'You are serious? You really liked it?' said Sophie.

'Really,' said James.

'You are very kind,' said Sophie. 'Of course, people are kind to one about such things and sometimes they are too kind. Sometimes it's better not to be kind at all but frank, so that one knows, as everybody else does, that there is always room for improvement. It does not do to be flattered into thinking that everything one does is perfect. I am very imperfect—'

'The proprietor thinks you are beautiful,' said James.

'There, you see, he is the kind of flatterer who will make me think I am,' said Sophie.

The proprietor re-emerged, bringing the coffee on a tray, the earthenware pot full, the cups rattling. He bowed the tray on to the table. He beamed at Sophie.

'Beautiful,' he said again, at which Sophie laughed and shook her head and James smiled. The proprietor chuckled happily as he disappeared. Anne returned to her chair. Sophie busied herself pouring coffee. James turned and eyed the view again as he stirred his coffee. The range of mountain heights was sharp under the light of the clarifying sun.

'If you want to sketch,' said Sophie, 'we don't mind.'

'He's dying to, aren't you, James?' said Anne. 'So please do.'

He opened up his sketchbook. With his pencil he began to put down soft, sweeping impressions. The sisters watched him, Anne with interest, Sophie with a sensitive awareness that images were changing for her. He was still sketching when they had finished the coffee.

Anne said, 'Do you think the proprietor will give us lunch? If not, we can drive up to Jajce and have it there. James?'

James allowed himself to be interrupted. He rattled his cup in the saucer. It brought the proprietor out after a moment or so. He blinked sleepy but amiable eyes.

'Lunch?' said James. 'In an hour, perhaps?'

The proprietor reached for the coffee pot.

'Good, yes?' he said.

'No, not more coffee,' said James in his now not quite so erratic German, 'food.'

'Ah, so. I do you good food.'

'In an hour,' said James.

'Good,' said the genial fat one. He looked at Sophie and Anne, his beam plumply happy for them. 'Beautiful,' he said yet again, then returned to his chair in the shady comfort of his café.

'Anne,' said Sophie, 'we have made a hit. Which is rather nice these days when it's only motor cars that make a hit with most men. Perhaps our good proprietor will treat us to an excellent lunch. We shall pay for it, you and I, because we would like to treat James for once, wouldn't we?

Isn't it intriguing to notice how people of rather stout proportions are nearly always much more affable than everyone else? Do you remember the story about the fat man of Salzburg? His smile was wider than his front door, and he was always smiling, and when he laughed the church bells shook, and the only thing that worried him were his extraordinarily large feet. He grew fatter each year and when at last he was so fat that he could no longer see his feet he laughed so much that the church bells chimed.'

James, for all his concentration, said, 'Oh, good God, Sophie.'

Anne said, 'But, Sophie, if he was always smiling and his smile was wider than his front door, how did he get through it?'

'Oh, he took a deep breath,' said Sophie coolly, 'and edged out sideways.'

James laughed.

'It's difficult for a fat man to hold a deep breath,' said Anne.

'Naturally,' said Sophie, 'there were times when he got stuck.'

'Then what happened?'

'He laughed,' said Sophie.

'And brought the house down,' said James.

Inside the café the sleepy proprietor chuckled. It was good to hear people laughing. They were all laughing, those three. They were nice people.

'I think we're interrupting James,' said Anne.

'Oh, I'm sorry, James,' said Sophie. 'Anne, let us leave him to it for a while. We can walk up to the top of the village and look around. There may be a shop. They sell braid and lace in some of these places.'

'Watch out for the fleas,' said James as the girls rose.

'Fleas?' said Anne a little uncertainly.

'They don't sell them, not in these places,' said James, 'they give them away.'

'Well, whatever they give us we'll share with you,' said Sophie generously. She and Anne walked up through the village. People began to materialize in doorways. The women in embroidered blouses and braided skirts were silent but curious. Here and there a shy smile peeped.

James sketched on for a while, then sat back. The mountains which were so clear in this light cried out for colour. He mused on them. It was very quiet without Sophie and Anne. One missed their infectious animation. He got up. The small church of whitewashed stone and red tiles stood back from the street. It was a simple, four-cornered building with a small open belfry. He walked from the tavern and turned to meander along the church path. The grass on either side already looked parched. There was a wooden bench. He sat down and sketched an outline. He looked up, at the belfry and the red roof, studied his outline and began again on a new sheet. He heard the sudden murmur of voices. The tavern had new customers. He finished his drawing, it did not displease him. But he would never make money at it. Not the kind of money he was beginning to think about. He would have to go back home some time and talk to the guv'nor about things. Things would have to embrace car designing. He returned to the tavern. He heard men talking but did not understand the language. There were many different tongues in the Balkans. But as he came round to the little patio, sheltered by faded awning, he heard someone say in German, 'Ah, so, an archduke is just as much an archduke in Ilidze as in Sarajevo.'

It startled him. He stopped. The voices stopped. In blank silence four men at a table looked at him. They were in dark suits, black hats and ticless shirts. They were swarthy, their faces impassive but their eyes flickering with suspicion. They knew him for a man who did not belong here.

'Good day to you,' said James. He moved and sat down. He had spoken in English, instinctively rejecting German. Three of the men were uncomprehending. The fourth responded.

'Good day,' he said gutturally.

James smiled and nodded. The proprietor came out and gabbled to the men. Then he turned to James and said in German, 'Soon, food. Good.'

'Good,' said James in English. There was not much difference. He began to sketch again. After a while the four men resumed their conversation, arms on the table, heads leaning in. The man who had responded to James had a fine, expressive face and eyes of brilliant brown.

His chin was dark with stubble and he had a pallor to his skin as if he had been too long out of the sun. James lit a cigarette and went on with his sketching, glancing occasionally at the pale man.

A shadow fell across the veined marble table and a hand placed itself on his sketch. He looked up. It was the pale man.

'What is this you do?' asked the man in German.

'You are saying?' said James in English.

'What's that? Come, you understand me. What is this drawing?'

James turned the pad and showed him. It was a likeness of the man himself.

'Perhaps not very good,' said James, resigning himself to German.

'Why have you done this?' The man was studying the drawing intently.

'Oh, the impulse of my kind.'

'What kind is that?' The man was curt, suspicious.

'I'm an artist of sorts.'

'Where are you from?'

'England. Oh, and Scotland.' James smiled. 'And where are you from?'

'Here,' said the man and waved an arm to expansively embrace all Bosnia, but his eyes were still on the sketch. 'Have you done this to show to someone?'

'Sometimes I show my work to friends. Would you like to have this?'

'I will have it.' The man ripped the stiff sheet

from the pad, folded it and stuffed it into his pocket. He went into the tavern. Rickety chairs stood around wooden tables, the tables scrubbed and clean. Behind the polished black marble counter was an array of earthenware coffee pots and china, bottles and glasses. The man called, 'Joja!' The proprietor emerged from the kitchen. 'Joja, who's that stranger?'

The proprietor shrugged. 'He came with two young women and asked for coffee and food. That's all I know.'

'So. The two women are up in the village, looking. What are they looking for?'

'Who is a magician? I am not. So how should I know? Listen, Dobrovic,' said Joja, 'sometimes people come in the summer to look and to buy braid. Then they go away. No one ever comes to stay.'

'He's not here to buy braid,' said the man Dobrovic. 'He heard Lazar say something, then he made a drawing. Of me. Look at it.' He took the sketch out and showed it to Joja.

'Ah, it is good,' said Joja with placating good humour. Dobrovic was a touchy fellow at times. 'You see? He's an artist. Sometimes artists come here too.'

Dobrovic spat on the floor.

'Artist the devil, he's a police agent more like. They come nosing too sometimes. This drawing, it's me, isn't it? A man with half an eye could see that. He'll show it to the police if I give it back to him and the police will ask me what I was doing at Kontic when I'm not supposed to leave Mostar.

Well, our number one comrade will be here soon and we'll see what he has to say about artists and prying women.'

'There's to be no trouble,' said Joja, 'Avriarches won't like it.'

'Is that roaring thief still running this district?' scowled Dobrovic.

'What can we do?' Joja spread his hands. 'The police at Jajce are in his pocket as much as we are.'

'You are, we aren't,' said Dobrovic, 'but he has his uses sometimes.'

Sophie and Anne returned. They arrived like the bright graces of summer. They made the four men stare. James was relieved to have them back. There was an atmosphere he did not like. He felt the men had been carefully watching him, scrutinizing him. Now they turned their eyes on the girls. Joja brought the food out. Anne and Sophie were delighted. There were trout, swimming in sauce, and salad containing something of everything, green with lettuce, red with tomatoes, rich with juicy cucumber and laced with sliced beans and peppers.

'Good?' said Joja with a confident beam.

'Lovely,' said Anne.

'Thank you,' said Sophie.

'Beautiful,' said Joja and smiled happily under his bushy black moustache. It was as well Avriarches was high in the hills. He might have been tempted by these two. They looked aristocratic. Avriarches liked high-born women.

'Ah, well, good appetite,' he said and went away.

He returned with a bottle of wine from a southern vineyard, and persuaded them to have it. It was just right, light dry and delicate. They enjoyed their lunch.

'Who'd have thought it?' said Anne. 'So out of the way, so small, yet such a good meal.'

'I don't think civilization stops beyond Vienna or is anything to do with the size of a place,' said Sophie. She wondered why the four men sat so silently at their table near the café door. 'I expect one could sit on the top of a hill and be just as cultured and civilized as a million people in a large city.'

'One could point to Diogenes, who lived in a tub,' said James.

'Was that civilized?' said Anne. 'Or uncomfortable?'

'That was mortification of the flesh for the purification of the soul,' said Sophie.

'Poor soul,' said Anne.

'This is hardly mortifying, is it?' said Sophie, dissecting her trout.

'It is for the trout,' said James. He engaged in light conversation with the baronesses, but felt the silence of the four men was a heavy, brooding one. They were drinking endless cups of coffee and saying not a word. The man Dobrovic referred to his tin pocket watch from time to time. At the finish of the meal James rose.

'I must pay,' he said and went inside. Joja woke up and stood up. He brushed his moustache and smiled.

'You wish?' he said.

'How much?' asked James.

Joja totted it all up on his fingers. He named an amount which James thought incredibly cheap. It brought Joja a handsome tip. He was more than happy.

'It was good?' he said.

'Very good,' said James, 'and thank you.'

'You go to Jajce now? Yes, very nice there. You go now.'

'We weren't thinking of that, only of returning to Ilidze.'

'Ilidze, that is nice too,' said Joja, 'you come back and see me another day, yes? Make you more good food. Ah, you are a fortunate young man.'

'You think so?' James liked the fat man.

'Beautiful,' smiled Joja and spread his hands. James knew what he meant and patted the proprietor on the shoulder. Joja bustled him out, anxious apparently to see him on his way with his young ladies. Outside a horse-drawn cart had pulled up and a man was dismounting. An earnest-looking man in a dark suit and wide-brimmed black hat. Dobrovic went to meet him. They shook hands. James received a little shock. The newcomer was Boris Ferenac. Ferenac saw him while his ears listened to Dobrovic. He said something to Dobrovic. Dobrovic rattled off a long sentence. Ferenac pushed him aside and strode to the tables. Sophie was finishing the last of her wine.

'Lazar,' said Ferenac, ignoring James. The

man Lazar got up and Ferenac pushed him inside the café, then turned savagely on him. 'You fool,' he said, 'with your mouth as loud as a donkey's – a German donkey's.'

'German – that was for friend Shuckmeister's benefit,' said Lazar, 'he fumbles about in our language. And how was I to know that man was behind me? But it was nothing he took any notice of.'

'Idiot,' hissed Ferenac, 'he's a man who'd take a lot of notice. He's heard things before and asked a child about me. He's supposed to be a teacher—'

'He's an artist,' said Joja.

'Oh, so now he's an artist, is he?' said Ferenac and sucked at his teeth. Life, it seemed, was no longer a matter of secretive smiles. It had become troublesome. 'He knows the son of Count Lundt-Hausen, the police superintendent of Vienna. I saw them together. Do you like the sound of that? I don't. He's drawn a likeness of Dobrovic and can no doubt do the same with the rest of you. But not with me. He knows me. He and I have met. This is a coincidence which is perhaps not a coincidence. And those damn women with him, they've been nosing about, Dobrovic says.'

'We weren't going to let them go, not until you came,' said Lazar.

'Look,' said Joja, 'don't make trouble, nobody keeps healthy on trouble, and they're nice people.'

'Shut up,' said Ferenac. 'If they're informers there has to be trouble and we're taking no

127

chances with the day so close. I don't want the police tapping me on the shoulder in Ilidze. Lazar, you go for Avriarches. He'll take care of the women. I'll look after the informer. We will make it seem as if Avriarches took all three of them.'

'Informer, bah,' said Joja, 'he's an artist, he's been drawing everything. It's madness to encourage Avriarches to take those young women, you'll bring the whole Austrian army and police force down on us.'

'Shut up,' said Ferenac again. 'A man who was a teacher with friends in high places, and who now says he's an artist hasn't come here at a time like this looking for things to paint. He's looking for us, for me. Well, he has found me. He'll wish he hadn't. Off you go, Lazar.'

Lazar slipped out. Joja looked worried. Outside Anne and Sophie were ready to go. They were putting up their parasols and James was fidgeting to get them moving. Ferenac came out and interposed himself.

'What are you doing here?' he asked James.

'I wondered if you'd recognized me,' said James amiably. 'It's a small world sometimes. Are you living in Bosnia now?'

'What is it to you where I live?' said Ferenac. 'But now we've met again, sit down and we'll talk. Joja will bring us coffee.'

'I've had coffee, thanks all the same,' said James, 'and we have to get back to Ilidze.'

'Ilidze?' Ferenac's eyes narrowed. He gestured. There were three other men now that Lazar had gone. The village was quieter than ever as they moved to bar the way to James and the baronesses. 'You,' he said to the sisters, 'go inside.'

Sophie drew herself up very coolly and said, 'I am not in your charge, neither is my sister.'

'Goodbye, Ferenac,' said James. He gave Anne his sketch book, then took both girls by the arm and moved forward, turning to avoid the men. The men shifted their position, presenting a more solid barrier. 'Don't be damned silly,' said James.

Anne trembled. Something very unpleasant seemed to be happening. James swore to himself. He felt he knew what it was all about now that Ferenac had arrived. It was all about assassination. The Archduke Franz Ferdinand was in Bosnia for the Austrian army manoeuvres. A good archduke is a dead one.

'You'll be wise to do as you're told,' said Ferenac. Joja came out and said something. 'Shut up,' said Ferenac and jabbed his elbow into the proprietor's round stomach. Joja gasped. 'You, my friend,' said Ferenac, 'get these women out of the way. Inside. Nothing will happen to them as long as they're sensible.'

'Let us pass, please,' said Anne bravely, 'then nothing will happen to you.'

James squeezed her arm. Sophie was becoming icy, looking at Ferenac as if his species could not be classified.

'You'll be carried inside if you don't walk,' said Ferenac.

Sophie felt James tensing with anger. She did

not want him to do anything foolish. She said, 'We'll go inside for a moment, Anne. Come along.' She turned and took Anne into the tavern with her. James followed in seething fury. Inside Joja stood pulling at his moustache, uneasily avoiding the eyes of the baronesses.

'I am sorry,' he said to James, 'it is not—'

'For the last time, will you shut up?' said Ferenac, crowding in with his men.

'For your own sake,' said James, 'let me tell you that various people in Ilidze know we're here. They'll expect us back this afternoon.'

'Expectations, expectations, ah, they burn in every breast,' said Ferenac. 'Well, there's time enough.'

'For what?' asked James.

'For a solution.' Ferenac gestured again. 'Take them upstairs, all of them.'

'You are the silliest man,' said Anne.

Ferenac, stung, shouted at her, 'You'll be sorry you said that, I'll show you who will feel the silliest in the end! Go upstairs, all of you! Do you hear?'

To Anne's horror a revolver appeared. It glinted in the dim tavern, its barrel snouting from the hand of Dobrovic. He gestured with it and the girls, with James, went through a tiny kitchen, full of heat from a wood-burning stove, and along a narrow passage to a staircase. They climbed to a tiny landing, the stairs creaking. Dobrovic, following on, pushed them into a cluttered bedroom which smelt of old wool and feathers. The angled ceiling was low and there was one small and not very clean window.

Dobrovic said, 'Stay here and keep quiet.' He locked the door on them and departed. They heard the stairs creak as he descended.

Sophie, looking around the room, said, 'This is not the better kind of hotel.'

'Then James must complain to the management,' said Anne.

James knew they were both shaken, although they could not have been cooler. He went to the window. It overlooked the rear of the tavern. Chickens scratched around on the hard brown earth. A well stood in the centre of what might have been a garden but looked more like a large, scruffy yard. It was bounded by a high stone wall against which peach trees clung. Beyond the wall were rows of the ubiquitous Bosnian plum trees.

'Damnation,' he said. He turned and inspected the room. A brass bedstead took up half the space. On it was an old feather mattress and odds and ends of junk. A table supported a bowl and pitcher and more junk.

'Those men, they're mad, aren't they?' said Anne.

'Fanatics,' said James, thinking of the Archduke Franz Ferdinand.

'What are we going to do?' asked Sophie.

'Frankly, I don't know,' said James. He ran a hand through his hair. 'Damnation,' he said again.

'Now, James,' said Anne. She was alarmed, she was not yet scared. She believed in the goodness of people.

James regarded the view from the window again. Beyond the stone wall on the right he glimpsed a corner of the church. He tried the window. The catch was rusty, the frame dry, the paint peeling. But the window opened. It was just large enough to let them out, except that there was a drop to the ground of about fifteen feet. A man came out from the back of the tavern and threw scraps from a bowl. It was Joja. The chickens rushed and scurried and pecked. Joja did not look up and James did not call. He felt Joja was well aware of him.

'What did that man Ferenac mean by a solution?' asked Anne.

'An answer to a problem. I think we're the problem.' James closed the window as Joja disappeared. 'I suspect they're going to keep us here until the Archduke Franz Ferdinand has left Bosnia.'

'What is the archduke to do with it?' asked Sophie. 'And what are we to do with them?'

'I think they're after the archduke,' said James. He could have said he also thought they intended for the archduke to leave Bosnia in a coffin, but the girls were worried enough. 'No, I'm not serious, of course.'

'Yes, you are,' said Sophie quietly, 'you know something.'

'I only know we've got to get out of here.'

The stairs creaked. Someone was coming up. Anne swallowed and Sophie steeled herself.

'It's Joja,' said James.

'Joja?' said Anne.

'The proprietor. Ferenac called him that. He's weighty on those stairs.'

The creaking stopped. The landing sighed.

'Quick, please.' It was a whisper outside the door. James pressed his ear to the panel.

'We're listening,' he said.

'They have gone,' whispered Joja, 'they have seen your car and mean to take it away. But one is still here. I will put a ladder to your window. But when you leave take it, hide it, it must not be seen or it will mean trouble for me. The wall, there is an opening to the church. Go, run, but do not cross the river and go up into the hills, go along the valley by the side of the river.'

'Good, Joja,' said James, 'we love you.'

'It is bad, bad.'

The landing squeaked, the stairs groaned. James continued to listen. He heard no voices downstairs. The man left behind was probably sitting outside. Joja would not have come up otherwise. If the man on guard was the pallid one, the one with the gun, he would be dangerous.

They could only wait. They stood by the window. In a little while they heard a small sound. They were too tense to speak, but Sophie managed a little nervous smile as James gave her an encouraging one. Beneath the window outside something scraped the wall. He opened the frame. The top of a ladder appeared. He looked down and glimpsed Joja disappearing. There was no time to waste.

'Sophie?'

'You go first, that is best,' said Sophie calmly.

133

'Yes,' said James. He put a leg over the sill. Both legs. He turned and found a rung with his right foot. Anne held the top of the ladder. He went down. The ladder was smooth and he slid most of the way in his haste. He planted his foot on the bottom rung and looked up.

'You, Anne,' said Sophie.

Anne went, agile and quick in her urgency. Sophie was out and on the ladder before Anne was halfway down. They left hats and parasols behind but took their handbags. James had left his sketchbook. The girls reached the ground in a froth of white underskirts. Quickly he hauled the ladder down. It was heavy. He took it to the wall and the chickens scattered as the girls followed him. He found the gap in the wall amid the peach trees, a triangular opening where the stone had crumbled away. He pushed the ladder through. He had to do that for Joja. He climbed, went through the gap, pulled the ladder after him and placed it in the long grass against the wall. He reached into the gap, helping the sisters up and through.

Someone shouted. The man Dobrovic was running from the back door of the tavern.

They hared away, the girls picking up their skirts and flying. Over hard ground and around bushes to the church. There was a wall there too and an old green door. It opened as James pushed. He bundled the girls through. Dobrovic came on in pounding chase. James went through the doorway and nipped behind the door itself. He watched through the crack as Dobrovic came running. Sophie and Anne turned. James gestured to them to go on. Dobrovic saw their whipping dresses and legs through the open door. He shouted again, his expression furious. He rushed at the opening and as he reached it James crashed the door against him. The impact of solid wood against face and body was traumatic. The door shuddered and Dobrovic dropped as if poleaxed, blood pouring from his nose. It gave James a feeling of giddy elation. That was a blow struck for fair virginity if you like! He turned to run, checked, stooped and thrust his hand into the bulging side pocket of Dobrovic's jacket. He brought out the shining blue revolver, thrust it inside his shirt and went after the girls. He caught them up, they flew over the church path and out into the street. The village was as silent as a graveyard. And every door was shut tight.

Nobody wanted trouble. James sensed the danger of knocking on those closed doors for help. Joja had said to escape up the valley. They crossed the street and took a worn, stony path winding down to the river. Sophie and Anne slipped and scuffled in their white, leather-soled shoes. James put his arms around their waists and took them downwards in a headlong flight in which six feet hopped, skipped and jumped.

'James!' It was Anne in heady exultation.

'I beg you, don't hang back, girls,' panted James.

Sophie said nothing, saving her breath for sustained effort. Only a slow-witted person would have failed to recognize the latent menace of those men, and she sensed that what James had recognized was a menace that was frightening. He was intense in his urgency to get her and Anne out of harm's way. But why? Why should those men want to harm them? James's cryptic reference to Franz Ferdinand had puzzled her.

They were rushing downwards, the sloping, winding path bordered by bushes and long wispy grass taking them in headlong flight to where the river, littered with fallen rock, danced and sparkled. They reached the smooth stony bank.

'Run!' said James. He knew they could be seen from the village above. They had to reach a sheltered way. In the distance the bald bank of the river gave way to bush and tree. They needed the cover it would give them. They ran. He was sweating. Anne's hair was tumbling loose, Sophie's bobbing. They gasped for breath as he urged them on. Discarding modesty they picked up their skirts and ran more freely. Anne ran hard and fast, supple limbs flashing. Sophie ran with long strides. Good girls, thought James. God, he had to get them out of this. His was the responsibility, he the one who had wanted to come here. He wondered if he should pray, but since he couldn't remember when he had last paid reverent devotions he decided that to call on divine help now might be construed as slightly impertinent.

Their chance of escaping close pursuit depended on how long it took Ferenac and the other two men to dispose of the car. It was the obvious thing for Ferenac to get it out of the way as quickly as possible. Its presence pointed positively to the fact that its occupants had been in Kontic, and the fact that Ferenac wanted to move it indicated intentions that were sinister.

There was quite a way to go along the hard, shelving bank of the river before they could reach the shelter of the straggling bush and pine. In places the ground was strewn with fallen boulders big and small, and their progress over these stretches was awkward and comparatively slow. The river sang cheerfully on their left, swirling around protruding stone and gurgling over submerged rocks. Farther to their left the hills rose barren, bleak and inhospitable, yet were tempting in the multitude of sheltering crevices they offered. But Joja had said not to go up into the hills.

They sped over a clear incline. The sun was hot, its heat brazenly trapped in the valley. Sophie's dress and petticoat whipped around her slender calves. Anne, a little more uninhibited, had hers hitched to her knees. White silk stockings were brilliant in the sunlight. James, running protectively behind the girls, experienced a moment of detached admiration amid his worries. Anne and Sophie, undeniably, had shapely legs. He urged them on. He was certain of one thing now. Ferenac meant to assassinate the Archduke Franz Ferdinand, either in Ilidze or Sarajevo, and was not going to be foiled by having anyone inform on him. Hell, thought James, if the idiot would only go back to Vienna and play his violin he would save the situation for himself and everybody else. But no, he had to go on with it and to remove anyone who stood in his way.

And if he could murder the archduke, what were three lesser people?

'I'm going to fall,' panted Sophie.

'No, you're not,' shouted James, 'you're not an old lady yet.'

Anne was sucking in great draughts of air. James came up with them, took Anne by the hand, patted Sophie on the back and ran with them. The pine trees drew them on. James saw they were sparser than they seemed at a distance and the girls would look like pale summer ghosts flitting through them. He glanced back. He saw no one in the bright valley. He glanced upwards. The village was well behind them now, away up on their far right. But they could still be seen from the place. There would be eyes watching them, for all those closed doors.

Sophie lost a pointed shoe. She stumbled and hopped on one foot. James retrieved the shoe and slipped it quickly back on to her slim stockinged foot.

'Thank you, James.' She was darkly flushed, her forehead damp, her hair spilling and her mouth open as she gulped in air.

'We must go on,' he said.

'I know,' she said and Anne, breathless, nodded. They picked up their skirts again and ran again. James followed. They reached bushes showing shiny leaf and plunged into the shelter of the foremost trees. The ground was softer, there was earth here which was saved from being washed by rain into the river by a ridge of stone that in the distance rose higher.

They ran between the trees until Anne gasped, 'James, we must rest for just a moment.' She stopped, sank to her knees and Sophie sank down beside her. James, affected by their physical distress, let them have their break. They were healthy girls but they were not international athletes. They were not trained for a long run.

After a short while he said, 'We'll walk for a spell now, we can't run all the time, I know. So come on, my lovely ones, they haven't spotted us yet.'

'Lovely ones? Oh, James,' said Sophie and laughed a little breathlessly. 'Have you looked at me lately?' Her loosened hair clung damply at her temples, her delicate make-up marked by perspiration. Anne was no better.

'You're both at your best,' said James. He helped them to their feet.

'You're a great comfort, James,' said Anne.

'I don't feel a comfort,' he said, 'I feel responsible. Come on.'

They went on, walking quickly through the sparse woodland, their feet crunching the dry needles, the air hot but finely scented. The hills rose high across the river, and on their right the slope covered with straggling bush ascended to the road.

'If we could climb up somewhere,' said Anne, 'we could reach the road, couldn't we?'

James shook his head.

'We can't show ourselves yet,' he said, 'we must keep to this valley for as long as possible. Ferenac and his men probably know every rock and blade of grass in this area, and they'll realize we'll need to get up to the road. Damn,' he said as the filtering light changed a little way ahead to glaring brightness. They broke from the trees and found themselves on a stretch of hard, sloping bank. The ridge on their left had fallen away, they could see the river again, a swirling, running flow. But there were more pines two hundred yards away. All the same, thought James, they would be out in the open for that distance. 'Damn,' he said again.

'Shall we run, James?' asked Sophie.

'Yes,' he said, 'and now, like the devil.'

They ran, the girls' shoes clicking over the smooth shelf of stone, the afternoon sun burningly plucking at their heads. Slender legs gleamed. James kept behind the girls, constantly urging them on. Two hundred yards, that was all. But the sloping shelf and the feeling that there must be eyes on their backs made the distance seem so long. When they reached the trees Anne and Sophie were gasping again. James turned and looked back. He squinted through the bright light, over the wooded stretch they had left and taking in the rising line of their retreat beyond. He caught his breath. Well beyond the vegetation a humped ridge showed like a sharp, undulating black line. Movement was breaking the line. A tiny silhouette showed. Then another.

'Oh, hellfire and brimstone,' breathed James.

He joined the waiting girls. 'Good,' he said cheerfully, 'you look fine. We'll need our second wind.'

'I think I'm on my fifth,' said Sophie.

'Well, make good use of it,' said James, 'because we need to run again. Go on, pick your feet up.'

Sophie and Anne did their best but the trees were thicker and brush hampering. They skirted bushes and ducked under low branches. James took the lead, breaking or holding a way through for his companions. They ran where they could and where they could not they at least had a respite from lung torture. The heat closed in on them and twigs reached to pluck at frisking skirts. James knew they were going as fast as they could and did not ask for more. The river seemed to be farther from them, hidden by another rising bulwark, yet it came louder to their ears, rushing and tumbling. Its insistent noise pounded at the hammering heart of Anne. She saw James kicking and savaging his way through tangled undergrowth in front and she was sure he was making demands on his repertoire of international adjectives.

The pines increased in density. They were hidden from any pursuers now. But that did not mean they were safe.

The skirt of Sophie's dress tore.

'Now that is tragic,' she gasped.

'I'll buy you another, Sophie, I promise,' said James, 'so come on.'

They went on, they struggled on and at times

they ran on. The pines began to thin. He hoped they were not going to lose their cover again. No, the wooded area stretched on. Even so, there was a weakness in the course they were taking. Ferenac and his men would know this was the only way they could go unless they emerged and climbed the dizzy slope to the road. And if they did emerge they would be seen. And they could not count on stopping a passing vehicle. Not in this area. Two carts a day along that road would be a good average. One motor car a month a high average. In any case, Ferenac would ensure that that avenue of escape was watched. The hills on the other side of the river were a temptation again, the huge boulders, the dips and ledges, and the crevices, affording hiding places.

Sunlight dappled the pines and the earthy ground as they hurried on, Sophie and Anne breathless but unwavering. James felt proud of them. To their left the stone ridge petered out and there was the river once more. It was bright and foam-flecked, running fast. The earth became harder, the growth poorer. James stopped objectively, the girls thankfully. Perspiration soaked them all. James wiped his forehead with his hand.

'I should rather like to sit in a heap of snow,' said Anne.

'Oh, sweet winter,' said Sophie.

James looked at the river. It curved at this point. It spanned a wide course, fifty yards or so. The opposite bank rose to merge with the foothills. There was a profusion of jammed boulders and the foothills themselves were split by dark, triangular fissures. But the river, how deep was it? The flowing waters sucked around the shallows, rushed and foamed around central islands of boulders.

'What do you think, shall we cross?' he said.

'In a boat?' said Sophie, dabbing at her face with a tiny handkerchief.

'James, are you sure they're behind us?' asked Anne.

'I'm afraid so, dear girl. I saw them. And they won't give up while they think we're in this valley. They know we can't turn back, only go forward. But they won't expect us to have crossed the river here. Frankly, it looks too damned rough. We're going to get very wet.'

'James, I have immense faith in you,' said Sophie, 'but are you sure we're only going to get wet?'

'Look, my sweet things,' said James, 'if we can cross here they'll not see us, the river bend is in our favour. Once across we'll get under cover. They can't turn over every boulder or poke their noses into every cave. Damned if I know for certain, though. But what do you say, shall we risk it?'

'We can't swim,' said Anne, eyeing the rushing river uncertainly.

'Well, there are other activities young ladies are far more graceful at,' said James, 'and in any case swimming isn't going to be the best pastime in that current. We've got to go across by making use of the rocks. I'll see what it's like.'

143

He buttoned his jacket and walked down into the shallows. He went on. The water was soon up to his calves, then his knees. And it was bitingly cold. He moved from one river-sprayed rock to the next, the level gushing and pulling at his legs. It was up to his thighs before he reached the middle and around his waist a moment later. It staggered him with its buffeting surges, but the standing boulders provided solid help. He was able to move although the river roared and foamed around him. Seconds were precious. In the middle of the river the waters tugged violently at him, but the wet, glistening outcrops of fallen stone were bastions of protection. Sophie, watching the tide beating at him on his way back, paled under her perspiration. If he slipped—

'Oh, be careful,' she whispered, her heart thumping painfully. And Anne, thinking of men who could not be far away now, breathed, 'Hurry, James, hurry.'

He splashed through the shallows, ran up the bank and back into the trees. He streamed water on the way, his face and hair wet from spray.

'I think we can do it,' he said, 'but I suggest you take your dresses off. They'll get soaked and heavy. I'm sorry, but I don't want you sinking.'

They did not argue. Sophie went a little pink, that was all. He turned his back. Quickly they removed their dresses. He took them, folded them tightly and tucked them inside his jacket. The girls were brightly, lacily delicate in waist petticoats and snowy corsets. And they were both pink now.

144

'Lead on, James,' said Sophie, her smile a desperate effort, 'and you hang on for dear life, Anne. I'll come with my eyes closed. I shall also pray.'

James took them down to the edge of the river. They stared at the menacing flow, at the spray and the foam, at the glistening boulders.

'There's a lot of it, I know,' said James, 'but it's only water.' And he went in, the girls with him, each using a hand to grip the belt on the back of his tweed jacket. Sophie shuddered at the icy cold of the water and Anne drew a hissing breath. James splashed forward, intent on crossing by the simple but precarious expedient of plunging from each sheltering rock to the next. But not every boulder was as near to the next as he'd have liked, and it was this that made the crossing such a risk. To lose a footing could mean being swept away.

Anne stifled gasps as the rising level icily embraced her legs and knees. She clung to James's belt and to Sophie's hand. The cold, surging waters were taking Sophie's breath. She felt the tidal pull at her feet. She hung on. James's tweed belt was strongly sewn to the jacket. Sometimes such belts were secured by buttons. Buttons would have ripped off. She thanked someone for the strong stitches.

James was the anchor, they were the chains. He brought them into deeper water, steadying them all against each solid sentinel of rock before plunging towards the next. Anne staggered as the river rose, surging, pulling and battering.

Her shoulder was squeezed against a shining boulder, the tide sucked her from it and she lost her footing on the uneven bed. And she lost her grip. James turned in the swirling waters, put one arm around Sophie's waist and dragged Anne mercilessly up by her hair as her face plunged in. They fought for their footing, Sophie panting, spray flying at her, and Anne coughing up water. James thrust them both into the lee of a huge bulwark, which stood up from the river like a misshapen obelisk. It protected them from the direct onslaught of the hungry tide. Foam lashed around them, the girls immersed to their breasts.

'James . . .' It was a wet, despairing gasp from Anne.

'Marvellous,' said James, and Sophie, chilled to the bone and rocked by the water, thought the fixed grin on his wet, dark face was almost villainously determined. 'But let's save the conversation for later. Go on now, we must.'

He kept behind them now, driving them forward, thrusting them, and they gasped and shuddered, fighting for handholds that were out of reach. He took hold of their sopping hair and they clenched their teeth at the pain as he bullied them through the rushing water and flying spray. He was not going to lose either of them and by their hair he kept his hold on them. Together they floundered and plunged from rock to rock. Each time the tide took Anne's footing he hauled her up and he thrust Sophie on, on. Splashing, desperate, the girls fought the river and James fought for them.

The level began to fall. It eased reluctantly away from soaked breasts and corsets, leaving round curves wetly outlined. It dropped to their waists as James, releasing their hair, bundled them forward. He grabbed their arms and rushed them on through thigh-high tide until they reached the shallows. Every second was now more precious than ever. From the shallows he rushed them upwards over ridged stone towards the boulder-strewn foothills.

He brought them up from the bank to the foothills and they began to clamber over masses of stone, James making for the nearest fissure. He looked back. The bend of the river hid that part of the valley they had traversed. He looked at the point from which they had made their crossing, at the trees from which they had emerged. There were neither sounds nor movements, except those of the river. But he stayed for a moment while the girls scrambled on. And suddenly, over the bright warm air, carrying above the noise of the river, came the muffled sound of a crack. That was the crack of snapping timber, by God it was. Someone was not far from the vital point.

'Oh, hell,' he muttered and leapt upwards after the girls. They reached a spot where the steep hillside began. James pointed the way to the fissure. They moved behind piles of rock which gave them cover. The fissure yawned. There was clear space in front of it and James brought the girls pell-mell over the ground and into the cave. Rushing from bright light into darkness made them stop. In front of them the blackness seemed impenetrable. Their breathing was strained and noisy. They blinked.

Sight came. The cave was high and deep. Distance darkened to invisibility. Exhausted, Anne dropped to her knees on the cool stone floor. Sophie leaned wearily against the wall, her undergarments plastered wetly to her body. She looked at James, his jacket distorted by the bundled dresses. He drew them out. They were wet.

'Oh, James,' gasped Anne.

'I know other young ladies,' said James, 'but I don't know any as brave and lovely as you two.'

'Brave?' sighed Sophie, her hair soaked into a lushly wet cap. 'James, I was terrified.' She slipped slowly down the wall until she came to rest. He went to her, took her hands and rubbed them. They were still chill from the icy river, despite her exertions. She smiled at him. 'I am glad it is you we are with.'

'I was rough with you in the river,' he said.

'Brutal,' said Sophie.

'Dear Sophie,' said James, and left her looking emotionally at him as he went to Anne. 'You, my sweet,' he said, 'seem very wet.'

'Oh, I am only half-drowned,' said Anne, 'which is not so bad as being fully drowned, is it?'

Her sopping underclothes, so revealing as they wetly outlined her, could not, he thought, have been more uncomfortable. His own were coldly, soakingly unpleasant. He rubbed Anne's hands.

'Walk about,' he said.

'But, James, I am worn down to the bones,' she said.

'Walk about,' he said, 'and you too, Sophie.'

Sophie, sitting gratefully against the wall but aware of creeping chill and wet discomfort, laughed weakly.

'When I was a small girl,' she said, 'I fell into a pond and when people had fished me out and someone had gone to fetch Mama, someone else told me to jump up and down. I was a very nice small girl and obedient, so I jumped up and down. It was to save me getting pneumonia, they said. But I squelched so much that I stopped and said I thought I would rather have pneumonia. I am not going to say I would rather have pneumonia now—'

'Sophie, walk about,' said James, 'or you'll freeze. Squelching is a minor consideration at your age.'

'My age? Do I look forty when I am soaked to the skin, then?'

James could have said she looked very wet and very endearing, but he only smiled, shook his head and went to the opening. He dropped on his stomach and peered out. He watched the river, the far bank, the straggling pines. He was soaked from head to foot but did not feel too cold, not yet. Excitement, fear and a touch of exhilaration all combined to keep his body nervously heated for the moment. He wondered if Ferenac and his men would be moving inconspicuously through the trees or boldly along the water's edge. He did not think they would all be together. One would be moving quickly ahead, others would be searching. He stiffened. The sound was not loud or angry, it was just perceptible enough to reach ears listening for it. It was the sound of someone moving through the pines. Someone moving slowly, searchingly. The crack of a snapping twig he had heard before had probably been made by the man in advance. This was a second man, a probing man. The hunt was being conducted quietly, thoroughly, by men sure of their quarry, sure that some time two young women would fall exhausted into their arms. And one man, James was sure, would have been sent by Ferenac along the road. He thought, as he strained his eyes, that he glimpsed movement among the trees but could not be sure. He stayed where he was without stirring a muscle. The faint sounds gradually receded.

By God, thought James, he and the girls had crossed the river just in time. Then he wondered about that. The moment would come, perhaps, when the hunters would sense the quarry had slipped them. If one man was on the road he would confirm he had seen nothing of the fugitives there. Ferenac would begin to look across the river and wonder.

James sighed. He looked around. The ground directly in front of the cave was clear, but there were rockfalls to the right, large enough to conceal someone crawling out on that side. The sun was beating down. He edged back into the cave. Sophie and Anne were walking briskly about. They had put their dresses on. They had combed their wet hair.

'Well done,' he said, 'that's the stuff of brave conquest.'

Sophie, pacing up and down arm in arm with Anne, said, 'Oh, apart from feeling uncomfortably wet, James, we are in excessively high spirits. But I beg you not to look at us because we are also hideously bedraggled.'

'I haven't noticed,' said James. The girls marched deeper into the cave. 'Um – may I suggest you take everything off except your dresses? It's too cold in here for you to dry out. You'll perish. There's a place outside where all your things will dry quickly in the sun without being seen.'

'We are to undress?' said Anne from the depths. She and Sophie had stopped walking about.

'It's not what I'd ask you to do in the Prater,' said James.

'Oh, I'm not disposed to endure uncomfortable modesty if there's a better alternative,' said Anne.

'Indeed, your suggestion is thoughtful and meritorious, James,' said Sophie, 'but will you please retreat a little and turn your back?'

He retreated to the cave entrance, standing close to the wall in shadow and looking out. The river was in disaffected flow, the trees lining the far bank in peaceful quiet. He took off his jacket, shirt and vest. He remembered the revolver. It was as wet as his jacket. He massaged his chest, keeping his eye on the view across the river. There were no sounds, no hunters, no menace. He heard whispers in the cave behind him, then Sophie's voice close by.

'James? No, please don't look, I am a terrible sight in just a damp dress. Here are our things.' He felt a heap of wet garments pushed at him and he gathered them without turning round. 'James, you will spread them very modestly in the sunshine, won't you?' Her voice was light, her only anxiety, seemingly, that which concerned the impropriety of a single and unattached young lady handing into his care delicate garments which no man should see unless he was married to her. 'You will consider them in a gentlemanly detached way, we trust, for we are both extremely sensitive and Anne is blushing—'

'I am not,' said Anne from farther back.

'Well, I am,' said Sophie.

'I promise every due respect and consideration, with my mind elsewhere,' said James.

'Thank you, James.'

She was delicious, thought James. They both were. They were making light of discomfort, embarrassment and the inescapable worry of the situation. He himself was beginning to feel frozen from the waist down. He crawled out, and the hot afternoon sunshine was a sudden touch of rapture. He slid along into the shelter of fallen rock. He laid the wet garments of the girls over the sunbaked lower rocks, spreading them out in the most practical way while trying to keep his mind on the promised level of detachment. All the same he smiled at frills, at lace. The four white silk stockings were a problem, their lightness and delicacy susceptible to breezes. He secured them by placing small stones on them. He laid out his shirt, jacket and vest. Keeping himself shielded he slipped off his shoes, long knitted socks and knickerbockers. He left them in the sun too. In his long woollen pants he crawled back into the cave. He lay close to the entrance, looking, observing, watching. He saw nothing. His wet pants were acutely chill. He heard the girls moving about, walking, pacing, keeping their circulations active.

'James?' That was Anne. 'Do you think – '

'We must stay here, you know,' he said, 'we can't risk showing ourselves even when our clothes are dry.'

'Yes, I see.' She did not argue but he knew she was disturbed. She was eighteen and young, she loved life and found people fascinating. But she did not know how to deal with men of violence. She did not understand them, she was removed from the causes which made thieves of some people and assassins of others. She was happy, why couldn't everybody else be? Sophie was more sophisticated, more inclined to coolly accept that there were indisputable reasons for some men becoming brigands, for some to be cynical about the wonders of life. Anne was life's uncomplicated love, Sophie was its poetic interpreter. Anne would give a husband laughter and sweetness, Sophie amusement and stimulation. And they would both give themselves, which alone would be a gift from life's warm treasury.

'James, are you all right?' That was Sophie.

'Fine except for wet woollens. Are your dresses drying?'

'Oh, we are almost whirling about,' said Sophie, 'and they are better all the time. They were not so wet as our other clothes. Have you seen anyone?'

'Nobody,' he said, but his ears pricked precisely at that moment. 'Oh, hell,' he said. Sophie and Anne froze into silence. He edged back a little as a man broke from the trees on the far side of the river. Not Ferenac. One of the others. The sun was dipping now and taking on the glow of late afternoon. The man came down to the river. He peered, scanning the waters, the banks, the boulders and the hills. He moved along the edge of the river. He took his hat off, wiped his forehead with the sleeve of his jacket and said something ferocious. Even at this distance the sound of his imprecation reached James's ears. The lightest of breezes carried it. James flattened himself. The man put his hat back on and walked slowly, squinting in every direction. He was retracing the line of hunt, moving in the direction of the village.

That meant Ferenac suspected the quarry had gone to ground. He had sent the man scouting back. Ferenac must know they were somewhere about. He would search until the light gave out.

And sooner or later he would decide the quarry had crossed the river.

James stayed very still. The coolness of the cave became a coldness. Anne's teeth began to chatter. The moving man disappeared. James told the girls to skip. Sophie said they would do their best but could not guarantee she would not fall flat on her face. They did their best while James stayed close to the entrance, watching, listening. He was cold now, very cold. But he did not move. The sun began its descent and the clear blue sky took on its first faint tint of gold. The drying garments spread on the rocks stirred. That, at least, was a comforting sign! James crawled out, slowly, cautiously. The undergarments were warm, all dampness gone. His jacket was only very slightly damp in places. He brought everything in. Anne came to take things from him, pattering up behind him. He looked very lean and masculine, she thought, in nothing but his pants.

'Thank you, James, you're a dear,' she whispered.

She retreated with the garments. Sophie received her things with sighs of bliss. She embraced them.

'Oh, sweet doors to paradise,' she said, 'what more can life offer than this?'

'A nice quiet journey back to Ilidze,' said James, pulling his dry socks on.

'What is that you say, James?' said Sophie from the depths. 'Oh, you are the most beneficent of men, all my clothes are beautifully warm and dry.'

James, a little smile on his face, said, 'Well, they all looked very enchanting in the sunshine.'

Anne laughed. Even in the dimness of the cave one could not miss the fact that Sophie was blushing, actually blushing.

James dressed. He heard soft rustles and swishes as the girls slipped their clothes on. The cave became darker as the sun dipped behind the mountains. He massaged his cold body. Long shadows crept over the river, over the trees. He wondered about Ferenac, whether he would give up. If he gave up he would probably change his plans. But he was not a man, in his fanaticism, to give up or to change his plans. Darkness, when it came, would restrict him and frustrate him.

It was going to be cold in this cave. He turned. The girls were pale glimmers of movement, but there was still just enough light for his eyes as he began to explore the place. He told the girls to stay where they were and keep their ears open. The cave narrowed at a depth of thirty feet, then opened out again and he saw the glimmer of still, dark water and a rocky ledge along the left-hand wall. He stripped off his knickerbockers and his still damp pants and vigorously massaged his chilled limbs. He put his knickerbockers back on but left the pants off. He was not very happy. They were in a damnable fix, no mistake. They had no food, no fire. The cave gave shelter but no warmth. Not until it was dark could they move out, and even then they would not be able to travel over these rocky foothills or the shelving riverbank unless there was a moon. Was there a moon? He cast his mind back over the last few nights. Damned if he could remember anything about bright moonlight.

He stamped around, reluctant to confront the baronesses with cold cheer. He saw the opening of the cave, the light outside was russet. He heard Sophie's voice, it sounded warm and reassuring.

'We need not worry too much, someone is bound to be looking for us. Papa and Carl for certain.'

'But they won't look for us here,' said Anne. 'Never mind, I am much more comfortable now, and we still have James.'

'And James still has us,' said Sophie, 'I'm afraid we're an awful responsibility for him. We must bear up and carry our banners bravely. I will recite the clarion call of the Habsburgs defying the Turks as James rides into battle.'

'Your imagination, darling, is sometimes stupefying,' said Anne.

James came stamping. The girls, for all their cheerfulness, looked peaked.

'What is that you have?' asked Sophie.

'My pants,' said James, 'they were trying to give me pneumonia. Shall we see if we can get away when it's dark enough?'

'Where you go, James, we shall follow,' said Sophie. 'My faith in you is tenfold. With any other man I should be afraid of breaking my neck. And some men, you know, exercise what I call such a distinctive carelessness when climbing hills in the dark that they are constantly breaking their own necks. I hope you will be very careful.'

'Sophie, you're a fund of sweet light,' smiled James, 'and I shall take care that nobody breaks a neck. Certainly not you or Anne. I'm too fond of you both.'

'And we are extremely fond of you,' said Anne, 'I don't know what we should do if you weren't here with us.'

'The fact that you're here at all is my fault—'

'You're not to say that,' said Sophie a little emotionally.

'I met that idiot Ferenac in Vienna,' said James, 'and for some reason he thinks I'm on his tail. He's a political creature.'

'It doesn't matter where you met him, what he is or what he thinks,' said Sophie, 'you are not to say this is your fault. You will upset me. I don't like being upset. I cry.'

'No, you don't,' said Anne.

'Yes, I do, and I will.'

'No, you won't,' said Anne.

'Sometimes,' said Sophie, 'the temperamental weapon of tears is woman's only effective one. James, what am I talking about?'

'How to keep smiling, I think,' said James. His nerves were on edge, his ears attuned more for the extraneous than this localized banter. But Sophie, he felt, was trying to induce cheer and avoid the dismal. 'I'll go and put my nose out for a while.'

He went to the entrance again. Outside the shadows were deeper, longer, the river a murmurous flow, the darkening pines quiet. He sat down just inside the opening, he looked and he listened. He stayed there until the sun had gone and twilight muted the colours. The temperature dropped. He stretched, rubbed his hands, blew on them and rubbed them again. The twilight deepened. Anne and Sophie walked and whispered. He listened for the extraneous sounds. The quietness outside carried an uneasiness with it. He stiffened as little noises suddenly carried too. They were the noises of moving men, from the foothills to his right. Damn, they had crossed the river themselves at some point. He retreated quickly and silently into the cave. Sophie and Anne came out of the darkness.

'Say nothing, they're not far away,' he whispered. He took their arms and led them through the narrowing passage into the black vault beyond, so much darker as the light faded outside the cave. The damp eeriness made Anne shiver and Sophie felt cold goose pimples rise at the engulfing blackness. In this inner chamber the ground inclined slightly downwards. James could not see the silent water, not in this darkness, but he knew it was there, somewhere in front of them. He had to get the girls up on to that ledge, above the still, black pool, and into a recess, their only possible hiding place. The ground became slippery and he knew they were at the edge of the water. The ledge was to the left. He kept hold of the girls while he put one foot up. He found the ledge and brought his foot down.

'There's a shelf wide enough to stand on,' he whispered, 'and a recess a little way along. Hold still while I get you up.'

He mounted the ledge. He reached down. Anne was a faint glimmer. He took her by the hands and pulled her up. He pulled Sophie up. They glued themselves to the damp wall and shuddered at its clamminess. But they made no sound and James loved them for their courage. He edged along, feeling his way, the girls following crabwise. He reached a rough, shallow depression in the wall and brought the girls into it, the shelf wider here. Anne gritted her teeth and Sophie fought to control her nerves as they all fitted themselves into the recess, James between the sisters, his arms around their waists, faces to the wall.

Then they could only wait. Below them the icy pool waited too, hungry to receive warm bodies.

They heard nothing but their own breathing for long minutes. They heard nothing of the men who silently approached the cave entrance. Sophie's heart hammered as the silence screamed at her and three bodies froze rigidly as with a rush and a clatter the outer cave was invaded. Boots pounded the stone floor. Fercnac, with two men, had burst in. Anne's right hand was over her mouth, stifling her frightened breath, and Sophie was conscious of the warning communicated by the tightening of James's embracing arm. No sound, stay still, stay still.

They stayed still, rigid bodies pressed to the wall. There was a light in the cave. The men had a torch. Oh, dear God, thought Sophie, they are men determined to get us. Why, why?

The light swept around the vacated area. Oh, by God, thought James, had they left anything there? Shoes? No. His pants? No. He had them folded and tucked inside his jacket, and the girls had left their hats and parasols in the tavern. But their handbags, which they had clung to with all the resolution of their sex? God, their handbags!

His urgent hands investigated. Sophie and Anne, in a nightmare of fear, frenziedly wondered what he was at. James discovered identifiable shapes and breathed with relief. The light moved, the beam fingering the blackness, finding the narrow passage.

'Damn them. Where are they?' It was Ferenac's voice, speaking in German. It sounded livid. He was answered by a mutter. 'The next, then,' said Ferenac impatiently, 'they're in one of these holes.'

But the man with the torch was moving down the cave, sweeping the light from side to side. It chased over walls, it pierced the darkness of the passage. It reached into the black vault and slow footsteps followed it. The beam swung, steadied and played straight down into the area of refuge. There were other footsteps and Ferenac's voice, echoing around the vault.

'Water,' he hissed furiously, 'stinking water. But we'll find them, they'll be in some hole we'll have to crawl into. They've got Dobrovic's gun and that gives them an advantage in the right place.' The light lingered on the black water, mesmerized by its menacing stillness. 'Come

161

on. What does it matter? If we don't get them tonight, Avriarches will tomorrow. Wherever they are, they're stuck. Come on.'

The beam retreated. The blackness descended. They heard the men moving out. The hardness of a revolver pressed consciously now against James's ribs. Until Ferenac had mentioned it he had forgotten it. He wouldn't even make a decent Boy Scout.

'Wait,' he whispered to the trembling girls, 'wait just a little longer.'

'Oh, James . . .' It was a distraught, almost imperceptible gasp from Sophie.

But he would not be trapped into moving yet. Ferenac had spoken in German. Why? To lull his prey in a language they knew? To bring them out of hiding as soon as they thought it safe? He would be wary of that revolver. Or were his companions German-speaking? Whatever the reason, it made James keep the girls on that ledge for long, agonizing minutes before he at last moved. Then he brought them free of it and helped them down, everyone moving cautiously. They edged clear of the water and around the wall to the passage. James knocked his head against projecting rock, but that was an insignificance compared with other things. They went through the passage into the outer cave. Outside the twilight had turned to dusk and the cave had the atmosphere of night. But at least they could see each other. Sophie winced.

'James, you've cut yourself,' she said, her voice strained.

'Just a knock,' he said. She and Anne were trembling, but he could have forgiven them an attack of hysteria at this point. He wiped away a trickle of blood on his forehead and said, 'Stay here a moment, I must take a look.'

Cautiously, warily, he put his head out. The dusk was bringing the night, dark night. He could see no moon. The river was almost invisible and the littered foothills seemed highly discouraging in the gloom. He could hear no sound except the murmur of the fast-flowing river. He listened intently for a while, then returned to the baronesses.

'I think they've gone,' he said. Anne, over-wrought, leaned against him. He put one arm around her. Sophie essayed a shaky smile. James gave her an encouraging one. 'I know,' he said, 'it was a near thing, wasn't it?'

'Near?' said Sophie. 'It was next door to doom for a moment'

'Oh, I was so scared,' sighed Anne.

James took her face between his hands. Her cheeks were cold.

'I'm proud of both of you,' he said and lightly kissed her. Sophie bit her lip and turned away. It was childish, she knew, but she would rather have liked a little affection herself. It was that kind of a moment.

'I heard that man mention a gun,' she said.

'Yes, I have one,' said James, 'I took it from the fellow who ran his face into that door. I ought to have thought about using it if they'd spotted us, but this is my first manhunt, and certainly the first on the wrong end, and I only remembered the revolver when Ferenac spoke about it. I also forgot to make sure until then that you hadn't left your handbags lying around here.'

'Oh, I see now,' said Anne.

'I must agree, I did think it the wrong time for you to be familiar, James.' Sophie managed a weak laugh. Their narrow escape was inducing light-headedness now. 'Do you think we shall be able to get away in a little while?'

'Come and look,' said James. At the entrance they peered into gathering darkness. In the west the sky was purple-black. Above them it was becoming inky. Without the aid of moonlight they would never be able to see their way over this terrain. Nor could they think about recrossing the river or climbing the slope to the road. And even allowing that they might make some progress along the foothills, every noise they made would carry. Which, if Ferenac and his men were still roaming about, would bring disaster. James felt the whole business was an absolute swine. How the devil was he going to get the girls out of it?

'We need a moon,' he murmured, bringing them back into the cave.

'Yes, that would be lovely,' said Sophie, 'and instead of everything being rather frightening it would all look romantic.'

'It would help us to see and save us breaking our necks,' said James, 'which is what I promised.'

'Men think in very practical terms, you know, Anne,' said Sophie.

'I am thinking in terms of a warm fire and hot food,' said Anne. 'Oh, it is so cold in here, isn't it?'

It was. And they were all hungry, thirsty and drained.

'Supposing you two try to get some sleep?' said James. 'We'll move as soon as it's light. I'll sit by the entrance for a while. Just in case.'

'James, exactly why are they after us?' asked Sophie. 'I think you know. Please tell us.'

They had a right to know, he thought. They had the courage to know.

'I believe Ferenac intends to assassinate the Archduke Franz Ferdinand,' he said, 'and I also believe he's aware I suspect him. Which is why his solution was to put me out of the way. Unfortunately, this has involved you two.'

'James, you aren't serious?' said Anne incredulously.

'He once said a good archduke is a dead one. I think he's very serious himself.'

'It makes sense of his desperate desire to get hold of us, for he knows you would go to the police,' said Sophie. 'James, I think I'm getting very frightened.'

'If he's that kind of a man,' said Anne, 'I think I'm going to be scared out of my wits.'

'I don't feel too happy myself,' said James, 'but he's got other things on his mind as well as us. We only have to worry about shaking him off. We'll do that as soon as it's light. It won't be difficult. Don't worry, we'll manage. Get some sleep. You must.'

Sophie and Anne were too tired to argue. They became a huddled bundle on the floor close to the wall, their heads pillowed on their white handbags. Anne shivered for a while, despite the warmth of her sister's body, but she dropped off, drawn into slumber by the compulsive inducement of exhaustion. Sophie lay awake, worried about James, surely colder by himself than she and Anne were together. The hardness of the ground made her hip bone ache but she did not move. Suddenly, surprisingly, she slept.

James, sitting close to the entrance, got up and walked about, warming his chilled blood. He blew into his hands. He glanced at the glimmering figures of the recumbent girls. They had given him brave companionship. The menace of Ferenac was an obscenity, but political fanatics were always the most pitiless. Who was the man Avriarches he had mentioned? Avriarches, felt James, carried further menace. What day was it when Franz Ferdinand arrived in Sarajevo? Tomorrow? The day after? Or was he to be killed by Ferenac in Ilidze? But Ferenac would not go to either Ilidze or Sarajevo if he thought the fugitives had escaped to inform on him. No, he would not go anywhere until the situation was clearly resolved for him.

Sophie and Anne moaned a little. They were restless on their cold, hard bed. They did not often come face to face with this kind of crisis, one that was such a frightening assault on mind and body. They moved in a rich, cultured and privileged society, remote from the rigours and hardships of the rest of the world. But it had not turned them into spoiled and bloodless caricatures. They had survived Ferenac and his hunters with courage this day, and without complaints or tears. James knew he must return them unharmed to their bright citadel of life, they deserved no less.

He heard a sigh, a rustle. They were finding the stone floor primitive, discomfort battling with exhaustion.

'James?' Sophie whispered his name.

'Can't you sleep?' He went over to her. Anne was fitfully dozing beside her.

'I've been asleep. It isn't the softest of beds, though.' Sophie kept to a whisper, not wanting to wake Anne. 'James, they won't come back here now, I'm sure they won't. So you must get some sleep too.' As naturally as she could she went on, 'It's not much good any of us being prim and proper, you know. You must lie down with us, we'll all keep each other warm. Please?'

She was being entirely sensible. His bone-weary condition tempted him. So did the warmth she exuded. She reached, took his hand and made the decision for him. He came down between her and Anne as she made room for him. She felt the coldness of his clothes. He must be frozen. She put her body bravely to his and her warmth generated both comfort and pleasure. He relaxed, using his folded woollen pants as a pillow. They pressed close. It was as instinctive as practical. In the darkness Sophie blushed to her roots. James was so undeniably masculine, so firm against her. She had been worried about him, now she worried about herself. There was a desire to be held, a desire to be wanted. She could not resist responding to the moment. She put her arms around him and drew closer. Warmly she snuggled. Sweet heat surged into her. She hid her crimson face in his shoulder because of the delicious excitement the physical contact brought.

James's chilled veins thawed and warm blood flowed.

Anne gave a restless moan, sought the comfort of another body. The three of them lay close. Sometimes they slept, sometimes they fitfully chased the elusive. The warmth was only partial, the hard ground inescapable. Aching hips awoke them, they turned, they twisted and they dozed in spasms.

Sophie turned for the hundredth time. There was coldness all down her front, warmth at her back. In turning she found warmth for her front. She cuddled, snuggled, found blissful comfort for one more short space and thought how good, how lovely.

James awoke. A dark head rested on his arm, a soft curving body slept warmly against his. Cold cramp made him curl his toes and stony ground tortured his hip. He moved. Sophie gave a dreamy whimper and clung. He stayed still. His hip went numb. Sophie murmured. He closed his eyes.

Sophie awoke. The fissure was grey with dawn light. Cold draughts besieged her back, but the warmth in her stomach and thighs was so good. Her open eyes vaguely surveyed a crumpled tweed jacket. It belonged to James. It was James. She was shamelessly, tightly aligned with him, her arms around him. A little tremor quivered through her and sensations of sweet pleasure disturbed her. His head lay on his folded woollens, his face was a little gaunt and his chin blue. The cut on his forehead was marked by dried blood. How hard his body was. Colour suffused her. So this was James. He was sleeping like the dead even on this uncharitable ground, with Anne cuddled up behind him. He was not an ordinary man. He was much more like the new image forming in her mind. And her images were never of ordinary men.

Slowly she withdrew her arms and sat up. She realized then how her body ached, how icy her feet were, how dry and wretched her mouth. And the hem of her petticoat felt coldly damp around her ankles. She stood up. Her knees were stiff. James moved and turned over. His head rested on her handbag. She picked up his woollens and went to the entrance. The light in the east was pale, the dawn still and silent. The sun would soon be up. She slipped off her petticoat and sidled into the open. She laid petticoat and pants out over flat rocks.

In the east the pale light strengthened and soft colour began to invade the neutral sky.

Chapter Seven

A man sat on a stone ledge high in the hills. In his fifties, he was black of beard and immense of girth. A shaggy fur hat was on his head, his dark grey woollen shirt was worn over a cotton one and his black baggy trousers were tucked into his boots. A cartridge belt was around his waist. A rifle, its butt on the ground, rested against the ledge. The man Lazar was talking to him.

'Describe them again, my friend,' said the bearded man, called Avriarches.

'The women? Again?'

'Again.'

Lazar described the baronesses. Graphically. Avriarches picked his teeth with a splinter of wood. Occasionally he spat. Sometimes he smiled. Lazar had a talent for describing women. Apart from that he was a rat-faced runt. Or so Avriarches thought.

'But you'll have to be careful,' said Lazar, 'Ferenac thinks they're aristocrats.'

'So you keep saying. Does it mean something to Ferenac? It means nothing to me. They're all the same under their petticoats. Except that these, who knows? I might send them back after a month or two and collect a pretty price for them. If I can catch them. If I don't I'll break someone's teeth for wasting my time.' Avriarches spat. 'You say they slipped Ferenac? Who is this Ferenac?'

'One of the chosen,' said Lazar.

Avriarches showed big teeth in a huge smile. It made Lazar shift uneasily on his feet.

'Chosen?' Avriarches' laugh was a gusty bellow. 'God must have come down in His world to choose a man who can't even keep a pair of flying petticoats in sight. What is he chosen for?'

'To put an end to the archduke. He must get to Sarajevo this evening to meet others there. He doesn't want these people to get there before him, he doesn't want them to get there at all. They know about him, he says.'

Avriarches, eyes wandering in apparently lazy fashion over the steep, sloping hillsides to the winding river far below, said, 'Idiots and incompetents, all of you. And what's one more archduke to worry about? There's always a dozen to take the place of the one before. Sit down. Don't move. Some of my men might be here soon. They shoot anything which moves in these hills.'

'I know that,' said Lazar. He sat, then went on grumblingly, 'It upsets people at times.'

'Oh, people,' said Avriarches carelessly. He surveyed the panorama above and below. The early morning sun was softening the bleak ridges. Far beneath them the river seemed a narrow, winding ribbon of shining light. Straggling pinewoods were tiny blotches of green. 'That is where the women and the man disappeared?' he said.

'Somewhere there,' said Lazar, pointing downwards. 'That's why Ferenac sent me up here to find you. Yesterday I only saw one of your men.'

'I don't appear in person for every pipsqueak. But so, last night I received your message. I was to come and collect the women. This morning, here I am, and you tell me they have disappeared, that I am to find them for myself.'

'They're hiding and if anyone can flush them out it's you,' said Lazar. 'We only ask that you let us have the man. Ferenac wants to silence him and Dobrovic wants to talk to him. You see, he almost killed friend Dobrovic, who has lost some teeth and needs a new nose.'

'Almost?' Avriarches was disgusted. 'He's a weakling, then. I know that Dobrovic, nothing more than another runt. The skinniest of my women could eat him.' The big Greek spat again. His eyes, as hard and as bleak as the stone, moved in restless search. 'See here, my friend, I don't like this. I hope I'm not being foxed. Look, there's nothing, and it's well after dawn. They wouldn't wait as long as this to creep out of their hole. Either they're not where you think or they've slipped your chosen one again. If that's the case, what am I doing here? My time, pipsqueak, is valuable. I'll wait only a little longer.'

He could wait patiently when necessary. It had a way of bringing its rewards in the end. He had learned this and so much else from his father, a man supreme in his trade, God rest his roaring soul. It was his father who had taught him that laws were made by authorities to cripple men. It was the duty of any self-respecting man to reject all laws made for him by governments. Strong men of inviolable self-respect made their own laws and cracked the heads of anyone who did not see eye to eye with them. True, his father had been forced to leave his country, Greece, because of the prejudices and hostility of successive governments, but all the family retained fine, colourful memories of their homeland. What a living they had made, what tigresses of women they had tamed, what a mote in every government's eye they had been. There you could dance on the top of a hill all day, drawing the fire of sweating lawmakers who couldn't have hit an ox stuck in a shop doorway.

Of course, when they had brought the army in to make things a lot more uncomfortable than the police, his father had finally left the country in disgust. But Bosnia had provided good new ground for a man of his ability.

He, Avriarches, had become chief of the band when his father, as drunk as a fiddler at a gipsy wedding, had fallen off a mountain ledge in the best traditions of his kind. He had not disgraced his father's memory. He could roar as loudly, rob as rumbustiously and, if necessary, cheat the devil himself.

It would be something to catch up with the Austrian women whom that pipsqueak Lazar had been on about. Especially if they were aristocrats. It offended the authorities mightily when he abducted any woman of substance. They kicked up the devil of a racket and swore to slit his throat or hang him once and for all. They often sent soldiers when he made this kind of trouble, but it took more than the provincial soldiers of Bosnia to corner Avriarches, son of Old Devilguts, as his father had been called. In any case, he usually returned women of substance after a month or so. Their fathers or husbands were glad to pay and to say nothing. No man liked to shout about the fact that his wife or daughter had spent a single night, let alone a month of nights, with Avriarches.

Austrian women. Yes, that would panic the Bosnian authorities and turn the Austrian governor red with rage. There would be swarms of police and soldiers. There would be a few fireworks, but they would bargain with him, like they always did, like they always had to when the safety of delicate hostages was in the balance. Well, life had been rather quiet lately. This could be enjoyable. And afterwards, a price for the pretty pair? No, not a price. A ransom.

Avriarches smiled hugely.

But that runt Lazar had better be right. If anticipation as pleasurable as this led to disappointment, he'd split the hills with the weasel's head.

He watched. He would watch for ten minutes more and then, if there was still no sign, he would call up his men and have them flush the whole valley. But better first to convince himself he could not localize the search.

James shifted. He winced at the cramping pains. He had slept, after all, and more heavily than he would have believed. The fitful naps had finally lengthened into spells of welcome sleep. Suddenly aware of light, he sat up violently. That was the light of a risen sun. Damn, he thought, they should have been up and away at dawn. And Sophie, for God's sake, there she was, sitting at the entrance, her back against the wall, her knees drawn up and cradled, her head resting. She was dozing in full view of anyone across the river.

He rushed at her, pulled her back into shadow. Her head jerked up.

'Sophie, you idiot!'

Sophie stared bemusedly for a moment. Then angry pride flushed her face.

'You are speaking as one idiot to another, I presume?' she said stiffly.

'Why the devil didn't you wake me?' He was dark, bristly, scowling. 'We ought to have been out of this place thirty minutes ago.'

She could have told him she let him sleep on out of compassion, that she herself had dozed when she did not mean to. Instead she said, 'I am sorry I am such a disappointment to you, but you will understand of course that I have the natural failings of every idiot.'

'Oh, Sophie.' He shook his head at her, brought her to her feet. Sophie, hurt and unusually sensitive, kept her face turned away. 'Sophie, don't you realize you could have been seen?'

'I've said I am sorry.'

Anne groaned and woke up. James went to help her to her feet. Anne winced at her stiffness. He checked his impatience, smiled at her and rubbed her hands. Sophie, comparing this with his treatment of her, turned her back on them, shocked to feel tears stinging her eyes. Anne winced again, this time at the pain of rushing pins and needles.

'We must go,' said James.

'Yes,' said Anne, 'but I look a dreadful mess, don't I?'

'We both do,' said Sophie in a tight voice, 'and James is a disillusioned man this morning.'

James looked at them. They were dishevelled, their clothes creased and dusty, their white shoes scratched and stained. But he saw beyond all that. He did not give a tinker's cuss for their state or care if they ended up looking like scarecrows as long as he delivered them safely to their parents. And the baron would be out again this morning, looking for them, that was certain, just as it was certain that he had been out looking for them last evening.

'Considering everything, you both look very good to me. Sophie, was I a little rough with you? I'm sorry.' He put an arm around her shoulders as he went to the opening, giving her a squeeze that asked her to forgive him. He felt her quiver. 'Sophie?'

'Oh, I am sorry too,' she said huskily.

'We'll manage,' said James. He put his head out and looked around. Everything seemed ominously quiet. The sun was on the river, the foam a frothy white around wet boulders. He licked dry lips. A quick dash down over the rocks and he would reach water. And be a clear target. No, they must wait before they ventured to the river, they must edge out of the cave and make their way along the foothills, using the mounds of strewn rock for cover. He glanced to the right and saw his pants and Sophie's petticoat laid out in the sun. The garments looked dry. A stiff morning breeze suddenly gusted, ruffling his hair and tickling the petticoat. It flirted with the lace hem and lifted it.

High above them Avriarches rose to his feet. He had been patient long enough. His eyes made their final search. They glinted. Far below, where the hillside rose from the sloping riverbank, he discerned the tiny flutter of something white.

He smiled.

'Wait here,' he said to Lazar, 'and when my men come show them the way I've gone. How long you'll have to wait will depend on how long it takes them to fill their bellies. They don't breakfast on goat's milk.'

He began to make his way down the ridged, precipitous hill. He was light for all his girth. He carried his rifle and hummed a song as he descended. The fluttering white had gone. But he knew where they were now.

*   *   *

James did not bother with his pants. He drowned them in the pool while Sophie put on her petticoat. Then they all emerged quietly and carefully and began to edge their way around the curving face of the hillside. Progress was slow, the jumbled piles of stone and the huge boulders as obstructive as they were protective. Feet scraped, slithered and slipped over layers of broken stone. The light was starkly bright after the darkness of the cave and Anne, heart in her mouth, felt they were as vulnerable as beetles exposed under lifted timber. Sophie was taut with nerves and James full of anxieties. But at least they were no longer cold. At times during the night they had all thought they would never be wholly warm again, but their scrambling urgency in the morning sunshine chased away all chills, and perspiration was soon wet on heated bodies. Gnawing hunger was for the most part strangled by knots of fear, but dry mouths became drier, their thirst made worse by the sight and sound of the river.

But James would not let them descend to the river, not yet. He could not see the course of the valley in front, for they were negotiating a long, sweeping bend of river and hillside. The vegetation thickened on the far bank. On this side the bank was a mass of fallen stone that spilled into the water. Footholds became precarious as the incline steepened, the girls leaning against the hillside and clamping to it at times. James urged them on. His sense of uneasiness made him sweat. Rocks and boulders lessened as the sloping bank shelved even more sharply. If any of them slipped they would tumble or slide all the way down to the river.

Anne kept gasping, 'Oh, dear, oh, dear.' But she went on and Sophie moved with her, face pale, teeth clenched, her pointed shoes a pain to her feet. Bodies were hot, the morning sun a hard brilliance on smooth stone. As long as they kept close to the hillside they could not be seen from the rear, the curve of the valley hid them. James breathed with relief as the slope became kinder. Spewed boulders again offered solid cover. The curve was straightening out, he could see more of the river ahead, the woodlands widening on the other side. He spotted a point where they might risk going down to the water. And at that point the river was so littered that there was a negotiable causeway of stone. There they could cross and take to the woods again and then, if all went well, climb the far slope up to the road, which lay a little distance back but which roughly paralleled the line of the valley.

'There,' he said, pointing to where the rock piles were like tumuli and would give them cover, 'we'll go down to the river there.'

'Water? Water?' said Anne, eyes showing dark rings. 'Oh, lead on, dear James.'

He took them down the slope between the high tumuli and they reached the river. They knew that at the water's edge they had no cover, but it was a risk they had to take. Anne and Sophie sank to their knees, cupped their hands and drew the water up to their parched mouths.

James lay on his stomach and dipped his mouth in. He knelt up and washed his face clean, taking the dried blood from his forehead. He looked back. He saw the curving line of the ridged hill and the heights above. They were harshly bright. Ledges and shelves were sharp. The briefest flash of reflected light leapt to his eyes as the sun ran along the polished barrel of Avriarches' rifle. James went cold. There was someone up there on those precipitous slopes. He strained his eyes but the flash did not recur.

'Come along, my pets,' he said lightly, 'we don't want thunder and lightning to strike. This way.'

Sophie and Anne stared at the causeway of jumbled stone. Foam and spray played around it in places.

'Are you sure, James?' said Sophie.

'It's better than getting wet.'

'Well, I still have faith,' said Sophie, 'and I promise you I shall not break my neck.' She smiled at him. 'I am not such an idiot as that.'

'Sophie, you're beautiful,' said James. He mounted the first stone and helped each girl up in turn. He led and they followed. The causeway was broken, uneven and slippery. Sophie took her shoes off, Anne followed suit. James took the shoes, carrying all four by their straps, and they moved from stone to stone. The spray showered skirts, rained around feet. Anne teetered and swayed, the river a foaming, angry rush on either side. Sophie steadied her, James looked back, turned and steadied them both.

The river wind whipped at them, warm and

brisk. It tossed the fair hair of Anne and wound it around her face. It took hold of the rich chestnut tresses of Sophie's hair and whirled them about her head. They stepped down, they stepped up, their stockinged feet clinging, James leading them the easiest way he could devise, and although their teeth were set and the rushing waters frightening they did not falter. He jumped into the shallows from the last rock. He carried Anne clear of the water to the bank and returned for Sophie. She let herself down into his arms. She was warm, flushed, and almost exhilarated. She put her arms around his neck.

'James, no one could say this is dull, could they?' she said.

'No one could say you are,' he said and carried her to the bank. He set her down. She and Anne slipped their shoes on and James hurried them up the bank into the shelter of the pines.

If he wondered about that flash of light in the hills, the girls did not. They had not seen it and he made no mention of it. Sophie felt a sense of comparative security in the woods, Anne a simple sense of relief that they could not be seen. They hastened over the carpets of dry needles. James veered to the right, wanting to see if the ascent to the road was negotiable. It was not. The pitted, craggy slope, marked by tufts of dry grass and stunted bush, was far too steep for the girls to climb. They had to go on. They went on. The trees and undergrowth became thick and lush, creating a humidity that made perspiration run. They flew on urgent feet whenever they could and fought their way through hampering undergrowth whenever they had to. Sophie kept losing a shoe, James kept retrieving it. Its heel began to separate from the sole. He hammered it against a tree.

'Thank you, James. I am responsibility enough without a silly shoe making it worse.'

They stood for a moment, breathing hard. Sophie, seeing how dishevelled Anne was, how the perspiration darkened her fair hair around her forehead and stained her apple-green dress under her arms, felt that she herself must look awful. Her garments were sticking to her body and heat that was clammy had her in its embrace. James would never sketch her again except as an object.

James, with his chin bristly, his dark, tanned face lined with sweat, said with a faint smile, 'What a bright, brave pair you are, I love you both. One day we'll climb a mountain together, all three of us, and stand on top of the world.'

'James, now you are thinking in very impractical terms,' said Sophie.

'Come on,' said James.

They resumed their flight. The sun climbed, a blinding brilliance in the blue sky. It made an oven of the woods. The strap of Anne's right shoe suddenly flapped loose, the button torn off. She stumbled. James caught her.

Breathlessly Anne said, 'Thank you, James, you are always there, aren't you?'

Sophie, seeing him with his arm around her sister and the smile on Anne's face, thought oh, this is terrible, I am beginning to be as jealous as a female Iago, and what did he mean, he loves both of us? He must love one of us more than the other, unless he meant he only loved us for our bravery. But I don't feel at all brave and if I were brave I should want to be admired for it, not loved. I should want to be loved for my weaknesses as well as my virtues. Oh, I don't know what I want except that I am all terrible nerves when he is close to me.

James knelt, using his handkerchief to bind Anne's shoe to her foot, running it like a twist of rope under the sole and tying it tightly around her instep.

'That will do very nicely,' said Anne, 'and do you think we're safe now? I mean, we haven't run into anybody, have we?'

'No, we haven't, not yet,' said James, 'but we'll go on.'

He continued to hurry them. He had not lost his feeling of uneasiness since they began their flight. The girls were desperately hot, their clothes sticky and hampering, their breathing noisy, and it was an effort to duck under every low branch. James kept forging ahead to make quick surveys of what lay in front, frequently bearing to the right to explore the possibilities of ascending to the road. Always the climb was too risky to attempt. Sophie thought they had lost him after a while and a little spasm of panic attacked her.

'Anne, quickly, we must catch him up.'

'Sophie—'

'Quickly!'

But James was suddenly before them, his face glistening with sweat. The girls stopped.

'Quietly now,' he said, 'there's a break in the trees farther up and a place where I think we can make our way up to the road. We can't go on like this for ever.'

They followed him as silently as they could. Sophie, despite the heat, kept shivering. Anne took her hand, wondering about Sophie's nerves. It was unpleasant for all of them, this feeling that those men must be somewhere about, but it was not like Sophie to give way to emotion. James would get them out of this.

The trees thinned and the sun poured through. There on the right was the ascent to the top and not far from the top was the road. It was easy enough for all of them to climb. But James suddenly froze. He leaned back on the girls to bring them to a halt. At the top of the slope on their right stood a man. It was Dobrovic, his face and head swathed in bandages and a rifle under his arm. He was moving, turning this way and that, alternately watching the road and surveying the valley. His thick bandages gave him a mummified look, but there was nothing of embalmed peacefulness about him. His movements were quick, restless, angry, and James sensed the man was savage with desire for revenge.

Sophie and Anne, glimpsing the figure, stopped breathing. Dobrovic glanced across the valley and signalled with his rifle. James construed it as a negative message. It was full of angry frustration. But it brought a response in the form of a shout, which sang through space. Dobrovic acknowledged it with a brief flourish of his rifle. He was not, apparently, able to do any shouting himself.

Under his breath James swore at the green-eyed gods of fate. Sophie fought sick disappointment and Anne sighed. They retreated to thicker cover.

'James, they know we're here,' whispered Sophie.

'No, they only hope we are,' he said, 'there's one man across the river so they can't even be sure which side we're on. It's damn bad luck having that character with the flattened face up there.'

They heard another shout. It was fainter but they felt its message boded them little good. A snapping twig froze them. It came from the river side of them. James pushed at the girls and they fled into the area close to the slope. Anne caught her foot, tumbled and fell. Sophie turned, James turned. He rushed at Anne, Sophie with him. Anne looked up as James helped her to her knees. She brushed dirt from her face.

'Ah, so.' It was a bold, amused voice. Anne and Sophie froze again. Avriarches, rifle in his hands, regarded them with a smile. They had never seen so huge a man. He seemed as wide as he was tall, so that although he did not command any more height than James he seemed ten times bigger. His large teeth gleamed amid red lips and black beard. His grey eyes were like polished stones. 'Dirty, yes,' he said, speaking German, 'even unwashed. But quite up to expectations. Sometimes people exaggerate, yes?'

Anne was in horror, Sophie in rigid fright and James in despair. One shout from this fat giant would bring Ferenac and his men racing to the spot. This, he felt sure, was the man Avriarches, whom Ferenac had mentioned. He slid his hand inside his jacket and shirt as Avriarches, in vast self-confidence, took time to study the rounded fairness of Anne and the aristocratic promise of Sophie. Being a man of boundless experience he could appreciate what lay beneath the dust and exhaustion of the cornered prey. Yes, they were a fine pair and he would lay odds that neither of them would be a disappointment. They might need a little fussing and coddling to bring them to sweet moods, but they would do, they would do very nicely. What was that pipsqueak of a man fumbling about for?

Avriarches grinned as he found himself looking at the blue snout of James's revolver.

'Drop your rifle,' said James quietly, 'and keep your mouth shut.'

Anne's blood rushed in wild hope. Sophie stared at James with eyes huge. Avriarches laughed. The noise came rumbling up from his belly and spilled in deep chuckles from his full lips.

'Pipsqueak,' he said, 'I've had a dozen like you for supper.' He laughed again. 'However, hot bullets give me indigestion. So, take it.' He tossed the rifle at James. But he did not let go of it. The butt leapt and the barrel slid smoothly through the brigand's hand, only to be gripped at the last moment. He impelled the butt forward and it smacked the revolver. The weapon dropped, struck violently from James's grasp. Avriarches put his foot on it. Anne sprang to her feet, a hand took hold of the back of her dress, wrenched and spun her like a rag doll. She fell.

James flung himself on his knees and grovelled in supplication at the feet of Avriarches, begging hoarsely, 'No, leave the women alone, let them go, I'll give you money, anything.' He abased himself at the booted feet. Avriarches, who despised cowards and considered their gutlessness should be forcefully brought home to them, kicked the snivelling runt in the chest. That is, he went instinctively through the motions but as his boot lunged up and forward James took the opportunity his ruse had given him. He caught the foot under his left arm. Instantly his other arm curled around the Greek's left leg. He heaved titanically while Avriarches was still grinning with surprise. The biggest man will fall if his legs are taken from under him. Even Avriarches could not defy the resultant force of gravity. He crashed like a lassoed bull. The ground came up and shook every bone in his body, driving his breath from him. James twisted free and scrambled for the revolver. Sophie seized the fallen rifle and with the primitive instinct of a creature fighting for survival, struck the head of the momentarily stunned brigand with the butt. His fur hat was off, his tongue shot out at the blow and he opened his mouth to roar. James kicked him in the jaw, the rifle butt struck his temple again and James finished the work, using the revolver to club the massive Greek senseless. The world which belonged to Avriarches spun under him and whirled him into black emptiness.

Chapter Eight

Avriarches came to. There was a thunderous pain
in his head. There was cramp in racked limbs.
He was stretched out on his back, spreadeagled
between trees. Nothing clothed him except his
long woollen vest that reached to his thighs. His
stripped and ripped clothes had been used to
bind his limbs and lash them to trees. Forked
pieces of branch had been thrust into the earth
to clamp his lower thighs. Any writhing movement would cause the rough timber to break the
skin and draw blood. Deep in his mouth was
stuffed part of his own shirt.

His livid eyes almost burst from their sockets,
for the ants were already there. Red and
scurrying, they swarmed to the writhing giant.
Despite the pinning timber forks his body arched
and thundered up and down, the choking gag
reducing his screams to wet gurgles. He jerked
with his arms until they threatened to unsocket.
Mother of God, he would be slowly eaten alive
unless Ferenac or his own men found him.

In his huge plunging he was the instrument
of his own torturing pain, the deadly forks of

barked wood scraping his thighs. A thousand ants climbed the writhing limbs to investigate. Avriarches bellowed and screamed, but emitted only strangled sounds.

Ferenac and his men entered the woods, drawn by the sound of a shot James had purposely fired from the revolver. He had also planted Anne's handbag back along the way they had come, Anne taking only her most wanted items from it and putting them into Sophie's bag. He had to draw Ferenac and his men into the woods, away from any points overlooking the river. The risk was a desperate one, the planted handbag a hope that would make Ferenac think they had turned tail and gone back to the village of Kontic.

James heard the hunters, the noises faint but unmistakable some way off. He shepherded the girls into the river then. The waters were deep at this point and only the foam-washed boulders prevented them from being swept off their feet. They made for the shelter of a cluster of boulders, standing high out of the rushing river. Desperation lent new courage, Sophie and Anne defying the icy cold and tumbling tide as James brought them within the shelter of the boulders. There they all immersed themselves to their shoulders. And there for the moment they had to stay and wetly freeze. The girls turned blue, the water slapping at their faces inside their stone shelter, the tide sucking at their legs. They clutched and pressed the stone. Anne's teeth chattered noisily and every breath was a wet gasp. Sophie clenched her teeth and breathed through her nose. James had his arms around them under the water, holding them. His gleaming wet face looked devilish. It wore something of a fixed, villainous grin, for despite everything he could not help thinking of Avriarches with undiluted relish.

They had downed that formidable man-mountain. James had made the girls wait at the edge of the wood while he dealt silently, speedily and mercilessly with the unconscious Greek. He knew that Ferenac and his men, raging around on both sides of the river, might flush him out any moment. But Avriarches had to be attended to. The few words the brigand had spoken had left James in no doubt about what was to happen to Anne and Sophie. It made him pitiless. He completed his work, leaving the stripped giant tied and spreadeagled. Then he had fired his shot and rejoined the girls.

They stood now in that icy water. Avriarches' rifle, wrapped in James's jacket, lay along a lower stone above the water. That rifle, together with the revolver, pocketed in the jacket, might be the final life-saver.

Sophie wondered if she would expire. She hoped not. She dearly wanted to live, she wanted them all to live. Amid fine spray she met James's eyes. He smiled very wetly. She smiled back and her eyes said, 'I love you, please love me.' As her limbs grew numb she heard Ferenac and his men savagely beating through the woods. James's look cautioned both her and Anne as they heard the distinct sounds of a man on the shelving bank. Above the noisy turbulence of the river the man's curses reached their ears. They gritted their chattering teeth and clung to the rocks and each other, the foam and spray flinging past them.

They heard the man scrambling along the bank. He was going back, parallel with the men in the woods, back in the direction of Kontic. Ferenac might find Avriarches now. James waited, forever governed by caution and the safety of his charges. The resilience of healthy bodies withstood the uncharitable embrace of the icy waters for minutes more, although lips as well as faces were blue. Summer heat meant nothing to this river. It was fed by cold mountain streams.

'Now,' said James at last. It took an enormous physical effort to leave their shelter, to force their suffering bodies through the tide to the other bank again. James would not chance the wooded side in case Ferenac had left one man scouting about. Desperation pushed them on, James behind the girls and using the wrapped rifle as a wall for their backs. Movement, however difficult, became a gradual tonic after prolonged, static immersion. They all knew it only needed one man to turn back, to break out of the woods, for them to be seen. But James thought they would have found Avriarches by now and that would turn them into a bunch of chattering furies for a while.

They fought the river, they lurched, swayed and fought on. They reached the shallows, waded through to the bank, then, streaming water, ran exhaustedly up over the incline to the littered foothills. There, in the shelter of piled rockfalls, they stopped. Anne sank down on a flat boulder, shoulders heaving, elbows on her knees and face in her hands. Sophie, gasping, pressed her back against the hillside, spread her arms flatly and closed her eyes. She breathed as if her lungs were squeezed. The sun smote her and her soaked dress glistened as it clung around her body.

'Well done, my braves,' said James in tender affection. He unwound his jacket from the rifle, which emerged clean, shining and wicked. His satisfied eyes reflected the dull glint of the metal. With the rifle was Avriarches' cartridge belt. They had not done so badly, no, not at all. He looked at Anne, she raised her head and smiled weakly at him. For all her wet, flattened hair and her loss of all make-up, he thought her brave and beautiful. If she married Ludwig, Ludwig would get a girl beyond price. He put out a hand and touched her cheek. 'We'll do them down yet, sweet one,' he said.

'You will, James,' she smiled.

He went to Sophie. She opened her eyes. She saw the smile in his own.

'James, please don't look,' she said, 'I am such a mess.'

'Are you? I don't think so. If there were only ten more like you the angels would dance. What's a slightly pink nose to any of the angels?'

'Oh, please don't be comical, I think I am quite over the edge.'

'No, you're not,' he said. His look was expressive of his intense belief in her. It stirred her every emotion. 'And we can't stand around, you know. My very brave Sophie, we can all make a final dash together, can't we? Look, do you see that point, where the river bends again? When we reach it you and Anne go on. I'll stop there. I have the rifle and revolver—'

'No! No, no, no!' Sophie, pale, flung the negative almost wildly at him. 'Oh, how can you even think we would let you do that! No, no, no!'

'Sophie—'

'Never, never! We must all go together.'

'Yes,' said Anne, coming up to them, 'we must all go together.'

'From the practical point of view,' said James, 'I—'

'I don't want to hear,' said Sophie, her mouth trembling, 'I hate practical points of view, they are all a danger to human relationships. We are all going on together and I don't care whether that's practical or not. I know at least that it's right.'

'Well,' said James, 'I—'

'No. It is not to be mentioned again. Ever.'

'Ever,' smiled Anne, who knew now why Sophie's emotions had been in the balance lately.

'Very well,' said James, 'but everything about you both has put me in your debt.' He turned, scouring the valley with anxious eyes. He seemed to have made so many surveys, seen so very little most of the time, yet Ferenac and his

194

men had never been far behind them. There was no sign of any of them now. 'Shall we go on?' he said.

'Yes, together,' said Sophie.

He risked everything to make the going as easy as possible so that they could move quickly. He took them down to the water's edge where the profusion of rockfalls was neither so thick nor so restricting. He made them run, telling them it would dry their clothes out quicker. The girls picked up their wet skirts and James had them going at a facile jogtrot. Their feet were aching and sore in sodden, splitting shoes, but James kept them at it. Go, go, go. The river ran with them on the right, sparkling, murmurous and winding. They took each bend gratefully, for each bend gave them extra cover. James carried the rifle, the cartridge belt around his waist, and he forgot his soaked garments in the vigorous exercise of the moment. Heat poured into him, but he smiled as Sophie and Anne ran on gamely. They flagged eventually and he let them walk for a while.

'James,' gasped Anne, 'you are very gracious. But oh, I am famished.'

'Think of other things,' said James.

They ran again in a while.

'Keep going,' panted James, 'not far now – be easy to cross in a moment – river's shallower.'

'That river again?' gasped Sophie. 'Oh, merciful Mary.'

A man, feet astride in the river, waders clasping his legs, a waterproof jacket around him, looked up with a frown as three figures came round a bend at a stumbling run. He delayed the throw of his line, his long rod quivering. James ran into the river, the girls lurching in after him.

Major Frederic Moeller, retired German officer and keen sportsman, could not believe such crass, outrageous behaviour.

'Damn and blast!' he roared at James. 'The fish, man, the fish!'

James panted something uncomplimentary about all fish. The major shuddered. Sacrilege added to asininity was unforgivable. The fellow was even waving a rifle in the most dangerous fashion. And by heaven, the women. They looked like camp followers, female ragtag and bobtail. He had never seen three more unappealing people, and he had certainly never known any to behave more thoughtlessly. They were treating the river like a paddling pool. Gypsies, by God.

He held James off at the end of his rod. James brushed it aside.

'Damn me,' said Major Moeller as the fellow splashed closer.

'Sorry, but we need help,' panted James, and as the German fixed him with a disapproving blue eye he resorted to the obvious to gain the right attention. 'My dear sir, if I may at this desperate point in their lives, I should like to present to you Baroness Sophie von Korvacs of Vienna and her sister Baroness Anne.'

'What? What?' Major Moeller was flabber-gasted. Baronesses? Those creatures? Two men standing on the right-hand bank viewed the river meeting with the stolidity of good and faithful servants. James gasped out the substance of the story. Anne and Sophie stood wearily in the swirling waters, faint to the point of collapse.

'So you see?' finished James.

'Good God,' said Major Moeller. He eyed James keenly and took another look at the young ladies, a shrewder look. Anne summoned up a little smile.

'It's all true, I assure you,' she said.

'Good God,' said the major again.

'Their father,' said James, 'is Baron Ernst von Korvacs, and the family is residing at present in Ilidze.'

'Major Frederic Moeller, at your service, my dear young ladies,' said the German, and bowed in his waders and clicked his heels muffledly on the riverbed. 'My car is up on the road. Gunther and Herman, my servants there, will render every assistance. So will I. Amazing. Astonishing. What the devil is the world coming to?'

Anne drooped. James slung the rifle, stooped and lifted her. He carried her out of the river and on to the bank.

'There, you're safe now, I think,' he said and set her down.

Major Moeller gave his arm to Sophie and waded through the water with her. She leaned heavily. He shifted his arm and put it around her.

'The damned scoundrels,' he muttered, 'but have no more worries, Baroness.'

'James has been so good,' she said faintly.

'Ah, that's James, is it? Thought he was going to shoot me when he first showed up.' A little chuckle from the major. 'Like him better now he's got that rifle slung.'

They grouped on the bank, Anne and Sophie almost dead on their feet. The major's servants hid their disapproval under impassive masks as they saw the assorted flotsam their employer had collected. Taking off his waterproof jacket the major wrapped it around Sophie's shoulders, then requested Gunther to lend his own jacket to the other baroness.

Baroness? Gunther gulped. He did not know whether to bow or fall down. He passed his jacket to James, who put it over Anne's shoulders.

'If you'll permit,' said Major Moeller to James, 'Gunther and Herman will carry the baronesses up to the car. It's not far but far enough. There are coats in the car.'

'Thank you,' said James. He felt elation born of a relief intoxicating. 'Major, could you drive the baronesses to Ilidze?'

'With the greatest pleasure,' said the major.

'Thank you,' said James again. 'Er – do you have any food?' He had seen a small hamper nearby.

'What a fool I am.' The major slapped a thigh in annoyance at himself. 'Of course there is food. Rolls, butter, meat and yes, something even better. Some schnapps. Gunther?' Gunther brought the hamper and opened it. The major swooped and drew out the brown schnapps bottle. Then he looked embarrassed. 'I have the failings of an old soldier,' he said apologetically, 'I drink from the bottle. I have no glasses. In such charming company I am ashamed of myself.'

'No, you are very kind,' said Anne, 'and we are very grateful.' Only the bliss of at last feeling safe kept her upright, and only her famished need of any form of sustenance made her take the bottle of fiery schnapps. Two mouthfuls turned her hot, pink and scorched. She gave the bottle to Sophie, who stared a little vaguely at it, then put it to her lips. The flame it lit in her throat made her clap a hand to her coughing mouth.

'Oh!' she gasped.

James drank gratefully. The liquor put a ring of heat around his exhilaration. Thank God for Major Moeller. The man looked a pillar of strength.

'We'll take the food to the car,' said the German, 'and you can eat on the way to Ilidze. We should go at once or those damp clothes will be the death of you.'

'Yes, now,' said James. He looked back down the river. There were no trees, only scrub and bush. 'I think I must wait for Ferenac.'

'No!' exclaimed Sophie.

Major Moeller nodded to Gunther. The sturdy servant lifted Sophie into his arms. She cried out. Herman bowed courteously to Anne. She was looking at James, who was squinting into the distance.

'No, you can't,' she said, 'you must come back with us.'

'Someone must take Ferenac,' said James.

'No, don't you dare,' cried Sophie, 'I will never forgive such idiocy. Major Moeller, stop him, make him come with us or we will stay too.'

Major Moeller looked thoughtful. He nodded to Herman and Herman stooped and took Anne up into his arms. The major picked up the hamper and placed it with considerate care in Anne's keeping. She cuddled it.

'Rest assured, my dear baronesses,' said the major, 'nothing foolish will be done and nothing foolish will happen. Gunther and Herman will take very good care of you meanwhile. Gunther, see that you drive them to Ilidze as quickly as possible. Then return at once for us. I will stay with our young man.'

'No, no one is to stay!' Sophie kicked as Gunther began to carry her up a winding path. 'Oh, no! James, please!'

'I shan't be long, Sophie,' said James.

'James,' said Anne, 'you had better not be.'

He watched with the major as the girls were carried up the incline, Sophie's last look one of anguished reproach.

'You think these scoundrels will come as far as this?' asked the major.

'I think Ferenac will definitely want to know if we've slipped him. He'll come all the way.'

'Ah,' said the major, and did not seem unhappy. He rubbed his chin. He was silver-moustached, healthily middle-aged and ruddily tanned. 'Permit me?' he said, indicating the rifle. James handed it over. He had not wanted to use it while the girls were with him. It would have drawn counter-fire. He had looked upon it as their last resort in the event of their being cornered. He would have had no choice but to use it then, although he would not have fancied his chances in a shooting match with Ferenac and his men. But out of his elation had come a lively desire to wait for the man who had relentlessly hunted them. A man who could plot assassination was sometimes, at best, only a misguided hothead, but a man who could hand over two innocent young women to someone like Avriarches was a first cousin to the devil himself.

Major Moeller beamed. He had broken the rifle open, examined the breech, cartridges and mechanism. He snapped the weapon shut. He caressed the smooth stock.

'From the Schroeder factory,' he said, 'and will suit us very well.'

'I hope so, it will need to,' said James. He could see them now, four of them, moving against the background of sunlit rocks and scrub. 'You are going to stand with me, Major?'

'If I may have that pleasure.'

'I'm very grateful.' James thought he and the German should be able to hold the men off long enough to ensure the escape of the girls. But Ferenac must be downed. To be certain of hitting him they would have to let him get close enough. 'There they are.'

'Ah,' said Major Moeller as he spotted the figures. A little light of battle glinted in his blue eyes. 'My dear James – if I may call you that

– might I suggest we take up a tactical position? I presume you did not mean we should literally stand.'

'The manoeuvres,' said James, as he and the major slipped down behind rocks, 'do you know when they finish?'

'Manoeuvres? What manoeuvres?' The major was eyeing with interest the approaching figures and the field of fire. 'Oh, the Austrian. They're finishing tomorrow and the Archduke Franz Ferdinand is arriving in Sarajevo the day after.'

'That means in two days.' James mused. 'Somehow, I think our friend Ferenac now wants to be there as well. I think he will have given up any ideas of taking the archduke on in Ilidze.'

'I see,' said the major, 'he's a bomb-thrower extraordinary, is he? It might be better to leave him to the police, perhaps?'

'It might,' said James, 'but for purely personal reasons I'd like to make sure he doesn't escape them.'

'Quite,' said the major. He smiled. 'But shall we take him between us? You point him out, my dear fellow, and I'll bring him down. On my honour, I shan't fail you.'

'Well, if it does get desperate,' said James, 'I've got this.' He brought out the revolver.

'A nice toy,' said the major, 'but don't wave it about, dear chap.'

'I think I'm going to like you,' smiled James.

They waited and watched. James lifted his head a fraction higher. Yes, four of them. All very distinct now. One was a big wide man, wearing only boots and long vest. Avriarches. Ferenac had found him, then. But the Greek moved stiffly, as if his legs pained him. He lurched rather than walked, and there was a perceptible wildness about him. There, thought James, is a man in pain but so bloodthirsty for vengeance that he was remorselessly driving himself to find it.

'Four,' whispered James.

'Well, we have six rounds, enough for all of them,' said the major.

'More than that,' said James, and opening up his damp jacket began to extract the cartridges from the belt around his waist.

'Reserves?' The major looked happy. 'What a fine thoughtful fellow you are.' He was cheerfully cool as he laid the rifle over the rocks and sighted it. 'Shall we take the fat one first?'

'Why not?'

'And then, which is Ferenac now? Can you point him out?'

James peered. There was the bandaged man and two of the friends he had muttered with at Joja's tavern. Ferenac was not there. That was a disappointment and a frustration. And a cause for deep thought. Ferenac had either chanced it and gone on his way to Ilidze or Sarajevo, or had turned tail. But then his men would have turned tail with him. Or had that roaring brigand, in his compulsive need for revenge, impressed them into his service? He was the kind of man to take all other men by the scruff of their necks.

'Damnation,' said James, 'Ferenac is missing.'

'Or lurking, perhaps? Such men are crafty, my

friend. What of these others? Are they important without him?'

'I rather think we're committed now,' said James.

'Quite so.'

The four men were only a hundred yards away now. Avriarches with his vast build dwarfed the others. Dobrovic had a rifle, so did the Greek, who had obviously insisted on commandeering someone else's. Major Moeller observed the targets with professional interest. They were out in the open and it would take them expensive seconds to reach the shelter of the nearest rocks. With the rifle butt firm in his shoulder he curled a steady finger around the trigger.

'It is agreed, then?' he murmured. 'We merely bring them down?'

'I think so,' said James, 'we'll leave the authorities to decide which of them should be hanged.'

'Very wise, my dear fellow,' said Major Moeller. In relaxed comfort he sighted and gently squeezed. The shot blasted the air with sound, echoing like a crack of thunder. Avriarches bellowed, threw up his hands, rocked back and pitched forward, a bullet in his right thigh. The bolt snapped back, then cleared the breech. The other three men stood in shock for a moment. Major Moeller squeezed again. Dobrovic plunged. In rapid succession came two more shots, each deadly in its accuracy. One smashed the third man's kneecap. The fourth man took his in the ribs as he made a wild dive for shelter. A revolver fell from his hand and clattered.

Dobrovic, a bullet crippling his left leg, writhed on the ground and clawed his way into scrub. Avriarches sat up shouting. He staggered to his feet, lurched like a drunk and fell headlong. He roared like a mad bull.

'My sainted aunt,' said James in admiration.

Major Moeller smiled modestly.

'Not too difficult at this distance. My dear James,' he said, 'I've won far more trophies for shooting than medals for campaigns. Had I missed any of them I should have asked you to blow my brains out. My boy, my thanks for such a splendid weapon.' He patted the rifle with all the pleasure of a lover.

'Thank Avriarches,' said James, 'it's his.'

'Is it? If you took such a piece from a man like that it's a great spoil of war and I regard it as yours.'

James, watching the wounded men crawling and heaving into what shelter they could find, said, 'Don't lose sight of the fact that they've a couple of rifles themselves.'

'And some nasty holes to go with them,' said the major cheerfully. 'We'll stay here, my dear chap, it's quite comfortable, don't you think? A little schnapps until Gunther and Herman return? They'll not return alone, depend on it. Your charming baronesses will see to that.'

'Well, I suppose while we stay here our hurt friends will have to stay there,' said James. 'Schnapps, you said?'

'Here,' said the major and pulled the bottle from his waders.

'Herr Major, your hand,' said James. They shook hands solemnly. James put the bottle to his mouth. 'Your health.' The schnapps was a further elation and mitigated to a pleasant extent the disappointment of not having bagged Ferenac.

'To you, my young friend,' smiled the major, and took a generous mouthful. 'And to your brave young ladies.' He took another. 'God in heaven, what a story, what a fine day's sport, even if you did wreck my fishing.'

A frenzied shot came whistling over their heads as they lay comfortably positioned inside their stone defences. Major Moeller refilled the rifle. Avriarches and Ferenac's friends were huddled behind cover. James heard the groans of Dobrovic, who had more than his wrecked face to worry about now, and he also heard the animal-like sounds of the maddened Avriarches. The brigand's rifle swung as he raised it, his booted foot sticking out. The major fired first. His shot split the sole of the boot and Avriarches rolled in agony, his rifle threshing the air.

'Can't have Fatty making a nuisance of himself,' chirped the major. 'More schnapps, James?'

They shared the bottle. They watched and conversed. Major Moeller was living out his retirement in Vienna. A widower, he preferred the lighter atmosphere of Vienna to the martial pomp of Berlin, and professed himself captivated by the elegance and hospitality of Viennese women.

'Not so – ah – majestic in form as the bountiful

matrons of Berlin, you know. Exquisite in the dance. I'm not yet too old, I hope.'

'For what?' murmured James.

'For waltzing. One can be on the retired list but not in the senile class, eh? What do you say, shall we drink to the ladies of Vienna?'

'Why not? Quality before quantity, shall we say?'

'Well put,' said the major, passing the bottle. A bullet sailed by. And another. A third smacked stone. 'Fidgety devils.'

'Nervous, I think,' said James, keeping a cautious watch on men in pain, discomfort and rage. He returned the bottle.

'English, my boy?' queried the major.

'Half. On my mother's side, God bless her. On my father's side, Scottish.'

'Ah, that accounts for it.' Major Moeller brushed his moustache. 'Fine fighters, the Scots. Remember Waterloo?'

'Not very clearly,' said James, enjoying his change of fortune, 'it was a little before my time.'

Dobrovic fired. The bullet smashed chips from sheltering stone. The major, with due regard for the stock of reserve ammunition, indulged in the luxury of a single response. Dobrovic's rifle, cocked over stone, was blasted from his hands. His yelling curse was like a scream. James, in new admiration for such shooting, patted the major's arm.

'Admirable day for the Scots, James. Waterloo. Thunderous. And old Blucher and his Prussians, eh? Formidable, the Prussians. Confidentially, never argue with one. Very proud and sensitive men. I'm from Hesse myself. Had one idiot challenge me ten years ago. Not being an idiot myself I insisted that the choice of weapons was mine. Chose rifles. At a hundred paces. Took his regimental helmet clean off. Hope you don't think I'm bragging, my dear chap.'

'I might have, half an hour ago, but not now,' said James.

The sound of another rifle cracked and sang. A bullet hit the ground to their right. James turned his head, the major trained his eye. There were men moving along the foothills on the other side of the river.

'Flanking party?' The major seemed interested but not perturbed.

'I think they probably belong to Avriarches, the big chap,' said James, 'and I suppose that could be their idea, to pass us, cross the river and then come up behind us.'

'Not a great problem,' said the major. 'May I suggest, James, that you watch our pained friends and I'll watch our new ones?'

He shifted his position to cover their flank. Bullets suddenly began to whistle around their bastion. The major, well aware it was covering fire, kept his head down and his eyes trained, watching the moving men as they negotiated the rocky foothills quickly and nimbly. He spotted one man on the hill itself, squeezed on a ledge, a rifle aimed.

'Keep down, James, he's looking for heads.'

James sank lower. At least they were unlikely to be rushed by the crippled band, and one could take one's eye off them from time to time. As he depressed his body a bullet screamed over his shoulder. The major fired as the man on the ledge jerked in the next cartridge. The man visibly shuddered and he lay groaning and perilously perched. The major resighted and as the first of the line of moving men reached a point directly opposite, he took him calmly and precisely. The impact of the bullet had the same effect as a blow. The man thudded backwards. His comrades rushed forward and dragged him into cover. A single man darted to make ground. The Major waited until obstructive rocks fractionally checked the impetus, then, ignoring the covering fire, brought the man to a halt. The black-clad brigand, a gypsy scarf around his head, seemed to stop in surprise and to poise himself for a new dash. Then he slowly spun and fell.

'Major Moeller,' said James, lifting his head, 'you're a damned marvel.'

'So are you, my boy, for providing this spare ammunition,' said the major. 'Might have been tricky without it, though I daresay we could have organized a fighting retreat. What do you say to firing off your revolver? Anywhere will do, except at me. Say about three shots. It'll make a useful noise and keep them all thinking. In any offensive, if you have to stop and think it's the beginning of having to worry.'

James fired three shots at Avriarches and company. Avriarches and company responded with blasphemy and several wild shots of their own. Bullets smacked stone and tore holes in the air. The major chuckled.

'Well done, James.'

'Frankly,' said James, 'I'm getting nervous.'

'Stuff of battle, my boy, healthy nervousness. But it won't be long now, rely on my men. When it's all over I'd be honoured if you'd call on me. I insist. No, damned if I shan't insist first on calling on you and the baronesses in Ilidze, if you'll permit. Best day's sport I've had in years. Capital. Keep down, old chap.'

He let go judicious shots at intervals, penning Avriarches' men across the river with his uncanny accuracy. And when the bandaged Dobrovic tried to crawl away he brought him back with a shot that singed his eyebrows. Angry rifles from the far bank spat in erratic intimidation from time to time, but failed to spoil the major's enjoyment of the engagement or James's cheerful appreciation of his new friend.

It was two hours before Gunther and Herman returned. Baron von Korvacs was with them, so was Carl. Father and son had just got back from one more fruitless search when Anne and Sophie reached the house in Ilidze. Because of Sophie's frantic pleading, the baron and Carl insisted on accompanying Gunther and Herman on their return journey. There were also two large cars full of police who, on arrival, immediately went to work. Avriarches' brigands began a mad scramble back through the foothills and up to the heights. Dobrovic and his two cursing friends, together with the vastly roaring Avriarches, were rounded up and carted off. James and Major Moeller came out of the line, finished the schnapps, greeted the grateful Baron Ernst with a cordiality that made him smile, then returned processionally to Ilidze with the police and the captives.

Sophie, lying on top of her bed, dreamt herself into the nightmare of flight for the hundredth time. For the hundredth time she plummeted into the abyss at the end of a river. For the hundredth time the shock awoke her. She turned, subconscious anxiety dragging at her tired body. She had slept, and for hours, after she had had a hot bath and much-needed food, but she would not get into bed, she was desperate for news of James. Anne had said she would not sleep at all until James got safely back, but she had gone down like one dead.

Sophie, after hours of sleep, was aghast to hear from her mother that James was still not back.

'Mama, I told him – oh, I knew they would get him – '

'He is at the police station,' said the baroness, who had feared the worst and was still in a state of blissful gratitude for the deliverance. 'He's there with Papa and Major Moeller.'

Sophie closed her eyes in the intensity of her relief, then opened them again.

'But why is he there? He's exhausted, starving. What are they doing with him, why should the police want him?' She went on distractedly. Her mother soothed her, made her lie down again, told her to sleep, told her she must sleep. Sophie tried to, a hundred times. It was late evening when she was shocked into one more awakening. The subconscious anxiety leapt after a moment into conscious awareness of voices in the hall below. She sat up. She heard her father.

'Come down again when you have had your bath. Carl and I will wait to eat with you. I think my wife will endeavour to provide you with a banquet. Well, could we do less?'

'Anything will do, sir.' That was James, and sounding so tired. Sophie came to her feet, her heart beating.

James came slowly up the stairs. The long questions, the many questions from the police had drained his elation hours ago. He was left only with the relief of knowing Sophie and Anne were safe, and even that was not quite such a bright light in his exhausted mind now. Unshaven, hollow-eyed, he could not remember precisely where the bathroom was, and that was what he wanted above all other things, a hot cleansing bath. He stood on the rectangular landing, the wide strip of olive-green carpet restful to his eyes. He speculated vaguely. A door opened. He turned. He saw Sophie. She was clad in something white, loose and very soft. Her eyes were dark, emotional, her mouth working.

'Sophie?'

'Oh, James!' She ran and flung herself against him. His response was immediate. He drew her into a warm embrace. After so much terrible worry Sophie slid into bliss. She hid her hot face in his shoulder. 'Oh, I am so glad you are back, but how could you send us away as you did? I have been out of my senses—'

'Dear Sophie,' he said and held her very close. Her warm, agitated body vibrated. 'Are you all right now? Let me look at you.'

'No,' she said muffledly, 'and I am not all right.'

'Why not? Everything has turned out quite well—'

'Well?' She was outraged but still kept her face hidden, still retained blissful contact with him. 'After your awful act of perfidy, sending us away, staying to have those men shoot at you, giving me hours of frantic worry, that isn't well at all. I am still shocked and distracted.'

'Let me see.' He put a hand under her chin and turned her face up. She was a beautiful Sophie, a laundered Sophie, her eyes very soft and looking as newly washed as her shining, flowing hair, her flush a warm, spreading pinkness. 'Yes, as I thought,' he said, conscious of his tired blood quickening because of the pressure of her soft, curving body, 'you are very well, Sophie. I must apologize for being so down at heel myself, but a bath and a shave should work some improvement.'

'No, James, no practical or sensible talk, please. Please?' She looked up at him, her colour deepening. She said breathlessly, 'Oh, if you will not, then I will!' And she wound her arms around his neck and kissed him without shame and in grateful love on his lips. It was not a light, fleeting gesture, it was an emotional, lingering betrayal of her need of him. It evoked warm, firm response which was not only electrifying but which so delighted her that she knew if her parents said she could not have James then she would never have anybody.

'My very sweet Sophie,' said James, and wondered what she would think of life in a Warwickshire cottage with one maid and a single pony and trap.

'You are saying that, you are calling me sweet? Oh, you are everything.' Her breathlessness came from her intense being. 'You were so good – oh, almost magnificent. Anne and I, we are so grateful, we always will be – except that I am much more than grateful, I am exceptionally loving. Oh, is that shameless, for me to say I love you? If it is, I don't think that fair at all, I should not consider you to be shameless if you said you loved me—'

'Oh, Sophie.' He could not resist her, her flushed loveliness, her way with words, and he swept her back into his arms. 'I should not have helped Carl change his wheel that day if I hadn't thought you to be the most beautiful thing I'd ever seen, even behind your motoring veil.'

'James? Oh, be careful, think of what you are saying, it is putting me in danger of my life.'

'Kindly advise me how.'

'How?' Sophie was irrepressible in this, her most delighted moment. 'But, James, you must know how weak we women are. When we are put into unparalleled bliss by the men we love we can die of it.'

'I think,' said James, kissing her chastely on the forehead, 'that before I can even begin to live up to such an unparalleled woman I'll have my bath. That might sharpen me as well as cleaning me. Go to bed. I'll talk to you in the morning.'

'Talk to me?'

'I'll kiss you in the morning.'

'That is better, James, much much better.'

Chapter Nine

Sophie awoke and lay in luxuriating bliss. A maid peeped in. She bobbed, entered and drew back the curtains. Sunlight poured into the bedroom. Sophie felt enriched by delicious comfort, sweet security and future's golden promise. The maid asked if she wanted anything.

Only James, thought Sophie.

'Nothing at the moment, Tica.'

The maid bobbed again and went out. Sophie stretched. She had had a gloriously deep sleep. Oh, the ecstasy of feeling so safe and so clean. Cleanliness today was a physical joy, the soft bed civilized enchantment. No more horrors, no more frightening waters, racked limbs and tortured feet. No more clammy heat or icy coldness.

Only James, who was quite unlike any of her imagined men yet quite irreplaceable now.

Her mother, informed by the maid that Sophie was awake, came in.

'Sophie? How do you feel, darling?'

'Beautiful,' murmured Sophie. Her hair, thickly draping the white pillow, lay richly, cleanly glossy again. Her eyes were slumbrous. 'Mama,' she said, then smiled. 'Mama, I'm so glad to be back with you.'

The baroness bent and kissed her daughter's cheek.

'And we are very glad and very grateful, darling,' she said. 'Would you like a meal sent up?'

'No, I shall get up. When is lunch?'

'Lunch has been served,' smiled the baroness, 'but we did not want to disturb you, we thought it better to let you sleep on.'

Sophie looked at the china clock. It was almost two. Heavens, how she had slept.

'That is the time? Oh, how disgraceful I am. How is Anne?'

'Quite herself again. She's up and about. She's talking her head off to Carl. Mostly about James. We are in debt to James, aren't we?'

'Immensely, Mama. Is he all right?'

'He is not complaining,' smiled the baroness.

Sophie wondered if James had said anything. No, perhaps not. Her mother would have mentioned it. He would speak to her father first. Formally.

'Mama, I was dreadfully scared, you know, especially when Avriarches appeared. I have never thought myself capable of swooning, but Avriarches, oh, he would have made the great Maria Theresa fall from her throne. There he was, a huge man – you have never seen such a monster – and suddenly, before one really had time to swoon, he was on the ground. James had actually upended him. But I shall never look romantically on brigands again.'

'Well, the authorities have him now, darling,' said the baroness soothingly, 'they have them all.'

Sophie was silent for a moment, then said, 'I can't feel sorry for him. He will make a villainous lump on the end of a rope. I suppose,' she added regretfully, 'that to wish him well and truly hanged shows how much such men can reduce one to their own, inhuman level.'

'Sophie,' said the baroness firmly, 'that isn't inhuman of you. It is, as your father says, very advisable to hang the occasional rogue in the interests of the rest of us.'

'Oh, I assure you, it's a lovely relief to have escaped that one,' said Sophie. 'Mama, where is James?'

'With Anne and Carl. He's been asking if he might see you before he goes.'

'Before he goes?' Sophie felt a little shock. 'Goes where?'

'To Sarajevo, with Major Moeller, an extremely pleasant man, to whom we are also very grateful. James says they have some business in Sarajevo and will be gone a day or two.'

'What business? He said nothing to me.'

The baroness regarded her daughter wonderingly.

'Sophie, you're very intense. Aren't you quite recovered? Would you just like to lie quietly?'

'Mama, I am exceptionally recovered,' said

Sophie, 'but I just do not want James going care-lessly off to Sarajevo.'

'Now what am I to understand from that?'

Sophie wanted to say that she was in such a sensitive condition about James that she did not wish to let him out of her sight. Instead she said, 'Mama, would you please tell him I should like to see him?'

'Very well, darling.' The baroness knew what was affecting Sophie. She was suffering from an excess of romantic gratitude. The baroness understood. She had herself suffered deceptive emotions as a girl, imagined herself in love a dozen times for varying reasons. Ernst had not been her romantic ideal when she first met him, and her feeling for him had only been one of affection. But by the time they were married she went into his arms with far more than affection. James was a very likeable man and they would always be in debt to him, but he was not as suitable for Sophie as Ludwig. 'Sophie, has something happened to you and James?'

Sophie's smile was a little unsteady.

'Mama, something has happened to me,' she said, 'and if it hasn't happened to James too you had better pray for me.'

The baroness did not protest or make a speech, she simply said, 'Is it so bad, darling?'

'I've had a sudden thought, Mama. About James. I think it will all depend on what he says to me. Will you please tell him that if he isn't required to go to Sarajevo immediately, I'll be happy to receive him in fifteen minutes?'

The baroness, affected by Sophie's obvious emotion, lightly touched her and said, 'I'll tell him now, darling.'

The maid went to fetch James twenty minutes later. Sophie received him in her room. Twenty minutes had not given her quite as much time as she would have liked, but there was really little more she could have done to better what she had accomplished, for she presented herself to him as an exquisite bloom of summer. She was slenderly, curvingly lovely in pale yellow. It set off the burnished brilliance of her chestnut hair and graced the aristocratic elegance of her form. She wished most desperately, after two days of feeling herself a dishevelled mess, to have James see her at her best. All the same, considering what was in her mind, it might have been a mistake, for to James she had an air of richness which somehow escapes those who may acquire wealth but are not born to it.

'Sophie, how beautiful,' he said. He took her hand and Sophie stared in almost horrified dismay as he lifted it and kissed it.

'What are you doing?' she said.

'Paying my tribute to a lovely Sophie.'

'Oh, are you indeed? I am thrilled,' said Sophie, loving him despite her dismay because he was so darkly cool – and to her new eyes – devilishly attractive. She looked at her slim fingers. 'My hand is very thrilled. But what is wrong with my face? Am I haggard? Are my eyes crossed? Has my nose taken a crooked turn? Have my teeth dropped out? You look very refreshed yourself, and not at all repellent. Well, if I am no longer quite the most beautiful thing you have ever seen you must close your eyes, because if you will not kiss properly again, then I must.' And she kissed him. It was a brief, almost angry kiss, but it destroyed James's cautious front. He put his lips very decisively to hers and kissed her so warmly and positively that her dismay vanished and she shut her eyes tight to hold back sudden tears of intense relief.

'James, oh, I thought – oh, I haven't turned into a frog, have I? You did kiss me last night and say sweet things, didn't you?' Her eyes were dark with appeal. 'I assure you, I am just the same today, only more so. That is, I am more exceptionally loving, and if you go to Sarajevo and don't come back until tomorrow that is twenty-four hours for me of not being alive. James, do you understand what I'm saying?'

James considered her with the seriousness of a man who knew that her striking fascination was presenting him with his greatest problem.

'I understand what I feel about you,' he said. 'On top of being irresistibly lovely, you're given to the kind of talk I can't listen to without realizing life could be very silent and empty for me if you weren't there. However, my lovely Sophie—'

'Oh, more of that, please.'

'However, my very sweet Sophie, much as I love you, and have done ever since you put back your veil, we must be practical—'

'Never,' breathed Sophie, 'never. I know what

being practical means to you. It means doing something which is going to upset me. I am not really disposed to cry about things but I am near to unleashing an ocean of tears this very moment.' He was not sure whether she meant this or was just using words, except that underlying vibrations were making her voice unsteady. 'I beg you, James, please don't say we must be practical, because in this case I know it means you are going to find reasons why you should not propose to me. You are going to say you can't afford me.'

He shook his head, caught halfway between a smile and a sigh.

'Sophie, my father will pay me a very good salary. More than that if I have a wife to keep. But I could give you little of what you're used to, what you're entitled to. We're not great landowners. You must realize—'

'No,' said Sophie passionately, 'no!'

'Sophie—'

'No. I won't accept your argument. It is so horrifyingly old-fashioned it would make some young ladies swoon.' Sophie was flushed and emotionally purposeful. 'No, I will not accept that at all. But I will accept your proposal. I wish to be proposed to. If you refuse, then I shall propose to you, and if you think that shockingly forward of me you only have yourself to blame. And if you turn me down I shall enter a convent.'

In the bright, sunlit room James eyed his glowing, dramatizing love a little hopelessly.

'Sophie, be serious.'

'You think I am not? I am very serious,' she said intensely. 'If you don't wish me to be your wife I shall become a bride of Christ. That is how nuns are looked upon in some orders, I believe.'

'Well, just look here,' said James, putting his hands firmly on her shoulders, 'there would only be one servant, two at the most, and a pony and trap – although a motor car would be no problem if you preferred—'

'All that? For me? I would have all that and you as well?' Sophie's emotion burst into delight. 'We should not have to live in a garret and exist on dry crusts? Then what is there to be so old-fashioned and practical about? Do you think I want a hundred mansions and a thousand servants? You do not know your Sophie, and I am your Sophie. You saved me from Avriarches and therefore you must claim me. James, do you have feelings and needs and desires? I do.'

'So do I, and they all concern you.'

She pressed herself close to him, her body trembling.

'Then please propose to me and marry me quickly.'

'You know I must first speak to your father,' he said, 'I want your parents to be happy about this.'

'Your responsibility is to make me happy, not my parents. Oh, this is quite frightening. My feelings, I mean. I am already thinking—'

'What are you already thinking?'

'That in between nursing our children I shall be able to sit in the garden and write some poetry.

We shall have a little garden too, won't we? Of course, I should not make that a condition, only a negotiating point—'

'We'll discuss all that,' said James with advisable gravity. 'I think we can work it all out. But I have to go to Sarajevo now. We didn't net Ferenac. He slipped us. As I know him so well the police think I can help to find him. I'll be back tomorrow or the day after and I'll see you then. I must see you then. Doing without you for a day or so is as much as I can manage.'

Sophie kissed him with warm passion.

'James, saying things like that is much lovelier than kissing my hand.'

'You will be careful, won't you?' said Anne. With Carl she was saying au revoir to James as they walked over the sanded drive to the gate. He was going to see the Austrian authorities in Sarajevo, and Major Moeller, hoping for more sport, was accompanying him. Baron von Korvacs, alarmed by the significance of James's story, had departed for Sarajevo earlier.

'Recently,' said James, 'I think I've learned to be very careful.'

'I can't comment on that,' said Carl, 'but I think you're a damned good friend, James. The police have located the Benz, by the way. Found it tucked into some woods this morning.'

'Oh, yes.' James smiled. 'I'm afraid the Benz slipped my memory a bit.' He looked at his watch. 'I really must go now.'

'Find that man quickly,' said Anne, 'and come

back to us soon. We don't feel quite complete without you now— Oh, who is that arriving?'

A cab drew up outside the house. Ludwig stepped out. He smiled and waved. They went out to him as the cabbie unstrapped his luggage.

'Oh, Ludwig, how good to see you,' said Anne, 'we can do with you.'

'Managed it earlier than I thought,' said Ludwig cheerfully. 'Sent your dear mama a telegram. Hope I'm not unexpected. James. Carl.' He nodded to each of them in his friendly way.

'Mama didn't mention it,' said Anne, 'but things have been happening. I'll tell you about them. Oh, thank you for coming.'

She felt happy as she looked at him. He seemed so debonair, so fresh, so much more the handsome, outgoing man than the dark brooding figures of her nightmare. Ludwig would never hurt her, never consider wrongs could be righted by tossing bombs that would injure the innocent. His eyes were laughing, his smile expressive of his pleasure at seeing her.

'My dear Anne, I'm delighted to be here,' he said.

'So am I,' said Anne, 'and I am going to monopolize you because James has to go to Sarajevo and Sophie is—' She stopped, glanced at James.

'Ah, yes,' said James.

Chapter Ten

Sarajevo. 28 June 1914. Sunshine, bunting, colour, crowds and the Archduke Franz Ferdinand.

The royal procession of motor cars had begun the journey to the city hall, where an address of welcome was to be given. The archduke and his wife were in the second car, a grey tourer flying the Habsburg pennant. Opposite them sat General Potiorek, Governor of Bosnia. The hood of the car was folded down to permit the cheering Sarajevo citizens a fine view of their distinguished visitors. It also allowed the conspirators to see their target.

They were seven. Among them were the three on whom the Black Hand pinned their happiest hopes. Cabrinovic, Grabez and Princip. All seven young men were positioned at different points along the Appel Quay, the processional route to the city hall.

An eighth man, a more independent and vainglorious assassin, sat up in the hills with the brigands of the captured Avriarches. He sat in fuming frustration, but he was not disposed to come down, for a Briton and two Austrian girls had eluded him and his cover was blown. Nor were the brigands disposed to part with him. He was, they said, as much responsible for the capture of their chief as anyone. They would see what happened to Avriarches before letting Boris Ferenac leave them. Since Avriarches was due to be hanged, Boris Ferenac would never know glory, only an unpleasant and premature death.

Flags waved as the archduke's motorcade entered the Appel Quay. In truth, the Bosnians were by no means as opposed to Austrian rule as the Serbians wished, and the Moslem population preferred an Austrian administration to the possibility of a Serbian one.

The conspirator first in line was a youth called Muhamed Mehmedbasic. He had all the hot desire of youth to destroy a tyrant, but not the nerve, and when the archduke's car drew level with him he did nothing but rigidly gape.

Cabrinovic, next in line a little farther on, was made of more fiery stuff. He had boasted, and loudly, that all he needed was opportunity. It came. He drew the prepared bomb from his pocket and struck the percussion cap against a lamp post. He took careful aim, the archduke's colourful helmet an emblazoned 12 o'clock point, and threw the bomb. But the driver of the ducal car had heard the sharp clear sound of percussion cap striking lamp post, and instinctively put his foot hard down on the accelerator as the bomb flew. It landed not in Franz Ferdinand's lap, it struck his gloved fingers as, seeing it coming, he threw up his hand to protect his wife. Deflected, the bomb hit the folded roof of the tourer and bounced into the road.

It roared into explosion, injured a dozen spectators and two men and a lady-in-waiting in the following car. The archduke was unhurt, although his wife sustained a minor scratch on her cheek as splinters flew.

The motorcade stopped. Confusion, loud and clamorous, came out of stunned silence. Cabrinovic, passionate with a sense of failure, swallowed a cyanide tablet. It was impotent from age and did him little harm. He leapt into the river. The water was extremely low and he lay in little more than a trickle. Four men, including a policeman and a plain-clothes detective, went in after him. One or two kicks were aimed at him before they pulled him out and hauled him off to the police station.

Franz Ferdinand, after making considerate enquiries about the injured, resumed his journey. His car sped past all other conspirators, and even Princip and Grabez were too confused by the sound of the bomb and their ignorance of the consequences to do anything but watch the archduke, very much alive, flash by. At the city hall Franz Ferdinand expressed himself angrily to the mayor, Fehim Effendi Curcic.

'Herr Mayor, one comes here for a visit and is received with bombs. It is outrageous.'

And having said that he composed himself and requested the mayor to proceed with the loyal address of welcome.

About this time James and Major Moeller had managed to divorce themselves from the confusion in Appel Quay. They had been looking for Ferenac and the unknown quantity represented by any other men with similar motives to his in mind. The Austrian authorities in Sarajevo had received James's story with interest, having been alerted by Baron von Korvacs. Uniformed police were everywhere, lining the route, and plain-clothes detectives were wandering keenly about. No one had been able to stop Cabrinovic throwing his bomb, but that did not mean others of his kind should be given the chance. Sarajevo was indignant at the attempt on the archduke's life, and as the police brought order out of confusion the anger continued as a loud buzz.

'Damnably close thing, James,' said Major Moeller, 'but it wasn't your friend Ferenac.'

'No,' said James.

'Is that it, do you think? An attempt, a miss, and peace for the rest of the day?'

'Damned if I know,' said James. It wasn't his cause, or the major's, but they felt involved. 'The fact is I've been as uneasy as a woman about it all since I first met Ferenac, and my intuition won't let it go away. I feel a sense of doom, and that's an old woman's feeling.'

'Well, my young friend, apart from Ferenac, who I feel must have done the wiser thing and gone home to his mother,' said the major, 'what are we looking for? More people like him? A furtive face, the shape of a bomb, an unshaven desperado or what?'

'Damned if I know,' said James again, looking around at people standing and people passing.

'Damned if I do, either,' said the major. 'Assassins, I suppose, try to look like ordinary people.'

'I wish they'd act like them. I'm at a high time of my life, I'd rather like peace, perfect peace.'

They began to walk, moving along the Appel Quay near the Lateiner Bridge, then turning into Franz Josef Street, Sarajevo's elegant shopping thoroughfare. They scanned faces. James felt their search was impossible. Instinctively he was looking for men with the same characteristics as Ferenac, men with secrets in their eyes, dark soulful men. He saw only people, all of whom wore an air of festivity for the day or concern for near tragedy. They were not people who seemed hostile to the formidable archduke, a more far-seeing man than Vienna gave him credit for. Perhaps under the eyes of the Austrian authorities the people of Sarajevo had learned to smile on all the right occasions, or perhaps they felt that Franz Ferdinand was sympathetic to the cause of self-determination for Bosnia. Serbia resented the Austrian occupation of the country, but the Bosnians of Sarajevo had flags and bunting out.

'It's a beautiful day,' observed the major, neat in a light grey suit, 'but the sport's a little more elusive. By God, I thought the police in Ilidze would never let us go.'

'What do you suppose we'll get, a reprimand or a reward?' smiled James.

The major chuckled and said, 'Either is worth the sport we had. I'm damned pleased to have made your acquaintance, I must say.'

'Mutual, I assure you,' said James, scanning more faces, 'especially when I remember the schnapps.'

'Kept us warm company, what?'

James looked as an elegant woman passed him. He thought of Sophie, so irresistible in her summer colour and her enterprising little turns of speech. She would always be able to talk him into some things and out of others. Well, he had made up his mind to propose to her, and his only obstacle now would be her parents. They would naturally want Sophie to marry one of her own kind. An aristocrat. Preferably an Austrian aristocrat.

He moved up and down the street with Major Moeller. It was lined with police and people, for the archduke's return route would take in Franz Josef Street. That, at least, had been the original intention. But because of Cabrinovic's bomb attempt this had been changed and the motorcade would proceed straight back along the Appel Quay. The public were not aware of this, nor the police, and so they lined Franz Josef Street in anticipation of seeing the archduke and his wife.

Major Moeller eyed a lady or two with a gentleman's interest and a man's appreciation. It relieved the unrewarding work of trying to spot would-be assassins. James eyed almost everyone he passed, although he realized, Ferenac apart, that he was unlikely to distinguish an anarchist from a municipal clerk. He did not have a policeman's nose or instinct for such work.

They heard some cheering, much of it sympathetic. Spectators visibly stirred. The archduke's procession, led by the mayor's car, was turning into Franz Josef Street. And Trifko Grabez, one of the three most promising conspirators, had just suffered a complete failure of his nerve. At the first bridge the archduke reached from the city hall, the Kaiser Bridge, Grabez stood in numb incompetence and let the car go by. He retired in a mood of maudlin self-disillusionment.

James saw the first car, the mayor's, enter Franz Josef Street. In a moment of confusion the driver had followed the original route, making this right turn instead of taking the rearranged route straight along the Appel Quay. Franz Ferdinand's car made the same turn in the wake of the mayor's car, for the archduke's chauffeur had not been informed of the changed plan. James watched. The royal car was not far away, a uniformed officer standing guard on the running board. He saw the archduke, in plumed helmet and white jacket, his wife in shimmering white by his side. Franz Ferdinand sat in broad, soldierly compactness. His wife, the Duchess of Hohenberg, though still shaken by the bomb incident, was smiling in response to the sympathetic cheers.

The car suddenly stopped as General Potiorek called the chauffeur's attention to the fact that a mistake had been made. It was a mistake that was to cost Austria her empire and Europe over eight million lives. The chauffeur began a reverse turn. Outside Schiller's well-known food shop, on the corner of the street, stood Gavrilo Princip, the last major hope of the Black Hand. The slowly reversing car came directly into line with him. James saw the young man step forward, and his long-lying uneasiness leapt into a full-blooded certainty that tragedy was imminent. He pushed forward but was blocked by spectators and police, and Princip, redeeming the failure of confederates, entered history. At a distance of no more than six feet he drew his revolver and fired twice. The shots were barely heard above the noise of the crowds. Franz Ferdinand, a bullet in his neck, continued to sit majestically and aloofly upright. His wife, a bullet in her stomach, also gave no immediate indication that she had been hit. General Potiorek was certain both shots had missed, since there was this entire absence of reaction from the royal couple. Princip was whirling about in a melee of enraged onlookers, and while this went on a brief examination was made of the apparently unharmed archduke and duchess. Nothing seemed amiss, but Potiorek ordered an immediate return to his official residence. Just as the car turned to proceed over the Lateiner Bridge the archduke's mouth spilled blood. His wife cried out and sank to her knees. Potiorek, violently alarmed, shouted at the driver to make all possible speed.

The police pulled Princip out of the hands of

citizens threatening to suffocate him or beat him to death. He was manhandled to the station, green with sickness, for he too had swallowed an aged cyanide tablet. He suffered no more than this sickness and some bruises. But Franz Ferdinand and his duchess were both dead half an hour later.

James and Major Moeller sat long in shock at a café table, silently aware of Sarajevo in panic, sorrow, mortification and anger. Shouts, cries and running people spoke of citizens conducting their own searches for anarchists.

In Belgrade, Colonel Dimitrijevic received Major Tankosic. The congratulations were sincere and mutual. Major Tankosic went to church later.

The assassination shocked Austria but did not intimidate her. The emperor, who had survived far greater tragedies, took the demise of Franz Ferdinand almost philosophically. The seven conspirators were rounded up. Under interrogation some of them were unable to conceal the Serbian origins of the plot. Accordingly the Austrian Foreign Minister. Count Berchtold, proceeded on the basis that the Serbian government was implicated.

Franz Ferdinand and his wife were unobtrusively buried at the dead of a rainy night, leaving Vienna in a state of mourning but not of grief for the unfortunate heir apparent. The archduke had not been one of the most popular Habsburgs. The capital spent one subdued night and then resumed its air of untroubled summer.

The new heir, Charles, was a likeable young man with a lovely wife. The emperor much preferred Charles. So what was there to mope about? There were always Habsburgs to spare.

The soft warm nights were beautiful, the lights radiant, the dance halls full and *The Merry Widow* playing to packed houses.

And the von Korvacs family, having abruptly cut their holiday short, were in residence again at their house in the Salesianergasse.

Chapter Eleven

Baron and Baroness von Korvacs had been shocked and grieved by the tragedy of Sarajevo. Back in Vienna they found it hard to hide their feelings, to re-enter the pleasurable diversities of their everyday life, and there was a quietness within the house for several days. Ludwig called after two days, apologizing for intruding on the family at this time but wishing to enquire after the health of Anne and Sophie. He was unable, in fact, to stay away longer from Anne. He had finally discovered it was Anne who engaged his serious affections and, as he had once declared to Sophie, such discovery must be followed by a vigorous pressing of his suit.

Major Moeller, who had also returned to Vienna, paid a courtesy call after four days. He came to see how the delightful young baronesses were after their shattering experience and to talk to the family again about the fateful moment in Sarajevo, when he and James had been close enough to see the shots fired.

'James always knew that something dreadful was going to happen,' said Anne.

'He did his best,' said the major, enjoying an aperitif, 'he passed on all the information he could to the police in Ilidze and the authorities in Sarajevo. It all pointed to a positive attempt on the archduke's life, but when rogues and villains are as fanatical as this bunch were, all the vigilance in the world can be set aside by the momentary freakishness of fate. If the archduke's car hadn't stopped, if there had been people close to Princip at that time – well, it is all if, if.'

'Poor Franz Ferdinand,' said Anne, 'I'm sure he meant to do so well.'

'Infernally hard on the emperor,' said Carl, 'he has had damned bad luck at times.'

'He will survive it,' said the baroness confidently, 'as he has survived other misfortunes.'

Sophie, standing at the drawing-room windows, suddenly entered the lists after a period of unusual quiet from her. She said, 'I presume James has survived whatever misfortunes he has encountered since he returned with us? Or does anyone know if he has gone off in search of other maidens in distress?'

This little burst of bitterness was so unlike Sophie that it produced a slightly shocked silence. Carl, standing near her, looked hard at her.

'It's not like you to be as ungenerous as that, Sophie,' he said.

She turned away, looking out at the gardens bright with the colours of summer. Carl, puzzled and curious, moved closer and peered at her. He was startled to see the glitter of tears. Sophie never shed tears, she could always deal with the ups and downs of life without resorting to a moist lament. It did not take him more than a second or two to understand. Sophie, previously so blithe and fancy-free, had fallen hard. Her predilection for James had been the most obvious thing about her recently. And she had seen nothing of him for days.

'Oh, that's all right, Sophie,' he murmured and squeezed her arm. She cast him a grateful but unsteady smile.

The baroness, aware of the upset aside, said lightly to Major Moeller, 'What is James doing these days, do you know?'

'Oh, we've met a couple of times. He draws and I jaw.' The major smiled. 'Can't get him interested in fishing, though. Nor in shooting. Pity. He has an aptitude for good sport, you know, but is shockingly lazy about it.'

'Not all the time,' said Anne. She glanced at Sophie. Sophie still had her back turned. 'But he's getting a little forgetful, isn't he? He promised to call.'

'Perhaps,' said Sophie, sounding a long way off, 'he's moving in more artistic circles.'

'James?' said the major. 'I hope not. That's certain death to any sportsman.'

The baroness found Sophie sitting in the garden later, a book in her lap.

'Sophie,' she said, 'Anne and Ludwig are going to drive out with Carl. Wouldn't you like to join them?'

'I don't think so, Mama,' said Sophie, 'I'm not really very good company at the moment.'

'It's been one thing and another, hasn't it?' The baroness was lightly sympathetic. Sophie did not look up. That caused a little inquisitive concern in her mother. The baroness, grateful to life and Ernst and providence for giving her three children quite matchless, would have gladly taken on the heartaches of all of them. But she always trod as tactfully and carefully as she could. She knew she must be particularly careful with Sophie, whom she felt to be the most intelligent of her children and yet the most sensitive. It was not like Sophie to suffer depression, however, or moods. She was equable where Anne was ebullient, and she warmed to life in her intense appreciation of it as Anne sparkled in her uninhibited enjoyment of it. 'Yes, one thing and another, darling.'

'Mama,' said Sophie in a suppressed voice, 'I'm quite recovered from one thing and another. I'm simply in the throes of a new ordeal, and I'm not enduring it at all well.'

The baroness, quite aware now of what was wrong, said gently, 'It's James, isn't it?'

Sophie smoothed the fluttering pages of her book and said, 'Mama, why doesn't he call? Ludwig has been every day, and Major Moeller, who is quite a new friend, has taken the trouble to come and see us. Wouldn't you think James would too? He isn't throwing us over, is he?'

'Throwing us over?' The baroness was slightly astonished. 'But I thought you and

James— Darling, I don't wish to interfere or jump to conclusions or ask the wrong questions, but I did infer from what you said at Ilidze that you and he were coming to an understanding. Was I mistaken?'

'I have a very worried feeling that I was, that I heard things he didn't really say. Oh, why doesn't he come and see me?'

'Shall I send him a note and ask him to call?' suggested the baroness.

'No.' Sophie looked up then. Uncertainty had diminished her elan but not her pride. 'Mama, he must call without being begged or persuaded.'

What have I done, she thought distractedly, that he doesn't?

James, in fact, knowing that the archduke's murder had deeply affected the von Korvacs and given the baron some official worries, had simply decided not to intrude on the family for a while. In any case, he needed a few days to think long and hard about marriage to Sophie. Yet for all the attention he gave to the ifs and buts, he knew he had already made up his mind to do what she had asked him to. Propose to her. Sophie, despite considering herself modern, still wanted a formal proposal. But did she genuinely understand that her horizons as his wife would not be the limitless ones they were now, when she had the world at her feet? She was quite lovely, she was creative, and she was blessed with wheedling voice magic. And the world did come to Vienna. It did not come to Warwickshire. Warwickshire, by comparison with Vienna, would be parochial.

He thought about it. He still had his room at the École Internationale, for Maude insisted he was more than welcome to it for as long as it suited him. She enjoyed his company, his presence at mealtimes and during the relaxing quietness of the evenings. Over lunch one day they discussed the Sarajevo tragedy and its possible repercussions. Maude, widow of a diplomat, had her ear instinctively to the ground, as well as friends in the service, and she frankly did not like what she heard about the belligerent nature of Count Berchtold's attitude.

'I think he means to accuse the Serbian government of being the instigators of the plot,' she said, 'I think he means to denounce Serbia and break her. Serbia, you see, has ambitions concerning Bosnia and Herzegovina, which are provinces of the Austrian empire. That makes Serbia a thorn in the flesh of Austria. Count Berchtold wants to remove that thorn, to destroy it. If he convinces the emperor that this can only be done by making war on Serbia, the consequences might be far more serious than he seems to think.'

'Why?' asked James.

'Why? My dear James,' said Maude, 'aren't you aware that the Russians consider themselves the protectors of all Slav peoples? If Austria does go to war with Serbia, Russia will go to war with Austria. The Germans won't stand aside from that. Their Kaiser has made that quite clear. They'll declare war on Russia. Russia has a pact with France. James, the whole thing could escalate in the most frightful way.'

'Austria at war?' James felt appalled. He saw Carl going off to fight and Sophie as a Red Cross nurse. 'That's madness. Madness can happen among lunatics, but not among nations. Can it? Not in this day and age, surely.'

But he knew one of the reasons why Baron von Korvacs had left Ilidze so abruptly was because he had been urgently needed back at his desk in the Foreign Ministry, which was in a state of outraged determination to bring Serbia to the whipping post. Kaiser Wilhelm of Germany had stoked the fires by assuring the Austrians he would support whatever actions they took against the anarchistic regime in Belgrade. Wilhelm had a particularly hostile eye for people who did not regard royal beings as sacred as divine ones.

'Well, it may not come to that,' said Maude, 'it will depend on what reparations Serbia agrees to make.'

The telephone rang in her office. She went to answer it. She returned to say that a lady, who would not give her name, wished to speak to James. James took the call.

'Hello?'

'I am speaking to James?' The voice was cool and unmistakable.

'Why, Sophie, how nice. How are you, how is everyone?'

'We are all alive, thank you.' Little vibrations

murmured through the coolness. 'May I ask what has happened to you? It's five days since you returned with us.'

'I've been quietly sitting things out. I thought your parents needed some quietness too, I know they were in a state of shock—'

'We all were. But we are still existing. You are very kind to think of us as being sensitively withdrawn from life, but you are also very cruel. I too have been sitting quietly, very quietly, wondering what was happening and what I had done. You have not called once, not once. Or telephoned or sent a single note. Major Moeller has called and so has Ludwig. He and Anne are beginning to hold hands. I am not asking for my hand to be held, only wondering why I feel so alone.'

'Sophie, I had to do some serious thinking, but I was intending—'

'Please don't interrupt.' The vibrations were uppermost now. 'I wish to tell you I'm not given to chasing after elusive or reluctant gentlemen and that I am only making this telephone enquiry because I thought the reason for your silence and absence was that you were either dying or at least desperately ill.'

'My very sweet Sophie—'

'As you are obviously perfectly well,' continued the vibrations, 'I presume you will suffer no painful physical distress in summoning a cab and getting yourself into it. And instructing the driver to bring you to this house. I will allow you one hour. Even the slowest cab should bring the most reluctant gentleman here in that time.'

'I assure you, Sophie, I shall—'

'You are to call on me. Now. At once. Immediately. You are a perfidious wretch and I am very unhappy.'

The line went dead. James looked at the silent receiver, smiled and placed it back on the hook. Sophie. Nature fashioned many women in irresistible moulds, much to man's confusion. It did not fashion too many quite as irresistible as Sophie. He had perhaps overdone things in staying away as long as this. But he had not wanted to seek a highly personal interview with the baron at a time when the assassination was still so fresh in that worried mind.

Well, he must go and see his unhappy Sophie immediately.

The telephone rang again as he was leaving the office. He returned to the desk.

'Hello?'

The voice came to his ear with a little desperate rush this time.

'James? Oh, thank goodness you are still there. What must you think of me? I was so ungracious and have hastened madly to call you back so that you should not have too much time to think about what a dreadful person I am. Please forgive me. Only I've been in such a dismal state. It seemed as if you had completely disappeared from our lives, and I began to think you had forgotten all about me or that I was an ungovernable embarrassment to you.'

'Ungovernable?' Her command of his language was delicious.

'Yes. I could not endure that. But I did not mean to be so dreadfully superior—'

'My sweet girl, you were superb,' said James. 'I've stayed away longer than I should, I know that now, but you weren't ungracious, no, not a bit. I'd say illuminating, rather. I was spellbound. I can listen to you for hours. I'm coming over now. Immediately. I've missed you. No one is quite like you. Believe me.'

'James, oh, that is so good to hear. Yes, please come at once. I am like a starved woman. And you have things to say, haven't you?'

'Yes. If you don't confuse me.'

Sophie bumped into Carl on her way upstairs to change.

'Sophie?' he said and felt distinctly relieved to see her glad smile. Sophie was a bright challenge to life and he hated seeing her down in the dumps.

'I must change, James is coming,' she said and hitched her skirts and flew.

'My dear girl—'

'My dear boy—' Her voice floated and sang.

James, thought Carl, would get a stunner, a shining light. Somewhere, perhaps, there was a stunner like Sophie belonging to another family. If so, he would like to meet her. She might take his mind off the Benz. His mother had recently made the observation that a man who was married to a motor car would not get very much out of life except fresh coats of oil.

'I'll look around,' he had said amiably,

'I might find a girl who'd make me a good mechanic.'

But a stunner, with something of Sophie's style about her, would please his mother far more and might just be more exciting than a mechanic.

'James is coming, Mama.'

'He's sent a note?'

'No, he spoke to me a little while ago on the telephone.'

'I didn't hear it ring.'

'Well, as the call wasn't for you its ring was not significant, and none of us can expect to hear everything when there's always so much other listening to do, and I think you were in the garden at the time. However, it was James I spoke to—'

'Darling, I haven't been in the garden.'

' – and it seems he's only been staying away because he felt you would not want too many people coming and going at the moment. That was kind and thoughtful of him, wasn't it?'

'You didn't think so yesterday.'

'I hadn't quite recovered from my ordeal.'

'Which ordeal, darling?'

'Oh, I'm better now, Mama, and am ready to receive James. Do I look suitably outfitted?'

'You look very nice and fresh.'

'I'd like to receive James in the library, then we shouldn't interfere with any other comings and goings.'

'I don't think we're quite like a railway station

246

at any time, and you're welcome to receive him in the morning room, if you wish.'

'The library would suit James better. It has a rather attractive masculine atmosphere. He'll be more at home there.'

'More at home? Sophie, I am hopelessly mystified. Do you have an understanding with James or not?'

'I have an understanding with him, I'm praying he has one with me. If you are hopelessly mystified, Mama, I am hopelessly committed. My pulse rate is alarming. And it's no good expecting anything to develop between Ludwig and me, is it? He's in love with Anne, you know.'

The library, with its walls of books and its brown leather chairs, had an air of cultured quiet. Sophie in a simple white blouse and dark green skirt was very much in keeping. As James was ushered in she turned, a book in her hands, the smile on her face masking the state of her jumping nerves. James in a brown jacket and cream ducks looked splendidly casual, she thought. She hoped he would see her, in the setting of the library, as a young woman of highly desirable grace and modesty whom he would feel quite able to afford as a wife. James actually saw her in a new style of elegance but in a quieter frame.

'James, you are really here?' Her poise was one of admirable calm, considering the pulse rate. 'I am aglow with relief.' She put the book back on its shelf and with a sweet smile extended her hand.

James saw through that at once. The ploy was one that dared him to take her hand and kiss it. Ludwig frequently kissed her fingertips. So did most of her admirers. Sophie was challenging him to declare himself a mere admirer or her faithful lover.

'My dear Sophie,' he said, and took her hand and kissed it. A little spark of fire flashed. 'And my very sweet Sophie.' He drew her into his arms, smiled into her wide-open eyes and kissed her lingeringly on the lips. That put out one fire but ignited another. Her pulse rate soared and she found it difficult to get her breath. Her anxieties and uncertainties flew. James was kissing her and in such a fashion that modesty flew too. She clung in abandoned response. Discovering her mouth he investigated it, pursued it and claimed it. Sophie closed her eyes and quite lost all breath. Was this a kiss? No, it was a sweet, imaginative communication between lovers, a beautiful meeting of long-lost lips. Five days, a whole five days. And, suddenly, all was poetry.

'Oh,' she gasped when he finally released her.

'Oh?' said James quizzically.

'I am quite faint.' But she was gloriously, breathlessly alive, her blood racing.

'If you fall,' he said, 'I shall fall with you.'

She could not unwind her arms but she felt herself capable of delivering a characteristic little homily. It helped her to recover herself somewhat.

'James,' she said, 'love can be very painful, you know, when one is at the mercy of a man who doesn't cross one's threshold for a year. Five days is almost a year. Well, long enough at least to have made me grow sufferingly thin.'

'Thin? It's not apparent,' said James, speaking from a position of telling proximity.

She would have liked to ask him to enlarge on that remark but they were not married yet, they were not even engaged, and certain avenues of conversation were closed to them by convention. She chose a path of penitence instead.

'James, I'm sorry I was so cross with you on the telephone, but I have had a bad time not seeing you, not knowing about you. I thought such depressing things, I thought perhaps I'd only imagined we had kissed and spoken together, that it was Anne you really love. You have always been so attentive to her. But you would not kiss me like that if you loved her, would you?'

'I'm very fond of Anne, but I think Ludwig is her man.'

'Oh, it's a sweet relief to know you aren't.' She put her hands on his jacket and began twisting a button. 'You will forgive me being so difficult and demanding, won't you?'

'Difficult?' said James, who thought her the captivating symbol of Vienna's enchantment.

'Yes. But five days really did seem an eternity and I began to think I'd been too forward, had flung myself at you.' She searched the button intently for possible faults, her face flushed, her lashes hiding her eyes. 'But you see, when you made me go with Major Moeller's servants while you stayed to wait for Ferenac and his men, I was frantic with worry and despair. I thought it was so dangerous and unnecessary after all you had done, and when you got back to us at last and I saw you – James, I couldn't help flinging myself at you, I was so terribly happy, but if you feel—'

'Sophie, you make even the little things sound monumentally striking. Will you marry me?'

'—I mean, I've been thinking, you see, that if you don't really feel—' She stopped her rush of words. 'James, what did you say?'

'Will you marry me?'

'Oh.' Sophie came out of breathless agitation and emerged from hiding. Her eyes swam in the warm waters of summer lakes. 'James?' she said, which meant she was asking for confirmation yet again, which was no less than any woman was entitled to or would want on such an occasion.

'Will you, Sophie sweet?' James in his insistence was compulsively obliging.

She flung herself back into his arms. She hid herself again. Sophie, for all her ability to meet ups and downs with composure, felt emotions that were devastatingly weakening.

'Sophie, am I to have no answer?'

'You are proposing to me, you are really proposing?' She came faintly from the depths.

'I think I've just proposed twice at least,' said James, wondering if he would ever have known what light and beauty and laughter meant had he not taken a year's sabbatical.

'Oh, you have saved me from an existence of gloom and misery,' said Sophie, and lifted her face to show him glowing light and laughter. 'Is it in order for me not to worry any more? Not to think about entering a convent? We are firmly engaged? We will marry?'

'When I've spoken to your father and informed my parents, we'll arrange a date. Will that do, Sophie?'

'Oh, it will do beautifully,' said Sophie, 'and it isn't painful at all now.'

'What isn't?'

'Loving you,' said Sophie.

Anne and Carl were delighted. Anne said that to have in the family the man who had upended Avriarches was quite the most historic thing the family had done. Carl said the Benz would profit too. Carl felt keenly appreciative of the match, for he was sure Sophie had committed herself heart and soul. That, unless James was fully alive to it, could be almost tormenting to someone as intelligent and independent as Sophie.

Carl wondered what it was about the demon of love that it had such an unpredictable effect on people. Sophie had surveyed the arena of life and made James her champion. On James that mantle now rested and Sophie would expect him to wear it bravely, proudly and unequivocally on her behalf.

A motor car, thought Carl, had its complications but providing you were reasonably good to it, it never became as unmanageable as people. Certainly it was never incomprehensible, as women were.

The baroness did not try to talk Sophie out

of the match. Sophie was desperately in love. She was not concerned with making a brilliant marriage, as she could have. She wanted James, no one else. But admirable and likeable though James was, the baroness knew his chief interest and occupation lay in sketching and painting. She had visions of him and Sophie ending up in a Paris garret, which though considered fashionable among very modern young people, was an uncomfortable environment for any married couple. It was not what Sophie was used to. However, James's father was Sir William Fraser. There must be sound connections and James must at least have long-term prospects. And one could not discount how he had saved Sophie – and Anne – from unthinkable disaster.

The baron, at Sophie's request, agreed to see James the following evening. In being late home from his office he did not endear himself to his tenterhooked daughter, but she readily forgave him because she knew he really was very busy. The Serbian question was invading every whisper and buzz in the Ballhausplatz, the Austrian Foreign Minister determined to present Belgrade with demands so humiliating that they would be rejected and war made inevitable. The baron felt depressed. Nevertheless, he received James cordially. His affection for the man who had delivered his daughters from terror was ungrudging. They retired to the library for a friendly but traditionally necessary discussion on the suitability of the match, in terms of how suitable was James.

Sophie tried to sit in calm acquiescence of the conventional, waiting in the drawing room with her mother. Anne and Carl were in the garden, relaxing in the evening sunshine. They would come in, Carl had said, when the champagne was opened.

'Mama,' said Sophie, 'it must be so embarrassing for James, this sort of thing. After all, it is the twentieth century and I'm not sure compulsory talks of this kind with fathers can't be considered an infringement of a daughter's right to decide her own future.'

'Darling,' said the baroness in her tranquil way, 'your father would not dream of infringing anyone's rights. He will only do what he thinks best for you.'

'Oh, I know.' Sophie rustled anxiously all the same. 'But James is a man, not a boy. It would be quite different if he were young and beardless—'

'Sophie, he is hardly aged and he has no beard.'

'You know what I mean,' said Sophie. 'Mama, how can we ask a man who virtually flung Avriarches and his cannon off his own mountain to prove himself to Papa? I do hope Papa doesn't pat him on the head.'

'Pat him on the head?' The baroness hid her smile.

'Metaphorically,' said Sophie. 'I suppose you realize that a talk like this implies I need protection?'

'Sophie dear, the experience and wisdom of

one's father do amount to a little more than the unlearned callowness of youth. He and James will get along very well together.'

'Oh, I will put my trust in Papa,' said Sophie. She got up and wandered restlessly about. 'Only if anything happened and James— No, I shall be resolute and allow nothing at all to happen.' But suppose her father considered James unsuitable simply because he wasn't rich enough or couldn't claim the very best connections? He would talk very kindly to James, very fairly and logically, and James might ask to be released from the engagement in what he would say were her best interests. Nearly all men had odd ideas about the best interests of women. Was it in her own best interests to break her heart?

She would never allow it, never. Nor would James in the long run.

The door opened. James came in. He was smiling. Sophie swept him from the room in a rush, begging him to talk to her elsewhere. James, set for a lifetime of indulging the whims of beautiful Austria, accompanied her amiably to the morning room. Outside in the Salesianergasse the traffic had divorced itself from daytime hurry and eased itself into an evening saunter.

'Please, what happened?' asked Sophie. 'What did Papa say to you?'

Her anxiety, the intensity of it, surprised him a little. She must know her own father. He himself had felt that whatever reservations the baron might have, he was not going to make his enchanting elder daughter unhappy.

'Sophie.' James took her anxious face between his hands and kissed the tip of her nose. 'Your father said you're a young lady of priceless virtue, high intelligence and persuasive argument. That I'm very fortunate to have won you where thousands have failed, and that he only asks us to take our time in setting the wedding date. It would allow your mother to see that everything was done properly. I thought him very generous and reasonable. He's a charmer, isn't he? We went on to talk about the balance of power in Europe, of which I know very little and he knows everything, it seems. I found his comments fascinating, his arguments convincing. I'm quite won over now to the survival of the Austro-Hungarian empire. Apparently, it's either that or the emergence of a greater German empire—'

'James!' Sophie beat at his chest with demanding fists. 'James, you beast, you are flying kites over my head. Speak to me of me, not of empires. Papa has said it's all right, that you may make me your most treasured possession?'

'Didn't I make it clear? I thought I did.' James was drawn into the brilliance of eyes compelling relevancies from him. 'Your father has no objections at all and is going to have champagne served. He also wishes your mother to arrange a small family dinner party in my honour. He thinks there'll have to be an engagement party as well.'

'Oh,' said Sophie, 'heaven has arrived at my door. James, are you pleased that I am yours now?'

James regarded her with the smile of a man who was not going to complain.

'Sophie, I don't think I've done too badly at all. I think I'm getting the best Austria could give. Yes, I'm very pleased.'

'Then I am pleased too,' she said. 'Actually, I am over the moon. Do you think— I mean, if you would rather do without an engagement party I shouldn't mind at all. I really only want a wedding. I'll talk to Mama. I must write to your parents and Mama must invite them here. Do you think they will like me?'

'They'll love you. I love you. Sophie, you're adorable.'

She put her arms around his neck.

'If you will kiss me,' she said, her eyes moistly soft, 'I will show you just how much I love you.'

Chapter Twelve

In mid-July Vienna swam in golden light. It mellowed old Franz Josef into having an official photograph taken that portrayed him in the rubicund health of balmy octogenarianism. In such a summer the Sarajevo incident became something for the statesmen to argue about, not the people. Serbia deserved a caning, but Franz Ferdinand and his wife, being demonstrably dead and buried, were better forgotten. Nothing could bring them back and the new heir apparent, Charles, was a much more attractive Habsburg. It was not the errors and omissions of the gloomy dead the Viennese preferred to gossip about, but the rich promise of the young and living. They did not like to turn their colourful taverns and coffee houses into funeral parlours.

However, there were some people the golden summer could not mellow. The Foreign Minister, Count Berchtold, for instance. He was adamant that a caning was the least Serbia deserved, and his belligerence mounted rather than lessened. With the German Kaiser's promise of support ringing martially in his ears, the Austrian

Foreign Minister felt he could command Serbia to jump over the Habsburg moon, with dire consequences if her acrobatics failed her.

The ordinary people did not worry much. Hardly at all, in fact. But then, as is generally the case with ordinary people, nobody really told them anything to make them worry. One or two newspaper editors did express concern at what might be going on in the underground communications linking the foreign ministries of Europe, but nobody worried excessively. There were exceptions, of course. Maude creased her forehead anxiously from time to time, then managed to startle James by referring to the possible pressure France might put on Britain.

'Hold on,' said James, 'for God's sake.'

Maude figuratively kicked herself. The last thing to bring joy to James, engaged to the beautiful Sophie von Korvacs, was a suggestion that the developing crisis would see Britain involved.

'I'm sorry,' she said briskly, 'that was a stupid thing to bring up.'

'Frankly, Maude,' said James, 'I've heard no one talk as seriously as you do about things.'

Maude might have advised him to have a long talk with Baron von Korvacs, whose position in the Foreign Ministry made him the best possible sounding board for his prospective son-in-law, but instead she said, 'I'm getting to be an imaginative old woman.' And she changed the subject by asking him about Sophie.

'Sophie,' said James with a smile, 'would handle

this Serbian situation with ease. Neither kings nor statesmen would be able to withstand her arguments, for she'd play from both sides of the fence at once. Her turn of phrase would induce euphoria. Incidentally, my father is a man of fact and logic. At some time in the future Sophie is going to stand him on his head.'

Sophie had told James that for the sake of his future he must not be modest. He was a man in ten thousand. His victorious confrontation with Avriarches, the bone-crushing man-mountain, had been proof of that. His father, therefore, must not only be grateful to have James working for him, he must be suitably appreciative of the valiant qualities of his son.

'But you mustn't think, dearest James, that I wish to push you into an argument with Sir William. I wish only to have him realize how very invaluable you are. You must know that I'm not at all concerned about whether we live in comfort or just make ends meet, but I should hope no one would so underrate you as to offer you a pittance.'

'I think we'll make ends meet.'

'I intend,' said Sophie, 'to work my fingers to the bone.'

'I intend,' said James, 'that you don't do anything of the sort.'

'Thank you, darling. Perhaps—'

'Sophie, however invaluable you think I'll be to my father, do you realize you'll be indispensable to me? I promise you you shan't be penned up, you can be yourself as well as my wife. You

259

can write your poetry, visit London, go to the galleries and the theatres—'

'Please don't,' said Sophie, 'or I shall get emotional. You aren't going to put me on a train every day, are you? We are going to be at home, aren't we, and have conversations? You are going to love me sometimes, aren't you? I can hardly be indispensable to you if I'm going up and down to London in trains.'

'I thought I'd go up and down with you. Not every day, of course.'

'Oh, I am no one without you, darling,' she said. 'We will get along together, won't we? Perhaps we will talk to your father together. I'm not too bad at talking to people, you know. Oh, I assure you, I won't be aggressive or unfeminine, I should not want your father to think I came from a family of boxers or footpads. But you see, I'm simply unable to bear not being part of all that is important to you, to us, and I should love to help you beard your father in his cage.'

'Den, I think you mean.'

'Very well. Den. You will be Daniel and I will be Daniel's wife.'

'Heaven help the lion,' said James.

Sophie wondered why he had not yet settled the wedding date with her. She felt she had already been forward enough, although it had been desperation which motivated her, and she did not want to press him further. He would come round naturally to agreeing the day when the engagement party date had been fixed.

The baroness, however, had a private word with

James two days later. She knew Sophie could not quite understand why James avoided the issue. James liked the baroness. He thought her a warm, affectionate woman who had bequeathed much of her charm to her daughters.

'James, please forgive me if I'm interfering where I shouldn't,' she said, 'but I understand the wedding date is still not settled. I think Sophie would like to plan for the day. Oh, please don't mention I've spoken to you, she would never forgive me. Will you think me silly if I ask whether there is anything worrying you, anything my husband and I could help you with?'

Something was worrying James. Not Sophie. The crisis. It was there, darkly looming. Yet the family seemed to behave as if it did not exist, although the baron was in the closest official touch with it. Maude was certain it was serious and Maude was not a scaremonger, she was an extremely practical woman. She was also shrewd and had maintained from the beginning that the wrong kind of diplomatic and political attitudes could lead to disaster. She was sure that Count Berchtold really did mean to crush Serbia, to have Austria annex that country and bring it into the empire to keep a stern and fatherly eye on it. The emperor was being persuaded that such action was vitally necessary. Maude said that if Franz Josef signed the declaration of war it would be because Berchtold had also persuaded him that Russia, for all her bombast, would not interfere. But Russia, said Maude, would never permit an Austrian annexation of Serbia. There would be a European war on a disastrous scale. James wondered if the baroness thought in those terms, if she even thought that a war with Serbia was in the offing. He did not know what the baron might have said to her, and he himself could certainly not speak for her husband. He could only put his worry across in the mildest way.

'Well,' he said, 'there seems to be something of a crisis concerning Serbia, Baroness, and I thought I ought to wait until it's all blown over. To be fair to Sophie the wedding should take place in an atmosphere of peace and harmony, don't you think? Nobody would want the occasion to be less than perfect for her.'

It sounded limp and uncomfortable even to his own ears. And the baroness was looking at him as if it was puzzling to hers.

'James, you can't think that anything dreadful will happen, surely? It's only a question of Serbia making suitable reparations. My husband has told me so. It might mean us taking a firm line with the Serbians, but that is all. It was a terrible thing they did, helping to plot the murder of the archduke. But whatever happened it would not affect you.' She wondered if he realized Sophie would go off her head if for some inexplicable reason the marriage did not take place. 'James, you have come to be a very good friend. I may ask you a question?'

'Please do.'

'It is just that you feel uneasy about this Serbian business? It's nothing to do with a change in your feelings for Sophie?'

James smiled. That made her feel better. It told her he did not need to equivocate.

'My feelings for Sophie are unchangeable,' he said, 'she is a great gift to me. It's only the crisis that's making me cautious about the wedding date.'

'I am so relieved,' said the baroness. 'James, Sophie is really rather an intense person. She is unable to trade lightly in emotions and affections, however lightly she may converse about them. I think you should speak to her, tell her you're a little worried about things and that is all. Am I interfering?'

'No,' said James, 'you're my friend and counsellor.'

'Good.' She smiled. 'You haven't forgotten the little dinner party we're giving for you at the end of the week? I thought you would like to have Major Moeller there, I think he has earned a special place with you and us. And you have earned a special place with the whole family.'

The following day the newspapers, which had indulged in fits of ferocity and intervals of reassurance, came out in speculative rashes. All concerning a punitive ultimatum to Serbia.

Baron von Korvacs, looking lined with worry, spent even more time at the Foreign Ministry. His wife asked him what was happening. He told her it was nothing. Well, nothing except discussions concerning the concessions Serbia would have to make.

'Don't let it disturb you,' he said.

'I'm trying not to,' she said, 'but I don't think you're very happy, Ernst.'

'We'll see, we'll see,' he said.

'There's the dinner party for James in two days. You must be home early for a change.'

'Yes. Of course.' The baron hesitated. 'Teresa, let it take the place of the engagement party.'

'Ernst! Sophie must have an engagement party. What would she think if we didn't give her one?'

'She might surprise you.'

'No, she shall have a proper occasion,' insisted the baroness, 'a splendid one. We must arrange a date at once. Sophie wishes the wedding to be as soon after as possible. She and James can better arrange the wedding when they know the date of the engagement party.'

'I know, my dear. I'll speak to you about it to-night.'

But he was home very late and went tiredly to bed. Dates still hung in the balance, as other things did.

James suggested a picnic, for the weather called everyone out of doors. Sophie would have agreed to eating a cold fish lunch al fresco in Greenland as long as James was there. Anne begged that she and Ludwig might come. Carl offered to drive them and took them to a spot miles out of Vienna, where it was gloriously peaceful and the meadows floated high and golden above the distant Danube. The day was radiant. It was a day for the old as well as the young, with

Europe sunning in the brilliance of its empires and kingdoms, the era brave with the majesty of kings and princes, with Queen Alexandra still its inspiration and Kaiser Wilhelm its proud, ceremonial mouthpiece.

Sophie never forgot that day of high summer, the purr of the Benz, the joy of being alive, the splendour of Vienna the golden and Austria the beautiful. And of Anne and Ludwig, patently falling in love, and James building a fire within a framework of stones and actually cooking meat for the picnic. He placed a piece of flat steel, punctured with holes, over the stones, laid thick slices of sausage on it and filled the air with the heavenly aroma of frying. Picnics were not a frequent occurrence among the von Korvacs. When they did have one it was a carefully planned operation involving many servants, speculations about the weather, consultations about what to wear, a journey with a slightly processional look and, finally, the picnic itself on a basis of organized jollity. There would be a lordly spread of cold meats, chicken and salads, eaten at a properly laid folding table and sitting in canvas chairs.

To have James in charge of the picnic meant no servants, no chairs, just the natural environment and simple improvisation. And sausage sizzling over an open fire. Heavenly, thought Sophie. Anne and Ludwig strolled in the high meadows. The Danube, a hazy and winding glitter, flowed far below. Carl, stretched on his back in the grass, panama hat over his face, awaited the food and wine. James had supplied everything. It was his treat, he said. He was down on his knees in front of the fire, using a long fork of Maude's to turn the sausage slices. Sophie put a hand on his shoulder, then caressingly touched his neck. He looked up at her. He was darkly brown. The sun got into his eyes and she felt, even though life was being so good to her now, that love could still be painful.

She said, 'Papa says it's not necessary to have a huge engagement party if we'd rather not. Mama says she has never heard of any engagement party not being necessary. I said I didn't mind either way, except that an engagement party must come before a wedding.'

'True,' said James, deftly turning a slice. He added, 'At least, on the whole.'

'To some people,' said Sophie, 'that could mean an engagement party getting in the way of a wedding.'

He knew what she wanted. A definite date. He had not yet talked to her in the way the baroness had advised him to. His worry was a gnawing, uneasy one. Austria was going to war, and even his imaginative Sophie did not seem to realize it.

'It might mean that to people like you and me, but it's not how parents see it,' he said. He channelled glistening slices of cooked sausage off the hot steel on to a plate. He put fresh slices on. 'When do you want the wedding, Sophie?'

Sophie, invited at last to be specific, said

earnestly, 'Oh, I would like it at the end of August. That is a long way off, I know, but—'

'It's next month,' said James.

'Yes, it's a long time, I have just said so, but there will be such a lot to do and think about. Darling, is it too long for you?'

The sun danced on her, warmed her, enriched her. James wondered how he had managed to win her. He ruffled his hair.

'We have to buy a house, Sophie,' he said, 'I can't take you home to a tent. I shall probably have to go back for a while and look around. When I return I expect your father will have got this Serbian business out of the way – I think he's one man who's up to it—'

'James, you are not trying to put me off, are you?' Her smile was valiantly bright, hiding her little feeling of sudden apprehension.

'No, never. Aside from everything else, my parents would never allow it.' He had written to them, enclosing a photograph of Sophie. He had received a brief letter of approval from his father, a long letter of happy surprise from his mother. 'Oh, we'll fix things, Sophie.' Lightly he added, 'By the way, you owe me a kiss.'

'James darling, you can have a hundred, a thousand—'

'Just one,' said James.

She looked around. Carl's hat was still over his face and Anne and Ludwig were dreamy, sun-hazed figures in the background. She bent and kissed James warmly and extravagantly on the lips. She did not know what the contact did to him, but it did the usual thing to her. It made her pulse rate leap.

'That's a debt very nicely discharged,' said James, returning to his frying.

'Debt?'

'I told you when I gave you that sketch of yourself that I'd let you know one day what I wanted for it.'

Sophie laughed. James, looking up at her again, saw her vividly alive against the pale blue canvas of the sky.

'Is that what you always had in mind to charge me?' she asked.

'Yes.'

'Well, I should have been happy to have made payment long ago,' she said.

'There's some interest due. Hot sausage ready. Will you call Anne and Ludwig?'

She said in an intense little murmur, 'I will do anything for you, James.'

'Sophie sweet—'

'Oh, it will be over soon, all this fuss about Serbia, won't it?' she said and went to fetch Anne and Ludwig.

They picnicked. They all ate hot sliced sausage with bread, olives, tomatoes and fat chunks of cucumber. James served the bread in crusty wedges. Everyone dipped into green salad and Carl poured the wine. They ate sitting on the grass, except for James who ate on his knees, keeping up with the demand for more hot sausage.

The day was a hum of summer sounds, of

laughter, breeze, murmuring grass and winging bees. They sat and talked when they had eaten, and they finished the wine. Anne and Ludwig took another stroll. James put out the fire and began to clean things up. Sophie tidied up. She sank to her knees beside Carl, who was having the laziest day. He was lying on his back again. She took the wine glass from his hand. He moved his hat off his face and smiled up at her. He looked young, strong and very contented.

'It's a good summer, Sophie,' he said.

'Oh, yes. I thought I had grown out of picnics, but I haven't. That is what the summer has done. There'll never be another one quite as perfect.'

'There never is,' said Carl, 'the best summers are always the ones you've had. O-eight was quite good. Anne's nose peeled. We're going to miss you, Sophie.'

'And I shall miss all of you. Terribly.' Sophie sat back on her heels. Her hat was off, her hair bright with sun-burnished tints. 'I'm a little scared. Wish me luck, Carl.'

'I do. The very best. You're the dearest girl. But scared? I've never heard you talk like that. They won't eat you, the British, will they? What's it called, that place you're going to? Warwickshire? Where is it?'

'It's not that,' said Sophie, 'I think I'll be able to manage Warwickshire. But I've never been a wife before. Carl, supposing I let James down? He's so practical himself, he can do things.'

'So can you. And James knows he's a man in

luck, he knows he's getting a stunner. He won't worry about the little things.'

'Carl.' She plucked at the grass. 'Carl, do you think there'll be a war?'

His relaxed look became cautious.

'Oh, I don't think so. Well, if there is, how long can it last? Not more than a month. We'd eat the Serbians.'

'Everyone is talking about it now. Except us. James doesn't mention it. Although he did say we ought to wait until the Serbian business is over before we fix our wedding. Carl, I couldn't bear it, not a war. Everything is so lovely and I'm really quite stupid with happiness. But if – if we went to war how could I leave Austria? I couldn't just go off and bury my head in the sand with James, I couldn't simply say goodbye to Mama and tell her the war was nothing to do with me. But I desperately want to marry James, to be with him. Carl, do you think he would stay here? Do you think he would live with us until it was over? Carl, would you talk to him? Would you, please? You and James are such good friends, and you're to be best man, aren't you? You could suggest he and I might live with the family as if you'd thought of it. You see, I don't wish him to think I'm running his life for him, he'll begin to give me odd looks and I couldn't bear that, either. Carl dear, could you just casually mention the idea to him?'

Carl had the clear-sighted, uncomplicated outlook of a young man to whom life was a matter of simple ideals and understandable principles.

Only recently had he begun to realize that life had its complex issues. And he felt an awareness of the intensity of his sister's emotions, all to do with the very complicated nature of her feelings for James. Carl had enough intelligence and enough feeling for Sophie himself not to laugh at her worries.

'That's the devil of a good idea, Sophie. I'll mention it to him at the right moment, rely on me. I'd have to get into uniform myself, of course.' Carl was on the officers' reserve list. 'But James is the type who'd want to help in some way, and I'm not so sure he wouldn't rather like to stay and see it through with us.'

'Carl, that would be wonderful.' Sophie seemed to float against the bright background in her relief. 'Oh, thank you, I'm so grateful.'

Carl reached and squeezed her hand.

'Couldn't let you down, Sophie,' he said, 'never.'

He watched her as she rose to her feet. She was worried. Well, a woman did worry more than men about war. To men wars happened. To women wars were forced on people. He wondered if Sophie's impending marriage to James signalled the first great irreversible turn of the wheel for the family. Sophie's going would begin the break-up. They would all miss her. Anne was vivacious and bubbly, Sophie was humorously delicious. Both his sisters were good to be with, both companionable. He had grown up with them in an atmosphere of relative harmony, Anne always the volatile spirit of the relationship, Sophie the resilient link which bound them. She it was who made it possible to bring about reconciliation whenever the harmony did get besieged by argument. Sophie had grown into a woman. Anne still had flashes of clear, bright idyllic youth. One looked at Anne and saw the joy she had in being young. One looked at Sophie and saw a woman ready for the more sophisticated wonders of life. She was a woman wanting to give now, because she felt she had been given so much herself.

I am having serious thoughts, reflected Carl, and for the first time in my life.

He felt he knew why Sophie had committed herself so unconditionally to James. Sophie had grown up. So had James. He had acquired the easy front of a man who had worked, who had lived out his youth, who had come to know people and had left awkwardness well behind. Sophie said she liked James because she could talk to him. Her natural love of words flowered when she was with him. She discussed poetry with him, which she seldom did with others outside the family because of her sensitivity concerning her own dedication to the muse. He could not imagine James would ever find her inadequate either as a woman or a wife.

Carl supposed his parents would expect him to make a suitable match himself soon. It was not something he had given a lot of thought to. He had not even sown his wild oats yet. It was expected of some men. Ludwig's father had once said that some women preferred a husband who had sown wildly but well, since she expected to reap the benefits of his experience. Carl doubted if his mother would agree with that. She would say that there was a tender sweetness in a husband and wife learning from each other, and that that was how God intended it to be. Should a man sacrifice nebulous wild oats for the sake of his mother? Carl thought it would not worry him unduly. Women were not constantly on his mind. Not as much, certainly, as the Benz. The Benz always made him feel warm with the pleasure of ownership. He smiled to himself. He was inclined, he knew, to shift to one side the necessity of thinking about one woman in particular. It was a help to a motor-car enthusiast that there wasn't one woman in particular. There was a highly engaging bevy at times of beguiling eyes and pretty faces, of attractive figures and peeping petticoats. There was enjoyment, careless rapture and the excitement of a world that was progressive, with countless years ahead. And there was no worrying involvement.

He imagined he would get married some time within the next few years. Out of the immediate future would step some divine girl who would make the same stunning impact on him as Sophie had made on James. If he could not quite picture every detail of his ideal, he was clear about one thing at least. She would be Austrian. He had travelled the countries of Europe without feeling any of them produced women superior to those of Vienna. If anything, it was the other way about. Vienna had an astonishing quota of superbly good-looking women. His mother would look around for him if he dropped only half a hint, and she would certainly not think it necessary to travel to Germany or France, Italy or Hungary. She would probably not go more than half a mile in any direction. She might not even leave the house but simply say, 'I'll invite so-and-so and her family to dinner, so-and-so is a charming girl and it's time you met her.'

He conceded he was taking his time to enmesh himself in the intricacies of serious life, that he was extending the years of irresponsibility. But at least he was harming no one. He had made no girl shed tears.

There was Helene, of course. Could he consider her seriously?

He decided not.

In any case, there was the Serbian question. Damned hard luck on Sophie if it took the gilt off her wedding day. Sophie deserved a perfect day. He was not affected himself. He had no commitments or involvements. He could fight the Serbians without making a girl weep for him. It would not last long and most generations were called on to fight for their country once at least. It looked as if the politicians weren't going to settle the matter in relation to Serbia. It was going to be left to soldiers.

All the same, because of Sophie he rather hoped now that the politicians would keep talking.

* * *

'James?' Carl spoke from under the bonnet. They had arrived home from the picnic and he and James were putting the Benz cleanly to bed.

'I'm listening.'

'I don't think it will alarm you, you're not that sort of fellow. But there might be a war. It's those damned Serbians— I must say, this engine is remarkably good on the oil. It's still quite clean too, have you noticed that? Did I mention it won't last long? It won't, you may rely on that.'

'Are we talking about the Serbians or the engine oil?' asked James.

'Oh, nothing to worry about,' said Carl casually, 'but I was just wondering about you and Sophie. A war might upset your plans a little. If it does happen – well, look here, would you consider staying on? You and Sophie, I mean. Just for the duration. With the family. We shouldn't take long to settle the Serbians.'

'If it's just you and the Serbians,' said James pointedly, 'no, it shouldn't take too long.'

'I thought you might consider the idea,' said Carl, emerging from the bonnet and smiling cheerfully.

'Has Sophie considered it?'

'Mmm? Oh, I expect she will when you mention it.'

'We'll see what happens,' said James.

On the evening of the small dinner party the baron telephoned from his office to say he was simply unable to get away in time to help receive the guests. He was profusely apologetic and hoped his wife would understand. She did, for she knew now that a crisis existed and that it was a serious one. But it must not be allowed to spoil things for Sophie and James. Ernst had known what he was talking about when he suggested the dinner party should be in lieu of an engagement party. There could be no glittering ball, which was what the baroness would have liked to give, if there was a war on. Ernst in his quiet way would very properly discourage it. Therefore, Sophie and James must have a happy occasion this evening.

There were only four guests. James and Major Moeller, Ludwig and Helene. Anne had rather begged for Ludwig to be invited. It looked very much as if Anne was becoming as seriously attached as Sophie. The baroness could not deny she would be pleased to have Ludwig marry Anne. So Ludwig came and Helene too. Helene would provide a pairing with Carl.

The small reception room was used for welcoming the guests. It was more intimate than the larger one, and a champagne buffet had been set up to precede dinner.

Sophie, wishing to dazzle James before settling down to be his earnestly inexpensive wife, wore a new gown. And it was not solely to dazzle him. It was for him, in acknowledgement of him, a reflection of what he meant to her. He was her lover, her protector, her saviour. Her poetic imagination dwelt on every descriptive word, and she was able to reconcile her abandonment to the flowery muse of a past era with her belief in herself as a modern young lady by remembering that self-expression could not be confined within the limits of what was popular and what was not.

The gown was a sheath of pale, lustrous gold, waisted to emphasize the slender sweep of torso and bodiced to enhance the contours of her rounded bosom. Jewels studded her piled glossy hair. Her eyes were hugely brilliant. She herself was brilliant, her mirror told her so, but when James arrived and looked at her, stared at her, she wondered if she had not overdone it.

'James?' she said apprehensively.

'Is that you, Sophie?' He smiled. He was darkly tanned and quite immaculate in his tails. 'Shame on you to look as beautiful as this. I'm stunned speechless.'

'But, James,' she said, 'I am only engaged once, so I did not want to look as if it was an ordinary occasion. I think it very auspicious and had to do my best to look auspicious myself. I will do?'

'You'll do for an emperor,' said James. He took her hand, bent his head and kissed her fingertips. Her eyes laughed at him. He gave her a wink and she sensed the fun they could get out of life together. 'Yes, my most auspicious Sophie.'

'Oh, my hero,' she countered demurely. She greeted Major Moeller, who had had the tact to stand well aside.

'My dear Sophie,' he said and kissed her hand with precise gallantry. 'I think you have James reeling a little. I'm past the worst weaknesses of youth myself, but all the same I am dazzled, by heaven I am. I've congratulated James. May I now give you my felicitations?'

'I shall be very happy,' said Sophie, and the major kissed her on each cheek. 'Thank you, dear Major Moeller. Will you take me to some champagne? I wish to become a little giddy.'

They all drank champagne. Anne, in sheerest sky blue, was happy for James, blissful for Sophie and contented with herself. Her mother, in white, competed with her daughters for charm. Helene, pink-clad, was in a flutter, talking excitedly to Carl about a war. Carl took her aside and explained cordially but clearly that the evening belonged to Sophie and James, not to any war. He understood her flutters but would she kindly make happier contributions to the conversation? Breathlessly Helene said she would talk only about the very nicest things.

But there were underlying tensions which neither the champagne nor the most cheerful conversation could quite dispel. The Austrian ultimatum to Serbia had been received. It virtually asked Serbia to skin herself alive. The speculative newspaper leaders had become messages of warning. However, dinner brightened the atmosphere. The two hanging chandeliers glittered with reflected light and the wine glasses sparkled with reflected colour. No one mentioned the ultimatum and no one suggested the baron's absence had anything to do with imminent war. The baroness did not want the occasion marred for Sophie and James, and in any case she had the compassionate woman's wishful belief that it was the responsibility of statesmen to avoid war, not to provoke it. However, the champagne aperitifs and now the dinner wine flushed Ludwig into indiscretion. He was as intrigued as his sister about the probable war and was bursting with a thousand unspoken words. Visibly more in love with Anne each day, he so far forgot himself in wanting to claim her attention that he suddenly put the cat among the pigeons by mentioning the ultimatum.

'And I hear,' he went on with cheerful excitement, 'that it's not a question of the emperor deciding if we're to go to war, but when.'

The ensuing silence was like a dull thud. It had been for Sophie's sake, the drawn veil, and she perceptibly paled as Ludwig pulled it aside. Anne saw the look on James's face, the tightening of his mouth, and her heart sank. She had adventured dangerously with James, he had won her lifelong affection during those hazardous hours, and nothing had delighted her more than his engagement to her sister. She saw now what he felt a war might do to him and Sophie. He was a man racked.

Major Moeller lifted his wine glass and regarded its amber contents fondly.

'My boy,' he said to Ludwig, 'it's hardly as clearcut as that, is it? I trust statesmen will see the wisdom of honourable compromise and continue to ensure life remains pleasantly undisturbed for some of us and improves for the rest. Anything else would interfere abominably with wandering comfortably about to call on friends or to find some decent fishing. Baroness, I can't say how happy I am to be counted among your friends here tonight. Really, I am honoured. And I am warmed by the special significance the occasion has for Sophie and James.'

'To have you with us is a privilege, Major Moeller,' said the baroness gratefully, and Ludwig reddened as Anne gave him a reproachful look. And James wondered sadly if the burying of heads in sand was because they too suspected, as Maude did, that the war would go far beyond a conflict between Austria and Serbia.

'This trout is heavenly,' said the major.

Sophie, recovering, said with a smile, 'Oh, but you have never sampled James's sizzling picnic sausage. That is ambrosial.'

'Fit for the gods,' said Carl.

James managed a smile. But he was quiet. Sophie noticed it and said desperate little prayers to herself. He had contributed hardly anything to the conversation, which was unlike him. She glanced at him. He was so sober.

'James, you aren't worried, are you?' she whispered. 'Please don't be.'

'I'm looking for bones,' he said lightly, dissecting his trout. But he was badly worried. Maude's latest observation had contained an indirect warning. Much as it would break her heart, for she loved Vienna, she said, she must seriously consider looking out her passport. Her return to England might be unavoidable.

The baron arrived at last. Entering the dining room he expressed sincere apologies to his family and guests for being so late and for his unsuitable dress. He looked tired and drawn.

'You're here, Papa,' said Anne, 'that's enough.'

'Ernst, we're halfway through,' said the baroness, 'but if you wish—'

'I need nothing except what is to follow,' said the baron, taking his place at the table. A servant filled his glass. 'I only hope James and our other friends don't think me entirely negligent. Perhaps half a host, as it were, is not as discourteous as none at all.'

'Honoured,' said the major.

'Papa, we are so pleased to see you,' said Sophie.

The baron smiled at her, then at James. James thought there was sadness in his eyes. At the end of the meal the baron rose to his feet. He waited until all glasses had been refilled.

'My dear family and friends,' he said then, 'there are times when a few words have to be said. I hope those I am going to say will not stretch into too many. I've heard many fifteen-minute speeches last an hour. We are here, aren't we, in honour of Sophie and James. The evening, I think, is an occasion to be happy for them. Between them, among other things, is compatibility.' He paused, then went on quietly but firmly. 'That is a hard-won state in the relationship between any man and woman. Some fail, but many do achieve it. Their example should guide nations, for between nations there must be a like compatibility. That is what nations owe people. That is what Austria and Britain owe Sophie and James. Sophie I regard as a treasure.' His smile for her was tender. Sophie's eyes moistened. 'James I regard as a valiant protector of that treasure. Their engagement I announce with warm pleasure. You will all join me, I'm sure, in wishing peace for them, in wishing a long and full life to them.' He raised his glass and his smile hid his sadness. 'My dearest Sophie, my very good friend James.'

'Sophie! James!' The table rose to them and drank to them. A speech was demanded from James. He stood up. Sophie, in emotion, took his hand and pressed it to her cheek. It brought tears to Anne's eyes.

'Baron, Baroness, and my friends, thank you,' said James. He knew he must say nothing about nations or peace, for the baron had said enough in his own quiet way, and to mention peace again would be an indirect reference to war. His words must be for Sophie, of Sophie. 'I agree,' he said, 'Sophie is a treasure. Quite priceless, quite unique. I don't admit to being biased, I do admit to being convinced. Sophie is able to enrich my life merely by being there, by her words and her poetry. If my voice ever fails me I'll borrow hers and inherit the earth. And I promise you that wherever we may be, Sophie will never fail Austria. Where she is there goes Austria. I'm afraid incoherency comes next, so if I may I'd like to take Sophie into the garden. I've not seen the garden at night. I should like to now, with Sophie. Thank you.'

Sophie clung to his arm as they went down the paved steps into the garden, illuminated by lights from the house.

'James, if you are afraid of incoherency,' she said, 'I'm afraid of being almost ready to cry.'

'Your father was very impressive,' said James. He realized the baron knew what might happen.

The night was balmy. The Modena Palace was ablaze with chandeliered fire and Vienna itself seemed roofed by a million lamps. Sophie, a silk wrap around her shoulders, turned to James, wanting to be held. But James was looking at the lights that were like fire. He was so serious. Familiar little apprehensions darted at her. But she said in her lightest way, 'Well, that was our engagement party, you know. I suppose we can say it's almost out of the way now. James, next month is suitable, isn't it? For our wedding, I mean. I must tell you, I'm quite nervous about it, I haven't had one before. But if we get married together, which is the usual thing, we should be a great help to each other, shouldn't we?'

James, knowing he was coming up to the worst and most unbearable moment of his life, wondered exactly what to say.

'Sophie, I'm not sure—'

'No, James, no,' she said, her forced lightness departing, 'you have proposed to me, I have accepted, we are firmly engaged and shall be firmly married. Please don't say we can't or shouldn't. We must get married, even if there is a war, and if there is then I should need you more than ever. James, I was speaking to Carl. He has mentioned to you what we might do, live here for a while, hasn't he?'

'Yes, he mentioned it, Sophie.'

'Darling, that would be very practical, wouldn't it, and you are sometimes in favour of being practical, aren't you?' There was a little desperation about her, the light from the house a pale glow on her face, the jewels like fireflies in her hair. 'We could be married very quietly, I should not mind a bit, and we could live here with the family until it was all over and go to England then. James, do you think that a good idea? It isn't what we planned, but we should be married and that would be rather nice, wouldn't it?'

'Sophie, my sweet,' he said. She put herself against him, he held her and felt her shivers. 'I must say things. Listen very carefully. You know, don't you, that Austria is determined to go to war with Serbia.'

'No. Oh, yes. But that has nothing to do with you and me.' She lifted her face and the apprehension was in her eyes. 'James, you are not saying, are you, that you will join our army and go to war yourself?'

'Please listen,' he said gently. 'When Austria goes to war with Serbia, Russia will go to war with Austria. Germany will fight in support of Austria. France will fight in support of Russia. Then the whole of Europe will go up in flames. Don't you read your newspapers, Sophie?'

'Yes,' she said, 'yes, but not politics, not wars. Politics and wars are the enemies of civilization, the enemies of people. James, what are you trying to tell me?'

'Sophie.' He drew her close. She was a brilliance in the warm night but her body was cold. 'Sophie, my sweet, I'm trying to tell you I may have to go home.'

'Home? To Edinburgh? To Warwickshire?'

'We live in Warwickshire because my father's main works are there. I may be forced to return there. Do you understand, Sophie?'

'No,' she said, 'no.' She wondered if he knew what he was doing to her.

'I think if you spoke to your father he'd explain all the implications to you, I think he knows precisely what they might amount to. If I go—'

'You mean to run away? From me? You would let our war make you do that to me?' Sophie thought she would go out of her mind at such cruelty.

'I shouldn't go to get away from you, Sophie. But Austria might not want me here.'

She stared up into his dark, sombre eyes and the summer night suddenly became icy cold. Like a shaft of freezing light the truth pierced her.

'Never,' she gasped, 'never! You couldn't! You would never dare to jilt me like that. If the emperor chooses to quarrel with Serbia, what is that to do with others, with Russia or Germany? Or with your country? Oh, but yes, if there's a war England would hate to be left out, she'll interfere as she always does and drag Scotland in with her. She'll do the least fighting and get the most spoils. Well, the emperor can manage without you or your England or your Scotland—'

'Dear heaven, Sophie,' he said desperately, 'don't you see? If France goes to war against Germany and Austria, Britain won't fight France, if she fights at all.'

That was the truth that had pierced her, the truth she had tried to reject with her anguished rejoinder. The appalling implication of what it meant engulfed her in pain.

'You'd go to war against us?' Shivering from head to foot, Sophie could hardly get the words out. 'You'd shoot at me?'

'For God's sake—'

'Only men could and would think in such terms! And you are worse than all of them, yes, worse, worse!' She was crying in her pain. 'You wished me to listen and I am listening, and you are talking about killing people who have been your friends, you are talking about going to war against me! Carl is as good as dead already, because what chance would he have against you? Oh, yes, you'll be heroic again, won't you? They'll decorate you for bombarding Vienna, killing my family and destroying me, because that is what you will do if you leave me and go to war against me.'

'Sophie, Sophie.' James understood her anguish. He shared it.

'Will you do that, will you?' She had torn herself from him, she stood icy and trembling, her head up, her eyes wetly glittering.

'How can I answer such a question as that? If

I go back home it will be because events make it impossible for me to stay. Sophie, do you really imagine—'

'You have said enough.' She spoke through shivering teeth. She felt herself already destroyed. 'I will say goodbye now, then. I have been very stupid, I have behaved like an infatuated girl. But I thought you loved me. You are like most men, aren't you? They love war better than any woman. I would have gone with you anywhere, I would have loved you, I would not have given you up for a thousand wars. I would not do that now. You are an iron hero, an iron Mars, a destroyer. I know now why you waited that day for Ferenac. You preferred war with him to riding back to Ilidze with me. Yes, I have been very stupid. I wish only one kindness from you now, and that is that you spare me the pain of seeing you again, whatever happens, whether there is a war or not.'

'Sophie,' he said, bitterly sad, 'you are wrong. I understand what makes you say these things. But you are wrong. Listen to me a little more.'

'No. No. No!' She turned, she ran. She entered the house in a rush and looked as if she could not see, as if the night had blinded her. She was white and she was so cold.

'Sophie, darling.' Her mother came smiling. The smile slipped as she saw Sophie's face and tragic eyes.

'I'm going up to bed,' said Sophie in a strange, wild voice, 'I've said goodbye to James. Please ask the others to forgive me.'

James took his departure a little later in an atmosphere strained and uncomfortable. He said nothing of his quarrel with Sophie. He was simply unable to. He and Major Moeller left together. They did not call a cab. They walked. It was not so late and Vienna was still dancing, still strung with gold and yellow lamps.

'Bear up, James,' said the major, concerned at his friend's silence, 'I know what's on your mind. It's on mine too. But it can't come to that. Damn it, there must be a few, wise men able to argue the hotheads out of it. It's unacceptable, the thought of friends going to war in this day and age. We've progressed since it was considered an honour to cut each other's heads off. My dear boy, don't think of idiots, think of men of wisdom. And think of Sophie. Never knew a more attractive girl, or a more entertaining one. Fine family. Splendid people. Some schnapps at my place, eh? Do, my dear James, Sophie's worth drinking to, what? Damn all fools, my boy, I'd like to see you and Sophie left in peace to enjoy life, and it is enjoyable if idiots can be taught not to interfere.'

'Let's try your schnapps,' said James, 'nobody's likely to interfere with that.'

They had their schnapps. The major had it because he liked drinking with James. James had it because of Sophie, because it was only the schnapps which helped blur the memory of her anguished eyes and bitter voice.

They parted at the major's door in the early hours, when Vienna was brooding on its way to grey dawn. James was a little foggy but still upright.

'Something's not quite steady around here,' murmured the major with confidential bonhomie, 'damn place moving about, I think. But we'll both get home on our feet, eh?'

'You are home,' said James, painful reality taking second place for the moment to alcoholic melancholy.

'Eh? So I am, so I am. Fortunate, that. Always lucky with the spin of the coin, you know. Always lucky in the friends I've had. Never got on with politicians. Think more of you than any of them. Don't forget that. God in heaven, James, they're trying to pull the carpet from under our feet. You know what I mean?'

'Yes,' said James, 'I do know.'

They shook hands very solemnly.

Chapter Thirteen

The Serbian reply to the ultimatum conveyed total surrender. But such unconditional compliance was quite unwelcome to Count Berchtold, who wished Austria to launch the war from a platform of high and unmitigated dudgeon. Serbia's failure to reject the ultimatum changed that to a platform of plain opportunity. The assassination had provided the opportunity and Count Berchtold was not going to be circumvented. It was not unreasonable to assert that Serbia would default on her promise of full reparations, and Austria, therefore, must act in anticipation of this.

Accordingly Franz Josef signed the declaration of war on behalf of the Austro-Hungarian empire, and the empire commenced hostilities by dropping bombs on Belgrade.

Russia, traditional protector of the Slav peoples, followed by declaring war on Austria. Germany, resolutely behind Austria at the beginning of the crisis, now ended a period of second thoughts and went to war against Russia. France, as Russia's ally, declared against Germany and began her overtures to bring Britain in on her side. The Germans began to advance on France through Belgium. The simmering pot erupted.

Baroness von Korvacs, emotionally loyal to the emperor, whatever course he took, and just as emotionally disturbed by all it meant, was called to the telephone at a moment when Carl had just received his mobilization orders. James was on the line. The baroness knew by now all the horrifying possibilities of escalation. British nationals were leaving Vienna as quickly as they could.

'Baroness,' said James hesitantly, 'forgive me for worrying you, but I must leave and almost at once. May I come and say goodbye?'

'Yes, I understand, James. Come and see us, please waste no time. The worst has not happened yet, though, has it? I pray it will not. James, whether or not Sophie will see you I don't know. She is terribly unhappy.'

'I'll come now,' said James, 'thank you, Baroness.'

The baroness found Sophie in the morning room, gazing out of the window at the traffic. The Salesianergasse was far busier than usual. Carriages and cabs, automobiles and people were moving with an air of urgency and excitement. Vienna was not depressed by the declaration of war, it was gripped by the same patriotic fervour as other European capitals. On many vehicles fluttering flags were mounted, and on many fair heads ladies had pinned their most colourful hats.

Sophie, still unable to believe James and his country could be so perfidious as to side with Russia and France, was numb, frozen and suffering. When told that James was coming to say goodbye she looked at her mother in pale-faced incredulity.

'Here? He's coming here? You'd let him into the house when he intends to betray us, desert us?'

'Oh, Sophie, I know how tragic this is for you, but that is unfair and unkind,' said the baroness. The tragedy was that Sophie was so intensely in love, so shatteringly robbed of love. She was affected in every fibre of her being, so obviously paralysed by the fact that James was putting his patriotic duty before his regard for her, before all his promises to her. To Sophie that meant he did not love her enough or want her enough. That, to Sophie, was the most unbearable wound of all, as the baroness was aware. But James could hardly be blamed for the decisions of politicians, nor could he be held responsible for consequences that would turn friends into enemies. He would be as unhappy about that as they were. 'Sophie, James is helpless. He can't stop this madness any more than we can. Can we stop Austria and Russia going to war? Can James stop his country joining in? Don't blame him for the blindness of statesmen in London.'

'I don't,' said Sophie tonelessly. She put her hands to her face, pressed her pale cheeks. 'I only know that when I most need him he is failing me. If he had any real feeling for us, for me, he would stay. I know it would need courage to do that, I know he'd be interned, but I prayed he would stand up and say he owed us too much to desert us. Instead he's going back to that hateful country of his, which means he's willing to fight against us.'

'Sophie, my dear,' said the baroness sadly, 'one is privileged in having friends, one doesn't demand that friends should consider themselves in debt to us. James has a duty to his country. He has to go back, you must see that.'

'I see that he feels he should,' said Sophie, 'what I can't see is why he feels he must. Mama, I never want to be in love again. Nor do I want to see James again.'

'That isn't true, is it?' The baroness was gentle, compassionate. 'Sophie, he's coming to say goodbye to us. That in itself under these circumstances takes a lot of courage. He'll be very unhappy. So you must see him. If his country does go to war it may be your last chance to.'

'Mama, I can't.' Sophie's eyes, dark from sleeplessness, put her mother in pain. 'Please don't insist. I think I would only say bitter things. I'd like to spare everyone that, I'd like to even spare James that.'

'Darling, I shan't make you, I shan't force you. I'll only say that if you don't see him you may later feel even unhappier than you do now.'

Sophie went silently up to her room. Carl, uncompromisingly on the side of his sister and knowing that the exodus of British nationals could only mean one thing, felt in all conscience that he would rather be absent too. But the baroness would not allow a second defaulter. So when James arrived Carl put in an appearance that was stiffly civil and extremely brief.

'You are going, I believe?'

'I'm afraid—'

'You need not explain. It was good of you to call. You'll excuse me? I have just received my orders to report. Goodbye.'

'Goodbye, Carl,' said James. He added, with the faintest of smiles, 'Thank you for Vienna. And the Benz.'

Carl clicked his heels, inclined his head and left.

Anne was close to tears. Preposterous rumours had suddenly become dreadful facts, and sheer inability to understand why made it so hard to know what to say to James. He was in difficulties himself. Anne, torn between love of her country and inalienable affection for the man who had saved her and Sophie from Avriarches, could not conceal her misery. The words she and James exchanged were awkward and inadequate, and neither mentioned what was uppermost in their minds. That Britain might enter the war against Austria and Germany. The baroness, looking on, wanted to weep.

'My very dear Anne,' said James in the end, 'I'm so sorry.'

'But you have to go,' said Anne at breaking point, 'there's your country, your family.'

'Yes,' said James,' and you have yours.'

'I am heartbroken,' said Anne, tears spilling.

'Oh, James, you'd not fight us, would you? You couldn't – you—' Sobbing, she flung her arms around his neck, kissed him distraughtly, then ran out. James sighed.

'You're not to blame,' said the baroness quietly. 'No one thought it would come to this, and who could have wanted it to? It is so sad, so shattering. We are going to miss you. You made our summer very eventful and you took great care of Sophie and Anne. We shall not forget that.'

'Baroness,' he said, 'I've had the most memorable summer. Vienna has been beautiful. But I shouldn't have enjoyed it as much as I have without you and your family. Please remember me to the baron.'

'He understands, I assure you.

'I know. Thank you for letting me come to say goodbye. I'm to meet Maude Harrison, our train goes in forty minutes, but I shall come back to Vienna one day.'

'Yes,' she said. She had told him Sophie felt unable to see him, for he had been in some hope when he arrived. His disappointment had been almost despairing but he made no fuss. She could not refrain from saying now, 'And Sophie?'

'I'd like to have seen her,' he said. His eyes, for a moment, seemed to look into a summer that was still here but for him had gone. It was a summer full of pictures of Sophie, vibrant with life, warm with laughter. 'I shall always remember Sophie.'

'She is not herself, James, do forgive her for not coming down.'

'Give her my dearest love,' said James. 'Will

you do that? Tell her I'll think of her and love her.'

As soon as he had gone the baroness made her way upstairs. Sophie was in her room, sitting at her dressing table. She was palpably shivering.

'Mama?' Her voice was husky.

'Yes, he's gone now,' said her mother, 'he's suffering as much as we are.'

'Are we suffering?' Sophie stared blindly into the mirror. 'I think you'll find most of us are in the streets cheering and waving flags. Perhaps when James gets home he will cheer and wave a flag. He'll get over us quite quickly, Mama.'

'He asked me to give you his dearest love, he asked me to tell you he will think of you and love you. I don't think he'll get over us quickly at all.'

Sophie paled to whiteness and put a hand to her throat.

'Mama?' she whispered.

'Oh, you have made yourself so miserable,' said the baroness, 'that you've been unable to think. That is what this is all about, isn't it, that you think he doesn't love you enough. He does, he's never been able to help himself, even I've seen that. He so much wanted to see you—'

'Oh, Mama,' said Sophie wildly, 'I've made the most dreadful mistake.' She turned, she jumped up. 'Mama, where has he gone?'

'To pick up Frau Harrison—'

'I must catch him, I must!'

'They are—'

But Sophie was away, rushing out and flying

along the corridor and down the winding stair-case. She flew from the house, down the steps, over the drive and out of the gates. Frantically she ran, her green dress whipping, people staring. She stopped, looked around for a cab. They were all full, all hired. She ran on again. She darted across the busy thoroughfare in front of cabs and automobiles. A cabbie paled and reined back his horse. A motor car hooted and swerved. She ran. She saw an empty cab and desperately hailed it. She asked the cabbie to take her to the Ecole Internationale, and all the way she rocked to and fro and begged the man to hurry, hurry.

The traffic was an impeding nightmare, she wanted to cry out in despair at every hold-up. Oh, James, James, please don't go yet, please wait. It took an eternity to reach the school. It was closed down, but a young housemaid was still there, making preparations for her own departure before locking the place up. Sophie spoke distractedly to her. Kirsti shook her head. No, Herr Fraser had gone, he was meeting Frau Harrison at the station, they were catching a train, going to England—

Oh, of course, of course! She should have thought of that, asked her mother before rushing out. She turned and ran while Kirsti was still speaking. The cabbie was waiting. He drove her to the station and she almost wept because the hold-ups were worse. Vienna was in patriotic exuberance, a city heady with the excitement of war, the streets full of people, the avenues thronged with vehicles.

And the station, when she got there, was a seething mass of soldiers and civilians. She did not know which platform to go to, which train he might be on, but discovered after frenzied enquiries that the last peacetime train with a connection at the border for Paris had left five minutes ago.

And that, her despairing heart told her, was the one he was on.

She searched the crowds, the faces, the standing trains, but she knew he had gone.

Life with its challenge, its excitements and its beautiful promise stopped for Sophie in that station. Out of high summer had come impossible war. Under the hammer of Mars dreams lay smashed. And James, her saviour, had run away, had turned his back on Austria, had turned his back on her.

It froze her anguished love.

BOOK TWO

AN EMPIRE LOST

Chapter One

There were disasters, tragedies, defeats. With few victories to offset the note of depression, Vienna gradually lost something that was never to return: belief in the invincibility and ordained purpose of her empire. In 1916 she also lost Franz Josef. He went to sleep one night and did not wake up. Perhaps he did not want to. He had served his time and more. He was eighty-six when he slipped peacefully away. He had been the resolute heart of the empire's ungainly body. When he had gone the empire had little heart left.

Baroness von Korvacs went into deep mourning. She had bravely withstood all the disappointments, all the defeats, but she wept on the death of old and imperial Franz Josef. Ernst was there to comfort her, so were Anne and Sophie.

Anne, married to Ludwig in 1915, when he was dashing and cavalier in uniform, lost him to the Russians in Galicia before she had scarcely begun to know him as a husband. He was wounded and taken prisoner, and Anne returned to live with her parents. Carl had survived so far, but was engaged in unimaginably hazardous warfare with the Italians in the Tyrolean mountains.

They all helped with war work. Sophie visited hospitals and convalescent establishments and frequently assisted with chores that did not require a young lady to have nursing qualifications. She faced up to this kind of work and to every other activity with an energy that was feverish. She also danced, because there were still men, officers and soldiers, who wanted Vienna to be a playground for them when they were on leave from the front. She danced as feverishly as she worked. She knew if she worked hard enough and danced long enough she would wake up one morning and find herself concerned only with Austria and the war, that the past no longer haunted her. She lost weight as she burned the midnight candles. She had the most eligible officers at her feet. She was tender to those who declared themselves in love with her but she could give none of them love herself. Her heart was frozen and would not thaw out. Never, before James, had she been remotely in love. Never had she thought love could be so ravaging, that it could take hold of heart and mind and common sense and reduce them to a state that lacked all reason.

At times she longed and ached for James, the enemy. And James was probably very busy killing her countrymen or her allies. From the way things were going it would not be long before he decimated Austria of all its young men. Then there would be no one left to dance with, no one to help her forget.

Of course, there was the reverse side of the coin. He might be killed himself.

What would be left then?

She received a proposal from a Captain Hans Doerffer early in 1917. He was dark, good-looking and amusing, and like so many of the fighting men talked about everything except the war. He made such a touching impression on Sophie that when he proposed to her in the cab on the way home from the theatre she had a moment of extraordinary aberration.

'Hans, I'm so sorry,' she said, 'but I'm already engaged.'

'Already engaged?' Captain Doerffer was puzzled. She had never mentioned it before and she wore no engagement ring. 'Already engaged, Sophie?'

In the dimness of the cab Sophie said, 'Yes, but I've lost him. To the war.'

'Oh. I'm sorry,' he said, 'I've been an idiot.'

'No, one can't escape reminders,' said Sophie, 'please don't worry.'

He studied her misty profile. There were no street lights to illuminate her. The lamps went out early these days. The darkness did give her this misty quality.

'Sophie, may I call on you? When I'm next in Vienna?'

Sophie knew how much most of them needed to fully escape when they were on leave, how much they were aware they could not escape.

They could only enjoy brief remissions, when they sedulously embarked on every carousing pursuit known to man. It was they, not the harassed citizens, who kept Vienna's gaiety alive, they who periodically descended on the capital and demanded not welcoming speeches, not propaganda, not reminders, but amusement. And it was an ungenerous citizen who begrudged them this, who said times were too bad or too serious for anyone, even soldiers, to dance instead of going quietly to bed. It was Vienna which called to the unattached men, for in Vienna there were so many beautiful girls and women, all beckoning like bright fireflies of the night. They, robbed of so many men, were ardent to please those who were left, those who still came when they had precious leave.

To Sophie, Captain Doerffer was a young man. He could have told her he felt old, but Sophie might have capped that by telling him she had lived a lifetime in a few years. They were, in fact, the same age.

She could not discourage his hope, or the chance of her own salvation. He was very likeable, he could in time be the one to unfreeze her.

'Yes, call on me, please do,' she said.

'With luck I should be here again before the year is out,' he said.

'I'll be here. I can't desert Vienna, though others have.'

'I'll take you dancing, Sophie.'

Dancing, she thought. Is James dancing? Yes,

if he's still alive. He'll be dancing with them all in Paris, perhaps. What else is left but that? Europe is a huge corpse and we who are left must dance around the coffin. I will dance. With anyone.

'Yes,' she said.

'And I shall probably propose again,' smiled Captain Doerffer.

'Be careful, be warned. Next time I may accept.'

She said goodbye to him. At home she stood before her bedroom window, her body cold and aching beneath her nightdress. Detached longing had become a very real one. It was like that so often. At times she thought the years of war were healing her wound, only for something to reopen it.

The night did not look as if millions of men were blasting each other into infinity. The sky was a silence, the stars fixations of impervious light in the vast canopy of indigo blue.

'Where are you, mighty Mars? Are you hurling thunderbolts? Are you destroying greater men than Avriarches? Or are you dallying in Paris, tormenting another woman into loving you? Or are you dead? No, never, for who could destroy you?'

She shivered as ice entered her body. The stars became tiny frozen diamonds.

'James, dear James. Do you remember Sophie von Korvacs? She is so lonely.'

She received a letter from Major Moeller in November. He was Colonel Moeller now. In

January his request for a return to active service was granted, and at the age of fifty-eight he had command of an artillery regiment on the Western Front. He wrote often to the von Korvacs, usually addressing his letters to the baron and baroness. This one he addressed to Sophie. He came to the reason why.

'The strangest news yesterday. I was at Divisional HQ. Can't tell you why, you'll understand. There were other regimental commanders present. One of them. Colonel Huebner, button-holed me, told me my name had been dropped in his ear last week. One of his batteries shot down a British plane. It landed behind our lines and the battery was cockahoop. Richthofen doesn't leave the gunners many to bag in this sector. Some of the men were able to pull the pilot clear before the machine went up in flames. He had a badly burned arm but was otherwise all right. Colonel Huebner went down to congratulate his men and to look at what they'd bagged. Burned out by then, but he saw the pilot. Despite his scorched arm the fellow was commendably cheerful. Would you like to know what he said to Huebner? "It's damned cold and damp on our side, Colonel, so I thought I'd drop in for some of your schnapps, if you've any to spare. I've an acquired partiality for it."

'Damned if it wasn't our friend James. What do you think of that?'

Sophie stared glazedly at words leaping from the paper. Her hand shook and the words spun. Mars had taken to the air and was unleashing his thunderbolts from the heavens. Oh, Olympus! Oh, dear and precious enemy!

She felt in giddy wonder. He was not dead. Her German allies had him safe and sound, and out of the war.

She read on, hungrily, dizzily.

'Like to have been there myself. Colonel Huebner thought him a cool devil. Remembering Bosnia I wasn't surprised. How do I know it was James? Well, it's an idiot's game, war, and a funny one. Colonel Huebner took him up to the regimental mess and gave him some schnapps, then asked him how he got his liking for it. And James said, "I shared a very fine bottle once with a friend of mine, Major Frederic Moeller. Don't know him, do you?" Huebner did, of course, and said so. So James said, "Give him my regards and a message, will you? Tell him that Sophie was right, it was nobody's business but the emperor's. Tell him to give her my love, if he can."'

The giddiness buzzed in her ears and she sat heavily down. It took a few moments before her swimming eyes could focus again.

'They'd cut away the scorched sleeves of his flying jacket and uniform and given his burns a light dressing. Huebner sent him to the casualty station for better medication and damned if he didn't walk off as calm as you like while waiting to be sent to a clearing centre. It was dark at that stage and no one picked him up. If I know James he got back to his own lines during the night.'

No, oh, no!

The letter shook again in her hand.

'I was bitterly disappointed at not seeing him myself. My dear Sophie, I tell you, I'd have shared another bottle with him. Honourable enemies, you know. What else would anyone have done with any friend who dropped in as an enemy?'

Oh, dear God, thought Sophie, this one should have been held safe and secure for me. James, how could you! You could have been safe for the rest of the war. Was it amusing to you, to send me your love and then to escape to fight me again? Colonel Huebner, whoever you are, why didn't you chain him up, why didn't you? He'll fly again and Richthofen will get him. Oh, James, couldn't you have thought of me just a little?

She gave the letter to Anne and her mother, saying in a flat voice, 'Isn't it odd, isn't it very odd? Here is a letter from Colonel Moeller, with news of James. You remember James? He was shot down and captured by the Germans. And they let him escape.'

'Sophie?' said Anne, seeing the pain in her sister's eyes.

'No one can survive all through this war, can they?' said Sophie. 'Especially an airman. There's only one airman who can. Richthofen. He'll get James now, don't you think?'

The baroness, who had begun perusing the letter, looked up and said, 'Sophie, there's nothing we can do for those who fight against us. What little we can do must be for Austria.'

'I know, Mama, I know,' said Sophie palely,

'but why did he escape? He'll only have to fly again. Does he want to die?'

'Sophie—'

But Sophie, so bitter, was gone. Anne went after her, caught her in the wide corridor leading to the domed vestibule. Sophie stopped, her face pale, her teeth clenched, her eyes glittering.

'Sophie, please don't.'

'I am not going to cry!'

'I know, but please don't be so tragic.'

'Why did he do it?' Sophie was distraught. 'I think of him so much, why doesn't he think of me a little?'

'Isn't it the duty of captured men to try and escape?' said Anne. 'Perhaps Ludwig will one day.'

Sophie found calmer breath.

'I hope he will, darling, I hope he will,' she said, 'you deserve that and so much more. You're a far better Austrian than I am. I'm a traitor, aren't I? I'm praying for my enemy when I should be praying for my country. Is that unforgivable?'

'No,' said Anne, 'never. When the war is over we can't still go on fighting each other, can we?'

'I shan't have the chance to fight with James. Richthofen will get him.'

She worked and danced more feverishly than ever then. She descended more frequently on convalescent soldiers, who discovered her aristocratic brilliance provided the strangest comfort. But it was comfort, because men who have been shattered by war acquire a sensitive awareness of the unseen wounds suffered by women. They understood every word she said.

'There, you see, I've managed to bring you some wine today. It won't bring any missing legs back, I'm afraid, but it will help you sing some sorry songs. Well, it is a sorry state we're in, isn't it? And, my dear gentlemen, it's beginning to show. On all of us. The emperor himself wears a very sorry face for one so young. And look at mine. Did you ever see anything sorrier? But listen to this. Misery, you know, is the most honest emotion of all. I'm so miserable myself I'm the most honest woman in Vienna. In the empire. Is there an empire? Well, whether there is or isn't, I exist very sincerely on my misery. In another six months at the outside I think we can all have a good honest howl together, don't you? Now, who will sing with me the lament to the fallen angels?'

They laughed. She laughed. They were all smiling as she left them a little later. They watched her go, the green lawn of the convalescent home a carpet for her elegant feet. They did not see the tears in her eyes.

Carl had not had leave for months, not been home for months. He was a major in command of a mountain regiment, fighting the Italians in a hard, bitter slog around the Tyrolean Alps. He wrote less frequently than he had done, and more briefly. The baroness worried about what the war was doing to him, how it was changing him.

'It's not a cause for worry, Mama,' said Sophie.

'How can you know that?' said the baroness.

'It's never a cause for worry when a man grows up.'

'Carl is still so young.'

'He was. He's now a man. I like him for it.'

Captain Hans Doerffer reappeared in Vienna in January 1918. He called on Sophie. He looked older, tireder, but was just as amusing. And still in love with her. For eight days they either danced or went to the theatre. He wanted her but was neither demanding nor tiresome. He did not flirt with her or worry her. He was glad to be with her, to watch her, admire her and talk with her. He had one advantage unknown to himself. He was a little like James. He was dark like James and he could be talked to, as James could. He liked to listen to her, as James did. Sophie, restless and loquacious, was never still, never silent. In eight short days she found in Captain Doerffer someone necessary to her, someone who could help her forget that Austria was bleeding to death, that the summer of her life had gone a thousand years ago and the winter was endless.

Anne said one evening, 'He seems very nice.'

Sophie, at her dressing table, said, 'He's going back tomorrow.'

'I'm sorry. None of them stay very long, do they?'

Sophie rose. Anne thought her so thin, so huge-eyed.

'Anne,' she said with a brittle smile, 'we're going to lose them all, aren't we? There'll be no men left in the end. Only Richthofen.'

'Sophie, don't.'

'I'm not bearing up as well as you, am I?'

'You're bearing up better than any of us,' said Anne, 'going to the hospitals and making yourself look beautiful when the rest of us look very glum. He is still on your mind, isn't he?'

'Hans? Captain Doerffer?'

'James.' Anne did not know how her sister and James could ever get together again. The Allies were tightening their hold on the Central Powers, and Austria was growing more embittered. The British naval blockade of Europe was strangling Germany and Austria. If Austria was broken beyond recovery Sophie would never forgive James. Or his country.

'James?' said Sophie, as if Anne had conjured up the unknown. But she thought oh, let me go, James, let me go. Don't possess me so, then perhaps I can make Hans happy. 'James?' she said again. 'Who is James?'

'Someone we both feel sad about,' said Anne.

'There's Ludwig,' said Sophie, 'he'll turn up, darling. And there's Carl. Let us feel for them. I am proud of Ludwig and Carl. And Hans is worth a thought too, don't you think? He'll propose again tonight or before he leaves tomorrow.'

'Do you want him to?'

'I must make someone happy.'

'Unless you love him, Sophie, you won't make

him happy, and you'll make yourself quite mis-erable.'

'Well, the satisfaction of sacrificing myself will ring my misery with a halo. Not many of us have haloes, darling. I shall marry Hans if he asks me.'

Captain Doerffer did ask. On this his last night they had danced until suddenly the strength ran from Sophie. He was concerned and took her home immediately. She recovered on the way and expounded in brittle amusement on him being the only man who had danced her off her feet. He escorted her from the cab to her door and proposed going up the steps. In front of the door, with the dark night shadows about them, Sophie looked into his earnest face. He smiled in hope, for Sophie was smiling too.

'Do you wish it so much, a wedding?' she asked.

'As long as you were there and as long as you wished it yourself.'

'Then,' began Sophie and stopped, the silence of the night broken by the noise of a solitary plane. A plane over dark Vienna. They heard it coming from the west, its engine harshly boom-ing and echoing, and because there were times now when the city, for all its traditions of revelry, withdrew into sombre quiet, the machine alone seemed relevant to the pursuance of life and war. Sophie, her face turned up to the echoing black cavern of the sky, was like a woman trans-fixed. Captain Doerffer saw her expression, one of strange, mesmerized wonder, and realized that she had simply gone from him. She was a dark world away.

So that was how she had lost her hero. He had fallen from the sky, shot out of it, and Sophie was listening to the flight of his ghost.

'Never mind, Sophie,' he said.

She did not hear him. She was following the noise of the invisible plane.

'Sophie, will you at least say goodbye to me?'

She drew a deep breath and came out of the night sky. James would not let her go. He was there, sometimes as a faint but insistent whisper, sometimes as an undisguised longing, but always in possession of her soul. She was sentenced to a lifetime of looking for him, listening for him, hating him and loving him. She could not make Hans happy. She could only say goodbye.

'Hans?' she said and lifted her face.

For all his regret and his realization that it would be of no help to him, he kissed her. Her mouth was soft, sweet, but so cold. And Sophie, apart from wanting to make the gesture, felt nothing. Only, after a moment, an impossible imagining of what it had been like when James kissed her on the day she fell into his arms.

'I think I understand,' said Hans, 'it's too soon, isn't it?'

'I'm sorry, I'm so sorry,' she said in distress.

'But I'll call again,' he said. 'In a year, perhaps. If I may, if I can.'

'A year?' She wondered how long a year could be.

'If I may. Perhaps they'll have gone by then, your ghosts.'

'I do have them, don't I?' she said.

'Not for ever. A year can work wonders, Sophie.'

But the year lasted less than a month for Hans Doerffer. On the Eastern Front the Russians, despite their revolutionary convulsions, still held their line. They even made the occasional assault. In one desperate Austrian counter-attack Captain Doerffer ran into a stream of bullets and out of Sophie's life. It added sadness to her bitterness.

'Mama,' said Anne on a day when things were going dismally for Austria in every way, 'do you worry about Sophie?'

The baroness, dejected by so much bad news but still resolutely coping with its effects on their daily lives, looked up from her sewing.

'I worry about Austria, darling,' she said. 'You're speaking as much about James as about Sophie, aren't you?'

'She still hasn't got over him,' said Anne. She was a quieter person now. The war made laughter and gaiety very much out of place these days. Her beloved Vienna was grey, food scarce and dear, fuel a constant problem. 'I think she still has hopes.'

'Nothing is more impossible now than Sophie marrying James,' said the baroness. For all her tolerance, even she had begun to feel bitter. 'She'll never really forgive him for leaving her, for going off to fight against us. Nor is she the kind to go on loving such a man. She's much too proud.'

'Mama, because of the war is that what you want to believe? It isn't like you to refuse to see the obvious. I don't think Sophie will marry any man if she can't have James. She would never really have married poor Captain Doerffer. It's rather terrible for her knowing James is on the other side. You'd think she'd hate him by now. We're a funny lot, aren't we? Not all of us love a man for the best reasons.'

'You may be right about Sophie's feelings,' said the baroness. She bit through a thread. 'But she and James are both going their separate ways and in a way that makes me doubt if they'll ever see each other again.'

'I wish Ludwig were home,' said Anne. She thought wistfully about her cheerful, easy-going husband. 'I'd like to have something out of this war.'

She had married Ludwig on a high note of excited love. If only he could come home they might have a child. That would give her a lovely reason for putting up with everything else. There was no reason why the Russians couldn't send him home. They seemed far more concerned with their revolution now than the war.

Chapter Two

Sister Margaret Kernan took one of the mugs of Bovril from the tray in the hands of an orderly. As she left the ward she hoped she would not meet Matron in one of the corridors. Matron would be sure to ask what she was doing, carrying a mug of Bovril around. She was lucky. Matron was in her sanctum, dressing down a slightly erring nurse with kind severity.

It was bright outside. June was almost on them. The red cross on the bodice of her uniform blazed. She looked around the terrace and out over the lawns and shrubberies. Some walking patients were out and about, some just dreaming. One was sitting on a white bench, a sketchbook on the table in front of him. She went down the steps of grey, glinting granite and over a broad sweep of lawn. He heard the crisp rustle of her starched uniform, glanced up, smiled at her and then gazed suspiciously at the mug.

'What's that, for God's sake? Not more unsolicited medicine?'

'It's your Bovril, as you know very well—'

'That's a winter warmer.'

'It's an all-year-round tonic,' she said, 'and what's this talk about unsolicited medicine?'

'Something between me and Nurse Paterson. Was it you who put her on to me?'

'Drink your Bovril,' she said, putting the mug on the table. She had a soft voice but a clear one, her enunciation disciplined so that patients had little reason to ask her to repeat herself. Her ancestors came from both sides of the border and had probably fought and murdered each other in the distant past. She had moved from Hereford to Derbyshire in 1915, when they had converted Hattersleigh Hall into a military hospital. Here her Celtic warm-heartedness was kept under professional control by her English coolness. 'I heard about Nurse Paterson.'

'Trapped me,' said James. 'She had the spoon halfway down my throat before I wondered what the devil she was up to.'

'She's new here,' said Sister Kernan, 'she thought you were Captain Davis. You were sitting on his bed, I believe.'

'Waiting for him to come back from the bathroom. Could have been serious.'

'You didn't actually swallow any, I'm told. But even if you had it would have done you no harm.'

'I'm advised by Captain Davis that it does extraordinary things to him.'

'Oh, fuss, fuss,' she said but she wanted to smile.

'Sit down, won't you?' said James, rising to give her the courtesy of half the bench. 'I know you're frantically busy as usual, but sit for a moment or two.'

'I can't, I really am busy.' She had snatched a minute to bring him his Bovril and breathe in some fresh air. 'And you're due in therapy at eleven. Try not to be absent-minded about it. Nurse Upton says you're never on time.'

'Tell her if she'll keep hoping I'll keep trying.'

She smiled. Captain Fraser was nearly as good as new. He had been gaunt on arrival. The sun was getting at him now, giving him a healthy tan.

'I must go,' she said, and went. He looked after her, her cap and uniform a dazzle in the sunshine. There were women and women. There was one who was unique. It did little good to look for someone out of the same mould. Sister Kernan was no one but herself, as she was entitled to be.

She spared herself a little more time in the afternoon. She talked first to some of the patients whose beds had been wheeled out on to the terrace, then went down the steps and crossed the grass to the white bench near an old apple tree. Year after year it produced a generous crop of fruit for the hospital, but last year the apples had been specked. A diagnosis had resulted in a lavish dressing of potash. The forming fruit this year looked as if the harvest might be abundant and healthy.

James got to his feet as she came up. He looked lanky in his hospital blues.

'Sit down,' she said, 'I can't stop.'

'Try and change your mind,' said James.

'Well, for a little while,' she said.

'Good,' said James and they sat down on the bench together. It meant a brief but pleasant few moments for both. They were friends. She was twenty-seven, her dark auburn hair tucked up, cap neatly perched, her features smooth and clear, grey eyes placid but perceptive. She had, after eight years of nursing, a capacity for absorbing the stresses of life in a military hospital. She was a woman of attractive, receptive wisdom, who could bring order to systems and reassurance to patients without either fuss or fret. Those who sensed the warm bosom that beat under the starched front confided in her, and she in her experience knew when to supply sound, practical advice that came straight from the head. When they wanted to be serious the wounded men talked to her. It was the young nurses they flirted with. Since the hospital was for officers there was an unavoidable amount of this kind of inconsequential skirmishing, despite the discipline enforceable on both sides. She did not mind that no one made inconsequential advances in her direction. It saved her having to discourage them. And at twenty-seven she had settled for the fact that she was on the shelf, in common with many women. The longer the war went on the more crowded that shelf became.

'Well?' said James.

'Well?' she countered.

'You needn't talk. It's not compulsory. Just put your feet up.'

'I can't stay—'

'There's no hurry for a while.'

'James, I simply—'

'The place won't fall down without you.'

'If someone should want me—'

'They can come and get you.'

'A hospital isn't run like a shop.'

'I'm glad of that, otherwise we'd simply be weighed and wrapped,' said James. 'But it won't hurt you to let it run without you for five minutes. Sit back, close your eyes and I'll watch out for Matron.' His smile was affectionate, and she felt the little weakness of any woman having a man trying gently to spoil her.

'You're very considerate,' she said. She knew he felt grateful to her, to the hospital. Most of them did, most of those whom skilful medication and conscientious nursing brought out of pain and into convalescence. He had known pain from a badly neglected and badly burned arm. He expressed his gratitude in his own way, slightly teasing. Other patients were like that. But Captain Fraser to her was not quite like the others. He was a man of pre-war attitudes, fashioned by customs and trends already considered dated. To her such men were always recognizable, not necessarily by their age. They had their own way with women, for they had been brought up to regard woman as a civilizing influence and that the least of her dues were courtesies. Captain Fraser almost always stood up for her, as if he moved in a world that was still gracious. He was one of the men who had been men before the war. The young men, the boys made adult by the war, were already a different breed. Flippant, reckless, casual. So were the girls who had suddenly found themselves doing men's jobs at eighteen and nineteen. They lived as if life was eating them up. It was to be expected. Captain Fraser belonged to the war now. It had to be fought, it had to be finished. But he also belonged to the generation which had been so buoyant, so hopeful, the generation which had seen a turn in the tide of social justice and a change in the intransigence of diehard government.

The boys, the young soldiers, were incredibly courageous, but so tragic as casualties, so bewildered. The men were as resilient as Job. When evening came and the hospital was at its quietest one could almost read their thoughts. She read them as reflections on how to get the war out of the way so that they could, perhaps, go and find the women they might have married but hadn't, or resume life with those they had. Captain Fraser rested very quietly sometimes, on his back, his eyes on the ceiling and as far away as a man could be. She never intruded, never asked him what it was that so possessed his mind.

No wife came to visit him. He was unmarried. His parents came from time to time, his mother came often by herself. She had grown up in the era that was gracious for the privileged, and looked it. She was tall, fair and still fine-looking. She had no airs, however, and it was some time before anyone realized she was not Mrs Fraser but Lady Fraser.

They came and went, the visitors. So did the wounded men. Some returned to the front, others went home to stay home because they were crippled or blind. A military hospital was a lodgement for the cruel consequences of war, a place for the pursuit of healing, for patching up, for the acceptance on the part of some patients for compromise and for the application of skill and compassion on the part of the staff. One remembered the patients, or some of them, for a short while after they had gone, but one's mind was almost wholly occupied by the needs of fresh admissions. New nurses had been known to periodically weep during their first weeks of duty, but after that one's emotions gradually became armoured by professionalism.

Captain Fraser was luckier than some. His arm, burnt from wrist to shoulder, had been in a critical state when he arrived from France. It had required such delicate treatment, such careful nursing. It still hung a little stiffly, but the seared flesh and scorched sinews had responded bravely after months of medical care. They were pleased with him and with themselves. With luck they would have him back in France and flying again in a month or so. The sinews were becoming flexible again. Prolonged physical therapy was his lot twice a day. He could now bend his elbow a little and stretch the furrowed limb and healing muscle. The scars were savage but even they would look less fierce in time, and he could always keep his shirt sleeve buttoned. There were other patients in far worse straits.

All the same he was a favourite with the nurses, even if with his dark bandit-like looks he was no Owen Nares. The nurses had their favourites. It could not be helped. Professional impartiality could not always withstand the undermining effects of one's more whimsical reactions. The way a man endured pain or the loss of a leg or an eye counted for much, but it was often the indefinable which softened the professional front.

They had kept Captain Fraser in bed for quite a time, the arm a painful mess and torture at the slightest knock or touch. He was not conspicuously heroic, he swore about it as much as any man, and whenever the massive dressing was changed he rarely failed to advise the nurse he'd just as soon have her put his arm back in the oven.

'How are we today. Captain Fraser?' Sister Kernan asked him once.

He stared at her as if she was touched in the head.

'I don't know how you are,' he said, 'but I feel frankly overdone.'

Other men made quips, jokes. It was part of the attitude, the atmosphere. No one could say, and she herself could not, why that remark of Captain Fraser's brought a more personalized touch to her professionalism.

They had become friends. There were traps available from Hobbs's Stables in the village, which could be hired by patients physically able and genuinely capable of handling the ponies, and Captain Fraser had taken her for rides into the dales on evenings when she was off duty. The outings could not be kept secret and she knew the nurses talked about her. Was Sister Kernan being courted? She was not. The excursions were companionable and pleasantly conversational. Captain Fraser did not flirt with her or make any advances at all. Nurses were understandable targets for men temporarily removed from normal life, and many of the officers were naturally amorous. They considered a crisp uniform added a touch of piquancy to a young woman's vulnerability. But Sister Kernan and Captain Fraser simply enjoyed each other's company, or so it seemed.

She wanted to relax now, to sit back on the bench with him, to be able to watch the comings and goings without feeling she was in neglect of her duties. He had this effect on her, inducing in her a wish that she had more time to spare.

'That's better,' said James, 'and it's not hurting, is it?'

'What isn't?'

'Letting a little time slip by.'

'You do so much of it,' she said, 'you sit out here and I watch you and you do nothing except let whole days slip by.'

'Not quite nothing. There are always pictures to look at.'

'Pictures?' she said.

'Moving pictures,' said James. 'I've discovered nurses never stand still, sisters never take time to stop and look, and doctors always hurry.'

Margaret laughed.

'It's like pictures of ants scurrying about, is it?'

'No. It's mainly pictures of young women with a very special appeal to the bedridden.'

'Oh, very fanciful. Not all of you are bedridden and not all of us are young,' she said.

'I'm drawing a general picture. You all look young. Only in Matron is there undisguisable maturity. Am I getting old?'

'I think you've a few years yet,' she said. 'Nurses, you know, are not really romantic creatures. We do have tender ideas about suffering humanity when we first enter the service, but we become very practical out of sheer necessity.'

'You may consider yourself the most practical person here,' said James, 'but most of the men in D Ward would fight lions and tigers for you.'

'Good heavens,' said Margaret. She sat up. She laughed. She sat back again. 'Well, I'm glad I know.'

'Oh, I'll bring on the lions to prove it if you like.'

'Please don't. War wounds are bad enough. Lion bites would be too much. By the way, you didn't say if you were included.'

'Among those fighting off the lions?'

'And the tigers.'

'My dear Maggie—'

'Sister Kernan when I'm on duty, please.'

'Naturally. In my case—'

'Concerning the lions and so on?'

'And the stand I'd make for you. I like to think I'd earn a mention in the newspapers.'

'Oh, lions eat man, you mean?' said Margaret.

'I rather thought in terms of man eats lions.'

She gave that some serious thought, then said, 'You'd be sick. But I'm very touched at being so well thought of.'

'You're sweet,' said James, 'despite your will of iron.'

She coloured a little and hoped it was not too obvious. She looked away, at the apple tree, and said, 'A will of iron stiffens my weaknesses. It's going to be a good year for apples, Captain Fraser.'

'I'm not on duty myself,' said James.

'I am, and I must go,' she said.

'I know. But tell me first, would you care to trot around with me for an hour or two this evening? I've booked one of Hobbs's traps.'

She was pleased but kept herself studiously reserved as she said, 'I'm not off duty until seven.'

'Seven till nine are the best hours on a summer evening,' said James. 'Would you like to come? I always enjoy it more with you.'

Smiling, she said, 'Shall I need my will of iron?'

'Why, did I try to kiss you last time?'

'No, you're always very well behaved with me. What you attempt with the nurses I don't know.' She got to her feet. James rose too. 'Your afternoon therapy, I think, Captain Fraser.'

Officially his rank was now Pilot Officer. In April the Royal Flying Corps and the Royal Naval Air Force had been merged to become the

Royal Air Force, with its own ranks. But at the hospital they still called him Captain. In April too Richthofen, the Red Baron, had at last been shot down, dying in his crashed plane. When Margaret gave the news to James he did not look elated. He looked disbelieving. 'Richthofen?' he said.

'Yes. Here, it's in the paper.'

He read the news item. The British had buried the German flying ace with full military honours. Richthofen deserved that, thought James, but he also deserved to survive. He was the greatest of them. They would be mourning him in Germany. And in Austria too.

He walked now with Sister Kernan across the lawn and up the wide stone steps to the huge paved terrace of Hattersleigh Hall. Here were the beds which had been wheeled out into the open air and tucked into the shade. As Margaret and James crossed the terrace one patient ventured a question.

'I say, Sister, who are you out with tonight?'

'Me,' said James. As they entered the Hall he said to her, 'I'll wait at the gates for you at seven.'

'Give me a little more time,' she said, 'say quarter past.'

'Done,' said James, 'quarter past.'

They walked along a wide oak-panelled corridor. The converted mansion was nineteenth century. During the winter the draughts dallied, frolicked and blew, but in the summer a welcome coolness invaded the place.

'Shall I take those things back to the ward for you?' asked Margaret.

'What a good sort you are,' said James, handing her his sketchbook and case of drawing implements.

'A kind of best chum?' she suggested.

'Well, that's a safe status, with a protective ring to it, isn't it?'

'I need to protect myself?' she smiled.

'Try to bear in mind,' said James, 'that there are a lot of us and only a few of you.'

He continued on to the therapy room while she turned into the corridor leading to D Ward. She took his things to his locker. For the first time he had used words which might mean he had a light-hearted flirtation in mind or something a little more serious. Or nothing at all. She hoped the evening would be as fine as the day had been, that it wouldn't rain.

She rather suspected she was ready to fall in love and it made her feel strangely unsure of herself.

It was a very fine evening indeed, as clear and as still as nature could devise. James was at the gates with the pony and trap at ten past seven. He sat in relaxed patience, waiting for her. The years were going. He was almost thirty-one. He looked his age, his dark features leaner, his frame fined down by the ravaging exigencies of war. But remembering that even Richthofen had fallen he knew himself lucky. For two and a half years he had served with the Royal Engineers in France. Then his request for a transfer to the Flying Corps was approved. He had his wings up four months later and was brought down after five months of combat flying. The German gunners pulled him out of his blazing plane and he spent a little while being courteously received by a Colonel Huebner, and the smallness of the world closed in on him when he found that the colonel knew his friend Major Moeller, back on active service and a colonel himself.

Colonel Huebner sent him under escort to the nearest casualty station. There they did their best for his arm and arranged for him to be ambulanced with some of their own wounded to a clearing centre, from where he would land up in a base hospital to receive more skilled treatment. But he elected, because of opportunity, to take a different course. He sat waiting, a blanket over his shoulders, his arm giving him the devil, Sophie at the back of his wandering thoughts as she so often was. There were comings and goings, the orderlies busy as the November afternoon turned quickly into dark, damp evening. They stopped looking at him and he felt himself becoming as unobtrusive as the anonymous wounded waiting for the ambulance to arrive. He got up and walked about. No one said watch that man, he's a prisoner. He moved out of the place in an idle, casual way. He took from a hook a German cap and greatcoat belonging to one of the orderlies and a few minutes later walked off wearing them. In the darkness no one challenged him, but he heard some German ambulances converging on the casualty station from the north. He knew he could not get back to the British lines without negotiating the massed German trench system, so he headed in the direction of the oncoming ambulances. They lurchingly passed him. He kept on and not long after found a churned-up road leading west. He took it.

A French family found him the next morning, sitting on the edge of a muddy ditch behind their house on the edge of a village. He had walked through the night and was now waiting for a miracle to happen or for modest manna to drop from the grey skies, or at least for someone who might know how to ease a burned arm that felt fiery. The French family took him across some fields to a farm. The farmer hid him for a day and a night, and then someone came and took him away in a deep vegetable cart. Close to the Belgian border he was handed over to people who specialized in helping escaped Allied prisoners. They took him across the border into Belgium, going north of Westroosebeke in Flanders and then heading south-west towards the coast. His arm made him grit his teeth and at the end of several days of endurance and close calls his Belgian friends managed to bring a doctor to him. The lifting of the original dressing was a fearsome work of medical art and the doctor, almost reluctantly applying a new, treated dressing, advised him to give himself up and allow the Germans to hospitalize him. If not, he was to be got back to the British immediately.

A young Belgian offered to get him through

to the coast north of Nieuwpoort. Here, by manipulation of Nieuwpoort's drainage locks, the area had been flooded in 1914 to halt Germany's advance. If they could reach this area at a point a mile inland, a specific point, a boat could be used to get him across the flooded canal region to the British side. It was a dangerous manoeuvre, one the Belgians would not normally undertake except when it had been carefully plotted and planned, as it had been several times. It was an impromptu operation this time, but the damp misty weather helped and so did the young Belgian Pimpernel's knowledge of the route and its hazards. They moved through the night, through the German lines two hours before dawn, launched the hidden boat while it was still dark and were on the grey, swirling waters as dawn mistily broke. Germans manning lookout posts spotted them then and for a minute or so, as the young Belgian pulled hard on the oars, bullets peppered the water uncomfortably close behind them. They reached the British lines in the first real light of day.

He had a brief stay in a base hospital and was then dispatched to England, into the care of specialists at the military hospital of Hattersleigh Hall. They informed him that from his own point of view he'd have been wiser to accept German hospitalization. His arm was a mess.

'What's the extent of my own point of view?'

'You've been carrying an arm about with you that's been in need of intensive treatment. We'll do what we can.'

They had done all of that. He was lucky. And in France the Americans had joined the Allies. That had to mean the end for Germany. He hoped it would be soon. He had had enough himself. Austria, he was sure, had had more than enough.

Austria.

He stopped his thoughts as Margaret arrived. He got down and handed her up into the trap, then climbed up beside her.

'Just a ramble, shall we?' he said.

'Let Poppy lead, we'll follow,' she said. Poppy was the pony. 'It's that kind of evening, isn't it?' She was still in her uniform but had freshened herself up and wore her blue cape. She looked crisp and colourful.

'It's perfect,' said James and headed for the winding lanes of the dales. He halted the pony before they had gone very far and they sat in the trap and looked at what the evening vista had to offer them. The colours glowed under the flushed blue sky, the sun in descent, little white cotton-wool clouds hanging in its path. In the west the horizon was like a rim of spreading gold, tipping the distant Pennines where they rose in uneven configuration. The Romans had crossed the Pennines, marching north to claim all they could of Britain in its lushest and wildest age. The Picts halted them and harassed them and made them think again about conquering the most northerly regions, and in the end Hadrian built his Wall to mark and hold the furthermost boundary of the Roman occupation. They had

333

left their marks on and around the Pennines. James thought that if one sat long enough and remained quiet enough the echoes of their legions could be drawn out of two thousand years of time. That is, if one's concentration was not broken by memories as strong and compulsive as his were. Memories that went back only a few years. He could not remember any reasonable period of time when his mind had been free of her. She would not go away, she was a vivid, obsessive recurrence.

Half a mile away the roofs and chimneys of a small village were shot with soft light. Smoke from one of the chimneys hung like fine transparent blue-black fabric in the still air.

'It's almost heartbreaking,' said Margaret.

'So much peace set against so much war?'

'Yes, and it doesn't make me forget the war, as it could, it makes me more conscious of it.'

'It won't go away for nurses, will it?'

'It won't go away for you,' she said, and looked ruefully sad. 'Dr Posford wanted to see you. I said I'd give you the message. You're going home tomorrow. You'll have to continue with therapy for a few more weeks, you'll be given a letter to take to your local hospital in respect of that.'

'I can't say I'm overjoyed,' said James, 'I'm rather settled in here. You need the bed?'

'Yes, and you don't, do you? Not now.'

'No, I don't, not now.' He sat there by her side, pensive. He had been expecting this but was not altogether ready for it. He had a decision to make and would have liked a few more days to think about it. In almost four years Margaret Kernan was the first woman since Sophie whom he had looked at with interest. Not that there had been many women, even on leave. And on leave they could only be remembered as pairs of eyes hinting at a desire to please. There was no coquettish flutter about Margaret Kernan. On duty she was calm, assured and unruffled. Off duty she was a pleasure to be with, a charmer. Physically she was as attractive as any woman, if one could forget Sophie's electric quality. Margaret, unlike so many restless wartime women, did not demand to be entertained, spoiled, flattered or made love to. In her company he felt pleasantly relaxed. And what was Sophie now but an impossible dream? Given the chance, how could he go back to her and ask for the years of bitter war to be discounted? She would hardly be sitting in Vienna waiting for him. Nor could he believe that other men, Austrians, would let her do that. One of them would have seen all he had seen himself in her, her irresistible sense of humour, her rich vitality, her love of life, her aptitude for engaging in all its diversions and her own striking loveliness. Such a man would have persevered, would have married her by now.

That conclusion, as always, made him inwardly wince. He could not forever live on thoughts of what might have been, punctuated by moments of painful resignation. That way led to a monastic future. To shut out all women because one had been lost to him was to deny life's purpose. Margaret, if she were willing to consider it, might give him the chance of a post-war future.

'No, I don't need the bed, not now,' he said again.

'They'll want you back, the Flying Corps,' said Margaret.

'It's the Air Force now.'

'Oh, yes. I keep forgetting.' She felt sorrow, and the peace and beauty of the evening didn't help. It imbued the sorrow with a touch of melancholy. She knew she would miss him. One did miss some patients for a while. She would miss him a little more than that. He would say goodbye, he would perhaps kiss her, as some of them did, and he would go and not be heard of again. Unless he was mentioned by a member of the staff who might spot his name in a casualty list. That sort of thing happened. Someone would say, 'We patched up Lieutenant So-and-so to no purpose, he's just been killed on the Somme.'

James flicked the reins and the pony ambled on. He was silent. But then, she thought, he often was, for all the talk they enjoyed in between. And he never mentioned what was on his mind. He did not use her, as other patients did, as a recipient for confidences. He had to have problems. They all did, those who had been to the front and had to return there. But whatever his problems were he kept them to himself. He never spoke of women, not in a personal way, but she did not think him a man who had passed all women by.

A farm cart approached, the shire horse plodding and pulling, the driver nodding under his shapeless hat. He woke up at the sound of the trap and drew over to let them by, touching his hat and smiling sleepily out of his ruddy, grey-whiskered face. The smile was for Margaret in her white cap and blue cape. She smiled back. They rounded a bend in the lane and stopped again. It was that kind of evening. They had no need to go anywhere. The world was before them, the sky limitless, the sun edging the Pennines with those streams of golden light, the world itself whispering with the sounds of verdant summer life. The wheatfields were high massed carpets of yellow and green, and the dales glided, curved and dipped, the colours a profusion of browns, greys and emeralds.

She had seen the view before, many times. But it was always different, always new, because the moment and the light were never the same, shadows never consistent. The greens were so changeable, sometimes deep, sometimes brilliant, sometimes sombre, and they embraced the stone outcrops in a variety of moods. She thought of the abundant generosity of nature and the inexplicable acquisitiveness of man. For all that nature gave him, man always wanted so much more. To get it he sometimes turned nature upside down.

She glanced at James. He sat in relaxed im-mobility, drooping a little, elbows on his knees, reins inert in his hands, his eyes quite far away. Because they were good friends and because he was to leave tomorrow she thought she might, at last, be a little intrusive.

'Is it a girl, James?'

'It's summer,' he said.

'This summer?' she asked.

'Well, there was a special one once. I thought it would never end at the time, but when I look back I wonder if any other could have been as brief. It should have lingered. It didn't.'

He did not say why it had been so special, so she said, 'All the summers were like that when I was a girl.' James set the pony meandering again. The lazy wheels drew up a little indolent dust. The falling sun touched her face with warmth and gilded the brass of the trap. 'That's how they seem in retrospect, anyway. I can never remember rainy days, only the warm ones and my father taking us on daily walking tours during the holidays. We could never afford hotels by the sea or even boarding houses. We lived in Hereford and with my parents there were seven of us. As schoolchildren we did see the sea once, on the Cardigan coast. We had a day trip by train. We thought the sand and the waves were wonders of wonders. My father said many places were like that until people invaded them. He said that once you could go to a place like Aberystwyth and walk along the shore for miles without meeting more than half a dozen other visitors. I remember saying that one shouldn't keep any wonders to oneself, it wasn't fair, they should be for everybody. My father laughed and said what sort of wonder would it be if everybody visited Stonehenge at the same time on August Bank Holiday?'

'Your father sounds like mine,' said James. 'Mine could also propound the unanswerable when replying to a question.'

'Fathers exist to profoundly propound,' said Margaret, looking at the rim of deepening gold, 'mothers are more practical. When I was walking out with my first young man—'

'Your first?' James gave her a smile. She responded with her pleasantly warm one. He thought her the kind of woman who would be handsome at an age when others looked old. 'Your first, Margaret?'

'James, I've not always been a vocational wall-flower.'

'You haven't even arrived.'

'Please raise my morale, do.' She laughed. 'But when I was walking out with my first young man I brought him home to Sunday tea. That was almost compulsory. No, it was direly compulsory. After he'd gone my mother, thinking in practical terms, said he was the most upright young man a girl could set her mind on. My father said a man as upright as that while he was still as young as that would turn a home into a church and every day would be like a Welsh Sunday. An adaptable Welsh girl might put up with that, he said, but as I was only part Welsh and my adaptability still unproven his advice was for me to keep a critical eye on the fellow. Although I was fairly enamoured—'

'Enamoured?' said James as they jogged down a gentle descent.

'Be careful.'

'No danger, not with Poppy,' said James reassuringly.

'I meant be careful, sir, how you mock me,' said Margaret. 'Well, although I was rather head over heels, shall we say, I was still very much my father's daughter, so I did keep an eye on my young man. I didn't find that too much of a strain as he was handsomely clean-cut, but I gradually realized it was my ears, not my eyes, which were hurting. I was being treated to long sermons, even if I only asked him the time. He spoke of time in terms of whether heaven or the devil was to prevail, and I felt he needed a pulpit more than me. So I gave him up. I knew I'd never be holy enough for him.'

'And the others,' said James, addicted to any woman with a sense of humour, 'you gave them up too?'

'Oh, they gave me up, I think.' Margaret laughed again. 'One by one. I was already interested in nursing and couldn't devote nearly enough time to any young man. I was given up by seven in one year, while I was studying and training to pass my exams. I qualified when I was nineteen and only nursing seemed important to me then.'

'It still does?'

'I think it has to be like that,' she said, 'I think at my age—'

'No age,' said James.

'At my age there isn't anything else. When the war does end there's going to be a depressing shortage of men and a depressing surplus of women, the women all needing to substitute something else for marriage. I'm fortunate. My substitute already exists and has been constant for several years.'

'It's not enough,' said James, pulling his peaked cap farther down to shade his eyes from the huge ball of golden fire.

'It has to be enough for me,' said Margaret.

'Work is satisfying, especially your kind of work,' said James, 'but it's still not enough, or shouldn't be. It can be creative, but not of life. Only people can create life. People are the result of life that went before and the propagators of life to come.'

'Are you trying to be profound now? What do you suggest, James, that some men take two wives? With two I suppose a man can double his propagation rate.'

'No, I mean that allowing for exceptions, as one always must,' said James, 'people aren't meant to live alone. There's no living creature designed by nature to be solitary.'

'James, I can't simply go out, find a man and tell him I'd like us to be creative together. To start with, he might belong to someone else. To become a non-solitary person I need help. Nearly all women do. Unlike men, we can't ask for what we want. Society demands modesty from us.'

He halted the pony again. The sun-fired Pennines advanced northwards and grey-backed sheep bunched on the rising slope of a wandering valley. The flushed western sky was slashed with red streaks.

She asked her question again.

'Is it a girl you think about so often, James?'

'It's Vienna,' he said.

'Vienna?'

'I've an obsession with the past,' he said, 'I need help too.'

She turned to him. She wished there had been more time, she wished the hours had not been so full of professional commitment, that she could have had something more than nursing.

'I only seem to get kissed at Christmas,' she said, 'when they hang the mistletoe.'

'Well, except at Christmas matrons and sisters are a little sacrosanct,' said James.

'You mean forbidden or forbidding?'

'Untouchable,' he said, 'but not to all of us.'

He kissed her. She lifted her mouth willingly, gave it warmly. The pony nibbled at the grassy verge and the evening was as silent as if the world had stopped.

'Thank you, James,' said Margaret, and he knew she would consider being asked, would consider whether their needs coincided.

'Margaret—'

'James, we all have an obsession with the past, we all look back. It's a sadness sometimes, knowing we can't actually go back. We can't even hold a second of time in our hands.'

It came out of that golden summer then, it came so clear and fresh, so well memorized, and the moment with it, the moment that was Sophie.

> *I stood on the bridge and watched the river*
> *Which passed by*
> *As life does*
> *For life is never still. Is it?*
> *It is only a transient moment*
> *That turns tomorrow into yesterday*
> *Each second comes and is gone*
> *As soon as it arrives*
> *Even a year is a time that has gone*
> *And tomorrow is another year*
> *Full of many things unknown*
> *That a day later are forgotten.*

No, never forgotten, he thought. And he knew that when it was all over at last, he had to try again. Despite all the bitter years, he had to.

'James?' Margaret's clear grey eyes held his. 'There's not enough, is there, for us? You have to go back, don't you?'

'Yes,' said James, 'in the end I must go back. To Vienna.'

Later that evening he watched the sun go down in a blaze of fiery purple. He wondered about them. About Sophie. About Anne and Ludwig. About Carl.

Chapter Three

The pass lay under the snow. When the summer came, if it ever did again, the melted snow would leave a rich green. But every winter was so long it seemed interminable. Locked in by the snow and the mountains, the pass was also barricaded by the iced sandbag bastions of war. On the north side were the Austrians, on the south side stood the Italians. Great barrier webs of barbed wire guarded the sandbag blockhouses and climbed the slopes on either side of the pass. The wire was draped in snow, which hung frozen from every strand.

For over three years they had fought for that pass, the Austrians in an endeavour to open up one more route into Italy, the Italians to get a footing on the soil of the Trentino region of the Tyrol. In France the opposing armies fought each other from trenches. In the Alpine territory the Austrians and Italians engaged in bitter and protracted mountain warfare. The men of both armies performed prodigious feats, whether at high or low altitudes, and amid conditions of intense cold, icy storms and enemy fire. They fought for and from ledges scarifyingly precipitous, they fought as they were commanded to, clinging to positions that were death-defying. Guns were dragged up to heights of three thousand feet, and from there they blasted cannonades that made massive mountains tremble.

Here, around the pass and for the pass, the Austrians and Italians had long set the pattern of attritional warfare. They had climbed the slopes and cut the wire, they had climbed higher and crawled along ledges and ridges to bypass the defenders, and when bright light came they had been literally shot off the mountainside by those who waited on their own ledges. They had attacked massively in attempts to smother the barbed wire and overrun the iron-hard sandbag walls, and they had died. When they used gunfire to smother the wire in rock, snow and ice they only left it quivering. Sometimes, because it was so difficult to move the guns once they were in position, opposing batteries ventured into the more devastating realms of war by trying to blow each other to pieces. Frequently the echoing, vibrating thunder of the guns brought in its wake the slow, rolling, snowballing thunder of avalanches, the gigantic walls of falling white liable to bury friend and foe in awesome impartiality.

The winter of 1918 had come early. It was bitter and biting even during the first days of October. The snow-covered strands of barbed wire began to create their patterns of strange beauty. The men looked lean, gaunt, and were burned black by the Alpine sun and winds. Sometimes only the fact that the Austrians stood north of the pass and the Italians south distinguished one from the other.

What counted was attrition, what counted more was to endure and survive attrition. They knew that. So they hated each other. They also, at times, loved each other. In this region, where fighting for every foothold was a hazardous exploit in itself, they were brothers as well as enemies. They all knew it was easier and safer to sit on the side of a mountain and wait for the other man to come than to go to him. The generals did not quite see it like that. They did not have the same attitudes as the men. They were not afflicted by boredom and a conviction that today was forever, that the war for the pass and the pass itself were symbolic of hideous permanency. The mountains would not change shape, nor the valleys, and therefore the pass was as it always had been and always would be. It could not be reduced and the war could not end.

'This is a pass that can never be taken, so what is the point of still trying to?' asked the Austrian commander of his staff.

'It makes the Italians worry about us,' said his staff.

The Italian commander said to his deputy, 'What is the use of any further offensive?'

'It doesn't do to let the Austrians think we've given up,' said his deputy, 'and I've heard that General Ponticori is considering the very original tactic of a night attack.'

'I hope he'll be here to lead it himself,' said the Italian commander, 'it will be very original indeed then.'

Despite the fact that the war was going so badly for Austria, the empire almost bankrupt, in their tremendous and prolonged mountain war with Italy the hardened Austrian troops yielded nothing. In this sector their headquarters were in the mountain village of Oberstein. Out of the line and into Oberstein marched the 3rd Company of the 54th Regiment for a brief rest. In command of the 3rd was Carl. Major Carl Korvacs. He had been campaigning in the mountains for the last three years after a year of fighting the Russians in Galicia. He was twenty-eight. He might, to the careless young, have been any age. His face, tanned to burnt mahogany, was drawn and bleak, etched by the bitter winds into hard lines. His blue eyes had long lost their warmth. They reflected the grey of wintry war as he marched his men through the snowy streets of the attractive little town.

He had not seen Vienna or his family for a long time. A respite for a week or ten days in Oberstein was as much as he and his men could hope for, and even then they would be subject to instant recall. The mountain ridges above the pass awaited their return. They were hungry for the warm bodies of men, those ridges, although a man did not stay warm for long. The living lay almost as stiff and cold as the dead after a while. The dead lay with ice and snow embalming them, preserving them, turning them so purely

347

white that they no longer made an impact on the eye. But eventually they would be gone, most of them, unclamped from their icy tombs by the compassionate hands of men whose duty it was to somehow climb down to them. And those who could not be reached simply stayed where they had fallen, as whitely mantled as the mountains until warm summer uncovered them.

Carl still believed in Austria. But he no longer believed in the war. His only affections were for his men, for their courage and endurance, for their acceptance of the impossible and their attempts at the impossible. His was an established, experienced company, full of veterans who had survived every risk, every hazard, every engagement, and senior officers knew that Major Carl Korvacs and the 3rd could achieve that much more than other companies. But there was something about Major Korvacs which made them prefer to give him his orders by a runner or by a field telephone. To stand face to face with him could be a little uncomfortable. His eyes could convey a cold blankness even as he was saying, 'Yes, Herr Colonel.'

He hated the pass. It represented the eternal stalemate and all mountain regiments disliked it intensely, although there were no areas of conflict they actually loved. A few months at the pass drained a man of what were left of his caring emotions and wrapped him about with a shell of indifference.

He saw his men quartered in the wartime barracks before making his way to a house called

Rosa Bella. He was to be billeted there for his rest period. The name itself, Beautiful Rosa, was sickly. His orderly, Corporal Jaafe, was already there, having gone on ahead to make sure things were right for him. Carl was not as tolerant of imperfections as he had been. The years of irresponsible rapture had gone, and for ever.

The house was imposing, its overhanging Tyrolean roof declining steeply, its timbers weathered and mellow, its chimneys smoking and creating circles of warm dampness in snow that still managed to cling. Corporal Jaafe opened the door to him. The square hall shone. The walls were adorned with pictures which Carl guessed were family portraits. The Trentino region of the Tyrol was Italian-dominated but still part of the Austrian empire. Some of the Italians, calling themselves patriots or irredentists, occasionally threw bombs as a sign that they wished the Trentino region to join with Italy, but the Tyrol was Austrian and had been since 1363, when by amicable arrangement it came under the jurisdiction of Duke Rudolph IV of Austria.

Carl, observing the paintings, noted that the faces were all Italian. Although the Tyrolean Austrians and Italians co-existed they never managed to look like each other. The Italians were as dark as those in Rome.

He stripped off his gloves and entered the drawing room. There Corporal Jaafe helped him off with his greatcoat. There stood a young woman. She was as stiff as a poker, inasmuch as her rounded form would let her be. She wore a crisp white blouse and black skirt. Her dark hair was neatly braided, and her eyes, overwhelmed by soft black lashes, were slumbrous with the smouldering hostility of the Tyrolean Latin for the Austrian overlord. Carl had seen that look before. He was not impressed. He turned to Corporal Jaafe.

'This is an Italian house,' he said in German.

'This is our house,' said the young woman in Italian.

'What is wrong with the house of good Tyroleans?' asked Carl of Jaafe.

Jaafe knew he meant an Austrian family's house.

'Herr Major,' he said, 'as I understand it there's no other house—'

The young woman interrupted, again in Italian. 'We are good Tyroleans in this house.'

'Who is this person?' asked Carl.

'She's Fräulein Am—'

'I am Signorina Amaraldi.'

Carl turned to her. Her dark fiery eyes clashed with his indifference. They were immediate antagonists, except that he cared very little and she cared passionately, patriotically. She was hotly Italian, which meant, as far as he was concerned, that it took little to make her spit and scratch.

'Are you an Austrian subject?' he asked.

'That is what our papers say.'

'Then speak German,' said Carl, 'or you will not be heard. You have a grievance, obviously. What is it?'

Pia Amaraldi, nineteen, an educated and

intelligent young woman and an avowed irredentist, could speak the official language very well, but was not going to yield to a brusque command from a hard-faced Austrian major.

'I have a protest, not a grievance,' she said, still in Italian.

'I did not catch that,' said Carl. He handed his cap to Jaafe.

Pia's crisp blouse stirred as her simmering fires grew hot.

'You have heard everything else I said.'

Carl could not be bothered to argue with her. They all had some complaint or other, those who were pro-Italy, stupidly forgetful of the fact that they were better off under Austrian rule than they would ever be under that of the erratic Italians. Italians would never make good politicians, only opera stars. They should stick to opera and leave politics and bombs alone.

'Very well,' he said curtly, 'what is your protest?'

'That we have told the military authorities more than once that we have no room to house soldiers. Now they have ignored us and ordered us to find room for you. There is no room.'

'Have you been spared billeted men up till now?'

'Yes.' Proud, defiant, she was not afraid to let him know which side she was on.

'Then you've been fortunate, fräulein. Show me the house.'

'That is not necessary.' It was another protest. 'You may take my word for it.'

'I can't,' said Carl, 'not without overriding the decision of the billeting officer. I'll see for myself. You may lead the way.'

She turned with an angry swish. She began with the ground floor, with the dining room, study, kitchen, outhouse and a sitting room. In the latter with its view of the mountains were two people, a handsome middle-aged woman and a twelve-year-old girl. Pia did not introduce them. Carl asked who they were.

'My mother and sister.'

Carl nodded briefly to them.

'I am Major Korvacs,' he said, 'I shall be staying here for a while.'

Pia's mother inclined her head. The girl smiled hesitantly, shyly. Pia frowned at her.

On the first floor were five bedrooms. He looked into all of them. Three bore the mark of occupancy.

'As well as your mother and sister, who else lives here?' he asked.

'I do,' said Pia.

'Who else?'

'There are relatives,' she said.

'No doubt.' The Italians were well known for the numeracy of their relatives. 'Living here?'

'They come to visit, to stay. Where are we to put them if you leave us no room?'

'I shall leave them one room. I shan't be here more than a week or so. I'm not on a long holiday. If I were I should be in Vienna, not here. What is this fuss you're making? Three of you and five bedrooms. And what is upstairs?' He pointed to the short flight leading to the second floor.

'There is only an attic up there,' said Pia, smouldering and fuming.

'Let me see it.'

'What is the point?' she said angrily. 'You have made your decision.'

He regarded her coldly. Angrier, she led the way up the stairs to a small dark landing. 'There,' she said, 'see for yourself if this is fit for anyone to sleep in!' She flung the attic door open. He looked in. It was full of junk, with an old bare truckle bed turned on its side against a wall. A small gable window let in grey light.

Carl, thinking of cold mountain bivouacs, said, 'There are worse places.'

She stalked away, she swished down the stairs. He followed. On the ground floor she turned to him.

'I am allowed to protest?' she said. 'Well, I have protested. You have decided. Supper is at seven.'

'You may dine without me. I shall be in bed.'

He was stiff and weary. The cold took time to thaw out from the bones. Corporal Jaafe prepared one of the spare bedrooms and half an hour later Carl was beneath the sheets and asleep. He slept solidly through the night.

The morning was crisp and clear. He saw the soaring white heights through the window, icy peaks ranging the wintry blue sky. Corporal Jaafe, arriving early from the barracks, brought him his hot shaving water.

He was spruce when he entered the dining

room. A buxom woman in a white cap and front bobbed agitatedly to him. No one else was present.

'Who are you?' he asked.

'Maria, signore— Herr Major.' Flustered, she bobbed her way out. Pia came in, clad in a dress of dark blue trimmed with white. She looked richly brunette.

'Good morning,' she said, 'that was Maria, our maid.'

'She wasn't here yesterday.'

'She doesn't live in now, she has her widowed mother to look after.' Pia hesitated, then said, 'Herr Major, I must apologize.'

He did not want apologies. He did not want to have to participate in trivial pleasantries. He wanted a few days doing nothing, thinking of nothing.

'There's no need,' he said.

'I was very rude to you,' she said, 'I am sorry.'

She was attractively penitent. He recognized it as a pose. Her hostility yesterday had been far more sincere.

'You've breakfasted?' he said.

'My mother and sister have, I have not.'

'Do you object to my sitting down with you?'

She saw that her apology had been wasted. She flushed. 'No,' she said touchily, 'I've no objection.'

She sat at one end of the table, he the other. Maria brought them coffee, rolls and some cheese. The coffee was weakly redolent of ground acorns, the bread black. Carl made no attempt at conversation. He ate the sparse meal without fuss and drank the coffee without comment. Pia watched him from under lowered lashes. He was not like most Austrian officers she knew, with their gallantries she thought shallow. Major Korvacs looked as if he had stopped treating life as a ballroom and war as a game long ago.

He rose to his feet as soon as he had finished. 'Thank you,' he said politely.

'If you wish the use of the drawing room?'

'Thank you, no. My own room is adequate and comfortable. I wish only to reside in your house, not to occupy it.'

Pia flushed again, hating him.

'I see,' she said.

He left the house a few minutes later. She watched him from a window. He walked briskly, stick in his gloved hand, his greatcoat buttoned to the neck against the cold. He would be a problem, she thought. He was arrogant enough not to care that he was in a house where he was unwanted.

Carl made the rounds of his resting men. They were in a relaxed mood at the moment, glad to be free for a few days from the soul-destroying atmosphere of useless conflict. They knew he would look in on them, but said little. He had made them the hardiest and toughest of mountain units, and if he was a more demanding officer than others, he was also one of the most respected. He had been promoted company commander two years ago. No further promotion happened. He had grown out of the acceptable mould. It did not worry him. His disbelief in the war as a great crusade had not affected his belief in his men. He knew Austria could not last much longer. He would be happy to finish the war as commander of the 3rd. He would be happy to finish it alive. But after four years each new day shortened the odds. Three times he had been wounded. The fatal bullet must be lurking somewhere.

He dropped in at Headquarters and lodged a curt complaint with the billeting officer, Major Wessel. To the effect that company commanders in from the line should not be housed with Italian families. That he would welcome arrangements to quarter him elsewhere.

'Impossible, Major Korvacs,' said Major Wessel. He saw the cold glint in Carl's eyes. 'True, true, I know that's a word you don't recognize but unfortunately I have to. However, I'll do what I can.'

'Thank you. At a pinch,' said Carl impassively, 'I'll share with you.' It was common knowledge that Major Wessel was very comfortably lodged.

'I'll do what I can,' repeated Major Wessel, equally impassive.

'I'm sure you will,' said Carl.

He took a long walk in the cold, crisp air, leaving Oberstein well behind. The mountain road, narrow, drew him upwards. The sky was an icy blue, the peaks brilliantly glacial. He went on until he had a clear view of the pass, away to the left, to the south. He stopped, turned and looked. He grimaced. That was what had drawn him. The unbreachable pass. He had left the ridges only yesterday, and gladly. But there it was, a sweeping white valley, the trenched lines black, like a series of dark winding gashes in the snow. He could not see the barbed wire but he knew it was there, extending far up the slopes. The sandbag emplacements looked ridiculously tiny. How deceptive was distance. He looked at the heights which, on either side of the pass, defied the most agile of mountain fighters. He wondered if it mattered now. It mattered to the respective corps commanders. One or the other would mount a new attack any moment. Whose turn was it?

The Italians' turn, he thought.

He returned to the house just before lunch. He glimpsed Signora Amaraldi at the front window. The door was opened by Maria. She looked flushed and upset. Pia swept into the hall, the skirt of her dress offendedly rustling.

'Major Korvacs, your servant—'

'Do you mean my orderly, Corporal Jaafe?'

'Yes, I do mean him,' said Pia. 'I do not mind him helping in the kitchen, but he is not here to run things or to take liberties. There will be no peace unless you make this clear to him.'

'Corporal Jaafe has a few duties here to attend to,' said Carl, 'but he's not known for being tactless. I've never had any trouble with him.'

'But you are not Maria,' she said with meaning. 'Maria is a good Catholic.'

'So is Corporal Jaafe,' said Carl. Hardened by four years of savage war, he felt this kind of complaint was a trivial absurdity. His expression told Pia so, but she stood up to him.

'He has insulted Maria.'

'How?'

'By forcing his attentions on her, by kissing her.'

'Oh?' His sardonic scepticism could not have been more pronounced. His reactions to the whims of women were no longer basically chivalrous. 'That has upset her?'

'Do you doubt it?' flared Pia.

He did. The complaint was not that Jaafe had kissed the maid, but that he was Austrian.

'She made it clear to him he had offended her?'

'She made it very clear. To him and to me.'

'Then I expect Corporal Jaafe feels as hurt about it as she does. To my knowledge she's the first woman he's kissed who didn't like it. Maria can therefore consider she's given as good as she got.' He walked to the stairs.

'Major Korvacs!' Pia's voice shook with anger.

'Fräulein?' he said politely, turning. The German form of address raised her temper higher. She knew it to be deliberate.

'I've always understood,' she said, 'that whatever the circumstances no Austrian officer would give one less than ordinary courtesy.'

Carl considered the point.

'I accept your rebuke, Fräulein Amaraldi. I'll speak to Corporal Jaafe. If he's there, please ask him to come up to my room.'

Corporal Jaafe, when he presented himself to

Carl, wore the old soldier's air of innocence, a time-honoured façade one tacitly accepted without being required to believe in it.

'What's the trouble?' asked Carl.

'Trouble, Herr Major?'

'In the kitchen.'

'Ah, the kitchen.' Jaafe seemed relieved that there was no more to it than that. 'Well, where else should I polish your buttons and clean your boots, Herr Major, where else should I press your—'

'I understand all that, Corporal Jaafe, but exactly why is there a complaint laid against you?'

'She is very Italian, Herr Major.'

'Who is very Italian?'

'The maid. Maria. She waves her arms about like a Neapolitan. I've only to put my head round the door and she's flapping about like an alarmed chicken and crying, "Out, out." If she could she'd have me shining your boots outside in the snow, which—'

'Which is out of the question, of course. It seems they don't like what they think is your proprietary air.'

'Herr Major, I merely come and go.'

'Quite so.' Carl allowed himself the flicker of a smile as the corporal polished a brass knob of the bedstead with the subconscious gesture of a man who automatically aimed for lustre on the face of metal. 'It goes without saying that you'd not force your attentions on the maid.'

'Herr Major?' Corporal Jaafe was the soul of innocence.

'Yes, what happened?' asked Carl.

'Ah,' said Jaafe as if remembering a trifling incident. 'Well, this is how it was, Herr Major. As you know, a woman who flaps her arms and runs about falls over herself like a blind acrobat. The least a man can do when this occurs is to catch her, and to be frank, Herr Major, it occurred this morning.'

'She fell over herself?' Not a muscle moved in Carl's face. 'And you caught her?'

'Fortunately, I was close enough to. But she's not a small woman, Herr Major, and as I caught her a little collision took place.'

'A collision?'

Corporal Jaafe coughed in the best interest of credibility.

'You'd not believe it, Herr Major, but it resulted in a kiss.'

'Your lips collided with hers? Extraordinary,' said Carl, 'and normally, no, I'd not believe it. In future perhaps it would be better to let her fall about. Similar collisions must be avoided.'

'Very good, Herr Major.'

Lunch took place in an atmosphere of contrived politeness, Pia addressing most of her remarks to her mother, who did not seem as if she considered this a favour. She appeared to be a quiet figurehead against the stronger personality of her daughter. The younger girl, Mariella, sat with her eyes on her food most of the time, though she occasionally essayed a shy glance at the uninvited guest. The fare was plain. No one had had anything better for months. Carl made no conversation at all. Not until Mariella was excused to go off to afternoon school did he mention that he had spoken to Corporal Jaafe.

'Thank you,' said Pia. Her mother gave Carl a little nod of acknowledgement. Since the absence of the father, wherever he was, placed the mother at the head of the household, Carl addressed his next remark to her.

'However, Signora Amaraldi, Corporal Jaafe's duties require him to use the kitchen from time to time. This is understood?'

Pia's mother, fingering the silver crucifix that hung from its fine chain and rested on the bodice of her black dress, smiled and said without animosity, 'Of course, Major Korvacs.'

Pia cut in a little testily, saying, 'As long as he does not give Maria orders or offend her in any way, Corporal Jaafe may use the kitchen, yes.'

'I think your mother and I have already agreed on that, fräulein,' said Carl, and that brought her hot blood rushing. He was daring to put her into what he thought was her place and to provoke her further by calling her fräulein when he had just given her mother the courtesy of the Italian form.

'My mother, Major Korvacs, knows I am to be consulted too on all domestic matters.'

'As you wish.' He refused to attach any importance to it.

He was on his way out again after lunch when

Pia appeared in the hall. She attempted a conciliatory smile.

'Please, I must apologize again,' she said, 'I must not get so cross, I realize things are as difficult for you as for us.'

'By comparison with other things,' said Carl, 'there's nothing here I find difficult. And is it so difficult for you, having one officer in your house and one corporal who merely comes and goes?'

'We are trying to adapt ourselves,' she said.

Carl, not disposed to engage in more trivialities, said, 'Where is your father?'

She hesitated before saying, 'He's not here.'

'Is he in the army?'

Again she hesitated. Then, 'Yes.'

He was prompted to ask, 'Which army?'

'The Italian army,' she said defiantly.

His blue eyes were cold. A number of Tyrolean Italians had evaded service with the Austrians to go and fight for Italy.

'Your father is an Austrian subject. If he's captured he'll be shot. You realize that?'

'We all realize it.' But she spoke quite proudly.

Carl left the house to stroll around the small snow-encrusted town. There had been a fresh fall in the night, but it was sunny now, the air invigorating, the layers of snow crisp and sparkling. Soldiers of various mountain units, taking a brief rest from the front line, were casually abroad. They were not noisy. They were men whose eyes seemed set deep in their faces, men aware they were still alive. It was often difficult, out there on the icy, bitter ridges, to decide whether one was surviving or not. One often felt dead. Oberstein represented bright, sunlit proof on a day like this that ordinary life and everyday occupations still existed. Civilians went about their business, farmers went up to sheds to see that their cows were still safe and warm under cover, and women queued at the shops for what was going. And the little cafés were always full, mostly of soldiers, though not offering the kind of coffee the Tyroleans were used to.

Carl got a little tired of returning salutes. He might have gone back to the house, to lie on his bed and think of nothing as he had promised himself. But that, if one indulged it too much, brought on a kind of moribund mentality which could eventually turn a man into a manic depressive. He had seen that happen to officers and men drained mind and body by months of mountain slogging, by the feeling they were in a war that had no end. At first, morose moods alternated with bursts of irritation. Later, introspective silences set in, became prolonged, and finally every emotion lay inert.

He might have joined fellow officers in the club set aside for them, but they would want to talk of the ifs and buts of war, they would want to talk of Vienna and the old days, and he was unable to engage in such conversations. He thought of his family. They were the only real figures to which his mind could relate. He had not been able to get to Vienna for fifteen months. He knew he might never get back. He could think about that without fear or prayers now. But he wanted to survive, to live on, to see his family again. Fortune had favoured him so far and his every instinct bore on self-preservation, probably because the margin of luck grew daily narrower.

He thought of Sophie. She would be suffering because of what the war was doing to people, to her. The rest of the family would be suffering because of what it was doing to Austria. Sophie's letters – she wrote frequently – were affectionate, descriptive and without heroics. She touched a little on her war work, but did not relate it to the glory of Austria, only to plain necessity. Anne had lost Ludwig to the Russians. Not permanently, perhaps, but unhappily. Sophie had lost her love to the British. That had to be permanent.

Looking back at the way he had parted from James, he could see only his own pompous absurdity. He could not clearly remember how James had taken it. Fairly quietly, he thought. He rather wished he could go back and say a different goodbye. He was older now, he had grown up. After four years a man did not indulge in a daily hate of the enemy. The hate only came alive when shot and shell were murderously piecemealing comrades and the only desire was to pay back in kind. Hate was impossible to sustain, and the things governments and generals said to whip it up were an embarrassment to most soldiers.

He was out of the little town now. In front the vista was one of ascending slopes and eye-hurting brightness. The sun was low, a huge disc of golden light tinted with winter red. He shook his head at himself, turned about and made his way back. He stopped at a café reserved for officers and had a cognac. He nodded to some he knew but did not sit with them. He was not sure exactly when he had shed the exuberance of patriotism for the mantle of disillusionment. Perhaps, while he still had some kind of exuberance, he should have married. There was a fundamental necessity about marriage, the one institution that remained stable through every crisis of civilization, the link between a man and a woman that stayed unbroken in spirit when the mightiest of other institutions were tumbling and crashing.

He had known a woman, the widow of a fellow officer in Innsbruck. Gerda, widowed for two years. Fragilely blonde in her black lace and desperately young. Wanting love. She was unlike Sophie, whom he thought independent enough, when all was said and done, to make her own life. He mentioned Gerda in this vein in a letter to Sophie, and Sophie in her reply had said, 'You are very wrong to assume it is easy for me to contemplate a life in which only my own face stares at me from my mirror.'

He did not feel himself able to offer marriage to Gerda, for of all things that embraced the risk of making her a widow again. But he offered himself. Her gratitude for purely physical love softened him for the brief time he spent with her, and at the end she neither begged him to return nor made any kind of claim on him. She only said, 'Thank you, Carl.' If the war did not prove fatal to him he thought he owed it to her to go back to Innsbruck. It was unimaginative to think marriage was advisable only within the context of mutually glorious love. He knew enough about life and people now to realize marriage was a creative state, not an Arcadian one, that each marriage was a tiny but vital factor in the whole structure of civilization. Each broken marriage was like a small link snapping.

He was walking again, back to the house through the snowy main street. In front of him he saw a young girl carrying her school satchel. Her dark hair hung in pigtails down her back. She was walking slowly. He recognized her as Mariella Amaraldi. He knew it was churlish to wish he did not have to bother with her. He caught her up.

'Good after-school time, Signorina Amaraldi,' he said in Italian.

She was startled. She was shy. She threw him a quick upward glance. She was a pretty young thing.

'Oh, signore. That is,' she said hastily, 'I mean Herr Major.'

'It doesn't matter. Life should not be as complicated as that for the young.' He smiled.

'Yes. I mean no.' She was flushed. She was also shivering, despite her warm coat and stout boots. She should not, he thought, be as susceptible to the cold as this.

'Aren't you well?' he asked kindly.

'It's nothing, signore.'

But it was not nothing. Her shivers were acute.

He knew the feverish mountain chill that could take the hardiest men by surprise.

'You must see your doctor,' he said, 'where does he live?'

'Over there.' She pointed.

'Come, I'll take you,' he smiled. One should not afflict the young with disillusionment.

Mariella did not argue. She went with him. Old Dr Caporal had come out of retirement two years ago, because the younger doctor had gone off to serve with the Army Medical Corps. The housekeeper answered the door. She was sorry but the doctor himself was not very well at the moment and was in bed. Was it serious?

'My young friend has a chill, I think,' said Carl. The woman brought them in and asked them to wait. She went upstairs, came down after a minute or so, went into the surgery and reappeared with a bottle of medicine.

'The doctor said this will do her no harm, whatever is wrong with her. If it is serious he will do what he can to see her. Tomorrow, perhaps.'

'Thank you. Something is better than nothing,' said Carl. He showed Mariella the bottle of medicine and they went on their way. She was shivering feverishly as she tried to thank him. He put an arm around her shoulders and hurried her home. He had to carry her up the steps to the front door. He glimpsed a face at the window, the moving curtain. Signora Amaraldi herself opened the door.

'What is wrong, what has happened to Mariella?' she asked in concern.

'A chill, I think. She's been to the doctor, we have some medicine.'

Pia appeared. She was instantly hostile.

'What are you doing with Mariella? Put her down.'

Carl felt icily angry that they should let their prejudices govern all their reactions.

'Don't be foolish,' he said, 'the child is ill. I'll carry her up to her room, if you wish. Do you have hot-water bottles? She should not be put into a cold bed.'

'Who are you to tell me how to look after my own sister?' Pia was hotly Italian. And he to her was an Austrian wolf, her pretty sister a trapped fawn. 'Put her down.'

'Give her to me,' said Signora Amaraldi in maternal worry.

Carl was incredulous at such behaviour, at the Italian insistence that anything was better for Mariella than help from an Austrian. It was bigotry gone mad.

'I'll put you down, Mariella,' he said gently.

The shivering girl, arms around his neck, had tears of distress in her eyes.

'Stop it,' she cried to Pia, 'he has been kind to me. Let him take me up.'

Her mother, reading the implications of the girl's flushed skin and uncontrollable shivers, said quietly, 'Herr Major, if you will carry Mariella up to her room I shall be grateful. I'll see to the hot-water bottles.'

Pia, chastened, followed Carl as he carried Mariella up the stairs to her room.

Chapter Four

Signora Amaraldi looked up from her fireside chair as Carl entered the drawing room. He asked how Mariella was. The girl had been put to bed half an hour previously.

'It's more than a chill, Major Korvacs,' said Signora Amaraldi, 'her throat is painful. I hope the doctor will be able to come tomorrow.'

'May I see her?' asked Carl.

She was no longer disposed to be aloof. She said, 'But yes, of course. Pia is sitting with her.'

She went up with him. Mariella looked small under the mound of bedclothes. Pia, at the sight of Carl, got up from her chair by the bed and fussed at the blankets like a woman uncomfortable. Mariella had not been very pleased with her, with the way she had treated Major Korvacs. He sat down on the edge of the bed and Mariella smiled faintly at him. His return smile was comradely. Pia thought then how finely etched his features were, how irresistible he must be to her little sister. Mariella did not yet fully understand why one must dislike Austrian officers, the instruments of imperial oppression.

'Hurting, Mariella?' said Carl.

'A little,' she said and touched her throat.

'Say ah.'

'Ah,' said Mariella bravely.

'More ah. Bigger,' he said.

Mariella opened her mouth wide. He peered, almost professionally.

'Tck, tck,' he said. Mariella understood. It meant she was ill but not seriously. The warm sheets and blankets felt so good around her feverish body, and she thought rapturously about sleep, except her limbs were so restless. Carl gave her another smile. 'Nasty,' he said.

'Mmm,' she conceded.

'Nothing to worry about,' said Carl, 'I had it myself when I was young.'

'Are you a doctor?' asked Signora Amaraldi as he got to his feet.

'No,' said Carl.

'But you are thinking something?'

'Only tonsillitis,' said Carl.

'There, that is what I said, Mama.' Pia burst softly in on the little conference. 'Tonsillitis, yes,' she said to Carl, 'she had it once before.'

'As your doctor may not be able to come,' said Carl, 'I'll have an army doctor call to see her. Just to make sure, and to give her a draught to get her temperature down and make her sleep.'

'Thank you, Major Korvacs,' said Signora Amaraldi gratefully.

'We're only guessing,' said Carl, 'we'll have to get that doctor. I'll walk down to the hospital.'

When he had gone Signora Amaraldi confronted Pia in the drawing room.

'Listen to me,' she said. 'We must take people as we find them. I must, at least, it's my nature. And you should. I don't wish to fight battles with Major Korvacs by being distant with him. It's unnecessary. He won't be here very long, he'll be sent back to the fighting soon enough. It would have been better if you'd made no fuss, if we had accepted him graciously. But you will insist on things being done your way, you are so like your father. Well, now I am going to do some insisting for once. I am going to insist on all of us being hospitable to Major Korvacs.'

'That's the same as being hypocritical,' said Pia, 'we wish to be free of Austrians, not to make friends with them.'

'What is being free, as you call it? We have all managed to live together so far and not everyone is as anxious to separate as you are.'

'Or as Father is.'

'Your father has always been single-minded. I can't understand you, girl. You've always been ready to smile on any Austrians when you've wanted something. Why is it so difficult with Major Korvacs?'

'He's here, in the house, he has forced his way in—'

'Nonsense,' said Signora Amaraldi.

'He's in the way. Any Austrian in this house is in the way. We must see that Mariella doesn't get too friendly with him.'

Signora Amaraldi threw up her hands.

'You make no sense, Pia. What am I to do with a daughter who has no sense? To be hostile is to make him suspicious. To be hospitable is to make him our friend.'

'I can't make friends of arrogant men,' said Pia.

'Arrogant? What are you talking about? He's a man who's been in the war a long time, he's had to fight hostile enemies for years and anyone can see he's not going to put up with hostile civilians as well.'

'The sooner he's gone the better,' said Pia, defiantly entrenched. 'He looks at one.'

'Looks?'

'As if one is inferior,' said Pia.

'Ah, that's it,' said her mother and became excited. 'That's it, but it isn't inferior he finds you, it's idiotic. He's right. There's no sense in your attitude, none.'

'I am not idiotic!'

'You're as close to it as you can be!'

'I'm not going around kissing him, if that's what you think I should do!'

Signora Amaraldi's laugh was short and exasperated.

'Well, if I were your age,' she said, 'I'd rather go around kissing a man like that than have him look at me as if I were a stupid donkey.'

'Oh, so now I'm a donkey!' Pia was flushed and angry.

'Like your father, as I've told him to his face more than once.' Exasperated mother and angry daughter squared up.

'Stop it,' cried Pia, 'you're upsetting me.'

'Listen to me, girl. Major Korvacs has been kind, he's bringing a doctor to Mariella. That's enough for me to know I'm not going to be distant with him any more.'

'Well, you're still a handsome woman, Mama,' said Pia, 'so perhaps you could go around kissing him. That would make him feel very much at home.'

'Girl, girl!' Signora Amaraldi threw up her hands again. 'You are hopeless, hopeless.'

Pia vibrated, her mother shook a finger at her. Suddenly they laughed and the confrontation collapsed.

The army medical officer confirmed tonsillitis. He provided Mariella with more medicine and a draught to make her sleep. Signora Amaraldi was grateful, demonstrably so. She conversed amiably with Carl over the evening meal. Pia made an effort too. Carl did not make the mistake of thinking they had taken a sudden liking to him. Simply, because of Mariella, he was less unacceptable. He was tempted to be frank towards the end of the meal.

'You're Italians?' he said.

'Yes,' said Pia firmly. Her black hair, her dark eyes, and her skin which tanned so easily, proclaimed her ancestry.

'You were born in Italy?' said Carl.

'We were born here,' said Signora Amaraldi, 'our family has always been here.'

'Then you aren't Italians but Austrians of

Italian descent,' said Carl. 'Has no one pointed this out to you?'

'We should not argue about these things,' she said.

'Signora, that isn't argument,' said Carl, 'it's fact.'

'We are Italians,' insisted Pia.

'Pia,' said her mother, 'it's better—'

'We are not Austrians,' declared Pia.

'I see,' said Carl. 'You're saying that the Normans who settled in England from the time of William the Conqueror are still French?'

'That is not the same,' said Pia, wishing he would not give himself such an air of cold superiority.

'You mean it doesn't suit your argument,' said Carl. 'You wish the Trentino to join with Italy?'

'It is right it should,' said Pia, 'the population is mainly Italian.'

'You mean that if the population of America should become mainly Italian, then America must become part of Italy?' Carl was caustic. 'You mean that if enough Hungarians were to emigrate to Australia, then Australia must accept Hungarian ownership? I should think such Hungarians had an obligation to become Australians. You obviously think otherwise.'

The logic was unassailable. Pia knew that to say no was to invite ridicule and to say yes was to destroy her argument.

'The Tyrol is not Austrian,' she said.

'It has been for six hundred years,' said Carl, 'and it has never been Italian. You have settled

374

here. Now you want to take it from us. Do you think you have a good argument?'

Pia's expression was almost fierce with frustration. Her mother smiled a little. Pia had never discussed the matter with Austrians, only with Italians whose points of view coincided with her own.

'It is not the same,' she said again.

'What isn't?' said Carl.

'What you have said about other people and other countries.'

'Naturally, you must stick to that or you have no argument,' said Carl. 'Well, as far as I'm concerned, signorina, I'd not want Austria to keep you. You may shout your slogans, draw your knives, throw your bombs and cheer for Italy. But you will take a long time to grow up. You will excuse me?' He put down his napkin, stood up, gave Signora Amaraldi a little bow and left the room.

Pia burst into anger.

'There, now do you say he isn't arrogant? Did you hear him? Everyone else is wrong, only he is right!'

'He's right about one thing. You will never grow up.' Signora Amaraldi shook her head. 'Your father never has. He'll still be making bombs when he's a hundred, if one doesn't blow him up first. I'm going up to look at Mariella. She's the sensible one in this family.'

Just after dawn the vibrating thunder of guns woke Pia. She sat up, listening to them. They heralded another fierce battle for the pass. The rumbling was cavernous, it made the house feel as if it was standing on trembling earth. She heard a hammering on the front door. She got out of bed and slipped on a warm dressing gown. Agitatedly she emerged on to the landing and met Major Korvacs in trousers and shirt. In the dim light her hair was a loose black curtain of softness about her shoulders, her eyes big in her startled face. But her warm Italian beauty was lost on Carl as he made for the stairs.

'Who is it, what do they want?' She was alarmed.

'I think they probably want me,' he said.

It was a runner from Headquarters. Major Korvacs was to assemble his company and march at once to reinforce Lamonte Ridge. The Italians were mounting an offensive. He had thought it was their turn.

He had his officers and men assembled and on the march forty minutes later. They reached the series of snow-covered ridges in an hour and in single file climbed tracks slippery with ice. The air was freezing, the morning grey and bitter, the dawn sun blanketed. They saw the gun flashes like tiny sparks of light far to the south, and the fire and smoke of shells bursting among the Austrian positions. The Austrians had their heads down. The reverberations travelled, rolled back and came again. The dull white slopes high above the valley were smitten by the shock waves of sound. Dislodged snow slowly spilled and banked, tumbled free and poured downwards in white masses. Above these masses, avalanching and roaring, powdered snow rose and hung like clouds. With the Italian guns reaching a crescendo of aggression, the scream and explosion of shells assaulted the outraged mountains and tortured the human ear.

Carl, at the head of his company, halted on a high ledge. Lamonte Ridge lay a little way beneath them, the long broad pass far below. Shells were bursting around the ridge, a wide rocky bastion of positional advantage manfully fortified with sandbags and stone, the sandbags now as hard and solid as the stone.

'We'll wait,' he said to Captain Freidriks. To climb down now would be suicidal. The shrapnel would blow them off the mountain.

'It's damn cold, waiting,' said Captain Freidriks.

'Frozen feet or shot-off head,' said Carl, 'we've got our choice. We'll wait.'

They waited. Their frosted breath hung until the icy shock waves fractured it. They watched the barrage, the running flashes, the flying snow, the splintered ice. The Austrians, dug in, kept their heads down as valley, heights and emplacements were pounded by the flame and steel of bursting shells. The Alps shuddered and bellowed like outraged giants.

The barrage eased, the flashes ran back. The guns became silent. The frozen sky brooded. In the south the Italians began to emerge like dark tiny spiders from the scarred lines of their redoubts. They came over their ridges, over their slopes, manoeuvring to outflank the broad frontal defences of the Austrians. Carl took his men down. Nailed boots bit into ice and snow, each man watching his comrade in front, to pull him back or rope him back if he slipped. The immensity of space and silence after the numbing, confining roar of the guns was an awesome assault on the nerves. One anticipated, after such a barrage, that an inferno of new noise would follow. Silence seemed the last thing the war could offer. The sudden sharp cracks of rifle fire that broke it were always conducive to absurd light relief.

Out they came from their cold holes, the Austrians, to man their sandbag trenches, culverts, blockhouses and emplacements. Carl had his men in position. Woollen-gloved hands beat together to make the blood flow and bring life to trigger fingers. Numbed toes squirmed around in woollen socks and cold boots.

They watched the distant Italians. Through his binoculars Carl saw them dark against the white, for even those who wore the camouflage of the mountain fighter could never, in movement, match the white of the snow. Their advance looked neither quick nor purposeful. They seemed to appear, disappear and reappear, creating constant patterns of changing movement. The desultory rifle fire stopped. The Austrians waited. Rifles opened up again, bullets flying from the south. Useless, thought Carl, from that distance. What were they playing at? His nerves began to crawl. The silence became complete again, and ominous. He knew what it might mean, that the Italians had drawn the Austrians out into the open, if those ledges and ridges and redoubts could be called open. Lamonte Ridge could.

He ordered his company back. There was one advantage about mountain fighting. You were not locked in a trench as on the Western Front. If you needed to move, and if you could, you had freedom to initiate a change of position, providing it did not constitute a retreat or the makings of one. He had the 3rd scrambling back off the ridge when the Italian guns opened up again. The shells began their whistling and screaming, and the thunder to roll. Shrapnel ranged over valley and heights, Austrians diving for holes and fissures, or walls of protective snow and ice. That was when a man hated the enemy. When he departed from the accepted formula and played tricks.

Carl, at the rear of his withdrawing unit, was still on the ridge when a shell burst behind him. The blast hurled him forward, lifting him from his feet. He felt as if a great hand had plucked him up and thrown him. He landed in snow, his head pointing downwards, and the space below was a limitless whiteness except for grey, jutting crags that the wind kept coated with ice but naked of snow. They whirled, those crags. He blinked his eyes. He was over the edge, with nothing before him but space, and the snow was already a warm wet bed under him. His lungs whistled to retrieve the air that had been driven from them. He felt no pain, only a loss of physical ability. His mind returned to work. It told him that if he moved he would begin his slide into the white void.

The guns roared, the slopes vibrated and the snow quivered and trembled. He heard exploding shells. Beneath him the snow lost all crispness as it yielded to the warmth of his body. It began to move. A rope came and landed softly by his head. He did not know if he could use his arms. He felt a wetness on his right jaw. He knew it was blood. He looked at the rope as the snow sank under him. Above the noise of the gunfire he heard Captain Freidriks call.

'Carl! For God's sake!'

It was his body that was slowly moving, not the snow. His numbed nervous system awoke. He reached for the rope just as his legs began to swing sideways from above. The rope frictioned through his gloved hand. He gripped hard, brought his other hand over and held on. He looked up. He was fifteen feet below the ledge. Captain Freidriks and several men, exposed to the gunfire, hauled him up, the rope twisted around his right wrist and both hands clinging to it. They brought him to the top. He was shaken but unhurt, and he moved quickly with the men into cover behind a sloping shelf above the ridge. The rest of the company were higher up.

Carl brushed snow from his greatcoat. He looked at Captain Freidriks and the men.

'Thank you, gentlemen,' he said and wondered if fortune was calculating the favours it had granted him.

'Our pleasure,' said Captain Freidriks. As Carl

put a hand to his face Freidriks added, 'You've a small cut, Herr Major, that's all.'

The fiends of hell seemed to be sundering the mountains as the red flashes of fire peppered the endless white.

'Have we cognac to spare?' asked Carl.

They knew it was an admission of necessity. They shared a frank consciousness of fear. Bravado was acceptable only in young recruits, who soon grew out of it. Flasks were produced, thrust at Carl. He extracted his own and passed it round. They each took a mouthful. He took two. The cold knot retreated from his stomach. The Italian guns hammered away. The Austrians had their heads down again. Some who had been caught by the second barrage were already stiffening, awaiting their white shrouds, which would not be long in forming today. The grey clouds massed, the dull light making the fire flashes redder. The snow came, the flakes huge, and the wind began to blow bitter. The guns stopped and the war around the pass stopped for the thousandth time, suffocated by the blanket of new snow. It whirled as it fell, hiding the dead from the living and the living from each other.

What use had it been, thought Carl, what purpose had it served, that assault by the guns? The profligacy of expending thousands of shells to hammer mountains and kill a score of men could only be put down to the curious self-delusion of generals, who saw grandeur in it and always thought one more attack would do it, although they knew it never did.

He stamped about. The shelf was full of white-misted figures doing the same. One could fight in the snow, one could lie in wait in the snow, but one did not let a snowstorm bury one. He felt he had spent years fighting a thousand engagements of this kind, with the weather as hostile as the enemy, and he did not know, any more than his men did, why the instinct for survival was so strong when all other feelings seemed dead.

The wind died. The storm of snow thinned and perished. Minutes later the sky was a clear, fresh-washed pale blue and in the sunshine the purity of the new mantle of white was beyond reproach. Carl took his company back into position again. Around the heights the figures of moving men were minute to the eye as other Austrian units manned their defences again. The sun cleaved the silence with brilliant light.

They waited. And then the Austrian guns opened up, battering at the mountain and valley positions of the Italians in a prolonged and revengeful bombardment. Angry at not being allowed to settle, the new snow slipped softly and wetly downwards, gathering weight and impetus that took it in plunging, white-foaming billows to the carpeted floors of chasms and gorges. Its booming descent muffled the noise of the guns.

Now the nerve-shattered Italians waited, but when the Austrian barrage lifted there was no attack. And no Italian assault materialized. The Italian commander had changed his mind. The snowstorm had reduced the will. Sensibly he let the battle rest. But the Austrians stayed on the alert all day, and when night fell they bivouacked in bleak and pitiless conditions. It snowed again a little after midnight. When morning came Carl and his company were withdrawn and allowed to return to Oberstein. The sun was out again as they marched in. Carl saw his men into the barracks and then made his way to the Amaraldi house. He had been away thirty hours.

Maria opened the door to him. She bobbed plumply. He nodded brusquely. Pia appeared in her white blouse and black skirt.

'Major Korvacs?'

'You must excuse my boots, signorina.'

She was not used to men like him. Most Austrian officers did not give a fig for her Italianism. All attractive women were fair game, especially in wartime. She avoided them as much as she could, although some could be useful in these days of severe shortages. It gave her perverse satisfaction to make use of them. They were so gauche in their assumption that they only had to flirt with her, to flatter her, for her to find them irresistible. If other women, Italian and Austrian, found them charming because they were still gallant, despite alarming setbacks, she resolutely refused to be impressed. They were Austrian and she was her father's patriotic daughter. Major Korvacs had come into the house that first day like the most arrogant of overlords. He was neither gauche nor charming, he was icy and formidable. But at least, unlike many other officers, he did not spend his time trying to put his arm around her waist.

What was he worrying about his boots for? She met his eyes. Their blueness was grey and there were lines around them. He looked tired, drawn, unshaven, and there was a cut on his cheek. An unexpected little tug of compassion weakened her.

'We are pleased you are safely back, Herr Major,' she said.

'Are you?'

Her mother came into the hall. It made him smile a little. They were always there in one way or another whenever he entered the house. Did they imagine he was going to make off with their silver?

'I am glad you are back, Major Korvacs,' said Signora Amaraldi, 'and if you would be so kind, when you are rested, Mariella would like to see you. She has been asking where you were.'

'She's better?' asked Carl from the foot of the stairs.

'Yes, she is, thank you.'

'We are grateful, please believe us,' said Pia.

'It was nothing,' said Carl and went up to his room. He wanted only a warm bed and a few hours of dreamless sleep. Corporal Jaafe, who had arrived in advance of Carl, came up from the kitchen with a hot drink. He suggested he might take Carl's boots.

'Yes,' said Carl. 'No, wait a moment,' He went to Mariella's room and knocked. Her soft voice answered and he entered. She was lying peacefully in her bed, her head resting on heaped pillows. She gave him her shy smile. He sat down. 'So there you are,' he said. Her temperature was normal, her youthful resilience triumphant. She looked warm and cosy.

'I am better,' she said.

'So you are.'

'I am having soups,' she said informatively.

'Soups are good for tender tonsils, Mariella.'

'Oh, yes, better than medicine,' she said. She looked earnestly at him. 'I heard the guns firing.' Everyone in Oberstein was used to the sound of guns.

'Noisy things,' said Carl.

'You were there,' she said.

'Oh, looking on.'

Wisdom was in her brown eyes. The cut on his cheek was a little raw. Pia, drawn by the sound of voices, arrived in the doorway. She listened as her sister and Major Korvacs chatted. He looked round and saw her. He got up.

'Mariella is doing well, isn't she?' he said. 'It's the soup, I think, not the medicine.'

'Would you like some?' asked Pia.

'Thank you, I would,' he said, 'though I don't think it will make me as pretty as Mariella.'

Mariella giggled. He patted her hand and went back to his room. Pia called to him as he reached the door.

'You would really like some soup now?'

'If it's to spare. Then I shall go to bed.'

She knew what it was like in ordinary times out there on those precipitous slopes, that it must be far worse as a theatre of war. She was an Austrian subject, but her sympathies were all with

385

the Italian troops. But it was suddenly difficult to look into the face of this man who had been fighting the mountains and the Italians for years. It was all in his eyes. Again she felt the weakness of compassion. His empire was battling for its life and he was asking only for some hot soup.

'I will bring it myself,' she said.

She hurried downstairs and hustled Maria into filling a bowl from the saucepan simmering on the stove. It must be just right, she said. She would taste it and did, making Maria grumble that no one had ever had to taste her soups before. Pia patted her arm and said it was delicious. It must be put on its plate on a tray, with a fresh napkin—

'I know, I know,' said Maria, 'but whether she'll want it, however much we fuss, I don't know. She had some only half an hour ago.'

'It's for Major Korvacs, not Mariella,' said Pia and astonished Maria by taking it up herself, for everyone knew the last person Pia Amaraldi would run about for was an Austrian officer.

Carl was already in bed, sitting up but leaning back, his hands behind his head, his eyes on the ceiling.

'Thank you,' he said as she put the tray down on the bedside table.

'It's very hot,' she said and wondered why she felt she would like to stay and talk to him.

'Thank you,' he said again. He was so detached she felt absurdly offended. She swept stiffly out.

He slept well, up to the dinner hour and past

it. Pia suggested to her mother that they put the meal time back. Her mother pointed out it was already back and that Maria wanted to go home.

'Should we wake him?' asked Pia.

'Let him sleep.'

'But he should have something to eat.'

'You're concerned for him?' Signora Amaraldi raised a dark eyebrow.

'Mama, I'm not as unsympathetic as you imagine. It's not against my principles to have Major Korvacs eat a little food.'

'Good,' said Signora Amaraldi.

Corporal Jaafe arrived from the barracks, refreshed after several hours' sleep. Pia asked him to go up and see whether Major Korvacs was awake and whether he wished to dine. Jaafe went up and came down again. Major Korvacs, he said, presented his compliments and apologies, the ladies were to proceed with their meal and he would go down to the officers' club later. He would have a light meal there.

Mariella having had her meal off a tray up-stairs, Pia and her mother dined alone. Pia was simmering with resentment.

'What's wrong with you?' asked her mother.

'What's wrong with our food, that's more to the point,' said Pia.

'I've known better,' said her mother, 'but so has everyone else.'

'It isn't that,' said Pia, 'it's because we're proud to be Italian. So he would rather not eat our food.'

'He was grateful for the soup, wasn't he?' Signora Amaraldi looked sensibly at the matter. 'And he has sat down with us at other times.'

Pia shrugged very expressively. She had said all she wanted to say.

Her mother looked at her with a smile when Carl appeared for breakfast the next morning. He was spruce, polite. Signora Amaraldi exchanged some pleasant words with him, but Pia was more polite than he was, refraining from bothering him at all. She did, however, ask him aloofly in the end if he enjoyed his meal at the officers' club last night.

'I ate it,' said Carl, observing a portrait that hung on the wall behind her. It was of a rosy face and black beard. Another relative, no doubt. 'It wasn't the worst meal I've had, but very near it. The best meals I've had in a year have been here.'

'Oh!' Pia's little exclamation of self-reproach was almost anguished.

Her mother said calmly, 'But, Major Korvacs, our food is so modest.'

'So it is everywhere,' said Carl, 'but here you manage to make it enjoyable.' He looked at Pia, whose mouth was trembling. 'Have I said anything to offend you, signorina?'

'No,' she said, 'I am upset through my own fault. I thought you chose not to dine with us last night because you had found us too Italian.'

Carl's darkly tanned face expressed mild astonishment.

'Our argument?' he said, stirring his coffee

substitute. 'There are all kinds of arguments these days. None of them means very much to me. Not compared with the argument of war. That takes up all my interest. When it's over I wish only to go home and mind my own business for the rest of my life. If other people still have arguments to settle, I ask only that they leave me out of them. I did not dine with you last night because it would have meant keeping you waiting. You have your times for your meals and I don't wish you to alter them to suit me.'

'But you had been out there on those mountains,' said Pia. 'We did not mind waiting. Mama will tell you so.'

Signora Amaraldi would have liked to advise her daughter not to press the matter. It was so obviously not important to Major Korvacs.

'Signorina,' he said, 'I appreciate your kindness, but it's quite wrong to think I did not want to dine with you.'

'It doesn't matter,' said Pia quietly.

He remembered something.

'The soup was excellent,' he said.

'Oh, the soup, yes,' she said.

He asked how Mariella was and if he could see her before he went out.

'She is almost herself again,' said Signora Amaraldi, 'and she will like to have you look in on her.' After he had gone upstairs she said to Pia, 'Why are you so upset?'

'Who is upset?' Pia was quickly on the defensive.

'First you're silly and unfriendly, now you don't

know what to be. You're used to men flattering you. Major Korvacs is too frank for you one day, too casual the next.'

'Mama, I simply wish he would go. I'm all nerves while he's here.'

'But he spends little time in the house and you've not been troubled by your nerves before. Well, he'll be gone soon enough, I expect. Those guns sounded so angry yesterday that I shouldn't have been surprised if one of them had blown him up. That would have settled your nerves, girl.'

'Oh, that's a wicked thing to say,' said Pia in distress.

'But isn't that what you like, hearing about Austrians being blown up?'

'Stop it!' cried Pia.

'Major Korvacs isn't going to live for ever. None of them do. He's already a man on borrowed time.'

'Stop it!'

'I tell you, girl,' said Signora Amaraldi warningly, 'no one is going to get much out of this war. Your father thinks we will enter paradise if the Italians win. Paradise, ha! It's likely that the soldiers who have died will be better off than some of those who survive. There's a look about Major Korvacs. Perhaps that is what he is thinking.'

'Mama, what are you doing?' cried Pia. 'You're hurting me. I won't listen, I won't.' And she flung her napkin down and rushed from the room. It left her mother wondering if Pia was at last finding there was more to life than Italian patriotism. Major Korvacs was a disturbing man.

Some women would want to break down that hard shell of his.

Mariella told Pia that she would like Major Korvacs to be her best friend. Pia responded by telling Mariella not to be silly.

'He's Austrian, remember,' she said, vigorously reshaping the girl's pillows.

'He's nice,' said Mariella.

'He's arrogant.'

'He isn't.'

'He has beastly cold eyes.'

'No.' Mariella's eyes began to brim. Pia swooped, put her arms around her sister and hugged her.

'Oh, I'm sorry, Mariella. There, forgive me, it's my stupid nerves. He's quite nice, yes, but it's no good wanting him for your friend, he'll be gone soon.'

'Yes, he'll go back to the war.'

'So you see, then?'

'Why don't you like him, Pia?' The young brown eyes were searching.

'It's not that. You know what it is. And I don't like him talking so much with you.'

'I won't say anything,' said Mariella, sinking comfortably back on the puffed-up pillows. The Madonna, pictured in sombre tints except for the glowing halo, looked down on her.

'Yes, but we had soldiers here once, looking. We don't want them again, do we?'

'Oh, no. Can I get up later?'

'We'll see,' smiled Pia.

Chapter Five

The day was fine. But Austria was reeling. And to make things worse, the Italians in concert with the British were attacking along the line of the Piave. Some units had crossed the river. The whole of the Tyrol, the southern bastion of the empire, was in jeopardy. At which the Austrians in Oberstein made a typical gesture of gay defiance. An orchestra of regimental musicians took over the town bandstand and in the bright morning sunshine played the popular airs of Vienna. The music drew soldiers and civilians alike. It was splendidly melodious, full of infectious Austrian bravura, and it made the listeners, Austrian and Italian, tap their feet.

Carl, hearing it, strolled into the little square. The bandstand, its octagonal roof shining in the light, was alive with the colour of uniforms, the glitter of instruments and the lilt of music. He stopped on the edge of the crowd to listen. The sky was palely blue, the Alpine sun warm, and the absurdly brave melody was like sparkling light in a world dark with suffering.

He had never consciously dwelt on what the

masters of light music meant to Vienna and Austria. Their compositions had been part of so much else one took for granted. The Strausses were indivisible from everyday Vienna. So had been the imperishable Franz Josef, who had perished, after all. So had been the beauty of the Ringstrasse at night and the loveliness of elegant women.

He stood, he listened and he remembered.

He remembered the extravagant excitement of crowded life, the reckless devouring of days because the years seemed inexhaustible, and the splendour of his parents at a Hofburg ball. The endearing charm of his sisters. It all seemed so long ago. But how permanent in its magnificence had the empire appeared to be then. How merciless now was the Allied desire to destroy it. Only Franz Josef, whose imagination inspired the Ringstrasse, had known how to keep the empire in being. What would follow its disintegration Carl did not know. Nothing that could match it, he thought. He smiled to himself. It was on the cards that if he lived to be an old man he would bore the young with tales of things he had never really noticed when he was young himself.

They were playing 'Vienna Woods' now. It was descriptive, it was also sad and bitter-sweet. He had never before realized the haunting quality of Johann Strauss's music, he supposed he had never really listened to it in the past. It had never been more than a pleasant accompaniment to happenings, to the flirtatious smile in the eyes of a girl or the laughter of his sisters.

Anne and Sophie. He wished them well.

Carl felt an intense desire to start again, to go back, to undo all that had happened since that day in Sarajevo, to have the world as it had been then, for all its faults. But, of course, in that world he had been one of the privileged. In today's world he was faced by the fact that Austria was losing the war. And whatever the outcome, however intense one's wish, nothing would ever be the same. He himself would never be the same, and even a mechanical marvel like the Benz would become utilitarian. Millions might benefit from the change, but thousands would be unable to adapt themselves to the new world or cease to regret the demise of the old.

He felt so old, though he was not yet thirty. He had seen so many comrades die, so many enemies fall. One went to war a naive young man and in the first battle became a seared old one. After the first battle one felt there could never be others like it, but there were, and with each battle the body and the mind both grew their armour.

He turned, brushing the arm of a young woman in a dark blue coat and hat. He murmured an apology. She saw his face beneath his cap, his features a finely drawn sadness, his eyes grey with the years he had lost. It made Pia catch her breath a little. And he was looking at her and not even seeing her.

'Major Korvacs?'

Yes, that was his name. He had contrived to drop the use of 'von'.

'Oh, I'm sorry,' he said, recognizing her.

'You were dreaming,' said Pia, who looked a warm glow of wideawake life herself.

'Not of anything important.' His smile was polite. 'Will you listen to that? They're finishing with the Radetzky March.'

He laughed. There they were, the empire's bandsmen, with Austria almost on her knees, playing the march composed by Strauss the father in honour of Marshal Radetzky for his great victory over Italy in 1849. That was the final trumpet note of defiance by Austria in this Italian-dominated region of the Tyrol.

It upset Pia. It upset her because it was so futile, because he was able to laugh with defeat staring him in the face and she could not, despite the promise of Italian victory.

'You are laughing at nothing,' she said.

'We're still sitting on our side of the pass. That's not nothing. Are you shopping, signorina?'

He had come round to calling her that and not fräulein, she noticed.

'No.' She had no bag so could not say she was. Her outing had no real purpose to it. She had left the house because she was so restless. 'There's not much to shop for, is there?'

'Ah,' said Carl as he stood in the sunshine with her, 'but when Italy takes over an abundance of goods and riches will fill the shops, and who knows, everything may even be free. Only to good Italians, of course.'

The music was behind them as they moved out of the square, the last notes of the march hanging in the air. Pia, flushed with anger, said, 'Please spare me your burning arrows, you are not the only one to have found war cruel and unkind.'

'Oh, it isn't over yet,' said Carl, 'we may yet confound the Jeremiahs. Since you aren't shopping, Signorina Amaraldi, will you join me in a cognac?'

'Do you wish to drink with someone you dislike so much?' she asked bitterly.

'I'm afraid you are suffering from my bad manners,' said Carl, 'I've forgotten how to be civilized. I don't ask you to forgive me but to take no notice. A man sorry for himself should have his self-pity ignored. It's the best way to bring him out of it. You're not a person anyone could dislike. There, that is a respectable café and we might have a cognac there. Signorina?'

She did not answer, though she walked with him to the café and sat down with him in the sunshine. The vista of mountains and sky was washed in white and blue, and the snow-capped roofs of the houses were brilliant. Carl ordered cognac, then asked Pia if that was what she wanted.

'I should not dare to say no,' she said stiffly, 'I don't like having my head bitten off.'

'Don't exaggerate,' said Carl. 'You and I have a frank understanding of each other. We established our clearly divided relationship on the day we met. You have been rude to me and I—'

'I have not!' She was so angry that it almost shocked her.

'Very well, signorina.' Carl regarded her thoughtfully. Her temper made her eyes look fiercely luminous. Her blue fur hat had a ridiculous feather stuck in it. Her mouth was moistly mutinous. Ready to spit? She was not like Anne or Sophie. She was lushly, smoulderingly Italian. He supposed some men liked that type. 'Shall we simply accept that we've been a little intolerant of each other and that we'll set the world a good example by leaving it at that? Signorina, a feather in a fur hat, that's the fashion now?'

Furious, she flushed, 'How dare you!' To be ridiculed on top of everything else was too much.

'I'm sorry,' said Carl.

'What is wrong with it?'

'Wrong? Nothing,' said Carl, 'the feather makes the hat look delicious. Quite the thing when everything else is so dire. Ah, the cognac.' The waiter set the glasses down. Pia, fury reduced to confusion, stared helplessly into Carl's eyes as he said, 'What shall we drink to, signorina?'

'I don't drink cognac in public,' said Pia.

Carl called the waiter back. Pia asked for a glass of white wine. Carl tipped the unwanted brandy into his own glass.

'Why didn't you say so before?' he asked.

'You gave me no chance. You were too busy cutting me down.'

'What a miserable devil I am,' said Carl, but she thought for once that his bleak eyes held a glint of amusement. The light was on his face.

And Pia felt a sense of shock at her reaction. She dropped her eyes, her gloved hands clasped tightly in her lap. The wine came. She took it up. Her body felt heated. The wine danced palely and pictures shimmered on its surface. She realized her hand was trembling.

'Signorina, what then shall we drink to?' His voice re-engaged her consciousness.

'Major Korvacs, please let us be friends.'

'We are friends, then,' said Carl, 'let us drink to that.'

He sipped his cognac, she her wine.

'Your family, they live in Vienna?' she asked.

'My family?'

'Your wife?' she said, eyes on her glass.

'My wife?' He seemed curious. 'You're interested in my wife?'

'She is someone to talk about, isn't she?' said Pia, wondering why she felt pangs.

'Is she?' said Carl. 'Well, she's a very unknown quality. I've never met her myself. I have parents and sisters, but no wife.'

'Oh,' said Pia and the pangs went away.

'I also have a Benz. In these days that's not such a worry as a wife.'

'A Benz?' said Pia.

'Motor car,' said Carl, and thought about the Benz and James and his sisters.

'Please don't go dreaming again, that isn't very flattering,' said Pia, then wondered what was happening to her that she could say something so silly.

'Do you wish to be flattered, signorina? No, I

think not.' Carl was ironic. 'That sort of thing is, in fact, unwelcome to modern women, isn't it? In the world that's coming all words must be practical, all actions useful.'

Agitated, Pia said, 'You have no right to say things like that to me.'

'I'm sorry,' said Carl and they sat in silence for a while. It did not seem to worry him. He had his cognac for warm company. She sipped her wine, grateful that it enabled her to keep her eyes lowered.

'How long do you have before they send you back to the pass again?' she asked when she was calmer.

'Do you mean how long before I'm out of your house?'

He was unbreakably hard. She had not meant that at all.

'I think perhaps you don't really wish us to be friends,' she said.

'But I speak Italian with you. Isn't that friendly?'

'Yes. Yes, I suppose so.' It was ridiculous, the things that were suddenly important to her. 'But how long do you have? You see, Mariella wishes you to be her best friend, and I should like to tell her you will at least not be gone by tomorrow.'

'You must know, signorina, that we are usually only out of the line for short spells. But Mariella?' Carl smiled. It diminished his bleakness and set Pia's emotions dangerously on edge again. She was alarmed at what was happening to her. 'We need say nothing to Mariella about going,' he said.

'I must get back,' said Pia. She did not have to, not immediately, but she felt she needed sanctuary and the reassurance of her mirror. Her mirror would tell her she was still resolutely Italian, wouldn't it?

'May I walk with you?' asked Carl.

Her sense of immediate pleasure was such that she was not sure if she would look into her mirror at all.

She said lightly, 'Oh, now I am flattered.'

It was only ten minutes to the house. She did not hurry and he measured his pace with hers. She asked him what his interests were and whether he would like to talk about them.

Was she off her head? thought Carl. What interests did she think he could have except in staying alive?

'I've few interests at the moment,' he said. 'What are yours?'

'Oh, I just have my family,' she said, and it did not occur to her that her omission of separatism represented to him a large hole in her answer.

'The English,' he said, 'always talk about the weather when they can find nothing else to discuss.'

'That must be very dull. They are dull too, I suppose.'

'Should you say that about your friends?'

'My friends?' Pia refused to concede. 'The English aren't my friends.'

400

'They're your allies, they're on your side, fighting for your Italy.'

Pia felt a rush of unhappiness.

'I am an Austrian subject, you have told me so yourself.'

'But I am quite aware you're an unwilling one,' said Carl. 'I don't think we should discuss that again. I met someone from England just before the war.'

'I'm sure she wasn't dull,' said Pia.

'She?' he said, and Pia felt herself the hapless victim of the set thought patterns peculiar to a woman becoming far too interested in a particular man.

'He?' she suggested.

'Well, he or she,' said Carl drily, 'he wasn't dull. He nearly broke my sister Sophie's heart. No dull man could have done that—'

'Oh, what happened?' Pia felt suddenly and intensely curious.

'What happened? The war,' said Carl.

'But,' she began, and then she said, 'Oh. I see. Oh, how sad.' She paused. 'I want you to know,' she said, 'that my mother sometimes says I'm a great donkey.'

'I can tell you,' said Carl, 'that in my time I've been the greatest of idiots.'

He was smiling. It warmed Pia. As they went up the steps to the house she said, 'Thank you, it has been very pleasant.'

'Pleasant?' said Carl.

'Well, we did not actually quarrel, did we?' she said. They parted in the hall. She sought her mother and found her in the cosy sitting room, darning some of Mariella's woollen stockings. One had to do that sort of thing these days. In the past old stockings had been given away and new ones bought.

Signora Amaraldi, watching Pia taking off her hat and shaking her hair, said, 'You came in together.'

'Yes.' Pia was glowing. 'We met by the bandstand. They were playing music, an Austrian regimental band, would you believe.'

'That's the Austrians for you. When they should be miserable they're playing music. So what difference is there between them and Italians?'

'Mama, I'm not going to argue with you,' said Pia, 'I'm going to say we must still be careful but that needn't stop us from being nice to him.'

'Haven't I been saying that myself?'

'Well, I am saying it too now,' said Pia.

Her mother used shrewd eyes on her daughter.

'While you're being nice,' she said, 'remember you've said we must still be careful. I think you must be more careful than any of us.'

'I'd never be indiscreet, never,' said Pia.

'I'm not talking about being indiscreet.'

The front door knocker sounded. Maria answered it, then came to say an Austrian officer had called. Pia went into the hall, a polite smile masking apprehension. A grey-haired major clicked his heels.

'Major Wessel, Fräulein Amaraldi,' he said.

'Yes, Herr Major?' She spoke in German. She was being careful.

'I wish to see Major Korvacs. Is he in?'

Pia heard Mariella's burst of laughter upstairs. Major Korvacs was obviously with her sister. She took Major Wessel up. She felt a little worried. Carl came out of Mariella's room and took Major Wessel to his own. Pia had lost some of her glow by the time she returned to the sitting room.

'Mama, I think someone has come to order Major Korvacs back to the front.'

'Perhaps that's all for the best,' said Signora Amaraldi.

'It isn't for him,' said Pia, 'he's done his share. Mama, four years. You can see that just by looking at him.'

'I have seen it. It was there when he first entered the house. Men go to war thinking it's not much more than a game. Major Korvacs discovered long ago that it has nothing to do with games at all.'

Pia swished restlessly about.

'I wish,' she said, 'you wouldn't be so wise and superior and know everything.'

'I don't know everything, but I know a little about men. And I know about you, with your Italian flag and other things tucked away in the attic.'

'Oh, hush!'

'Suddenly it isn't so simple, girl, is it?'

'Is anything?' Pia would not be drawn.

'Are you beginning to think that Austrians are people too?'

'Oh, I've never been as prejudiced as that! There are Austrians here, people we know and have lived with. But we are Italian—'

'Then let us go and live in Italy and not plot to throw bombs at people we've lived with.'

'I would never do that, you know I wouldn't! Oh, you're as unkind as he is sometimes—' Pia broke off and turned her back.

'Ah,' said her mother, 'he's been telling you you have no sense, I suppose. Well, you'll have to change your ways to impress a man like him.'

'I wouldn't do that for any man,' said Pia proudly, 'I'd want always to be myself. Mama, please, I'm only saying Major Korvacs has been in the war a long time and that we should be sympathetic.'

'I know exactly what you're saying,' said Signora Amaraldi. 'If they're sending him back to that pass, however, it's prayers he'll need, not sympathy. And we must hope the military authorities won't ask us to lodge anyone else.'

'We must be firm,' said Pia, 'we have to keep the room ready for Major Korvacs when he comes back.'

'Oh?' Dark eyebrows lifted. 'There's a change in our standing as a fine old Italian family, is there?'

Pia, restlessly picking up china ornaments and replacing them, said, 'Mama, there's Mariella. She likes Major Korvacs very much, she wouldn't want anyone else here. She'd want us to keep his room for him—'

'Are you crazy, girl? Do you think we're keeping

a hotel or pensione, with rooms reserved? Major Korvacs is a good man, yes, but you'll be storing up trouble for us all if you encourage the authorities to keep lodging him on us. As far as I'm concerned, he's more than welcome, but you know as well as I do that feelings aren't important. Ah – or are they?'

'I have simply come to understand I can't blame Major Korvacs personally for Austrian oppression of Tyrolean Italians.'

'I've never felt oppressed. You have, your father has. Look at me, Pia, instead of walking around in circles.' Signora Amaraldi looked long and hard as Pia faced her. 'Listen to me. What do you think your father would say if he knew you'd been walking out with an Austrian officer?'

'He would say it was a big song and dance about nothing, because I've been walking out with nobody! I met Major Korvacs by accident and he saw me home. Did I ask him to? No.'

'Good,' said Signora Amaraldi, 'it's as well not to invite trouble, it knocks at one's door all too often without being asked.'

'You seem comfortably off here,' said Major Wessel, looking around the spacious, well-appointed bedroom with its marble-topped washstand, polished tallboy, wardrobe, dressing table, pictures and chairs. The bed itself was huge, its brass gleaming.

'I wouldn't deny that,' said Carl.

'You'll appreciate how short we always are of suitable accommodation,' said Major Wessel, 'and we felt we had at least found a reasonable residence for you, even though it was Italian. If you can hang on for another day or so I think we can offer you accommodation with an Austrian family. The house of Pietro Amaraldi isn't quite the right place, I know, but—'

'Pietro Amaraldi? Should that name mean something to me?'

'It does to others.' Major Wessel stood squarely to the window, from which the view was of glittering snow. 'Pietro Amaraldi has been agitating for years to have the Trentino region unite with Italy. He's a leading irredentist.'

'And head of this family?' Carl was not very interested.

'Yes,' said Major Wessel, too old to be anything but an administrative officer and frankly glad about it. 'The authorities intended to put him away somewhere when Italy declared war, but he saw it coming and slipped us. However, he was captured, with thousands of Italians, at Caporetto last year. But he escaped. The authorities would like to get him back. We searched this house some time ago. He's the kind of man outrageous enough to come calling on his family. It's believed he's back in Italy now. Very wise of him.'

'It saves him getting shot,' said Carl.

'Yes.' Major Wessel turned. 'You've found the family unfriendly?'

'Not at all.' Carl's smile was thin.

'Well, they're not in a position to be too out-spoken, although they have land and farms in the area and consider themselves better than others.'

'True, the family portraits do look down on one.'

'The farms are managed and worked for them,' said Major Wessel. 'I imagine it's a blow to their pride to have to quarter a military man.'

'My pride has felt no blow,' said Carl, 'why should theirs?'

'They're so damned Italian,' said Major Wessel. 'But look here, I didn't want you to think your request had been pigeonholed. In two days at the outside I can promise you—'

'Yes, thank you,' said Carl, 'allow me to see you out.'

They parted on fairly friendly terms at the front door, then Carl went back up to his room. Pia, talking to Mariella, heard him. Mariella had just asked if she could get up.

'Yes, after lunch,' said Pia, 'but wrap up warmly.'

'Oh, I will. Pia, someone has just been to see Major Korvacs.'

'I know.'

'He's not going to leave us yet, is he?'

'I shouldn't think so,' said Pia,' I'll find out.'

She knocked on his door a minute later.

'Come.' His voice sounded wetly muffled.

Pia looked in. He was cleaning his teeth at the washstand. He wiped his mouth on the towel.

'Signorina?'

Pia said very casually, 'Oh, it's Mariella.'

'Yes?'

He was always so calm, so much in command. Her father could fire off a thousand hot-blooded words for every precise one spoken by Major Korvacs. She could have dealt so much better with her emotions if he had been like most of the other Austrian officers she knew, extrovert and reckless.

She said, 'It's just that Mariella asked whether you have to go.'

'Not immediately,' said Carl. 'Major Wessel is the billeting officer. He called to offer me the opportunity of alternative accommodation in a day or two.'

'Alternative accommodation?' Pia thought she had never heard such woodenly unattractive words.

'It's nothing personal,' said Carl, 'simply that I put in a request when I realized it was inconvenient for you to lodge me here.'

Pia stared at him. Humiliation crimsoned her.

'Oh, how could you! Major Korvacs, how could you! Oh, to do that, to insult us so! I shall never forgive you!' She swept out, she ran to her room.

He appeared at lunch, as correct as ever. Pia would not look at him, but her mother was more philosophical.

'You are leaving us, I understand, Major Korvacs,' she said as they began their lentil soup.

'Yes, in about four or five days,' he said, 'I doubt if our rest period will last longer than that.'

'Four or five days?' Signora Amaraldi looked puzzled. 'But Pia said—'

'No,' interrupted Pia angrily, 'I only repeated what Major Korvacs said.'

'Yes, that he was moving to another house in a day or so.'

'I was offered that,' said Carl. He broke a piece of black bread.

'Yes, because you had made a request.' Pia was vehement. 'Mama, we are insulted—'

'Pia!' Signora Amaraldi flashed her eyes at her daughter.

'When I saw Major Wessel out,' said Carl, spooning soup, 'I told him I was so comfortable here that I wished to remain. Certainly, I've no wish to leave my young friend Mariella until I have to. She's to get up this afternoon, she tells me. We've arranged to play chess.'

Pia was reduced to devil-provoked speech-lessness. Oh, he was out of cold hell, this one. Deliberately he had let her make an idiot of her-self. Had he enjoyed that? Did he dislike her so much?

Finding her voice she gasped, 'Oh, you are impossible, you told me you were moving to another house, you said nothing about remaining here!'

'I said I'd been offered the chance to move,' said Carl. 'Signora Amaraldi, in the middle of my answer to her question, your daughter vanished.'

'Ah, she never stops to think,' said Signora Amaraldi, 'she runs and rushes where everyone else walks. She has no head, Major Korvacs.'

Bitterly Pia said, 'Yes, I have told him I am a senseless donkey.'

'Let us enjoy the soup,' said Carl, 'it's very good.'

'Major Korvacs,' said Pia, while her mother watched her out of knowing eyes, 'when I next ask you a question will you please not reply in such a deceptive way?'

'If you will promise to stay and listen,' said Carl, 'I'll be as straightforward as I can.'

Signora Amaraldi smiled. Pia bit her lip.

Chapter Six

To keep Mariella cosy and to give Major Korvacs
no reason to complain, Pia saw to it that the
drawing-room fire was ablaze that afternoon.
The piled logs crackled and the armchairs grew
warm. The chess table was moved close to the
fire. There Mariella and Carl sat down to play.
Signora Amaraldi, who enjoyed domestic tasks
and accordingly worried less about the shortage
of servants than Pia did, settled herself in her
chair with a basket of sewing on her lap.

Mariella, fire giving her a glow, turned the
chess pieces out of the box.

'I'm white, that's Italian,' she said with
adolescent ingenuousness, 'you're black, that's
Austrian.'

'Black, hm,' said Carl. 'Very well, my young
friend.'

'I shan't mind if you win,' said Mariella.

'I'll be racked with shame if I don't,' said Carl,
'you're only half my size.'

'It's brains that count, not size,' said Mariella.

'Ah,' said Carl, 'that's a different kettle of
fish.'

'Never mind,' said Mariella magnanimously, 'you are still nice.'

'Thank you,' said Carl, 'you are quite my best friend.'

They began the game. Mariella was good and played with youthful, earnest confidence. Pia, who had been upstairs, came in. She had changed into a brown velvet dress. It gave her a rich, lush look. She had recovered from her lunchtime brush with Carl.

'May I watch?' she asked, putting her hands on an armchair.

'As long as you don't talk,' said Mariella.

Carl got up and brought the armchair forward so that Pia could sit next to her sister. Pia thanked him and asked who was winning.

'I am,' said Mariella, 'but Carl is doing awfully well for someone without much brains.'

'Oh, Mariella!'

'I didn't say that, he did,' said Mariella. 'Well, he as good as said it.'

'Yes, he is like that,' said Pia, 'he doesn't always plainly commit himself.'

'Hm,' said Carl, considering his move.

'There, you mustn't talk,' said Mariella to her sister.

Pia watched. Her mother watched. Carl played thoughtfully. Mariella played happily. She wriggled and enjoyed bites at her knuckles, but all her moves were made decisively.

Carl kept saying, 'Hm.' But he was relaxing for the first time in months. The firelight was cosy, the atmosphere friendly. His bleakness eased.

He smiled at Mariella's wriggles. Pia covertly watched him. The hard lines of his sunburnt face softened in the glow of the fire, and she thought how fine-looking he was. She could not quite understand some of his moves. Whether he was only a moderate player or simply wanted to make Mariella happy by letting her win, she didn't know, but certainly his play was either indifferent at times or a little suspect. Mariella kept saying, '*Mama mia,*' in slightly shocked surprise. She also tck-tcked in sympathetic regret but did not allow this to affect her earnest dedication.

'Check,' she said after an hour.

'Hm,' said Carl and pondered. Pia thought there was a smile in his eyes. He moved his king. Mariella pounced with her queen.

'Checkmate,' she said with sorrow for his downfall and relish for her victory. The one came with a shake of her head, the other with a winning smile.

'Hm,' said Carl. He surveyed the Austrian debacle. '*Mama mia,*' he said.

Mariella laughed, Pia laughed. Signora Amaraldi smiled.

'Never mind,' said Mariella.

'Massacred,' said Carl, 'and by my best friend.'

And Pia felt a strange little sadness. His country was in its last desperate fight for survival. He had been soldiering for Austria since 1914 and if Austria went down he would go down too. For four years he would have fought in vain and many of his friends would have died in vain. But there he was, making Mariella happy, a smile on his face. Perhaps against the tragedy of a broken empire he realized defeat in a game of chess meant nothing. As a fervent supporter of the Italian irredentists she should be feeling glad that the Austrian empire was tottering. But she was not. It disturbed her.

Mariella stayed up for the modest dinner and was then happy to go back to bed. Major Korvacs had been very agreeable, especially to Mariella, who was beginning to hero-worship him a little. Pia had not let her nerves show. The harmony had spread to the kitchen, where Corporal Jaafe, with the old soldier's artfulness, was making astute dents in Maria's Catholic purity. At the moment he was helping her with the dishes prior to seeing her home on his way back to the barracks.

In the dining room, the meal at an end, Carl suddenly said, 'Signorina Amaraldi, your father is Pietro Amaraldi – correct?'

Pia, caught off guard, looked startled. Her mother sighed.

'He is my father, yes,' said Pia.

'An irredentist,' said Carl.

'Is that what he's called?' she asked as casually as she could.

'Is it?' said Carl.

'He has been called a patriot,' said Pia.

Carl looked at her. It made her feel she had a retarded intellect.

'By the emperor?' he asked sarcastically.

She was in dismay. He was cold again. And she

was suffering from loyalties confusingly divided now. A few days ago she would have been proudly and defiantly Italian, but it was not so easy at this moment. Her eyes begged her mother for help.

'Herr Major,' said Signora Amaraldi calmly, 'we are good Austrian subjects most of the time. Now and again we are a little Italian and say silly little things, but we are as sad about the war as you are. I will tell you, yes, my husband Pietro is called a patriot. He too says silly little things. About politics. He has gone off with other Italians and left us very embarrassed.'

'So I believe,' said Carl. 'Well, what does it matter now? Austria has tried to hold the empire together, believing it to be more of a blessing than a curse, but the cracks are getting wider and Vienna will fall into the abyss unless a miracle happens. I can't produce that miracle and you, signora, being Italian, would not wish to. To you it is better to be governed badly by Italy than be governed in any way by Austria.'

'I have not said so.' Signora Amaraldi made her point quietly.

'Perhaps I'm quoting the opinion of Tyrolean Italians generally,' said Carl. 'There's nothing I can do about it, though as an Austrian I regret it. With things as they are I see myself bowing to the inevitable.'

'But Austria is still fighting,' said Pia, a little distressed. She did not know when she had felt so uncertain about what she wanted. It had all been so simple before, all in sharp, divisible black and white. Now there were so many shades of grey. 'Major Korvacs, you haven't given up, have you?'

'No, I haven't given up, I'm still in the position of having to obey orders,' said Carl. 'With you I've merely established my views. I concede your Italianism. So with that out of the way, what is to be done? Might I suggest chess? Would you care for a game, Pia?'

Pia was newly startled. He was smiling. A little ironically, perhaps, but not unkindly. And he had called her by her name at last. Austria was breaking on all fronts, her father was not important to him and he wished to play chess.

'You aren't going out?' she said.

'Would you prefer me to?'

'Oh, no.' Her colour rose. 'No, of course not, not if you would like to play chess. It won't be too dull for you?'

'Pia, do you want to play?' he asked.

'Oh, yes.'

'Then let us be dull together,' he said.

She managed a light laugh at that.

'I will just go upstairs first,' she said, 'and see you in the drawing room.'

When she came down a little later her mother was in her fireside chair, Major Korvacs was feeding the blaze with logs and the chess table had been set out.

'Mariella is sound asleep, Mama,' said Pia. Her mother nodded and Pia sat down with Carl. Her father had taught her chess and she was excellent. She opened the play. It did not take her long to realize he was a better exponent than

416

he had seemed in his game with Mariella. He had indulged her sister. He did not indulge her. He was absorbed in the play, as if he had set aside the war and what was happening to Austria. He sat with one elbow on the table, his chin cupped, face as weathered as if he had spent a lifetime battling with the winter winds and summer heat of the mountains. He did not look like a Viennese dilettante, nor like the oppressive Austrians her father had taught her to hate. He looked like a soldier in a mood of relaxed peacefulness.

The game began to go her way. He got into difficulties with his queen, made two very good moves to ease the situation and said 'Hm,' a little later when the piece again became vulnerable. It was the first time she had heard anything from him since the start of play.

'You're not in hopeless trouble,' she said.

'I'm pulled out of position,' said Carl, 'and hopelessness is just around the corner, signorina.'

She hesitated, then said, 'I'm Pia.'

'It makes no difference, I'm still all over the place,' said Carl. He ran a hand through his hair in the most natural gesture she had seen him make. She willed him to move his queen's rook to trap either her king's knight or bishop. He made the move. She had the choice of saving one or the other. She moved her knight, leaving him to capture her bishop. He seemed a little surprised. She knew, and supposed he did too, that two bishops are considered stronger than two knights. In surrendering one of her bishops

417

she could have been guilty of an elementary mistake, especially as she did not seem to have gained any tactical advantage.

'Why did you do that?' he asked.

'What did I do?'

'Gave up your king's bishop.'

'Major Korvacs,' said Pia, 'that's almost like cheating.'

'What is?'

'Trying to make me disclose my tactics.'

He looked up from the board. Their eyes met. Pia felt swamped by weakness.

Carl, taking her bishop, said, 'Your move.'

'Yes,' she said and surveyed the board without seeing it. Several seconds elapsed before clarity came out of turmoil. They played on. It was quite stupid, but she wanted him to win and she knew he was going to lose. At chess she could always instinctively see ahead. Carl had to reflect on the pros and cons. She did not quite know what to do when she eventually saw the opportunity to mate him. She passed it by and made an innocuous move.

'My dear young lady,' said Carl.

'I am happy with it,' she said, keeping her eyes on the board.

During the next fifteen minutes they made three moves each. Hers were all negative.

'What are you doing?' said Carl.

'Trying to beat you at chess.'

'Trying not to, you mean.'

She coloured and said, 'Well, you didn't try very hard against Mariella.'

He regarded her thoughtfully. She would not look up.

'Pia, I concede,' he said with a smile.

'Would you like a second game?' she asked.

Carl looked at the china clock on the mantelpiece and said, 'Perhaps tomorrow? I must go down to the barracks now and see how many of my men are drunk. Thank you for showing me your skill. You'll excuse me? Signora Amaraldi?'

'Goodnight, Herr Major,' said Pia's mother.

Pia felt it was a little flat without him. She wished he had won, that she had managed to let him. It was silly, but it was there, the wish. Her mother went to the windows, drew back the heavy velvet curtain and looked out into the night.

'It's snowing,' she said.

But they heard Major Korvacs go out all the same.

Signora Amaraldi, settling herself down again, said, 'Pia, you're being very nice to him.'

'Please, Mama, don't start that again.'

'No sense,' murmured Signora Amaraldi, gazing into the fire, 'no head.'

'But you must agree,' said Pia, 'he's really rather nice.'

'We're both agreed on that now, but there's no need to overdo it.'

'I am overdoing it by playing chess with him?'

'No, by worrying about him—'

'Who is worrying about him?' said Pia.

'. . . and talking about him.'

'That's ridiculous.' Pia shrugged off the

absurdity. 'Anyway, he's not the sort who'd appreciate either of us worrying.'

'Oh, he can stand on his own feet,' said Signora Amaraldi, 'he has learnt how to do that, I think. He's gone down to see his men, and on a night like this. His is the best mountain unit, did you know that?'

'No, I didn't, and how do you?'

'Anyone who knows anything about the Austrian troops in these regions will tell you that, if you ask them. Of course, some of us are interested only in the Italian troops. It will be a good thing when this war's over and Major Korvacs, if he's lucky, can go quietly back to Vienna, to someone who's waiting for him.'

'Someone?' Pia felt a rush of anxiety. 'Mama, he's engaged to be married?'

'How should I know? But a man like that, there's bound to be someone wanting him.'

Pia's relief was such that it alarmed her.

'Mama, you're only guessing. First you say waiting, then you say wanting. You're confusing yourself.'

'Wanting and waiting, one leads to the other,' said Signora Amaraldi. 'And waiting, ah, women do their share of that, as Holy Mary knows. A man, he kisses you, loves you, then goes off somewhere, anywhere, and soon enough he's having a good time and you're sitting and waiting for him, knowing he won't return until it suits him. Your father is that kind of man.'

'Do you think Major Korvacs is having a good time, knowing he has to go back to the fighting, knowing his country is losing the war?' The impulsiveness of Pia's protest made her mother sigh for her.

'I'm not talking about men like Major Korvacs, but men like your father.' She shook her finger at Pia. 'Yes, you may look at me, girl, you've always been his echo. I've managed to keep my mouth shut, I've managed to live with our Austrian neighbours. I haven't gone around saying that when Austria is beaten everything will be wonderful for us. You'll see, we'll all have to work just as hard and the only difference will be that the Italians will take our taxes and tell us what to do instead of the Austrians. Ha! A year after it's happened you'll wonder why you were so naive. But all people are foolish, everyone wants something off the moon and will follow anyone who promises it to them. You and your father and others, you've promised the moon itself to the Tyrolean Italians, you've called the Austrians bitter names and said we must get rid of them. I've said nothing, I've gone along with you and your father because I'm his wife and your mother. But I don't believe it's all going to be wonderful, not because I'm not a good Italian but because I've got sense. So has Major Korvacs. You and your father call the Austrians tyrants. Well, now we have one in our house and you don't know what to make of him, do you, or of yourself? Because you realize he isn't a tyrant. You'd like him to be, then it wouldn't be so confusing for you, you could hate him very healthily—'

'Mama, don't, oh please don't,' said Pia desperately.

'We've never had Austrians in this house before,' said her mother. 'Now we have Major Korvacs and I tell you, Pia, from now on we should both make up our own minds about politics and people. We should learn for ourselves without believing what others tell us. No wonder you're confused, no wonder Major Korvacs makes you feel unhappy. But perhaps it won't last. Perhaps when he's gone or eventually gets blown to pieces you'll be able to tell yourself he was an exception, you'll be able to forget him and go back to being a proud Italian patriot again.'

'Oh, Mama, may God forgive you,' cried Pia and ran from the room. Her mother did not call her back. For too long Pia had been her father's unquestioning echo, existing in a climate of emotive politics that nurtured the growth of prejudice and violence. It was about time she listened to voices other than her father's.

In the officers' club they talked about the rumour that the Austrian High Command intended to make one last great attempt on the pass. Success would relieve the pressure on the Austrian divisions desperately trying to stem the advance of the Italians and British across the Piave.

Carl listened and said nothing. He had heard it all before during the last six months. One more great push to turn the tide. More shells, more men, more determination. He knew what it would mean. The valleys and the chasms would simply receive bigger heaps of dead.

He left the club late. He walked slowly back to the house. He could see no future except that which embraced crushing defeat. In France even the Germans were in retreat, their Hindenburg line broken. He would have liked to turn about, to face Vienna and to walk home, to the gracious home of his parents, to feel clean and civilized again amid the familiarity of all that he had so carelessly taken for granted. He would have liked to see Sophie again, and Anne. Curiously, he felt he would also like to see James again, even if only for James to understand he had come of age now.

Pia let him into the house. He apologized for being so late.

'Oh, it doesn't matter, we—'

'Goodnight, signorina.'

His abruptness dismayed her.

'Goodnight, Major Korvacs,' she said.

He turned at the stairs. He knew he'd been brusque. He had no right to inflict his greyness on others.

'I'm sorry, I had things on my mind,' he said. His coat collar was turned up, his tanned face hard from the cold night. 'We'll play chess again tomorrow, shall we?'

'It must be when Mariella is in bed.' Pia summoned up a smile. 'She will be jealous otherwise.'

'I've made a conquest?'

'Yes,' she said in a low voice.

'That's unfortunate, isn't it? Someone must remind her I'm Austrian.'

Pia trembled.

'Oh, how can you! That is so unkind.'

'But necessary, Pia. Goodnight.'

He fell asleep without effort but when he was awoken he felt he had only just closed his eyes. The noise, a creaking floorboard, had been enough to bring him instantly alert. He lay for a moment, his nerves on edge.

The floorboard creaked again.

He sat up. Silently he slipped from the bed. He rustled into his shirt, trousers and jacket, for the bedroom was chilly. He went to the door. He opened it, slowly and noiselessly. The house was in pitch darkness. But he heard faint, indistinguishable sounds. From above. He waited until his eyes adjusted to the darkness, standing at the open door, thinking. Did it matter? Would it affect the course of the war, whatever he found, whoever he found? All the same he was curious.

He silently crossed the landing and took the short flight of stairs to the attic. He saw a dim light under the door of the attic. He walked to the door, and carefully though he trod a floorboard creaked. And another. He found the handle and opened the door. The attic, lit by two candles, was eerie with frail yellow light and flickering shadows. A man was there, a man who stood squarely to the open door and so looked directly into Carl's face. Pia was there, too, rooted, staring.

'You, I think,' said Carl to the man, tall, broad

and bearded, 'are Pietro Amaraldi. A patriot, I believe.'

'I am the Amaraldi.' The man's voice was deep, strong, resonant. 'And you are an intruder in my house.'

'But you, if you had any sense, are the one who should not be here,' said Carl.

Pia was anguished, trembling. Her father was nerveless, purposeful, a dark unmoving figure amid the wandering shadows.

'The floorboards creak, Austrian,' he said, 'they tell me when someone is prowling about. Well, you have done your prowling and finished with it. You just have time to say your prayers.' He raised both arms. The revolver clasped in his hands pointed at Carl.

'No!' cried Pia.

'Dead dogs are the only commendable ones,' said her father.

'Don't be a fool,' said Carl.

Pia darted, frantically reaching for the aimed revolver. But it barked twice in rapid succession. The bullets tore into Carl's chest. He staggered, shuddered and fell. Pia froze, the blood draining from her face and retreating from her agonized heart.

'No,' she whispered in pain, 'no. Oh, Mother of God, no!'

'What else could I do with an interfering dog?' said her father and slipped the revolver back into his belt.

Pia ran to Carl, dropping to her knees beside him. He lay on his back outside the door, in the dark shadows, the weak candlelight from the attic scarcely touching him. His blood oozed inside his shirt and jacket.

'No,' whispered Pia again, 'no, no!'

Her father stooped, ran his hands over Carl and nodded with the dark sombre satisfaction of a patriot who had done what he had to do and done it well.

'It had to be,' he said, 'they're all the same, all nosing around in search of good Italians. Well, this one has had his day. Go down and get his socks, his boots and his other clothes. We'll take him out of the house and leave him somewhere. He was out this evening, wasn't he? Very well. He did not come back. You understand? He did not return here. Someone shot him in a street. It happens. Come on, girl, get up. You don't want him left lying here, do you? Go on, bring his greatcoat and the other things.'

Pia, numbed by anguish and tragedy, stared up at her father, the great Amaraldi, a leader of Italian irredentists, a man determined to take the Trentino into the warm arms of Italy. He and Pia had both heard the floorboards creak and had known it would not be Mariella or her mother. And Pia realized her father had not thought twice about the necessity for murder. For Pietro Amaraldi there could be no compromise.

'Why, Papa, why?' she whispered brokenly. 'He was not that kind of Austrian, he did not deserve this.'

'Are you mad? There's only one kind of Austrian. Leave him and get his things. He's joined the others who are better Austrians now they're dead.'

But Pia was frozen. Someone came climbing the stairs. Signora Amaraldi appeared on the dark landing, a woollen dressing gown around her, her hair loose over her shoulders. She looked at the tableau of drama, at the still form of Carl, at the kneeling Pia and at the tall, heavy figure of her bearded husband.

'They woke me, the shots,' she said in a strangely calm voice, 'but Mariella is still sound. You're lucky, Pietro. If she had woken and come up to see what you had done, this house would have rocked to her screams. She loved this man. He was kind to her, spared time for her. In her innocence, what did she care that he was Austrian? You have murdered a good man, a fine soldier. If God will forgive you, I will not. Do you think only Italy deserves patriots, do you think yours the only cause that matters? What gives you the right to put any man to death?'

'What are you talking about, woman?' It was not in the nature of Pietro Amaraldi to accept or admit, even for a moment, that any member of his family was not as dedicated as he was or could think differently from him. For as long as he could remember he had campaigned for the Trentino to become part of Italy. He had risked his life far too often to have it put in careless jeopardy by an Austrian officer who was an un-invited guest. 'Was I to let him take me, hand me over? You'd have been taken too, all of us, even Mariella.'

427

Signora Amaraldi, white-faced and rigid, looked down again at Carl. She crossed herself. Icily she met her husband's dark, fanatical eyes.

'You understand nothing of life, of people,' she said. 'Do you know what Major Korvacs would have done? I'll tell you. He'd have told you not to put your family at risk by staying here, by having us hide you and feed you. He would also have told you that Italy could have the Trentino as far as he was concerned. He had lost his illusions, he knew what the cold hard facts of life and war were. For four years he had fought for his country. But he still cared for people. He cared for his men, for Mariella. Your politics meant nothing to him. He would only have told you to go. But to you patriotism and politics must be fed with blood. So you murdered him. Perhaps you and Pia feel happier now. I do not. I am weeping for him. And for you, for both of you.'

'Mama, no,' gasped Pia in anguish. 'Oh, please, I am weeping too.'

'It's not to be wondered at when your mother makes crazy speeches like that,' said her father. 'Get up.' He pulled her to her feet. 'You must do as I ask, Pia. It's necessary. For all of us. Get his things. Get them.'

'What are you going to do with him?' asked Signora Amaraldi.

'Dress him up to his greatcoat and cap,' said her husband. 'Then we'll take him away and leave him where it will look as if he's been assassinated in a street. I'll fire two shots. Then I'll go. I can't stay here now. The swines will come looking, they'll search this house from top to bottom, knowing he was quartered on us. They'll have their stinking suspicions. You'll have to clear the attic of all traces. Pia, do as I say. Do you want us all shot?'

Pia went down like a pale ghost. Her tears were locked frozen inside her lids. She collected up Carl's things, the necessary things. Her limbs moved mechanically, her mind as drained as her heart. She took the items up to her father. He was quick and expedient, and unmoved by his act of murder. He was used to making decisions, to desperate extremes, to committing himself. Pia stood shuddering, wondering if she would ever be able to close her eyes again and if the pain would ever go. Her father stooped, pulled Carl up and hefted him over his broad shoulder. Carl hung limply. Pia led the way down to the hall. Her mother descended with them, opened the front door and looked out. Oberstein was asleep, shrouded in whiteness. She crossed her self again.

'Go with God, Major Korvacs, and forgive us.'

'You've turned into a crazy woman,' whispered her husband fiercely. 'Go on, Pia, lead the way. Go down the street and turn right, that's the way to the Austrian Headquarters. He came from there, he must be found on the route. If you see anyone, come back to me, I'll be following. There'll be the usual night patrols out, so take care. Ah, you're the one I can always rely on, Pia. On your way, girl.'

Pia went. Her father waited a little while, then

followed, carrying Carl. The door of the house closed. The night was cold, icy cold. The snow hung on the mountain slopes, on every ledge, and it hung on every roof in Oberstein. There were no lights, but the snow whitened the darkness. The surface of the streets was slippery. But Pia did not care if she fell and slid into eternity. The tears unfroze and ran down her face. They blinded her eyes but she went on. Her father, a patriot, must be protected. Nothing could bring Carl back.

Oh, why did you come to our house? Why didn't you let me stay as I was? Why did you make me love you? I could not love you, but I did. Now we have murdered you.

They found a place. The nearest house was forty yards away. Her father set Carl down in the crisp snow close to a wall. He laid him on his back, his greatcoat unbuttoned, for the bullets had directly entered his jacket. His cap was dislodged and Carl, at peace, had his face turned up to the night sky. Pia, tears streaming, could not help herself. She knelt beside him and touched his cold face, his closed lids. Grief engulfed her. Oberstein, asleep, was his graveyard, Vienna lost to him.

'I'm going to fire two shots,' whispered her father, taking the revolver from his belt.

'Not into him! No, never!' hissed Pia.

'Of course not, foolish Pia. That would make four bullets in him, not two. Then I'll go. You get back to the house. You mustn't be seen. I'll look after myself. You'll hear from me. You'll hear from Italy too when the Austrians go down. They've lost the war. It's only a matter of time. What are you crying for?'

'I'm crying for us, Papa, for us,' she wept, then stiffened on her knees. Her fingers on Carl's eyelid detected the faintest flutter. As her father looked round she put her hand over Carl's mouth. And his mouth was warm with the faintest of breath. Oh, sweet Mother Mary, he was not dead, not yet! But she knew her father must not be told. 'Go,' she gasped, 'go before a patrol comes, go!'

Her father fired his two shots into the air and slipped away. Pia, he knew, had sense enough to vanish. But Pia stayed there, slipping her frantic hand inside Carl's jacket to feel his heart. Was it beating, was it? Oh, please, dear God, let it be.

It was. So faintly, so weakly, but it was.

But he was lying in the cold, killing snow.

With her father gone Pia flung herself over Carl, pressing to him, giving his cold body the warmth of hers and crying like a child.

They found her there, with him, close to him, the Austrian night patrol. They had heard the shots.

431

Chapter Seven

He came out of a long, disturbing dream, a dream of decimating war. The ceiling danced, slanted, keeled, then slowly righted itself, becoming blankly and whitely still. There was a figure nearby. White too except for the red cross on her cap. She smiled at him.

'So,' she said.

His chest was tight, his lungs pained him as he breathed. She took his wrist and counted his pulse rate.

'Ah,' she said.

'Ah,' said Carl. It was as much as he wanted to say.

'Don't talk,' she said briskly.

He was not inclined to. Drowsy, he lay there looking at the ceiling and trying to get his brain to work. The room was small and smelt of disinfectant. He wondered what had happened. He drifted back into sleep. When he next awoke a man in a white coat was bending over him, lifting his lids, looking into his eyes. The nurse stood by.

'So,' said the medical officer.

'So?' said Carl and the nurse smiled.

'Good,' said the doctor, 'very good.' He spoke to the nurse, then left.

'What's good?' asked Carl, his chest feeling heavy.

'You are,' said the nurse, 'but don't talk.'

He was better the next day. He remembered. Two officers from Headquarters came to see him, to ask questions. He shook his head negatively, still disinclined to talk, and the nurse said he shouldn't, anyway. They left. Carl ruminated. The luck was still with him. Even as Amaraldi had fired there had been an instant of time to tell himself he was not going to survive, after all. Pia had tried to save him. That was worth remembering.

The heavy ache in his chest turned into a pain, but it was bearable. And in the afternoon the nurse said he could talk a little. Having said it, she left him to himself for a while. So he could only talk to the ceiling. The ceiling was blankly unresponsive.

The following day the doctor had a look at him while the dressing was being changed.

'Well?' said Carl.

'Good,' said the doctor clinically, 'very good.'

'Very good feels like indigestion to me,' said Carl.

'Don't talk,' said the medico, 'breathe in. Good. Out. Good. Hurt?'

'A little,' said Carl.

'Quite so,' said the doctor and left. He was a busy man.

Five minutes later the nurse said there was a visitor for Carl. He had had visitors earlier. Captain Freidriks and two of the men.

'What visitor?' asked Carl. One of the officers from Headquarters was back, perhaps, wanting to get his story from him.

'An anxious young lady,' said the nurse. 'She's tried to see you before but you haven't been up to visitors until now. You may receive her for a short while.' She went out and after a second or so Pia came in. She wore a warm black coat and fur hat to protect her from the wintry cold, but she looked chilled and pale, her mouth working agitatedly and her eyes dark with pain. She closed the door and leaned against it, seeking its support for her trembling body.

'Signorina?' said Carl in polite enquiry.

'Oh, Major Korvacs,' she whispered. She struggled desperately for control. She did not know how to meet his eyes. 'Oh, I'm so glad you're alive, I—'

'My condition has been officially described as very good.'

'Oh, I am so ashamed.' Her eyes begged her desire to lay despairing family remorse at his feet. 'I am so terribly ashamed.'

'Please. Sit down,' said Carl.

She was emotionally grateful for the bedside chair. Her self-control was dangerously frail. She plucked at her gloves, her head bent, and she fought the rush of bitter tears.

'Oh, but it's a miracle, isn't it?' she gasped.

434

'That I'm still alive? Well, it's a great relief, Pia.'

Pia? He was calling her Pia? She darted a bewildered glance at him. He did not seem grim or accusing. Only curious. But he was pale under his tan.

'I am so unhappy, so dreadfully sorry,' she whispered, 'please forgive us. No, it isn't possible for you to forgive us – but you are alive, that is a wonderful answer to our prayers. I thought, we thought— Oh, Major Korvacs, it was so terrible—'

'You're not going to cry, I hope,' said Carl.

'I have been crying all night, all day,' she said, her head bent again, her hands feverish in her lap.

'You can stop now. Visitors are supposed to bring smiles, not tears.' He did not want to make the issue emotional.

'Major Korvacs—' She swallowed. She could not stop shivering. The tears were perilously close, even though she had wept so many. It had been unbearable at home, with Mariella asking questions and her mother racked with despair. 'Oh, believe me, I am truly glad—'

'You've said that.' Carl was laconic. 'Where's your patriotic father?'

'He has gone.' Anguish besieged her. It was a terrible effort to talk about her father. 'He went soon after.'

'Not before time,' said Carl.

'Major Korvacs—'

'I meant to boot him out of the house.

Didn't he realize he was involving his whole family?'

'That was what my mother said, that you would just make him go.' Pia looked desolate. 'But he was so sure of himself. Oh, I've been so wrong, so silly.'

'So have I in my time. What happened after the – ah – accident?'

She told him. She held nothing back, except how she had kept him warm, kissed his lips, breathed her life into his. She had explained to the Austrian patrol that she was worried because he had not returned to the house, not even by one in the morning, that she went looking for him and heard the shots. She told them she did not see who had fired them.

'You see, he was still my father,' she said. 'But I thought afterwards that you would naturally tell the true story.'

'I haven't recovered yet,' said Carl, 'so I've said nothing so far. You're very frank, Pia.'

'I am ashamed.' she whispered, 'I shall always be ashamed. Oh, you will get better, won't you?'

'I am better,' said Carl, 'even if not quite recovered. I realize now why you didn't want me in your house, why your maid was so nervous of Corporal Jaafe being around. Your father was living in the attic, of course. Food had to be supplied to him, things taken up and down.'

'Yes,' she said, pulling at her gloves again, 'but, please, you are not going to do anything to Maria?'

'Never mind Maria. Your father was there that

day when you showed me round the house?'

'Yes, but well prepared. We knew you would be coming. He was in the attic, yes, but safely hidden, in case you had made a search instead of just an inspection.' She took a deep breath. 'Major Korvacs, your wounds, are they bad, are you in pain?'

'Thank you, no,' he said politely. He felt fairly comfortable. The tenderness seemed to have moved to his ribs. 'You went up to your father that night?'

'Yes.'

'That was what woke me, the creaking floorboards. They gave us both away.' Carl's look was direct, Pia's eyes averted. 'Were they kept purposely loose?'

'Yes,' she confessed, 'some on the stairs too. You have to walk well to the left. I forgot to that night, I wasn't thinking. My father had been getting restless with you in the house.' She shivered, unable to shut out that night. 'My mother, oh, she is so distressed and unhappy, even though she's so thankful to know you're alive.'

'Yes,' said Carl. He did not feel any need for useless recriminations. It was enough to know that this unhappy girl had stayed with him instead of leaving him to die. 'Tell your mother I'm too deep into the real war to worry about the one your father is fighting. If he's gone off to wage more politics, let him. He's only one of thousands who turn life upside down for the rest of us on the pretext that it's good for us. But it isn't patriots or politicians who bestow the

437

worthwhile benefits on mankind, it's doctors, scientists, chemists, inventors and others like them. I accept the solution, Pia. I was shot in the street. By someone I didn't recognize. I know now what to say to questions from Headquarters.'

Pia was palely disbelieving.

'Major Korvacs?' she said huskily. Despite her relief at his escape from death, her despair at what had happened had been laying its dark hands on her every thought.

'You must stick to what you've said and leave it at that,' said Carl. 'I don't want to be bothered indefinitely by inquisitive people from Headquarters. Has anyone been to see you?'

'Yes, they asked questions and looked around. They were stern but not unkind. I told them what I told the patrol and they seemed to think that because I was with you when the patrol arrived it counted in my favour.'

'Oh, we Austrians would rather be gallant than suspicious,' said Carl.

Pia, bemused by what seemed so hard to believe, said hesitantly, 'Major Korvacs, what do you mean when you say we must leave it at that?'

'I mean you must say nothing about your father, you must stand by what you've already told the authorities, that you came out looking for me, that you found me.'

Pia's eyes suffused.

'You mean you forgive us?' she said huskily. 'You are not going to report my father?'

Carl felt a tightness arrive in his chest because he was talking so much, but he wished to put this girl and her mother out of their distress and worry.

'I'm not concerned with your father,' he said, 'only his family. You're not responsible for him, neither you nor your mother. All I want to do is survive this war, not take on the extra problem of worrying about hot-blooded Italian separatists. We'll forget what happened. How will that do?'

The warmth that invaded her cold body was borne along on a sea of hot, rushing tears.

'I— oh, I don't know what to say,' she whispered.

'You can say whatever you like as long as you leave the wonders of Italy out of it. If you wish to enjoy your fractious politics, Pia Amaraldi, then do so. Politics make some people very happy. They only make me feel sorry for the world. But you are young, burning, idealistic. Perhaps I envy you your enthusiasms, your future. I don't know. I think you should prepare yourself for disappointments as well as rapture. You may find an Italian government just as difficult to tolerate as an Austrian one. What's the matter?'

Pia was sobbing, her face buried in her hands. The two shots fired at Carl had shattered her. Her beliefs were in doubt, her faith in her father gone. Her burning desire to see an Austrian defeat and an Italian victory had been suffocated by anguish. Her pride was broken and Carl's cynicism was crucifying her.

'Oh, I'm sorry, I'm sorry,' she sobbed.

'Stop crying,' said Carl, but not unkindly. 'All

I'm telling you is that you won't always be young and burning.'

'Oh, that isn't important. It's you—my father—I didn't know he meant to do that. Please believe me. I didn't even know he had taken his gun out—'

'You must forget all that,' said Carl, 'didn't you understand me?'

'How can I forget?' Pia's sobs racked her. 'You will get better, you will come and stay with us again, won't you? No, how could you do that? You could never come to our house again, not after what my father did. Oh, my mother is so unhappy.'

'Tell her not to be.' Carl watched her dabbing at her eyes and nose. She was a young woman of ideals who had been shocked by a moment of violent reality. Patriots who threw bombs or fired guns were heroes from afar to those who supported them. It did not look quite so heroic close to. But she was resilient, she would get over it. When Austria finally crumbled she would be out on the streets with other Trentino Italians, waving her flag. But her distress touched him. He said, 'Would you like to play some chess? I'm not supposed to do much talking. Or lecturing. But chess is for thinking. Do you have time to stay for a game? Or a few moves? It would be better than crying, Pia.'

'Chess?' Pia's tears reached their moist end. 'Oh, Major Korvacs, does that mean you've forgiven us, that when you are better you will come to our house again? It has been so terrible for my mother, and Mariella hasn't been able to understand. We could not tell her, could we?'

'I thought we had settled all this,' said Carl. 'Now look here, tell your mother that when I come to see her I'll talk to her about Austria, about Vienna. But not about Italy. Or the war. Or your father. Do you understand?'

'Yes,' breathed Pia in emotional gratitude and love. 'Oh, thank you. I'll see the nurse about a chess set.'

'There's a set over there.'

She brought it and laid it out on the bed table. The nurse came in.

'It's time, fräulein,' she said.

'Be an angel,' said Carl, 'let her stay a while longer for some chess.'

'Very well, you may play a little chess, then,' said the nurse and left them to it. Pia was so out of all her senses with relief and happiness that quite genuinely her opening moves were as scatterbrained as a child's. Carl was on to the nonsense.

'What are you doing?' he asked.

'I'm trying my best,' she said, 'but I have had rather a bad time lately and I'm not quite myself yet. In any case, I just like to play, I don't care all that much about winning.'

'It's no help to me if you don't put me on my mettle, Pia.'

'But you have had a bad time too, much worse than I have.'

'I'm not a cripple,' said Carl and made a very decisive move.

'Even so,' said Pia, 'we should just play for fun.' And she made a countering move that was a deep, threatening challenge.

'God in heaven, that's fun?' muttered Carl.

They called it a draw twenty minutes later. Pia realized he was tired, he had lines around his mouth. She tried to say goodbye as calmly as she could. But it took her an effort to say, as she reached the door, 'May I come tomorrow?'

'You'll find it very boring,' said Carl.

'Please, may I come, may I come each day?'

'Of course,' said Carl.

Pia almost flew in her haste to get home. She had been existing in a state of despair. Now, suddenly, she was reprieved, the whole family was reprieved. Her mother had been a figure of tragic self-torment. It was like coming out of darkness into light to be able to fly home and tell her that Major Korvacs was better, was going to recover, had received her and been so kind, so generous. He had even wanted to play chess with her. And when he was out of hospital he was going to call on them. And oh, Mama, what do you think? Nothing was to be said about Papa. Major Korvacs wanted it all forgotten. He was going to say an unknown person shot him in the street.

It brought her mother out of shame and despair.

'We'll do as Major Korvacs says, Pia, we'll do everything he says. I think I'm glad for him in one way now. He won't have to fight again. By the time he's recovered the war will be over and they'll send him home to Vienna to convalesce, if they have enough sense and compassion.'

Vienna? Pia's divided loyalties were torturing her now, and it did not make her any happier to realize that if he returned to Vienna she would never see Carl again. Her relief at his recovery was intense, so was her gratitude for his generosity, but her animation died.

She took Mariella to the hospital the next day. Her sister had begged that she might go. She had been told that Major Korvacs had been seriously wounded. She accepted that unquestioningly. Ambulances were commonplace in Oberstein. But she had not been told until yesterday and she had been full of questions until then.

An Austrian colonel was leaving Carl's room as Pia and Mariella arrived. He looked searchingly at Pia. Her heart had an uneasy moment.

Mariella was excited but shy. Carl was propped up on heaped pillows. He smiled to see her. Pia thought he looked drawn. Mariella was bright in a green coat and knitted hat. Pia was in dark red, a colour that defied the brooding clouds of winter. Her fur hat was glossily black. She was nervous again, still haunted by her father's deed, and the glance she gave Carl asked anxiously for reassurance. But Carl was smiling at Mariella.

'Oh, I hope you don't mind,' said Pia, 'but she so wanted to come and she will only stay a little while, I promise.'

'Good afternoon, little sister,' said Carl.

'I am happy to see you,' said Mariella with the grave courtesy of the young. 'You have been in the war again.'

'Carelessly so,' said Carl, 'I should have kept out of the way.'

'Soldiers can't keep out of the way,' said Mariella, a little proud for him.

'Ah, there you are, my sweet friend,' smiled Carl, 'that's war for you. How are your tonsils?'

'Oh, they are famously better,' said Mariella.

'Open your mouth,' said Carl. Solemnly she opened it, bending so that he could observe her healthy, yawning gap. 'Mmm, yes,' said Carl, 'now close your eyes.' Mariella closed them. He popped a boiled sweet into her mouth, a luxury which had come to him by way of a shared Red Cross parcel. Mariella blinked, savoured the sweet and smiled in delight. She kissed Carl on the cheek. Pia envied her sister the simplicity of unprejudiced youth. Mariella was already strong-willed enough to resist either deliberate or environmental indoctrination. Her likes and dislikes were founded on her natural instincts, not on lectures, harangues and overheard conversations.

'Tell Pia that if she's going to stay a while she may sit down,' said Carl.

'Pia, you may sit down,' said Mariella.

Pia sat down. Mariella and Carl talked. She was curious about his wound. Carl unbuttoned his pyjama jacket and showed her his chest bandages. Mariella frowned and shook her head.

'Someone did it to you,' she said darkly.

'The bullets did it,' said Carl.

'An Italian,' said Mariella and with a little fierceness that startled Pia.

'Oh, fortunes of war,' said Carl, and he and Mariella talked about other things in the fashion of friends who never experienced awkward pauses. They went on until Pia gently interrupted.

'Mariella—'

'Yes, I have to go now,' said Mariella without fuss. In the most natural way of a friend she kissed Carl on the cheek again and said good-bye. Her going brought back Pia's nervousness.

'You're worried?' said Carl. With his bleak smile he added, 'The miracle has happened? The Austrians are suddenly winning the war?'

The Austrians were not. The Italian 18th Corps and two British divisions were well across the Piave and had split the Austrian forces. Defeat looked inevitable, in which case the Italians and British would swarm into the Tyrol.

'I've stopped thinking about who is going to win and who is going to lose,' said Pia. 'Perhaps nobody is actually going to win. I've only been able to think of why you are lying here. My mother asked me to tell you that whatever happens because of the war she will always be on your side, always believe in you. She says she is not as proud of us as she was, but is very proud of you. Oh, you see—'

'Yes, I see.' Carl wondered about her, about her insistent self-flagellation. 'Let me tell you

445

this so that we can have done with it all. I've lost faith in many things, in governments, generals and the common sense of people. But I've been privileged to know the men of our mountain regiments and I've known Italian men of the mountains too. The men of my own unit I shall always remember, those who have gone and those who are still alive. And I love my family. I've been very lucky. These things are all that count with me. Colonel Gruber was here just before you arrived, asking questions. I told him what I said I would, and that I've no idea who shot me. Nothing more need be said, Pia.'

'I understand,' said Pia. Her hands were clasped in her lap, her red coat and glossy black hat an enrichment of her Latin beauty. 'You have had enough of war, of killing, you would like it all to end. And you are sorry for people like my father and me.'

'No, just your father. You have ideals. Your father only has politics. I know you now, Pia, and I hope your ideals won't just become politics. Or do you wish to be Italy's Joan of Arc?'

'Oh,' she said unhappily, 'I only wish you would not be so hard on me.'

'I don't mean to be. I'm an old man, I think. You're a very lovely young woman.' Carl smiled as colour rushed into her face. 'Has no one told you that before, that you're lovely?'

A number of men had. But not Carl. Not until now. Pia wondered if life would ever be the same for her, ever hold again for her the stimulation of being her father's daughter, of being a passionate patriot. It was right, it must be, for four hundred thousand Tyrolean Italians to be brought under Italian rule. But to achieve that Austria must be defeated and broken. So must Carl.

'You aren't very well,' she said, 'or you would not be paying me compliments.'

'My condition is desperate but not serious,' said Carl, quoting the general who lacked a sense of reality but not of optimism. 'Shall we play chess?'

'If you would like to,' she said. There was nothing else she could say, despite all she wanted to. She had no rights, no privileges, except that of being able to visit him. And that was more of a humane obligation. So she played chess again with him. With an effort she concentrated. She was always a move or two ahead of him. Carl was not without occasional flair, but time and again she forced him into purely defensive tactics.

'Check,' she said in the end. Carl switched the position of his queen. Pia moved a knight. 'Checkmate, yes?' she said with strained brightness.

He conceded with a smile.

'I'm well beaten, damn it,' he said.

She could not hold back a little emotion then. She said, 'No, you will never be that, you will survive all bad luck and disasters, Major Korvacs.'

'Hm,' said Carl.

She decided she must be more natural with him, more as Mariella was.

'And you must stop trying to sound like an old man.'

447

'Oh?' he said.

'Yes, you must stop saying hm, hm. You're not an old man.'

'Hm,' he said. He coughed. He reached under a pillow, extracted a handkerchief and put it to his mouth. He coughed into it, wiped his lips and said, 'Thank you.' She asked him thank you for what? 'For the game and the advice,' said Carl.

He looked a little more drawn. It worried her. She said, as she rose, 'I may come tomorrow?'

'I'll beat you tomorrow,' said Carl.

She was restless at home, depressed by her imaginings, which all concerned a future that seemed to offer so little when once it offered so much. She could not sit still and especially she could not sit for long under her mother's eye. When Mariella's bedtime came her mother went up with the girl. Pia went up a little later. She always spent a few minutes saying goodnight to her sister. Mariella had some information to impart. News and that which mistakenly passed for news at the time had a way of being communicated lip by lip at school. The current news, exciting to the shining-eyed Italian children, was that Italy was winning the war.

Pia, tucking her sister in, listened as Mariella said, 'Is it exciting, Pia? Are you excited?'

'Are you?' Pia ducked the question.

'Not awfully.' Mariella, dark head comfortably bedded in the pillows, looked gravely up at her sister. 'You see, the Austrians aren't fighting us, are they?'

'They're fighting Italy.'

'That's not us,' said Mariella.

'It is really,' said Pia and heard her own lack of conviction.

'No, it isn't. We aren't Italy, we're Austria.'

'We're Italians living under Austrian rule, you know that. It's right for Italy to win as far as we're concerned.'

'Then Major Korvacs isn't our friend, is he?' Mariella looked sad. Pia leaned and kissed her.

'He's your friend, Mariella, so you are his. It's not his fault that Austria is fighting Italy.'

'Would you like to marry him, Pia?' The question came knowingly from the observant girl. Pia flushed.

'*Mama mia*, what are you saying, little one?' she said. She turned away, picked up Mariella's folded dress and hung it in the wardrobe. Mariella smiled.

'If I were old enough,' she said, 'I would marry him.'

'Mariella, that's silly.' Pia was hot, suffering.

'It's not. I am Austrian,' said Mariella.

'You aren't!' Pia swung round. Mariella lay in calm, composed grace. 'You're Italian.'

'No. I've looked at maps. Anyway, I want to be Austrian, I want to be on his side.'

'Mariella, hush!' Oh, thought Pia, Carl has wrecked this family. 'If your friends heard you say such things you'd have no friends.'

'If they were like that I shouldn't want them,' said Mariella proudly.

Pia sat down on the edge of the bed.

'Oh, Mariella, it's become so difficult, hasn't it?'

'I want Austria to win,' said Mariella, 'I don't want the Italians to come and take Major Korvacs away. They'll take all our soldiers away and make them prisoners.'

'No, the war will be over then,' said Pia, 'and prisoners will be released, not taken. Mariella, wait – our soldiers?'

'We're Austrian,' said Mariella stubbornly.

Pia accepted that she was in confused limbo herself. It was heart-breaking to realize Mariella was also affected.

'Don't speak like that,' she said. 'What has got into you?'

'Nothing,' said Mariella, 'but Mama says we must think things out for ourselves. You ask her.'

Pia swept down into the small sitting room. Her mother looked up from needlework. She was never able to sit doing nothing.

'Mama, what have you been saying to Mariella? Do you know she's just told me she's Austrian?'

'We're all subjects of Austria.'

'That isn't the same as being Austrian.'

'I haven't told Mariella what she is,' said Signora Amaraldi. 'She's thought it out on her own. She's been looking at maps. She showed me one. She said, "Look, we belong to the same country as Major Korvacs."'

'Oh, how simple that is,' said Pia bitterly. 'Mama, don't you see, Mariella is too young to understand that it isn't simple at all. She mustn't go around telling her friends she's Austrian.'

'She won't.'

'She might. Then they'll think we're traitors.'

'They may think what they wish,' said Signora Amaraldi. 'I clear my conscience before God, not my neighbours.'

'Mama,' said Pia, 'it could be dangerous for Mariella.'

'Yes,' said her mother, 'that is what such things are about, girl, that is what patriotism can be about. Intolerance. People wish to live with each other but there are a few who won't let them. Mariella might say something, yes, she might. And someone will say why should she think differently from us? And they'll pull her hair out. She'll come home crying. That is what your father's patriotism is about. Intolerance. It's taken me a long time to open my eyes. Are yours still shut, Pia, even now?'

'No, Mama, no!' Pia felt tears that hurt. 'But what are we to do? We must be on Italy's side. Oh, I am so unhappy.'

'Because of Major Korvacs?' Signora Amaraldi sighed.

Pia, so restless, so depressed, said, 'I can't forget my father deliberately shooting him, I can't forget the look on Carl's face— Major Korvacs. I thought how he had fought all through the war only to be murdered by us. I can't sleep at night. Can you sleep, Mama?'

'Sometimes I lie awake. Pia, I know why I'm unhappy, I'm not sure I know why you are. Are you in love? Is that it?'

'No,' said Pia desperately, 'no.'

Her mother laid aside her needlework and stood up. She put her hands on Pia's arms and turned her. They faced each other. Pia's mouth was tightly compressed. 'Pia?' It was an affectionate enquiry. 'Are you in love?'

Pia swallowed her pride and rushed into anguished confession.

'Oh, yes, I am, and I don't know what to do about it or what's going to happen to me. He thinks I'm only a silly dreamer who loves Italy. Oh, that's funny. Yes, funny, because for days I've been asking myself what has Italy ever done for me that I should want to wave the flag for her? But it's terrible as well as funny because I feel like Mariella, I want to be on his side. I want to be Austrian as well as Italian.'

'You are. We all are. But sometimes we have to make a choice.'

'Mariella has been looking at maps,' said Pia, 'I've been looking at books. Major Korvacs was right when he said the Tyrol has been Austrian for centuries. We're saying part of it must join with Italy because there are more Italians than Austrians. That's what happened to Texas. It belonged to Mexico. Americans went to live there and when there were enough of them they said Texas rightfully belonged to the United States. Is such a thing right? Am I wrong because now I'm asking is it right for the Trentino to be taken from Austria and given to Italy, which has never owned it? Papa would never forgive me for even thinking it.'

'He needs forgiveness, not you,' said Signora Amaraldi. 'Oh, how silly we all are, making such tragedies of politics until suddenly one person is more important than all our ailments.'

'Oh, I'm not a bit important to Carl, you know.' Pia's smile was mirthless. 'Just a young political creature. Mama, how did it happen? He walked into the house as if he owned it and I thought I'll show him. And now look. I'm off my head about him. Mama, what am I to do?'

'If I were you,' said Signora Amaraldi briskly, 'I'd forget what he thinks of your politics and simply look your very best for him. He's not a man who sees a woman and worries about whether she's Italian or Russian or Greek. He's come a lot farther in life than that.'

'But he's not going to be impressed by my wearing my best hat, not when his country is breaking apart,' said Pia. 'Oh, if Austria goes down, Mama, what can I do for him?'

'If he's as important to you as that, Pia, buy two new hats and wear them both.'

'Both?' Pia laughed shakily. 'Mama, we're being rather silly, aren't we?'

'Yes,' said Signora Amaraldi, 'and it's not much of a change, is it?'

Chapter Eight

Pia did not put on two new hats or even one when she visited Carl the next day. She wore her blue coat and hat, which he had seen before. But she had taken care with herself and looked like an Alpine picture postcard with the extra dimension and the quality of animation. Carl's eyes acknowledged the picture but he made no comment. He did not seem to be any better physically than the day before, and she thought he should have been. He coughed a bit from time to time. They talked and then played chess. He was friendly, naturally so, and it warmed her. It pleased her immensely that the game ended in a draw. Only at the last moment, when she was on her way out, did he say something that upset her.

'The news is good, Pia?'

'Good?' What did he mean when for him all the news was awful? 'Good?'

'For Italy.'

The Austrians were in disorganized retreat from the Piave.

Pia trembled.

'Mariella doesn't think so,' she said bitterly and left with her eyes wet.

She arrived on the following day in her dark red coat and black fur hat. It was her favourite outdoor wear and made her look as if she had just emerged from a Christmas box. The coat was damp with snow all the same. She took it off and shook it. Her deep green dress had a rich velvety sheen.

'Yes,' said Carl.

'Yes?'

'Didn't I mention it before? You're young and beautiful.' Propped against the raised pillows he smiled at her. 'Is there someone in the Italian army thinking about you?'

'No! There isn't!' There was a flash of her old spirit. 'There's no one. But if there were, why should you think he has to be in the Italian army? Why not the Austrian? This is the Austrian Tyrol, we pay our taxes to Austria, we learn and speak German, so how do you know I'm not as good an Austrian as I am Italian?'

'I made a very ordinary comment,' said Carl, 'you don't need to fly as high as that to put a flea in my ear. Sit down and let us be friends. Friends are better than donkeys.'

'Well, you should not assume people can only communicate with their brothers and sisters,' said Pia. She thought him paler beneath his tan, but his drawn lines made him so finely good-looking that she badly wanted to touch him, kiss him. 'Mariella sent you this,' she said. She had been doubtful about it but Mariella had said she must take it. It was a watercolour painting of the imperial Austrian flag. Underneath it Mariella had carefully lettered in German, 'Long Live Austria.'

'Good heavens,' said Carl, touched.

'It's to let you know she's loyal to her best friends.'

'Kiss her for me,' said Carl.

Pia, striving for the lightest of rejoinders, said, 'Actually, she asked me to kiss you for her. May I do that?'

He looked up at her. Under her fur hat her face was warm with colour.

'It'll be a brave deed, I'm not the most kissable object.'

She stooped to kiss his cheek, but her lips would not obey the rules of modesty and found his mouth instead. For a second she communed in warm bliss with him, then straightened up, her colour warmer, her heart thumping painfully.

'That was quite courageous,' smiled Carl. 'Thank Mariella for me. Can you read German well?'

'I think so,' she said.

'There's a Vienna newspaper over there. It's a week old, but would you care to read it to me?'

'You wish that?'

'You've a very good voice,' said Carl, 'all Italians have.'

She sat down and read the paper to him. Her heart did not take long to sink. The news items

456

sounded like a catalogue of gloom, doom and disaster, and it appalled her to realize what it must be doing to Carl. But he made no comment. She wanted to stop. He began to cough. She looked up. Horrified, she saw what he had hidden from her before. He was coughing blood into his handkerchief. She stared in heartbreak and panic. He wiped his mouth carefully.

'Go on,' he said.

'No, I can't. Major Korvacs—'

'It's nothing, it's not going to kill me,' he said. 'Go on.'

How could she? He was ill, bleeding inside, and if he died her father would be a murderer and she would never sleep again. She put the paper aside and stood up.

'I'm going to see the doctor,' she said, white with emotion.

'Don't do that,' said Carl, 'sit down and finish reading.'

'No!' She was fierce. 'You're supposed to be getting better, but you're not. Oh, don't you see, my mother and I will never be happy again unless you recover, never be able to look people in the face. I'm going to find someone. I am, I must!'

She rushed out. But seeing someone, finding someone, was easier said than done. She had only ever been concerned with Carl, with going straight to his room. She had not noticed very much else, except that the hospital seemed a busy one. Now she realized just how busy. The bustle of the place alarmed her. It gave her a strange feeling that Carl was no longer considered important. They had extracted the bullets, patched him up, given him a bed and his own room because he was a company commander, and provided a nurse who looked in on him now and then. And that was as much as they could do for him. There were newly wounded casualties from the mountains. There always were. And with the worsening of hospital supplies and the hurried transfer of some doctors to help with the casualties of the Piave battles, Carl was not likely to be operated on again unless he reached the door of death. They were taking a chance on him now, hoping he would cure himself. Pia's certainty about all that made her frantic.

She could find no nurse, no doctor and no orderly who would listen to her. She had no standing. They knew she was Italian, and how many Italians had Austrian sympathies? She was only in the way, and the wards were full of men far closer to the grave than Major Korvacs. Stop worrying. He is all right. Please go away.

She managed in the end, however, to find the only person she really knew there, Carl's nurse. The nurse spared her a moment.

'Please, something must be done,' begged Pia, 'Major Korvacs is coughing blood.'

'So would you if you had a lung wound.'

'He'll die. He's dying now. And no one is doing anything about it.'

'Calm yourself, fräulein.' The nurse was composed, though shades of sorrow made her want to weep. She had seen men die in the

458

hospital, had felt regret for them all. But now Austria itself was dying. Who could not weep about that? 'Major Korvacs is not in crisis.'

'I know what that means,' said Pia, her face pale but her eyes looking ready to catch fire, 'it means he isn't going to die until next week.'

'Nonsense,' said the nurse. 'In any case, after tomorrow there will probably be no more operations here. Major Korvacs will be going with other patients to the hospital in Bozen in the morning. We are evacuating all casualties except those it's impossible to move.'

Bozen? Bozen? That was fifty miles away, which might as well have been a thousand. Pia stared at the nurse in entreaty.

'Then Major Korvacs is one of those,' she said, 'he can't be moved, not when he's coughing blood.'

'More can be done for him at Bozen than we can now do for him here, fräulein.'

'Are you sending all the wounded to Bozen because the Italians and British are coming? But they won't harm wounded men and may bring their own doctors.'

'We are retreating,' said the nurse, wanting to be on her way, 'and no one is going to leave wounded men behind unless it's unavoidable. With exceptions everyone in this hospital is going to Bozen. You will excuse me, please?'

Pia returned to Carl. She felt drowned by despair.

'Major Korvacs, they've told me the hospital is being evacuated.'

'Oh, yes,' he said as if it had little significance. 'Events have caught up with us. We must go. Tomorrow there won't be time for even a brief game of chess. But look, Pia, I've written a note to your mother to reassure her. And another one to Mariella. They're in here.' He handed her a sealed envelope. 'Remember me to them both. And thank you, Pia, for what you did for me that night, and for trying in the first place to stop your father using that gun. And for coming to visit me. You're an excellent chess player. You're also very sweet.'

Pia felt he was freezing her out of life itself. He was saying goodbye and he thought, perhaps, that he was saying it kindly. She supposed that judges sometimes passed death sentences as kindly as possible. It was not much help to the condemned.

'They can't send you to Bozen,' she whispered, 'they can't. You're too ill.'

'I must go,' he said and she knew he had accepted coming defeat. His empire was in its death throes. Imperial Austria, so long the arbiter of Europe's history, was bankrupt and beaten. Centuries ago, in its infancy, it had checked and hurled back the swarming Turks and saved Europe from the barbarism of the sultans and their janissaries. Europe had forgotten that, forgotten the great Metternich and the humanity of Maria Theresa. Pia knew she herself had not wanted to remember. Carl had never apologized for imperial Austria, he had fought for it and commanded the finest and hardiest of mountain soldiers. She did not think her father, in any reckoning, would be counted the better man. But her father and the other patriots would inherit the Trentino. After four years of war what did Carl have? An injured lung and a broken empire. The hospital staff were making plans to evacuate. It was probably what the doctors and nurses wanted to do for Carl and the others, to save them the final bitterness of falling into Italian hands.

All the same, she did not know what she would do if he went.

'Please,' she said, 'don't go, you're not well enough. Please stay.'

'I prefer to go,' he said, 'can you understand that?'

She could and did. But what he could not understand himself was that because she and Mariella and her mother would never see him again, they would never have the chance to give him love in place of her father's hate.

'The weather, it will kill you,' she said desperately.

'The weather and I are old friends,' he said. 'Old enemies even. My dear Pia, don't be so worried. I'll survive. We had an abrasive first meeting, I know, but we are friends now, aren't we? I wish you a good future under your Italian flag, but make sure you tell Mariella I'm very proud of the flag she's given me. The Austrians have had days when they've danced in the streets. It'll be your turn any moment. Do you remember the music from the bandstand? That was a brave Austrian finale, wasn't it? Goodbye now.'

She could not speak. Silently she put on her coat. She was being sent away, with a note for her mother and another for Mariella. Nothing for her, nothing. Shaking, she went to the door and opened it. She turned.

'I am not going to dance in the streets,' she said, 'never, never, never!'

She ran from the hospital into the cold, wintry darkness of the afternoon, but it was no darker than her bitterness. She could not remember how she walked through the streets, how she reached home. She gave her mother the envelope from Carl. When she said the hospital was to be evacuated and that Carl was going to Bozen her mother said, 'I'm glad. A man like that should not end up as a prisoner of war.' And when she told Mariella, her sister said very clearly, 'Good. I don't want the Italians to get him.'

'I know. Oh, Mariella, things are never what we want them to be, are they?'

'When I'm older I shall go to Vienna,' said Mariella, 'no one will make me go to Italy, no one. I'm Austrian.'

The news next day was climactic. The Austrians had been negotiating a ceasefire with Italy, and an armistice was agreed. On Italy's terms. Which meant, among other things, that Italy would take over the Trentino region of the Tyrol. The Italians in Oberstein did not take long to pour into the streets and dance in the snow. Intoxicated by Italy's victory, boldly defiant of the Austrian garrison and ignoring the bitterness of Austrian residents, they celebrated in anticipation of changing the Austrian administration for the government of Rome.

Excited friends called for Mariella. No one was going to school, everyone was to dance and sing.

'Come, Mariella, come, come,' they cried, and Mariella had too much instinctive sense to declare herself unwilling.

'Wait till I get my coat,' she said and they waited in the hall while she went up to her room. When she was putting on her coat she said to Pia, 'I must go out with them or they'll throw stones at our windows.'

'Mariella, you're wiser than I am,' said Pia affectionately. 'You make your decisions but you think first. I feel I've made all my decisions without thinking at all. But it's right for your friends to celebrate, so don't feel they're insensitive. It's difficult for us, it's natural for them. We're no longer good Italians, and we ought to be, we should be.'

'I know what it is,' said Mariella, 'you think it's wrong for a good Italian to love an Austrian. That's silly. He sent me a very nice note.'

They went down the stairs, Mariella's friends claimed her with shouts and laughter and they all ran out into the street. Pia stood at the drawing-room window and watched them. They were caught up with other children, with people, all singing as they made their way to the square. This was the day her father had sworn would come. This was the day she herself had awaited. She did not feel rapturous, only bitter that events had robbed her of anticipated joy. The day was an impossible one for her. Carl's world had fallen and smashed. And instead of being in his hospital bed, as he should, he would be up, waiting for the ambulances to assemble and collect patients. Oh, it was suicidal to go on such a journey on a day so cold.

Her mother entered the room.

'We should go out too, Pia, it's what we all wanted, the end of the war and an Italian victory. But it's too wintry for me, and I'm not in the right spirit.'

It was that night on the attic landing which had spoiled it all for them. And it was wintry, though the sun was shining and the mountains glittering. The night's snow, a white cloak over the little town, was, thought Pia, a brilliance to the Italians. It must seem like a shroud to the Austrians. They would not be out in the streets, they would be weeping in their homes.

'Mama,' said Pia, 'those wounded men from the hospital, they'll freeze to death before they get to Bozen.'

'No, no, they aren't going to climb up and down mountains to get there,' said her mother, 'they'll go by road, to Tai today and for the night, then on to Arraba and then to Bozen. There's a very good hospital at Bozen. They'll sew up any holes Major Korvacs has been left with.'

'If he doesn't die on the way,' said Pia.

464

'Pia, your father had his say with Major Korvacs. Now perhaps God will have His turn. If your father couldn't kill him, and there's no more fiery sword than his, God won't let the weather do so.'

'Mama, what am I going to do?' Pia's eyes were on people, dark shapes against shining white, but her mind was on the ambulances and the preparations for the retreat to Bozen.

'You must do what all of us should now, Pia. Think of Italy and the Pope and the King instead of Vienna and the emperor. We shall become Italian citizens now. It's what Major Korvacs said in his note to me.'

Signora Amaraldi.

We are going, you will remain. You will have new loyalties to observe, I must keep my old ones. Any moment you will be free to give allegiance to Italy, while I cannot desert Austria. I need to see Vienna. Briefly I have known your family. I am honoured. There is nothing I hold against it, nothing. I hope, in turn, I've given you no cause to think badly of the country I represented while I was in your house. Forgive me that I can't keep my promise to come and see you. I send, if I may, my love to Mariella.

My felicitations to you.

Carl v. Korvacs.

'Mama, it isn't as simple as that, you know it isn't,' said Pia.

'No, not for you. For you it's going to be very

difficult, for you realize, don't you, that this armistice will bring your father home?'

Pia closed her eyes. She could not hate her father. She had been his pride and joy, his most faithful follower. But that was all gone, that relationship, shattered by the cold, deliberate nature of his act.

'Mama, his friends will have heard how he shot Carl. They'll think him a hero. He'll walk around as one. I know now I don't speak the same language as he does.' Pia saw a glinting rooftop from which the snow had slid. She saw how sharply blue the sky was, how icy it looked. She thought of the road to Tai, the Austrian columns, the despair of defeat and retreat, and the ambulances jolting over the frozen road. Some Austrian families were moving out, wanting to get to Innsbruck or other places before the Italian troops arrived. Pia turned from the window. No one could say she had not thought about the decision in her mind now. 'Mama, I am going with him, I am going with the hospital staff and the ambulances.'

Her mother did not throw up her hands or beat her forehead. Quite calmly she said, 'He has his soldiers, Pia, perhaps they'll go with him.'

'According to the armistice, the soldiers are supposed to stay where they are. Let me go, please. When he's in hospital in Bozen he'll have no one to visit him.'

'He won't be alone, Pia.'

'I'm going,' said Pia intensely, 'I must.'

'Yes, I know you must,' said Signora Amaraldi.

'Go and stay with your Benino cousins in Bozen. It will be a long journey, Pia, and a cold one. Take your warmest clothes and what money there is. When you see Major Korvacs tell him we understand about our new allegiances but we are first his friends. If I were sensible I'd stop you, because I think you may break your heart. But you must go, I see that. Nothing else is going to be of any help to you.'

The road was narrow, winding and icy. In the distance it had a hard glitter to it, which seemed a promise to be kinder underfoot. It never was. One unit of troops escorted the hospital wagons and ambulances, and that was Carl's company. His officers and men marched doggedly and silently, rifles slung. Orderlies drove the ambulances and supply carts. Doctors and nurses either rode aboard vehicles or marched with the soldiers. The ambulances with their Red Cross markings ground and creaked along, carrying wounded who could not walk. The senior medical officer wondered why he had ordered the evacuation. No one at Headquarters had said it was advisable or necessary, but nor had anyone commanded him to cancel the order. He had carried it out with his staff, he supposed, because he felt that was what everyone wanted. Some staff had been left behind to look after the more serious cases. He liked the way several nurses marched with the soldiers. He was grateful for the soldiers. Their presence gave comfort, even pride. They were grim and bitter but not demoralized.

Austrian refugees, mainly women and children, trudged in batches within the column of soldiers. Breath escaped like steam from every mouth, but the blood stayed warm. It circulated and invigorated.

Pia, carrying a heavy case, wore her dark red coat and black fur hat. The coat was warm, the hat cosy and a vanity. She walked steadily in stout boots, moving past groups of civilians, the collar of her coat turned up. She hoped no one would know her. The Austrian women might not take kindly to the presence of an Italian on a day like this one. She kept her eyes on the ambulances in the van of the march. Soldiers looked curiously at her, for she seemed very much alone for one so attractive. Some eyed her admiringly, some sympathetically, not realizing she was Italian, not dreaming she could be. But eventually there was one man who looked at her and knew her. She felt his eyes on her. She turned her head and saw Corporal Jaafe. He was not quite like the Jaafe who had kissed Maria and seen to the requirements of his company commander. He looked grim and silent, his rifle slung, his pack high on his back.

She did not know whether to expect animosity or resentment from him. He altered his line of march until he was walking beside her.

'This is a bad day, fräulein.'

He did not sound hostile. Perhaps he related her presence to a need she had to escape, even though she was Italian.

'Yes, very bad, Corporal Jaafe.'

'They say we're better off here than in Vienna, that it's not good at all in Vienna. Can you believe that?' He nodded at the snow, the frozen wastes and icy road. 'Can you believe there's more to be had here than in Vienna? If there is, then all I can say is that thunder and lightning must have razed Vienna to the ground.'

'You know that can't be true.' Pia, the weight of her case dragging at her arm, worried and wondered about which ambulance Carl was in. 'Oh, things are bad at the moment, but life must have something good to offer you and your comrades after so many years of war. Defeat can't be the only consequence for brave men. Vienna isn't razed to the ground, and even if it had been it would rise again.'

'But who'd have thought things would turn out like this?' Corporal Jaafe shook his head. 'They must be bad for you too if you're having to leave.'

'I'm going to relatives in Bozen,' she said, 'it's more Austrian than Oberstein.' The implication that she preferred an Austrian environment was a natural reaction to Jaafe's sympathy.

'But how long will Bozen be safe, that's what I'd like to know,' he said. 'You're by yourself, fräulein, without your family?'

'Yes, for a while,' said Pia. She was fiercely glad she had come, she would have gone crazy had she stayed home. It was not going to be easy. If the weather turned, conditions would become pitiless, and what Carl would say when she turned up to visit him in the Bozen hospital she didn't know. She could not hold back the question hungry on her tongue. 'Corporal Jaafe, where is Major Korvacs?'

'He's here, of course,' said Jaafe, his boots crunching. 'That's why we're here. They said no Austrian units were to move, but when we heard Major Korvacs was getting out of bed to march to Tai today, we all said we would go too, never mind what the Italian High Command said. We will lay down our arms only when the Herr Major commands us, not the Italians, not even the emperor. Major Korvacs is the one who's looked after us. We were the best fighters of them all, fräulein, and don't you forget it. We still are. No one is going to stop us going where Major Korvacs goes.'

'But where is he, in which ambulance?' asked Pia, her eyes on the lumbering vehicles ahead, all of them horse-drawn. The slanting sun cut across them, picked them out.

'Ambulance? He's not in any ambulance. He's up there, leading the company, with the other officers. He's taking us all home, all of us. He's going to march us into Vienna, take my word.'

'Oh, no!' Pia was tragically alarmed. 'Corporal Jaafe, he'll kill himself.'

Corporal Jaafe turned his old soldier's grin on her.

'He's better on his feet than his back, fräulein, I tell you that for nothing.'

Pia, in wild agitation, said, 'You mean he says he is. Oh, don't you see, he knows he's going to die and he wants to do it heroically, on his feet.

Oh, it's wicked, it's stupid. You must stop him—'

'Not Major Korvacs,' said Jaafe, 'he'll outdo the devil himself. Don't you worry, fräulein. Here, give me that.' He took her case. 'I'll stow it in one of the carts, you don't need to carry it.' He stopped to wait for a baggage cart to grind up. 'You go on, fräulein, keep walking, don't get cold. I'll catch you up again.'

Pia went on, well aware how the coldness could creep into boots, woollen stockings, into feet and legs, if one did not keep moving. She was grateful for Corporal Jaafe's paternalism but frantically worried about Carl. Her eyes searched the winding column, but she could not distinguish individual figures at the head of it. She walked more quickly, working her way past soldiers and coming up with a group of trudging women.

Carl marched with the sun on his face. The light was brilliant, reflected and accentuated by the inescapable walls of icy white. He did not look back. Had he done so he would have seen the slopes that swept down to the pass, the pass that had meant everything and now meant nothing. The air was so clear, so sharp, so tingling. He drew it fearlessly into his lungs. It pierced them but he did not cough. And the pain that had nagged seemed only a lurking tightness.

On either side of him and behind him marched his officers. He knew they were watching him, waiting for weakness to show. But what was his life, any single life, against the canvas of Austria's defeat? A million better lives had already been lost for the empire, a million widows or mothers wept for them, and not one of those lost lives had changed the course of the war for the better. Relentlessly, remorselessly, the Allies had hacked away at the empire, destroying the intangible qualities that had held together a dozen different nations, scores of different peoples. What was an empire but the indefinable host wherein unity fostered amid disunity, keeping its members from each other's throats?

His officers were silent. The extended columns were silent. It was all silence except for the sound of marching feet and creaking wheels. They had spoken all their words during the years of war. There were no more. Defeat marked their end. Defeat was silence. Even in France the German armies were approaching the end of the road.

The silence did not last for ever. It was suddenly broken by women's voices raised in anger, and the anger turned into a chorus of jeers. A sharp, solitary cry of pain pierced the jeers.

Carl stopped and turned.

'What's happening?' he asked. A soldier came leisurely along the side of the halted column. Ahead the ambulances creaked on. 'What's happening?' asked Carl again.

'They've found an Italian woman, Herr Major,' said the man.

'Well?' said Carl sharply.

'Herr Major, I wouldn't put it past them to skin her alive.' The soldier seemed regretful but otherwise indifferent. Perhaps everything else loomed far bigger. Even the troops nearest

472

the noisy melee were looking on without doing anything. Carl strode down the line. He reached the women, a dozen or more of them. They were hysterically angry, surrounding a woman down on her knees in the icy road. Carl caught just a glimpse of her, her back to him and snow on her red coat. The women were pushing, slapping and tongue-lashing her. Her hat was off, hands at her hair. She seemed to disappear as her tormentors closed tighter around her.

'What are you doing?' Carl's voice was biting, harsh. The women turned. They were fairly young, their husbands in the Austrian army, and they had preferred to leave their homes rather than come face to face with Italian troops. They wore their masks of anger glitteringly, tears not faraway. They looked at Carl, at his bleak eyes, his hard, drawn face. His expression was unforgiving for the angry, the unbridled, the revengeful. He understood their feelings but not their brutality. They became silent, uneasy. 'Has defeat made savages of us?' he asked.

The woman on the ground, hidden from him, shivered as she heard his voice. Corporal Jaafe arrived. He stared at the scene, at Pia on her knees, trembling, her face in her hands. He approached Carl, whose eyes were on the Austrian women.

'Herr Major—'

'See to her, whoever she is,' said Carl.

'But Herr Major, she's—'

'See to her,' repeated Carl, and marched back to the van of the column, where his officers awaited him. He moved on with them and the dour cavalcade of retreat resumed its trudge. Something nudged its way into his mind. A colour. A glimpse of dark warm red. And words.

They've found an Italian woman.

He stopped again. He swung round. He saw her clearly then, not so far away, a black fur hat back on her head and Corporal Jaafe brushing snow from her coat. Warmth rushed into Carl's body. He knew then the real reason why he had kept silent about Pietro Amaraldi, why he had protected Signora Amaraldi and her daughters. Because of all of them and one in particular.

'Pia!' He called to her. 'Pia!'

She looked up. She saw him. He was outlined by the sun and the mountains. She saw him stretch out his hand and heard him call again.

'Pia, come!'

She gasped. She ran, her eyes hot, the floodgates threatening. She ran past the soldiers, over the ice and snow. She ran into his arms. Carl held her and his compassionate comrades turned away.

'Pia,' he said, 'my sweet foolish Pia.'

'Carl?' Her tears spilled. 'Oh, let me come with you, please let me — I'll ask for nothing, only to come to the hospital and visit you—'

'There'll be no hospital,' said Carl, 'and ask me for love.'

'Love?' Her swimming eyes were in disbelief.

'Whatever I've lost,' he said, 'I've plenty of that to give. That's better than nothing, isn't it?'

'Carl, you are saying you will give me love?' she said.

She was a warmth against him, a woman.

'You have it,' he said, 'is it what you want, Pia?'

'From you? Oh, yes, yes,' breathed Pia, oblivious of armies, victories, defeats and even the unfurling banners of patriots, 'from you that is everything I want.'

Chapter Nine

It came. Defeat. Total, absolute, overwhelming. With it came the collapse of the empire. The abdication of the young and earnest emperor. The demoralization of Vienna, the starvation of its people. All food supplies had been cut off weeks before the Armistice. The Socialists took power provisionally to work desperately for a democratic Austria.

Baron von Korvacs stared greyly into the face of ruin. The baroness and her daughters and her servants looked for fuel for the fires and something to eat. The markets swarmed with the hungry and the markets had almost nothing to sell. Money values plunged. Costs soared.

The victors arrived. The Viennese received them numbly. Sophie saw British uniforms and stared strickenly at them. The Allied Peace Commission began to reorganize the city administration with the help of the new government. Returning soldiers flooded the streets, adding to the difficulties. They had come to see what Vienna had to offer them after four years of fighting. Vienna had nothing, only a grey despair and a soul in limbo. The soldiers' hopes turned into disillusionment, disillusionment into violence and anger. There were riots because of the shortage of food, fuel and miracles.

But there was a minor miracle one day. The telephone in the von Korvacs' residence rang and when Sophie answered it, it worked. There was a girl on the other end of the line, a girl who announced herself as Pia Amaraldi and was desperate for something to be done about Carl. They were in a little Alpine town. Heiligenblut. Carl was resting there, with his company. He had a bad chest wound. But he was going to march his company all the way back to Vienna. It was madness. There were no trains, so little food. Someone, please, must come and take Carl home. He would not listen to her. He laughed at her. Could his father not do something? Please, please.

Sophie communicated the message and its urgency to her father. And the baron, who had served the empire faithfully and with distinction, went immediately to one of the ministers of the new government. The minister listened to him and stared at him. Had the baron taken leave of his senses? What could be done for any individual soldier when conditions were as they were and there were thousands stranded in those dead theatres of war? The baron should remember there were only people now, there were no privileged persons.

Sophie, in despair for Carl, in despair for

Austria and the grey years ahead, felt she had been emptied of all life.

In December the door of the house in the Salesianergasse was opened by one of the few servants still employed there. The evening was bitterly cold, the caller a British officer in cap and greatcoat of RAF blue. It was James. The servant looked hard at him, recognized him and courteously invited him to step in and wait.

The baron and his wife were in the drawing room when the servant announced the name of the visitor.

'What?' The baroness looked up in shock and embarrassment. 'Who has called, who did you say, Heinrich?'

Heinrich repeated it was Herr Fraser, except that he was in uniform now. The baroness turned to her husband. She and Ernst, terribly worried about Carl, had been racking their brains. They had also been trying to compile a list of assets and liabilities, of servants who would have to go and the one or two who might be kept on. In addition they had been consulting a list of small properties for sale. They would not be able to afford to stay here. But who would buy their house these days?

'Fraser? Did you really say Fraser?' The baron, a tired, exhausted man and very grey of hair, looked up over his glasses.

'Yes, Excellency. He wishes to know if you'll receive him.'

'Show him in,' said the baron after a moment's hesitation.

'Ernst?' The baroness was in doubt.

'We must receive him, my dear.'

James, divested of his greatcoat and cap, was ushered in. The spacious room was cold, the fire tiny, meagre. The baron and baroness were on their feet, receiving him formally. He was older, harder, but very recognizable, his dark hair falling familiarly across his forehead. But his squadron leader's uniform was a reminder of a war lost and an empire gone. The regime they had loved, honoured and served had been catapulted into oblivion. James had had a share in that.

'Thank you for seeing me,' he said.

The baron inclined his head but did not offer his hand. Nor did the baroness extend hers. Whatever liking the baron had had for James had been worn away. Not by defeat alone. The baron could understand defeat, could accept an honourable one. But Austria faced unimaginable humiliation. He found that unforgivable in the Allies. The fate of what remained of the once great Habsburg empire was to be decided by political opportunists like Clemenceau and Lloyd George. Neither the baron nor his wife could forget the part Britain and James himself had played in Austria's destruction and their own ruin, and they could not advance their greeting beyond polite stiffness.

'You are well?' said the baroness with a civility that was painful.

James knew that the restraint of similar civility on his part would get him nowhere. He had not come merely to exchange awkward courtesies.

'Well? No, I'm not,' he said, 'I've been in Vienna three days and I'm sick, devastated. It's taken me all those three days to find the courage to call on you. I've been talking to people and I know you've had an unbearable war. But I haven't had the happiest of times thinking about you.'

'We have grown older more quickly, perhaps,' said the baron, 'but at least we aren't lying dead in some mountain crevasse or some muddy trench. We have survived, but I'm not sure whether survival is going to be endurable. There is so much talk about recrimination when already so many lives have been lost and so much destroyed that might have been spared.'

'Yes, I know,' said James, who had had four years he would rather forget.

'But the war itself, that is over, thank God,' said the baroness. She had lost much of her lustre and well-being. She was starved of the warm flesh that had given her figure its look of handsome maturity. She looked like a woman robbed of something dear and precious. Old and golden Austria had died on her. She had never thought the day would come when she and her family and servants had to go their separate ways each morning in search of food. Coffee, on which the Viennese doted, over which they had spent so many enchanted hours, days and years, had long since disappeared. Sometimes one was lucky enough to get a substitute, although one did not feel fortune's blessings when one was drinking it.

James did not look as the Austrians did, she thought. He looked neither hungry nor bereft, though there was something about him which had not been there before. A hardness, a quality of implacability, as if in all his purposes he would always get that which he most wanted.

'Carl, Sophie and Anne,' he said with an interest he did not disguise, 'may I ask about them?'

He was aware he had not been invited to sit down. They had received him but it was beyond them at the moment to make him comfortable. Clearly they did not wish him to prolong his call. He understood. But he would have liked them to know he was grieving for Vienna too.

'Carl is well, Sophie and Anne are well,' said the baron, but it was another politeness, wooden and lacking conviction. The baroness's mouth trembled.

'Are they well? Please tell me,' said James.

'Carl,' said the baroness and swallowed. 'Carl has a bad chest wound. He's down there, in some mountain village. We had a telephone call about him yesterday. There's a girl who is desperately worried about him and we've been trying so hard to find out if we can get him home. But it's easier these days to move heaven and earth than bring a wounded man home from the Alps. And Anne is—'

'A moment, Baroness.' James was on to the

baroness's vulnerability. He was here to campaign for Sophie. He had quickly found out that the baron's elder daughter was still unmarried. He meant to campaign without qualms. 'This mountain village. Where exactly is it?'

'It's called Heiligenblut, it's impossibly out of the way, north of Lienz.' The baroness knew there was a reason, other than polite enquiry, for the question. The Allies were the conquerors, the men of power, and James represented that power. A little flame of hope sprang. 'The girl is Italian. I can't think how Carl came to be mixed up with an Italian—' She stopped.

James, knowing why she had stopped, said with a faintly ironic smile, 'Yes, there were Sophie and I, we became very mixed up too. Loving one's enemies is very painful, Baroness, I assure you. Perhaps that is what this girl has found. We'll see. Can Carl be reached?'

He was so decisive, like a sudden clear strength in the house.

'There is a telephone number we have tried to call back,' said the baron, 'but there are always breakdowns, breakdowns.'

'Will you let me have it?' said James. 'I want Carl to stay where he is. I'll not have him shunted about. I'm serving on the Allied War Relief Commission and there are some things we can get done that you probably can't.'

Perceptibly the baroness softened. The flame of hope burned brighter.

'Could you, James?' His name slipped out. 'Would it be possible? The Italian girl said he

482

intended to march his company home to Vienna, she said he would kill himself doing that.'

'I rather fancy Carl might be going for what we call kill or cure,' said James. 'I'll get him to stay where he is if that means we reduce the odds. Give me that telephone number. What is the girl's name, if she's the one who does the talking?'

'Pia Amaraldi,' said the baron and gave James the number.

'James, we would dearly like to have Carl home, to look after him here,' said the baroness in impulsive gratitude. 'We could not thank you enough. He has fought such a good fight for us, for Austria, all these years.'

James thought. He knew he could forge his re-entry into the family. But it was not that alone. It was Carl, whom he had known and liked, one of the few who had fought all the way through.

'Then he deserves better than a telephone call,' he said, 'though I'll make that first. Then I'll go myself. If necessary I'll take a staff car and a couple of men. I'd like to see Carl. I presume,' he said with the ghost of a smile, 'that I'll have to transfer to a horse and cart at some stage. If I can find a horse that hasn't been eaten. Salzburg, that's the place. Will you leave it to me?'

The baroness glanced at her husband. Ernst was still a little aloof.

'We will be happy to leave it to you, James,' she said, 'and you will sit down for a moment, won't you?'

'I don't think I should stay, not this time,' said

James. 'There must be an interval for adjustment, especially when things are so bad for you. I can't expect you to behave as if nothing has happened. I shall be in touch. Meanwhile, Anne and Sophie? Will you tell me how they are?'

'Anne is here,' said the baroness, 'but Ludwig, her husband, we last heard of in a Russian prisoner-of-war camp. But since their revolution we've heard nothing, nothing at all. And Sophie—'

'Yes?' said James, noting her hesitancy and the baron's stiff silence.

The baroness could have said that Anne believed Sophie had been waiting all these terrible years for him, but she herself was doubtful whether the feelings of either of them had survived. So she said only, 'Sophie is out, James.'

'How is it you're a member of this Commission?' asked the baron, breaking his silence.

Again the suggestion of a reminiscent smile from James.

'I went into the lion's den,' he said. 'That's to say, I had an interview with my father. I wanted to get back to Vienna as soon as possible. The one way of ensuring that was to get myself appointed to the Commission. Some string-pulling was necessary. Because of what his infernal machines meant to the war effort, my father is able to corner the right people in the corridors of power. I don't make a habit of asking him to use his influence on my behalf. Let me be frank, Baron. For once, I didn't hesitate. There's Sophie, you see.' He caught the baroness's startled look. 'I'm still not cured of Sophie. I've spent four years thinking about her. That's ridiculous? Perhaps it is. But there's no one else. Only Sophie.'

The baron took off his glasses and polished them. The baroness did not know whether to be helpful or discouraging. But after four years, four long and tragic years, his first thoughts had been of them, his first suggestion that of helping Carl. She could not give him discouragement. While she could not forgive his country, she could begin to forgive him. All his hopes, in any case, were entirely in Sophie's hands. Someone must tell him where he could find her.

'James—'

'We are very reduced.' Her husband's quiet interruption seemed to convey the message that discouragement was necessary. 'And we can expect no concessions from your side, we can only look forward to losing what little we do have left.'

'You must know, Baron,' said James, 'that if it were all in my hands you would get your empire back.'

'Ah,' said the baron with a touch of reminiscence himself, 'we did have a talk once, I recall—'

But Anne came into the room then. She saw James. Her eyes widened and misted, her mouth quivered. James felt a shock, a pang. Her parents were thin. Anne was thinner. Youth and beauty had been fined down by the tragic consequences of Sarajevo. If only he had been closer to that student, Princip. If only.

Anne had suffered heartache as well as hunger. Heartache for her lovely Austria and for Ludwig, who might be dead or just alive. But she could not be bitter towards James. There was the war, yes, but there were so many other memories, all drenched with the fragrance of summer. She came up to him, she smiled and put out both her hands. He took them and pressed them with unchanged affection. Theirs was a gesture of peace and reconciliation.

'My dear Anne,' he said.

'It's over at last, isn't it?' she said unsteadily. 'And you are up and we are down. Oh, we are very down but we shall be up again. James, I am so glad to see you, so glad you came through it all and have come to see us.'

James thought her almost heartbreakingly courageous. The war had laid its cruellest hands on women like Anne.

'And I am very glad to see you,' he said.

'You and I, we aren't too old to do things better, are we?' she said. 'We will see there are no more wars, that friends don't have to fight each other, won't we?'

'I shall never again fight my friends,' said James.

'Anne,' said the baroness, not far from tears, 'James is going to help us get Carl home. He's on the War Relief Commission and means to go and find Carl himself.'

'I'm in a position to oil wheels, you see,' said James, 'and I'll bring Carl home, I promise, even if we both have to ride back in a turnip wagon.'

'Oh, you'll do it,' said Anne with an overbright smile, 'it will be nothing to the man who downed Avriarches and dropped in for schnapps with a divisional colleague of Colonel Moeller's.'

'Oh, he got to know about that, did he?' said James, gratefully aware of a warmer atmosphere.

'He wrote to Sophie about it,' said Anne, who felt sure she knew why James was back. 'He was only sorry you did not give him the opportunity to offer you his own schnapps.'

'In a war,' said James, 'who needs friends with enemies like Colonel Moeller? Do you know if he's all right? I'd like to think so.'

'Oh, he was bearing up very well the last time we heard, about five weeks ago,' said Anne. 'James, could you do something about my poor Ludwig? Could you, please?'

'Everything I can, but it's going to be a lot more difficult.'

'I know,' said Anne, 'but I'm going to pester you about it, I'm not going to be at all proud. I mean, you're still our friend, there's only been a long nightmare in between, hasn't there?'

'Yes, Anne. Which is why something positive must be done about Ludwig as well as Carl.'

Ludwig at this moment was nearing Bratislava in Hungary. He had a right leg as stiff as a board, his stout crutch having become a close friend. He was in company with a thousand other Austrian scarecrows, who had been marching for months across revolutionary Russia.

'James,' said Anne, 'you are going to be a great

surprise to Sophie, you know. And you will have to wear a thinking head on your shoulders.'

'Is it possible to see her?' asked James and looked at the silent baron. The baron said nothing. The baroness left it to Anne, who had no reservations.

She said, 'If you want to see her now, she's at Sacher's. She went there, she said, to celebrate honest misery with sorry friends. Perhaps you'll be in time to save her from actual lamentations, James, and to bring her home. She said she would not be late. We are staying home to be privately miserable, although now you're here to help us, I don't think we're quite as miserable as we were.'

'I think I'll go to Sacher's,' said James and looked at the baron again. The baron smiled wryly.

'I advise patience and understanding,' he said.

'I advise love, James, unqualified and unconditional,' said Anne.

'Go to Sacher's, James,' said the baroness softly, 'and thank you for remembering us.'

Sophie, keeping a promise to her convalescent friends, was celebrating catastrophe with them in the red and brown bar of Sacher's Hotel. The bar was full and therefore warm. It was one of the few places still retaining an air of gracious living, Frau Sacher still dispensing service, though not from the same bountiful cellars, with old-world charm. The portrait of Franz Josef was still on the wall. Perhaps it would soon come down.

Perhaps in the new order of things it would have to. British and French officers were present. Serving on the Commissions, they had begun to frequent Sacher's. Sophie took absolutely no notice of them. She would not look at them. Especially she would not look at the British. She wondered how any of them could come among a starving populace with their well-fed robustness. There were Viennese women with them, women who were defiant of disapproval because they were lonely and hungry and hoped that some time during the evening their escorts would lead them to food.

Sophie sat at a table with her friends. She was tautly thin but just as striking, her features almost aquiline from privation so that her eyes looked hugely luminous in her pale face. Other eyes, discerning eyes, might have perceived the blank emptiness behind the luminosity.

With her wounded companions she drank wine. Frau Sacher saw to it that she got the best of what was available, for the men were her guests and Baroness Sophie von Korvacs would not be disposed to accept less than that for any of her friends. With these friends she shared the wine, with them she toasted their battles, their wounds and their future, although they knew and she knew that there was no future. She was vivacious, amusing, fascinating, beautiful. They all loved her. How were they to know she felt even emptier than they did? Their eyes were on her, smiling at her, admiring her, and the words fell from her lips in brittle streams.

'So, you see, my courageous ones, what is there to worry about for any of us? We are as far down as we can go, aren't we? We have nothing. We have even lost Hungary, which fed so well at our imperial table. Therefore, this must be our last night of sorrow, for from now on there is only one way to go and that is up. The mightiest ship can capsize but it can sink no further than the seabed. How is that for a solace to take back with you tonight? It should be good enough to put you to sound, happy sleep, don't you agree? I shall sleep without a care in the world and when I next come to see you I hope you'll be dancing.'

'Will hopping do?' smiled a man with a smashed kneecap.

'I will hop with you,' said Sophie and smiled in return, though she wanted to weep, to weep for all of them, all the crippled, unsung heroes of Austria. But she had kept every tear at bay for four years. And James would not be shedding any, not that man of iron. If he were still alive he would be ablaze with medals, and in triumphant London the women would be around him like dazzled moths, reaching for him, kissing him. Let them, let them! Vienna was an empty shell, holding nothing to draw him back. But perhaps, when the city was at its darkest and coldest, his ghost would stand on her doorstep. Only his ghost. Austria, whom he had rejected, whom he had helped to crush, would never allow his living body to enter her borders. For four years he had been in desertion of Austria and of her too. He had left her to eat her heart out. She had no heart now. No love could survive years as interminable and as bitter as these. There were no emotions, no vibrations, only a terrible, desolating sense of unending winter. She smiled again, looking at the bottles. They were empty too, except one. 'There, you see, that is the last of the wine. Drink it, my very good friends. Do not drink to the emperor. We have no emperor. But if you must drink to one Habsburg, drink to Franz Josef, the old and august one, for he polished our jewel very brightly for us.'

But they drank to her. And Sophie smiled brilliantly for them.

She rose to her feet. Despite an empire lost, despite her frozen heart, she looked in her dark, glossy-feathered hat and pre-war fur coat, and in her starved, slender beauty, as if she alone personified the memory of proud and imperial Vienna. Every Allied officer there raised his eyes to her. She saw none of them, she looked through all of them. She smiled again at her convalescents and said goodnight to them.

She turned to go and looked into the face of James.

Her cold blood rushed. A sensation, almost of eerie fright, struck. His was the dark, drawn face of ravaged but triumphant Mars. Richthofen had not got him, then? No. It was Richthofen who had fallen from the sky.

'Sophie?' A quiet appeal for reconciliation. 'May I take you home?'

Strange fire touched her ice. But there was so much pride in her, so much bitterness, so much defeat. And he had come back in the arrogance of the uniformed victor. She looked at him out of huge, blank eyes.

'Sophie?'

Sophie walked straight by him and out into the cold night and wondered wildly what she was doing. It was James, James, and she had cut him dead. Had it been James? So intense, so real, so alive? Ludwig seemed to have gone from the living, and Carl, according to a desperate Italian girl, was dying on his feet. James alone was unconquerable. She walked, her heart beginning to hammer, every sense in wild confusion. The wind was icy, but strangely, madly, her blood was hot. But the bitterness made her walk on and her pride made her walk with her head up. And the wine engaged light-headedly with her hungry body.

James? She had seen him? Then what had she done? Walked out on him. He would not dare to follow, not after that.

But she heard him behind her, his footsteps insistent. And her blood pumped crazily into her heart. He caught her up and walked by her side. He said nothing. She flung her head higher, her teeth clenched, the bitter wind stinging her taut face. She walked faster. He kept pace with her, kept close to her.

'I'm not going to leave you,' he said.

Not going to leave her? Did he know what he was saying? He had left her on that station all those years ago, he had left her to go to war with her. She walked on, head high, and every dead emotion came to life and the wine chased her thoughts into a giddy whirlpool. Vienna was so dark, so icy with winter, the lamps empty of light, the night as bitter as death. The dead leaves blew out of unseen heaps and skittered and rustled over the cold ground. Those without homes, and there were thousands, huddled together for warmth in every protected corner of the old, narrow slums. But the streets through which Sophie walked, with James dark and obdurate beside her, were empty and hollow. When had Vienna ever been so dead? James and his English and his Scots and all his other allies had turned the birthplace of emperors into the graveyard of Austria. She could not look at him, speak to him, forgive him, yet what was making her heart hammer so wildly if not the coursing blood of renewed life? She felt the purpose of his presence. He meant to corner her, defeat her and add her to his triumphs. Her lungs began to fight for air and she could not contain the surging vibrations of her newborn blood. It pumped through her starved body and fed brilliant light into her brain.

He heard her sigh. It was like a faint breeze dying in the face of paralysing cold. She fell. He caught her, held her. Stricken, he saw how white her face was, how heavy her lids lay. He lifted her and she hung like one lifeless in his arms. He began to carry her home.

Summer came again for Sophie. The light was so bright, the sun so warm. She was running, swooping, not in fear but in pursuit of life. And life received her as James opened his arms to her.

Her eyelids trembled, lifted. There was no light, no warmth, only a sensation of weakness. Except where arms were around her.

James felt her stirring.

'Sophie?'

She spoke at last, in a whisper.

'Who are you?'

'Years ago, Sophie, we knew each other.'

'Yes. Many years ago. You may put me down, please.'

'Put you down? I will not. Are you mad?' He was almost grim. 'My God, you're starved, you weigh nothing, you should not be out. What have you been doing? Drinking wine without food inside you? Venturing into the realms of fantasy? Don't you know there's been a war, that even in Vienna it's not safe to be out by yourself at night?'

Sophie, in a state of physical weakness and indignity, felt outrage swamping her senses. What was he saying, what was he talking about, did he think that after all this time, after all her heartbreak, she only wanted to listen to a lecture?

'Put me down,' she said wildly.

'I will not. If I put you down what will keep you standing up?' He was shocked, horrified, placing the necessity of getting her home far above everything else, even his desperate wish to reclaim her. But she had not forgiven him. He had to give her time, or in her pride she would freeze

494

every word he spoke. He was going to have to start from the beginning again with Sophie. But he would have her. He would not give her to any other man. 'Sophie, I'm taking you home. Please make up your mind about that. I'll put you down when we get there, not before.' He tried to sound kind. Sophie did not answer. But she turned in his arms and weakly her arms stole around his neck. She hid her face against his coat. He felt her shiver. Her teeth were clenched again, her heart hammering again. He carried her quickly down the deserted silence of the Salesianergasse and turned into the drive of the house. He carried her up the steps to the door. There he set her gently down on her feet. He knew what it might do to her pride if he attempted to carry her into the house. Sophie swayed. He reached again for her. She fell into his arms, shuddering violently. James felt racked.

'Sophie? Are you all right? Sophie?'

And suddenly Sophie was weeping, weeping the tears that had frozen on the day he left her. To James it seemed as if the long conflict had been mankind's worst obscenity. He rang the bell urgently, then put both arms around her again.

'Sophie, my darling Sophie, what have we done to you?'

'Nothing, nothing – I am only dying – that is all.' She was sobbing on his chest. 'Oh, I thought Richthofen would get you – and I prayed for you – I should have been praying for Austria.'

'Sophie, there hasn't been a day when I haven't

thought about you. But I know what you must feel. I do understand. You're all right now, you're home. I won't distress you. I'll leave you now, but I'll—'

'Leave me?' Her voice gasped its way through strangling sobs. 'Oh, dear God, you would leave me again?'

'Sophie?'

'Oh, love me, James, please love me,' said Sophie.

It was Anne who opened the door, who stepped aside as James, lifting Sophie into his arms again, carried her into the house and out of her long cold winter.